IT WAS THE BEST
OF ALL POSSIBLE WORLDS...

The young country of America—from the wilderness outpost of Fort Detroit to the cosmopolitan city of Philadelphia, from the remote *Wees-konsan* to the settlements of the Ohio Valley—this is the country of Owen Sutherland: soldier, diplomat, and founder of a great frontier trading company.

IT WAS THE WORLD
TURNED UPSIDE DOWN...

Revolution, civil war, Indian hostility—Owen Sutherland's America is in turmoil. He must fight for his family and friends, for his company, and for his country—a fight that begins with

DEFIANCE

The Third Powerful Novel
in the Northwest Territory Series

THEY WERE THE
MEN AND WOMEN OF
THE OLD NORTHWEST

OWEN SUTHERLAND. The frontiersman and trader who would fight for both Red and White—and for the country he believed in.

JUBAL SWAIN. The giant, red-bearded, one-handed renegade leader pillaging for himself and others, ever ready to kill.

NIKO-LOTA. The Delaware Indian whom Owen once saved. He had a debt to repay and vengeance to reap.

ELLA SUTHERLAND. She was Owen's aristocratic bride, bringing civilized ways to the frontier.

LUCY SWAIN. She longed for her missing children and revenge for her murdered husband, even if it destroyed her.

BRADFORD CULLEN. He wanted a trading empire with no rivals—and spies, politicians, and hired killers could all be used against the Sutherlands.

JEREMY BENTLY. Owen's noble young stepson, he took his place among the valiant men of the northwest.

SALLY COOPER. Once Pontiac's slave, she was now a lovely yo   woman, torn by her love for two fine me

By Oliver Payne from Berkley

NORTHWEST TERRITORY SERIES

Book 1: *Warpath*
Book 2: *Conquest*
Book 3: *Defiance*

NORTHWEST TERRITORY·BOOK 3
DEFIANCE

OLIVER PAYNE

 Created by the producers of
**The Kent Family Chronicles,
Wagons West, The Australians,
and White Indian Series.**

Executive Producer: Lyle Kenyon Engel

BERKLEY BOOKS, NEW YORK

DEFIANCE

A Berkley Book/published by arrangement with
Book Creations, Inc.

PRINTING HISTORY
Berkley edition/March 1983

Produced by Book Creations, Inc.
Executive Producer: Lyle Kenyon Engel
ISBN: 0-425-05846-8

To Suzanne and Yuri

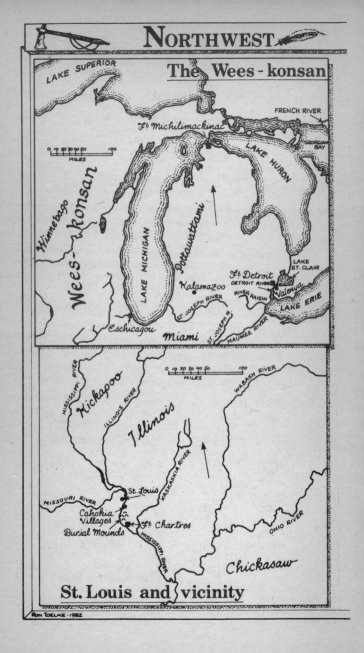

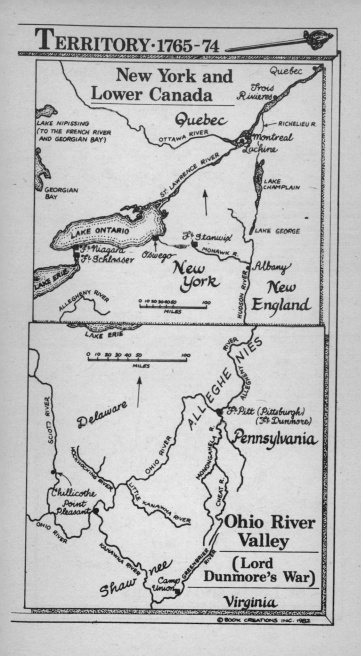

TERRITORY·1765-74

New York and Lower Canada

Quebec

Trois Rivieres

LAKE NIPISSING
(TO THE FRENCH RIVER
AND GEORGIAN BAY)

Quebec

OTTAWA RIVER

RICHELIEU R.

Montreal
Lachine

GEORGIAN
BAY

ST. LAWRENCE RIVER

LAKE
CHAMPLAIN

LAKE ONTARIO

LAKE GEORGE

Ft. Niagara
Ft. Schlosser

Oswego

Ft. Stanwix

MOHAWK R.

Albany

LAKE ERIE

ALLEGHENY RIVER

New
York

HUDSON RIVER

New
England

0 10 20 30 40 50   100
MILES

LAKE ERIE

0 10 20 30 40 50   100
MILES

Delaware

SCIOTO RIVER

HOCKHOCKING RIVER

OHIO RIVER

ALLEGHENY RIVER

A L L E G H E N I E S

Ft. Pitt (Pittsburgh)
(Ft. Dunmore)

Pennsylvania

LITTLE KANAWHA RIVER

MONONGAHELA R.

CHEAT R.

Chillicothe

Point
Pleasant

OHIO RIVER

KANAWHA RIVER

Shaw nee

Camp
Union

GREENBRIER RIVER

Ohio River Valley

(Lord Dunmore's War)

Virginia

© BOOK CREATIONS INC. 1982

That the colonists, black and white, born here are freeborn British subjects and entitled to all the civil rights as such is a truth not only manifest from the provincial charters, from the principles of the common law, and acts of Parliament, but (also) from the British constitution....

—James Otis, *Rights of the British Colonies*, 1763

Mr. Otis has raised his voice bravely and nobly in the cause of freeborn British subjects in America, white and black, but there is no mention in his writings of the red face. If untold thousands of Indians are not to be considered freeborn subjects of the same king as the eloquent Mr. Otis, then how is it that every treaty we have signed with our sacred mark refers to us as subjects? Do these documents lie?

—Owen Sutherland, writing as the venerable Indian sage Quill

NORTHWEST TERRITORY·BOOK 3
DEFIANCE

PART ONE

Gathering of Waters

chapter **1**

WEES-KONSAN

West of Lake Michigan, in the wilderness known to Indians as Wees-konsan—the Gathering of Waters—a young bull moose stood in an icy pool, feeding on water-lily sprouts. Though his antlers were no more than downy twigs on his massive head, the moose was lord here, powerful enough to intimidate even the hungriest of wolves. Content and secure on this sunny June afternoon in 1765, he had survived the most dangerous season for his kind, when thawing ground turned to mud, miring large animals, trapping them until they starved or were killed by predators.

Now the ground was dry, and he was safe from attack as he browsed in a cove at the border of the swollen river that wound through pine forest and aspen grove on its way to the Mississippi, the Father of Waters. When his antlers grew fierce and thick he would be more than a match for any wolf pack stalking the herd, and only human hunters could fell him, if they were brave and skillful enough. Human beings he avoided if he could, or charged if he could not. In this pool he was alone except for butterflies hurrying from wildflower to grass, from bunchberry to wild calla poking through the water's surface. The sound of wind rattling aspen branches or rushing through the pines was lost in the roar of the river, and even the whistling of the swans in a nearby lake was hardly audible above the swirling rapids.

Yet the moose heard something in the distance. He raised his head, ear twitching, water dripping from his snout. Listening, he scented the wind, snorted once, and took an uncertain step toward the stony bank. The sound came again, and he hesitated. It was like the cry of a wolf, yet not a howl of hunger but of fear. The wail came again, startling bluejays that hurtled from their tree and squawked above the river in excitement. The moose lumbered out of the pool, unafraid but ready for

3

whatever was approaching from upstream, and crying louder now, like an echo on the wind. Standing in the shadows near some pines, the moose chewed steadily on water plants that hung from his mouth. When something appeared at the bend in the river, he stopped chewing and waited, curious and placid.

Whirling around the bend, a shattered log raft steered by two white men headed directly toward the cove near the moose. Kneeling precariously at the back of the plunging, awkward raft, a gangly blond fellow tried to hold their course for the cove by ramming a long pole into the water and dragging it along the riverbed. At the front of the raft, the other man lay on his ample stomach, using another pole to fend off rocks and driftwood in their path. It was this chubby one whose terrified cry had sounded like a wolf in the distance.

Again he shrieked, "Land! Land! In there! That pool! Get us in! Get us in! Help, dear Lord! Help!"

With one hand, the chubby man poled at obstructions, and with the other he shoved his grimy wig back onto his bald head. His face was red with exertion, his fine linen blouse split across the back, and like his friend, he was completely soaked from a long and losing battle with the river. The raft struck driftwood at the entrance to the pool, jarring the heavy prone one, whose name was Nate Breed, and again knocked the wig askew on his head. Meanwhile, the collision nearly threw the other man—the thin, blond one—overboard, but still kneeling, he held his balance, his long legs splayed between separating timbers that had broken their lashings. This second man was Melvin Webster, whose inexperienced but game pole work was all that stood between them and a frightening trip along another turbulent stretch of river. In their struggle neither Mel nor Nate noticed the bull moose calmly chewing and looking on, just forty yards to their right.

At the last possible moment, with the current mercilessly pulling at their fragile raft, Nate let out a howl of anguish and dropped his pole, ready to leap into the shallows. But Mel did not give up. He got to his feet, risking his life, and jammed the pole into a mass of driftwood and rocks, preventing the raft from spinning away. This maneuver further spread the timbers apart, and Nate gasped, expecting his friend to drop through. Mel kept his balance, however, using every muscle in his wiry body to keep the raft near the mouth of the inlet. With his legs he forced the timbers together, and driven by utter determination, he held the pole in the rocks. With a deft and powerful wrench of his body, Mel swung the raft into the pool, where it spun lazily, once, then twice, toward the shore. It stopped with a gentle bump.

Muttering thanks to the Lord, Nate lay on his stomach, groaning and wheezing, and Mel collapsed onto his back, knees up, eyes closed, grateful to be alive. After a little while, they recovered and dragged their raft ashore. It was loaded with supplies, trade goods, some bundled Indian peltry, and miscellaneous bags, heavy frying pans, and tent gear. They stumbled onto land, neither of them noticing the angry, diving, chattering jays and not seeing the bull moose still watching them from twenty yards away.

The moose chewed languidly as Nate clamored, "Why the hell I ever listened to ye in the first place is beyond me!" He strained to haul the beaver pelts from the raft, and through his teeth he went on, "I shoulda come out here alone! Too soft, that's what I be! Too soft just 'cause ye be blood kin, an' I pitied ye wastin' yer life in White Plains with Granny Breed!"

On he went, complaining as he worked, but Mel made no reply, laboring quietly to pile their goods on a high place where they would make camp. Ignoring Nate's grumbling, Mel anxiously rummaged through an oilskin sack and pulled out a paper that unfolded into a map. Seeing this, Nate roared and clenched his fists.

"Aye, read yer damned treasure map!" He sneered these last two words. "Yer damned heathen Injun treasure map's what got us into this!"

"Spanish map," Mel said, his voice deep and slow, a sharp contrast to Nate's falsetto squeal. Mel was angular, a homely fellow in his early twenties, with blue eyes and a slight stoop to his bony shoulders.

"Spanish heathen! Injun heathen! Don't make no difference!" declared Nate, whose body was as strong and stubby as Mel's was long and slender. "I should never've let ye spout on about that map an' Injun treasure mounds an' such! God's wounds, Mel Webster, yer a doodle-brain! An' I'm as much a doodle-brain for not knowin' better than to listen to ye!"

Mel laid the map out on a flat rock and placed stones on the corners so it could dry. He then began removing his wet linsey shirt and trousers, muttering all the while, "There is a treasure, I tell you! And this map'll get us to it!" He threw down his drenched shoes and glared at Nate, who was hanging his own clothes on a bush in the sunlight. "If you didn't like this search you should've said so back at Detroit, or before that at Niagara, or at Albany, or even at New Brunswick—"

"Enough!" Nate bawled, wringing out his bob wig, which was short and braided in a knot where it covered each ear. Like Mel, he had a stringy beard, and with his bald head and heavy belly, he looked more an oriental mystic than the New York barrel maker he was by trade. "Enough talk about what shoulda been! A year back I believed ye! After all, ye be my cousin, an' I trusted all them rumors that a scholar what kin read Latin an' Greek an' Spanish an' whatever should be keen enough to know what was what when it comes to treasure maps! But, no, ye be a danged doodle-brain when it comes to treasure maps, cousin, an' ye drug me through the woods from Detroit to Michilimackinac to . . . to wherever in God's name we be right now!"

As though realizing for the first time that they were somewhere unfamiliar and perhaps perilous, Nate glanced around, peering into the dark woods and up at treetops, though his untrained eyes did not detect the moose. Mel distracted Nate by kicking a stone into the pool.

"This was as much your idea as it was mine, cousin," Mel pouted, putting on a dry smock of drab linen. "You wanted to come out here and trade for peltry, and you wanted treasure, too. I never said I knew exactly where it was. Anyway, it wasn't I who bought that worthless raft from the Winnebagos!"

That got a snarl from Nate, who gave his wig one final squeeze before suspending it on a branch. Then he turned and pointed a finger at Mel, who looked away.

"Now listen good, Mel Webster, 'cause I ain't gonna say this again! It was my idea to buy a raft from them redskins, is right! Why? 'Cause there ain't no other way to get safe through this here outlaw country! Even Injuns is afeared to come through here! The raft was my idea because I didn't take to traipsin' through these piny woods with a pile o' peltry and trade goods on my back when all the while them renegades might be layin' in the treetops, ready to ambushcade us!"

Mel gave a noise of disgust and began picking up branches for a fire. He mumbled, "We should have bought a canoe—"

"Canoe?" Nate howled in scorn. "Listen to the woodsman! Did readin' about bark Injun boats teach ye how to drive one? Eh? Did yer scholaratin' tell ye how to steer an Injun boat through them rapids? Eh?"

Mel kept collecting wood, knowing Nate was right: He could not handle a canoe very well, much to his own annoyance, for when he had come out here with his cousin in Bradstreet's army last summer, he had intended to learn the ways of the wild. But he was still a novice.

Nate found some dry clothes and continued, "If we didn't buy that there raft we'd never git through outlaw country without gittin' our throats slit! Think on that!" He snapped his fingers at Mel, who grimaced.

"We're still not through outlaw country, raft or no."

Nate blinked as he thought about that, and then looked around once more. He went to get his rifle, which was with their goods, and cleaned out the wet powder in the priming pan. It was time they collected themselves, repaired the raft, and got out of this beautiful but dangerous country before the warnings of the Winnebagos upstream proved true. For half a year this region had been terrorized by a band of renegade Americans, French, and half-breeds under the command of a giant named Jubal Swain, a killer who preyed on trappers and traders for hundreds of miles around.

In this remote country, which was crisscrossed with busy trade paths, Swain's force was virtually unopposed. The British Army was widely scattered and had suffered heavily in the 1763–64 uprising led by Pontiac, the Ottawa war chief. The Indians themselves had paid dearly when traders were forbidden to go out during the war, and lead ball and powder were completely cut off from the redskins. Poorly armed, disorganized, and weak from a winter of bad hunting as a result of the lack of ammunition, the Indians of Wees-konsan were unable to attack the hidden stronghold of the outlaws.

With no military garrison closer than Michilimackinac in the north or Detroit to the east, the country under Swain's domination was without law, and no one was safe here. Only the strongest villages were able to protect themselves from attack, but that ability was diminishing with the rumored growth of the outlaw band, said to number thirty hard cases and their women, as well as a few children. Nate rammed home a bullet in the barrel of his rifle. He felt a cold chill run down his spine to think of the peril they faced until they got through to the settlements of French *habitants* farther south at the confluence of the Mississippi and Illinois rivers.

He rested the rifle against a tree, then turned to Mel, who

was blowing at tinder he had struck ablaze by holding the priming pan of his unloaded rifle against it and firing the powder.

Nate said, "From what them Winnebagos told us, we'll soon be at a big Injun town where we kin hire some redskins to take us out; they might even canoe us all the way back to Niagary."

Mel looked up sharply. "Back? What about the treasure mounds . . . the map—"

Nate let out a growl of frustration and hissed, "I give up! I want to trade like everybody else out here! I want furs, not dreams! We poked around Detroit all autumn 'cause ye thought the map told ye to! After all that rootin' in dirt ye was wrong, ye made a mistake—"

"Miscalculation," Mel muttered, turning his attention to the flickering blaze that was sending up a billow of gray smoke.

"Miscalcee—misclacu—whatever, it was a mistake, an' it cost us precious time an' money! Then ye drug me off to Michilimackinac afore winter, an' there we sat keepin' warm in the midst o' mangy redskins an' pushy Redcoats! Poxy women, thievin' half-breeds, bad food, moochers, an' no Injun treasure mounds! That was all a miscalcu . . . lation! There! That was a mistake, too!"

Mel had the fire going, and he opened a canvas bag of pemmican as he answered, "The map doesn't say just what region the mounds are in, but once we're there I'll know it by the landmarks! It takes time to—"

"Time! Hah!" Nate tossed over the frying pan and fetched a bottle of rum from his knapsack. "I ain't got time to root through mud, an' dig holes where there ain't nothin' but dirt, nor freeze all winter with moochin' Redcoats an' pushy Injuns! Time? My time run out! I'm goin' back to Niagary an' trade, not treasure hunt!"

Mel stamped angrily around the clearing, slashing balsam branches with his ax, cutting saplings for a lean-to, all the while thinking of a good reply to Nate's argument. But his cousin again was right. After months of hunting in the northwest they were no closer to finding the Indian burial mounds. Some years back he had read of the mounds and fabled treasure in a Spanish book about explorations in the northwest. According to the book, an explorer had heard of a treasure in sacred mounds built by ancient civilizations. Before returning the book to the Spanish tutor who then had taken it home to Spain with him, Mel had copied the map now drying on the rocks, some of the ink smudged, but otherwise undamaged.

What could he tell Nate, who had plodded with him through the wilderness in spite of government regulations forbidding unauthorized whites to enter Indian country? They had taken the chance of being jailed, attacked by hostiles, or now murdered by renegade whites—and for what? A century-old map and a dream born in Mel's fertile imagination had spurred them on with visions of great treasure, but his constant research using existing maps and charts had failed to convince them they were on the right track.

There was one other hope for Mel, and that lay in their course down the Mississippi to the canoe routes heading east. A likely location for the treasure mounds was somewhere there. He had studied every available tract or journal on travels in the northwest, and one of his prime choices for the site of the mounds was on the Mississippi, though he had no idea just where.

First, however, they had to get out of the Wees-konsan before they were discovered by outlaws. They must bind their raft's timbers to make it strong enough for the run down to the Mississippi—an estimated four more days of travel. Even if they had decided to return to Detroit, they were on the wrong side of the watershed for an easterly trip to Lake Michigan; unlike a canoe, the raft was too heavy to be portaged. There was no means, save by water, to get their small store of furs and wares out of these woods.

If only Nate would not be so pessimistic, so skeptical, their search would have been more exhilarating and exciting. Though Mel was a greenhorn in the wild, he was an avid botanist, self-taught. He was never bored, often sketching new plants and animals he encountered. He kept a detailed journal of his experiences, making the expedition a source of profound enchantment for him, but Nate had no such interest and found every step painful, every setback or delay a torture.

Even now, gathering balsam to thatch their lean-to, Mel took interest in the shoots and buds, the insects and the birds. This preoccupation always annoyed the more practical Nate, but nothing restrained Mel, who peered at the black and gold butterfly resting on a pink wildflower. Then he saw the bull moose, staring, chewing, now just fifteen yards away.

Mel's first impulse was fright, for even an inexperienced traveler knew the fury of an immense moose when angry. Mel froze, but gradually his fear diminished as he stared at the animal. The moose was untroubled, not aggressive at all. Smitten with a rush of good feeling that the moose apparently trusted him, Mel even thought he might go slowly toward it and stroke its nose in a gesture of affection and assurance. He glanced about for a succulent to take to the giant but was interrupted by a call from Nate, who was busying himself with their meal.

The moose was unperturbed. Mel smiled, then wondered whether he could frighten it off by clapping his hands and shooing. He tried that, but the moose merely stepped into the water for another mouthful of lily shoots. Mel chuckled, felt wonderful about life, and went back to the campfire.

After Mel moved away, the moose lifted his head and gave a snort of surprise and challenge; but Mel did not hear it, nor was it meant for him. The moose had seen movement in the trees nearby. Shadows were closing in, living shadows that caused the great beast to snort once more, throw his head back, and lumber away, fleeing in terror.

Mel heard the moose crash among the trees, and he turned in time to see it vanish into undergrowth. He wondered what he had done to startle the creature. He did not see the danger lurking, moving along the edge of the trees...a danger so deadly that even a bull moose ran for his life.

That night, rain came down heavy and loud, roaring in the trees and on the river. Far downstream from the camp of Nate and Mel was a sandy spit of land with a newly built shelter, where two men sat at dawn huddled in blankets against the damp and chill. The campfire had long ago been drowned by the downpour, their lean-to was a lonely shadow against the dull greens and grays of the misty woods, but they were comfortable enough, dry, and well fed.

One lay on his side upon a blanket spread over a bed of soft balsam. He was reading a book, and a rifle and sword lay close at hand. Dark, weathered from wind and sun, he was a strongly built fellow in his thirties, with clubbed black hair and a two-months' beard. His trade blanket covered a fringed buckskin shirt worn over a light linen smock that reached partway down his legs. In doeskin leggins, with moccasins and such a tawny complexion, he might have been mistaken for an Indian if not for his curly hair and light gray eyes. He was Owen Sutherland, a Scot who made his living as a frontier trader. A former officer in the famed Black Watch Highland Regiment, he was at home in this forest, though his youth had been spent deep in books such as this volume of Voltaire's *Candide*.

Beside him, sitting with knees up, chin on forearms, a big Chippewa named Tamano gazed glumly at the rain. Tamano was a fine-looking man, big like Sutherland, with long hair, prematurely gray, that fell over his shoulders. He wore buckskins beaded with bright reds and yellows, decorated with colored shells and porcupine quills. Pulling his own blanket over his shoulders, he shuddered as a gust swept through their campsite.

Sutherland chuckled and turned the page. Tamano stared at his friend, who was too engrossed in reading to notice. Tamano watched a moment longer, eyeing the strange collection of letters and pages whites loved so much; he shook his head, and turned back to the dismal rain that seemed not to let up. They had been in this campsite too long, Tamano thought, and he did not like it. For almost a week they had used the spit of sand as a base while they scouted through the woods for some trace of Jubal Swain and his renegades. The Scotsman and the Chippewa had sworn to track Swain and ultimately to kill him, to put an end to his treachery in the northwest. Now they were convinced the outlaw's stronghold could not be far away. Stray parties of Indians told of frequent attacks and slaughter; fleeing trappers had lost all they owned—peltry, traps, and bait—to roving killers who sprang unexpectedly out of the forest to strike ferociously and plunder or destroy.

If not for this heavy rain, Sutherland and Tamano would have broken camp before dawn and made their way southeast, where they expected to find Swain's camp. Now they must wait before moving on, both aware of the risk of discovery. Swain was cunning and cruel, and if they did not move soon they were likely to be spotted and themselves become the quarry.

Tamano was uneasy. His eyes flitted along the treeline and back toward the beginning of the spit. This site had been chosen because there was only one approach by land, and they had a good view of the river and the far bank in case danger came from there. A canoe, turned upside down close by, was ready to be launched as soon as the storm let up, and they would be on their way eastward. Portaging over high ground, then following a river running toward Lake Michigan, they would continue their search, asking at villages, querying travelers, searching through scenes of death and desolation until they located Swain's lair. But that would be all they could do for now; the outlaw band had become much too large for Sutherland and Tamano to take on by themselves. They would have to return to Fort Detroit, their home, several hundred miles due east. There they would gather a strong force of fighting men and come back to wipe out the thieves and murderers before they grew numerous enough to dominate a vast area from the Illinois River to Lake Superior.

Already Swain's outlaws had diverted great quantities of stolen furs southward to French and Spanish settlements on the Mississippi—furs that should have been traded by Indians to the Frontier Company, the trading firm in which Sutherland and Tamano were two of the principal partners. If Swain enriched himself at the expense of the Frontier Company, which could ill afford even one bad trading season, then the firm might very well fail. As a result, many who had put their trust in Sutherland's bold and innovative scheme to ally traders, merchants, and trappers as partners in a free association would lose all they owned. There were good reasons to defeat Jubal Swain, and they were anxious to get on with the job before winter, when the annual trading season began in earnest.

Sutherland laughed to himself and lay back, the book on his chest. Tamano smiled at his friend, whom he had known since wilder days ten years ago when the Scotsman had been captured and tortured by Ottawas under the powerful Pontiac. Instead of pleading for his life, Sutherland had laughed at his tormentors, moving their hard hearts with his courage until Pontiac himself commanded the ritual be halted. Then Sutherland had been adopted, washed in the winter river to rid him of his white blood, and named Donoway, "fearless in the flames."

These two had come through much together, marrying sisters of another Ottawa leader. Sutherland's wife had been murdered in 1763, and in his pursuit of the killer he met and fell in love with an Englishwoman who now awaited him as his wife back at Fort Detroit. Last year the uprising of Pontiac had been crushed, and the British were consolidating their hold on the northwest territory that once had belonged to France. Yet for all the strength of British arms, the northwest was too huge and too impenetrable to be policed or ruled by law. It was up to men such as Sutherland and Tamano to take the law into their own hands and overcome the lawless.

Sutherland chuckled again, and Tamano said in the language of the Ottawa, "Hey, brother, you like this rain?" Sutherland looked up, humor in his eyes. Tamano nodded. "Yes, perhaps you enjoy this rain. You are like the bear holing up in winter, and you like it here as long as you have white man's letters to keep you from thinking about Swain and bad weather!"

Sutherland sat up, stretching the stiffness from his bones. He yawned as Tamano took the book from him and puzzled over it. Sutherland reached to turn the book right-side up; Tamano fumbled with it, looked skeptical, and turned it upside-down again.

"Looks better this way," the Chippewa muttered, his eagle feathers flickering around his face in the wind. "Tell me, Donoway," he said, returning the book. "What do these letters mean for you? Can they stop the rain? Hunt game? Can they tell how to find Swain?"

Sutherland slid the volume into a pouch, saying, "I wish books could tell such things, brother, but they're more . . . more to illuminate your mind."

Tamano grunted and looked at the lowering sky. "Sunshine illuminates, but there's no sunshine, just rain. If letters illuminate only your mind, they're a waste of time."

Sutherland took out his clay pipe and a small sack of tobacco. "White men have to illuminate their minds in times like these when politics are changing so fast and ideas are pouring down like rain—"

Tamano laughed heartily. "Books like sunshine, and ideas like rain! You have a strange culture, you whites! You should have stayed Ottawa, Donoway. You need another washing to drive out your white spirit!" He laughed again, all the while conscious of their surroundings of the forest and the river.

"Listen, Tamano, whites need intellectual illumination, just like this book gives, because we're too complicated for our own good. Without illumination to keep the peace, there'd be millions of people at each other's throats. Right now there's such confusion in the American colonies that without illuminated thinking, colonists would be fighting each other and the soldiers . . ."

Inspired by reading Voltaire, Sutherland rambled on about the rising tensions between England and the colonies over the mother country's right to tax Americans without permitting representation in Parliament. As he listened and watched the woods, Tamano filled his own pipe and puffed away while Sutherland told about taxation riots in New York and Boston, the destruction of the homes of government officials. The scene Sutherland depicted was one of increasing bitterness on both sides, bitterness that was dividing Americans, pitting one side against the other over the question of civil liberties, government, commercial rights, and social justice. Among the most important points of contention was whether Parliament and the British Army should continue to govern the rich northwest territory or—as the colonists desired—turn it over to colonial rule.

For the most part, Tamano was hard put to understand anything having to do with the white man, but when Sutherland explained that the fur trade upon which they both relied for survival was affected by the colonial dispute, the Chippewa listened.

"If Parliament gives the colonies control of the northwest territory, the powers that be in America will parcel it out and sell it off to profit the land speculators," Sutherland said. "That means Indian lands will be bitten off piece by piece, through war or forced treaties, until there is no more Indian land—and without the fur trade, the Indians cannot survive."

Tamano asked, "And does that book tell you what is right and wrong in all this?"

Sutherland relit his pipe, which had gone out while he had talked. "Sort of. It's the story of a young man who wants to believe that this world is the best world it can possibly be, but he meets so much misfortune and sorrow that he can't find comfort in this philosophy."

"Then why were you laughing?"

Sutherland smiled, recalling the wry, ironic humor of Voltaire. He took the book out of his pouch again and began to read parts to Tamano, translating as best he could from French to Ottawa, using Indian notions to explain European ideas. Soon, Tamano was chuckling at Candide's innocent stupidity, and he liked most Sutherland's interpretation of the book's moral:

"No matter what misfortune we encounter, we must learn to work without theorizing, to cultivate our own gardens and make them flourish no matter what is happening in Philadelphia or Boston or New York."

"Tamano's squaw cultivates our garden," the Indian said thoughtfully. "She needs no French books to tell her that." He looked up at the sky. "Hey, the sun is coming back. Tamano is hungry. Let's eat some fish."

As the wind tore a ragged blue opening in the clouds, Sutherland picked up his rifle and went down to the river's edge, where a mess of trout were squirming in a net submerged in a pool. Sunshine suddenly poured down, warm and invigorating after the mist and rain.

Sutherland hauled up the fish, sunlight sparkling on the dripping water, and turned to go back to camp. Then a shout from the river caused him to drop the catch and whip up his rifle, cocking it, ready to fire. What he saw were not Swain's men, but Mel Webster and Nate Breed, clinging to their disintegrating raft. Waving forlornly to him, they floated through quiet water into the shallows. In a moment, Tamano was at Sutherland's side, and they dragged the battered pair ashore, laying them on the sand, trying to still their frightened babble.

"We surrender . . . we surrender," Nate mumbled, shocked and pale with fright, quaking from head to foot. All the while he fumbled with his disheveled wig, which, like the rest of him, was wet from a long night on the water. "Spare us, let us go . . . no more, gentlemen! Spare us! We've done . . . ye . . . no harm! Ye have all . . . our goods! Grant us our lives—"

Sutherland patted Nate's face while Tamano stood guard, rifle raised as he searched for any pursuers. It was obvious these two had been struck by Swain's men, and they were lucky to have escaped.

Mel groaned and tried to sit up, but he was as weak and exhausted as Nate. "In truth, sir, you have all we own! Spare our lives, and I'll tell you about . . . dear Lord! I'll tell about the map you've taken, the trea—"

"Hold on, hold on!" Sutherland demanded, shaking them both hard. He did not recognize them from their stay in Detroit last year, for many people had come into the fort at the time. The two men were making no sense, and Sutherland said, "You're in no danger now! Hush, gentlemen! Take heart! Come to your senses. Can you walk a little way to our camp?"

Astonished not to be in the hands of killers, Nate and Mel looked at one another, their eyes bleary and darting. Gaining some strength and hope, they got up. Sutherland helped them to their feet, but when Nate saw the fierce Tamano, his knees buckled, and Mel caught him before he fell. With Sutherland's aid, they returned to the fire Tamano had built. Plying the greenhorns with rum and food, Sutherland got the harrowing story of how the renegades had come storming out of the trees, whooping like devils and brandishing tomahawks.

"We just got away!" Nate said through a mouthful of bread and rum. "How we got away I'll never—" Then he glanced at

Mel, who was eating slowly, and said, "Well, I reckon my cousin here did have somethin' to do with us escapin'."

Nate said they had dashed for their raft, leaving behind all they owned, the outlaws on their heels. At the last moment, Mel had turned and fired his two pistols at the attackers, wounding a couple and startling the rest, slowing pursuit long enough to float the raft.

"They hadn't expected us to respond so smart an' quick!" Nate nodded, feeling somewhat proud. "Them varmints ate some gunsmoke, an' they didn't like it one bit, no!" He munched away, while Mel stayed silent, empty pistols still stuck in his belt, though he had no powder or ball.

In the next moment, Nate thought of all they had lost to the renegades, and complained that they were utterly destitute in the world. He did not say it, but even Mel's precious treasure map had been lost to Swain, who undoubtedly would preserve it, thinking it might one day help him to understand the lay of the land in this largely uncharted region. Swain would not know the map was a key to a treasure, but Mel, and even Nate, prayed he would not destroy it, and that one day, somehow, they might recover it.

As Nate told of the sudden attack, Sutherland took stock of Mel and guessed there was more to the young man than first met the eye. Tamano said he would check upstream to see whether the outlaws were coming this way. He went to the canoe, which he turned over and shoved off toward the far bank.

Nate was saying, "Upon my honor, Mr. Sutherland, no two travelers were ever less deservin' of such heartless treatment at the hands of rogues, brigands, rascals . . . ." He looked up to see Sutherland go toward the river, rifle in the crook of his arm.

A moment later, Sutherland turned quickly. He ran back to the camp and kicked dirt onto the fire, to the protests of Nate, who had not finished his meal. Mel was on his feet, sensing danger, and he grabbed the bullet pouch and powder horn Sutherland threw him to reload his pistols. On the river, Tamano was paddling swiftly for shore.

Nate looked around, bewildered, then understood. Letting out a wheezing gasp of fear, he jumped up, and was quickly tossed Sutherland's knapsack. They hurried toward the water, where the Chippewa's canoe shot over the surface like an arrow.

Sutherland soon had most of their gear, food, and weapons at the river's edge. The other two men stumbled along, dropping things, clumsily hurrying, though no longer confused; the presence of Sutherland and Tamano gave them a confidence they had never felt before. Sutherland rushed them wading through the water and into the craft.

"Swain?" the Scotsman asked Tamano, who nodded, held his rifle ready as he knelt in the stern of the canoe, and peered upstream. Sutherland saw movement, as of deer drifting along the edge of the forest at the far bank. There were at least eight men, some with feathers, others wearing felt hats and fur. As Mel got into the canoe, Sutherland saw another group slipping along the near shore, moving rapidly, silently. So far, they had not seen his party, which was largely concealed by the sandy spit and some thick brush. But as soon as the craft put into the current, the four of them would make good targets. They could wait no longer.

While the outlaws homed in on the smoke from the smoldering campfire, Tamano and Sutherland paddled strongly out from behind the spit and drove downstream, away from the advancing renegades. There came a shout close at hand, where other outlaws had come out on the near shore, just thirty yards from the fleeing canoe. Sutherland fired his rifle without hesitation, and a figure staggered and fell forward into the water. The remaining attackers opened fire, and Sutherland and Tamano paddled with all they had.

Neither paddler could shoot to defend them, but Mel snatched up the Chippewa's rifle and leveled it on the nearest enemy. Before he could fire, a shot sang past so close that it nipped his neck, drawing blood and causing him to recoil in pain.

"Keep your head down!" Sutherland blared, and Nate obeyed, hunching below the gunwales of the craft.

Mel leveled the rifle again, taking careful aim. By now the outlaws had all seen the canoe, and they poured lead into it, several bullets striking the fragile bark, though fortunately above the waterline. Still Mel held his aim and fired coolly. A man in the trees went down, wounded. Nearby, Sutherland saw someone he recognized: Jean Dusten, an aging, short Frenchman who had joined Pontiac's uprising and was a fugitive. Hastily, Dusten fired and vanished in the shadows to reload.

Tamano steered the canoe close to a rocky out-crop, and suddenly another figure appeared at point-blank range, rifle raised. Mel let him have both pistols, and the man crumpled without firing. Sutherland whooped, and Mel's eyes burned with battle fury, his body quivering with rage.

They paddled on, bullets whistling past, splashing into the water, causing the hairs on the back of their necks to prickle. Then they rounded a bend, entering fast, turbulent white water that bore them out of sight. Now they were safe, though they would be unable to continue their search for the exact location of Swain's hideout; the woods were filled with too many of his men. But they still knew enough about the general vicinity of the outlaws to consider their scouting mission a success. They would head back to Fort Detroit, portaging their canoe and following the rivers east. Then, at the fort, they would find enough men to volunteer to come out and destroy Jubal Swain once and for all.

chapter 2

NORTHWEST OUTPOST

Two weeks later, far to the east on the straits between Lake Erie and Lake Saint Clair, Fort Detroit bustled with excitement at the arrival of the sloop *Trader*. The supply ship of Owen Sutherland's Frontier Company, this smart little vessel beat her way up the channel in bright sunshine, a puff of smoke and clap of her swivel gun saluting the stockaded fort that sprawled on a bluff on the western side of the Detroit River.

The arrival or departure of a ship or canoe brigade was always a special occasion at this remote trading post, and by the time the *Trader* came abreast of the palisade and dropped anchor, Detroit throbbed with a great commotion of residents and soldiers on their way to see the ship. Previously quiet on this splendid spring afternoon, the dirt streets of the outpost were transformed into a noisy mass of folk strolling to the landing. There they would watch the unloading, get the latest news from the east or abroad, and observe what sort of goods the Frontier Company had chosen for the trade this year. Layabouts, cardplayers, vagabond Indians, off-duty soldiers, French *habitants,* Anglo adventurers, half-breed laborers, and canoemen called *voyageurs* made their way through the fort along with a host of sporting children. Flowing past rude log cabins, neat whitewashed cottages, and larger log trade warehouses, this was a bright and colorful crowd of scarlet and white uniforms, fluttering feathers, red sashes and caps, fine beaver hats, buckskins, and drab linsey.

No other place in all America had attracted such a cross-section of folk, from soldiers to trappers to scholars and ruffians. Detroit was the point of departure for the most distant northwest, a land still unknown. Beyond this fort, the country was so vast and shrouded in deep forests that even the boldest hunters, white or red, had not roved to its ultimate borders. The fantasies of American, French, and British peoples crystallized here in this isolated collection of log and bark. When outsiders thought of Fort Detroit, they conjured up romantic dreams of a frontier without end, of a life free of social limitations, where strength and courage were enough to guarantee prosperity.

That dream, though unrealistic, was why Detroit had changed so much since 1760, when British troops took command at the close of hostilities between French and British empires in America. No longer was Detroit a sleepy community of *habitants* who fished, farmed, or traded for a carefree subsistence living. Now there were at least six hundred newcomers from the east, many of them former colonial militiamen who had come out last summer with Bradstreet's expedition to pacify the lakes tribes. These were people with imagination and vision, most with the will to brave the rigors of wilderness life and put down roots.

While philosophers in Europe were idealizing the natural life and declaring the sacred purity of natural law, these frontier people were ready to hew that life from the endless forests of America, to trade with Indians, settle, and prosper. The vanguard of America's future was crowded along the Detroit River, though their original hopes had largely been dashed, their dreams proven to be only dreams. The British government had sharply curtailed white movement in the northwest, which was declared Indian country. Required to purchase licenses, all white traders were forbidden to come and go as they pleased at the forts. Too many unscrupulous men had debauched the Indians, cheated them, turned them into drunkards, and enraged the warriors, causing the great rising under Pontiac that had devastated nine British posts as well as the colonial frontier.

Men who had come out to Detroit with the idea of buying Indian acreage cheaply and reselling it to latecomers were disappointed to learn that the government forbade all private purchases of Indian land. Strict rules and regulations frustrated these free spirits who saw the untamed land as rightfully theirs, not the Indians'. Much English blood had been spilled to defeat the Indians and their French allies during a century of terrible, cruel warfare. Regulations caused deep resentment against the army.

Thus Detroit was in a state of disgruntlement as the *Trader* dropped her sail snapping in the breeze and let herself be towed to the landing by a whaleboat. Restless, eager to be about the business of winning their fortunes, the people of Detroit were

distracted from their boring routines to watch the ship arrive.
There would be news of home, letters or newspapers to stir
the melancholy loneliness of some. There was always hope
that official dispatches would permit whites to invade the northwest and exploit it as early colonists had exploited the Eastern
Seaboard and made it blossom into one of the richest regions
of the earth.

In charge of this rough-and-ready horde was Lieutenant
Colonel John Campbell, a tall, stern Scot of late middle age,
who strode through the fort on his way to meet the ship. The
appearance of a vessel was as much a pleasure and distraction
to him as to anyone else. His duty was a tedious and thankless
one for a professional soldier who, over several decades, had
seen the worst and finest moments of British arms. At Detroit,
Campbell was chief constable in a rowdy, tough community;
he was the enforcer of laws that in some areas were impossible
to enforce. He had the task of overseeing trade, of pacifying
restless Indians, of protecting government property, and of
preventing illegal settlement.

Standing between French, British, and Indian blood enemies
who coveted the same land, Campbell had meager strength
with which to do his duty. A few more than one hundred men
of the Royal American Regiment, the 80th Light Infantry, and
his own Black Watch Highlanders were not enough to patrol,
inspect, defend, arrest, frighten, or control frontiersmen and
Indians. More than once he had sent soldiers to drive unauthorized squatters out of their newly built homes, and had
burned those homes to the ground. His was the unpleasant duty
of British commanders in every post of the northwest and along
the border between the colonies and Indian country. Often the
army was despised by those they were supposed to protect.
Good men such as John Campbell were accused of being no
more than agents for wealthy commercial interests who wanted
to keep the new lands for themselves, preventing wholesale
settlement that would divide the land among smallholders.

But without Campbell, without beleaguered army garrisons
that were so poorly supplied and understaffed, the northwest
would be drenched in blood. Indians and whites would fight
to the death; French and Americans would slaughter one another; Virginians would fight Pennsylvanians for country claimed
by both colonies, and New Englanders would kill Yorkers over
land that royal charters said belonged to each of them.

As Campbell made his way to the water gate, he was the

image of authority. Tall and resplendent in his scarlet coat and black tartan kilt, he walked purposefully in the company of two other men. One was Ensign James Parker, an Englishman in his twenties, who was an officer of the Royal American Regiment. Parker's uniform was also scarlet, but with buff tunic facings, smallclothes, and breeches. His unit, known as the Royals, was commanded for the most part by British and mercenary Swiss officers, and was made up of Americans trained for wilderness war. He was a good officer, though poor, as were many ensigns who had no family connections in high places.

As the officer in charge of inspecting all goods that came to Detroit, he was responsible for preventing smuggling as well as for collecting duties laid upon the fur trade. Like Campbell's, Parker's duties were difficult to carry out, though he was capable and intelligent and well liked by most merchants and traders. Nevertheless, Parker was in the unenviable position of administering unpopular regulations, and it was he who often sat in judgment of civil disputes related to commerce. He labored admirably to be fair and honest with people who often had no understanding of what those concepts meant.

Just behind Parker and Campbell was the man who relieved him of the paperwork related to the trade: Farley Jones was a scowling, thin-lipped creature of indeterminate age, who hunched over whether he sat or stood, and who never had a good word for anyone. Lugging a heavy ledger, ink, and quill pens, Jones shambled along behind the officers. His long, hooked nose probed the dust that filled the air, his eyes were slitted and beady. He had the annoying habit of clicking his cheap false teeth, making a surprisingly noisy sound that unnerved more genteel folk and tickled the rougher sort and children, who enjoyed mocking him. As handsome and fine as the two officers were, Jones was ugly and decrepit, his clothes in need of a wash, his pallid face crudely shaved, and his threadbare stockings hanging down to his calves.

No one liked Jones, but he had connections back east, and when he had come out with Bradstreet's army last year he bore letters of recommendation from persons important enough to win him a place as chief clerk for the garrison. For all his unpleasantness, Jones was a sharp accountant, hard to fool, and more than a match for most devious merchants of the northwest. None could slip untaxed or mislabeled goods past him; he knew his business, and he was indispensable to the overworked Campbell and Parker.

About to make their way through the densest part of the noisy mob pushing out through the water gate to see the ship, these three men passed a cabin with an apple-green door and polished brass fittings. There in an upper window appeared a beautiful blond woman in her early thirties who waved to them and called down to ask what all the commotion was about.

Campbell and Parker lifted their hats in salute, and the colonel said, "It's your company's vessel returned from Fort Niagara, Mistress Sutherland! If you'll do us the honor, we'll escort you to the landing."

Ella Sutherland, the wife of Owen Sutherland, gave a cry of excitement and asked them to wait. She closed the window against the dust and hurried from her small bedroom, which was prettily furnished with a curtained maple bed, a French walnut dresser—with real drawers, which were something special on the frontier—and a warm-colored hooked rug. In the far corners were a crib and a small bed for her sons. Ella went quickly down the narrow, winding stairs, paused to straighten a small painting of her family estate back in England, and entered her living room. Here, too, furnishings were more comfortable than elegant, though they spoke of good taste and a love of plants and flowers, which adorned tables and windows.

Ella threw a knitted shawl of undyed wool over her shoulders and glanced at her sleeping son, Benjamin, who was nine months old and liked to nap on an elkskin covering the settee. She arranged her long hair at a mirror, then opened the door, letting in the noise and hubbub of the street.

There was much more clamor than she had anticipated, and she stopped in the doorway, watching Farley Jones hop about, with something brown and furry twisting and snapping at his legs. Jones was trying to hit whatever it was that clung to his stocking, but he was off-balance carrying the ledger and writing implements. As Campbell and Parker were taken aback at first, a crowd quickly gathered to watch the clerk being spun round and round by . . . Ella gasped in dismay to see it was Sniffer, her older son's pet otter.

"No, Sniffer! Stop! Stop!" Running into the street, Ella screamed at the animal, which was sleek and elongated, using its body to whip the helpless Jones around.

Ella and Parker got on opposite sides of the rapidly spinning clerk, but Sniffer scampered faster, evading their grasp, angrily shaking his head as he bedeviled the clerk. Jones swore and swung the ledger uselessly at the otter. The people began to shout and hoot in delight, roaring with laughter as Jones, too dizzy to stand up any longer, collapsed in a heap. Ledger, ink, quill, and bony limbs were all tangled in the dust. Horrified, Ella shrieked at Sniffer, who ambled away, triumphantly escaping to the cabin.

"Oh, my word, I am sorry, Mr. Jones!" Ella exclaimed, trying to lift the fellow to his feet. She would have succeeded, except that he was so dizzy he fell down again.

Sputtering and clicking his false teeth, Jones raged at the vanished otter. When he turned his anger on Ella, Colonel Campbell interrupted and roughly hauled him up.

Swaying, Jones spat out, "Colonel, I demand that animal be destroyed at once! It's a menace, a danger, a beast—"

"Now, now, Mr. Jones," Campbell said in his deep burr. "Let's regain composure, shall we?"

Jones fought for control, all the while glaring at Ella, who was pale with embarrassment. Campbell maintained his decorum, but he was sympathetic with Jones, who fortunately had not been hurt by the otter. As Ella was the sister of Major Henry Gladwin—the former commander of Detroit who last summer had returned to England—Campbell was reluctant to scold her for the animal's attack. Just then Ella's son Jeremy appeared. The ten-year-old was sandy-haired and fair like his mother, her son by her first husband. He retained the name Bently to honor the memory of his natural father. Nervously biting his lip, he apologized to Farley Jones, who haughtily looked the other way, his beak in the air.

When Jeremy asked innocently, "Sir, what did you do to him to make him so angry at you?" the clerk swung around on the boy.

"Do?" Jones squealed, his rattling teeth nearly escaping. "What did I do? Why you little—"

"Yes, Mr. Jones," someone from the crowd demanded, "tell us just what you did to the innocent little thing!"

Everyone turned to see Reverend Angus Lee, a young Presbyterian minister, push the spectacles back on his thin nose and step forward. Lee looked very much as though he were going to give a Sunday sermon on the wages of sin.

Jones blustered, but before he could get very far, Reverend Lee told Campbell, "I saw it all from the door of my residence,

Colonel; Mr. Jones saw the otter sleeping peacefully in the road, and he gave it a spiteful, nasty kick—" Lee did just that to the air, his frame agile and light, and he nearly lost his broad-brimmed felt hat in the demonstration.

Jones squealed again and shook both fists above his head. "A lie! That's a goddamned lie, Minister!"

Lee's watery eyes widened. Jones realized what he had said, stammered, and appealed to Campbell for support. By now the officer had lost his sympathy for Jones, though he knew better than to dismiss the incident out of hand. He turned a grim eye on the sheepish Jeremy.

"Master Bently."

Jeremy winced at being so addressed by the most important man within a thousand miles. Yet he compelled himself to meet Campbell's steady gaze and did not waver.

"Master Bently, your otter is rather known for his ability to create mischief, is he not?"

Jeremy swallowed hard. "I . . . ah, sir, I have heard it said, yes, sir."

"Now, young man, your pet is to be kept clear of Mr. Jones from this moment on. Do you understand? Yes? Well, I hope so, for if that otter causes any more serious mischief in the confines of this post, he will be destroyed."

"Dest—But, Colonel, you can't—"

A touch from his mother and a stern glare from the commander silenced Jeremy. His jaw shut with an involuntary snap. There was a burning in his eyes, and he could not keep his lip from trembling, but still he looked directly at the officer.

"Very well," Campbell said with a sigh and looked at Jones, who obviously was disappointed that nothing more severe had been done. "Let this pass, man. Come, we have king's affairs to conduct."

Jones tramped away, jamming the quill behind an ear. Colonel Campbell bowed to Ella and asked whether she would accompany them to the landing. Glancing at the downcast Jeremy, she said she thought it best to attend to some more immediate matters; she would come down after a while.

The two officers departed into the crowd, and Ella told Jeremy to go to the cabin. Then she thanked Reverend Lee for his kindness.

Lee chuckled, closed his eyes, and said, "It did me good to see that sniveling quill-pusher get what he deserved!" He opened his eyes, which twinkled with mischief. "Did you see how little Sniffer whirled him round? Spun him like a human top! Clever, it was—" Then he caught himself in such an un-Christian attitude, touched his lips with his fingers, and stifled his hilarity. "After you have done your motherly duty, Mistress Sutherland, I would be honored to escort you to the vessel."

After Ella lectured Jeremy and said he must remain behind in the cabin and see to Benjamin, she and Lee walked arm in arm through the water gate and down the gentle slope that led to the landing. They were good friends, having come out here together in the spring of 1763, just before the brutal Indian uprising began. Lee had officiated at the marriage of Ella and Owen that autumn, and as the schoolteacher of Jeremy, the minister was always a welcome guest in the Sutherland house.

Lee knew Ella was worried that Owen had not yet returned from scouting out Jubal Swain's stronghold, so he tried to cheer her up with general banter about the fine condition of the company ship now being unloaded alongside the wharf. Lee also was concerned about Owen, remembering how obsessed he had been about running down the murderer of his lovely Ottawa first wife, who had been slain by a *voyageur* renegade. It was in the course of that consuming quest for revenge that Sutherland had come to know Ella. As a widow whose American husband had died of wounds sustained in the French and Indian War, she had come with Jeremy to Detroit, intending to return to England with her brother, Major Gladwin. Then all that had changed. From the start, Ella and Jeremy were smitten by Sutherland, who fell in love with her and was charmed by the boy.

As Ella and Lee strolled to the ship, the minister wondered with concern whether Owen's new and happy family would be threatened by another vendetta to punish Swain for the murder of Garth Morely, a merchant partner in the fledgling Frontier Company. Then Ella caught Lee's attention by waving enthusiastically at the ship, and Lee peered ahead to see two familiar faces on board.

"Why, it's Peter and Mary!" Lee exclaimed and waved, too. They hurried down to the landing. "They weren't supposed to be coming out."

Ella said he was right. She had seen Peter and Mary Defries, a young married couple responsible for much of the company's affairs in Montreal, just six weeks ago, when she and Owen had gone east to attend the wedding of Jacques Levesque and Angélique Martine, two other partners in the company. At that time, the Defrieses had not said they were coming out. Ella hoped nothing was wrong in Lower Canada, where Frontier Company furs were sent for shipment abroad, and where trade goods were procured to be taken up to Indian and half-breed traders employed by the firm.

Ella's joy to see her friends overcame worry, and she rushed onto the landing as Mary came carefully down the rickety gangplank, her year-old daughter Jeanette squirming to be put down. Mary was a beauty. Blonder than Ella. Mary was just twenty, a cheerful, spontaneous young woman who had overcome much adversity in her life. The child she carried had been conceived in an Indian village, where she was taken as a prisoner after her father and brothers were murdered by hostiles. The baby's father was a soldier who later died fighting alongside Owen Sutherland after the Battle of Bushy Run, which had broken the back of Pontiac's rebellion. Mary knew there were those who whispered that raven-haired Jeanette was the daughter of an Indian war chief.

Ella and Mary embraced, and the bright blue cape and hood Mary was wearing fluttered in the breeze, nearly engulfing Reverend Lee as he shook hands with big Peter Defries. Fair, good-looking, and massively built, Peter contrasted with the slight minister, who happily took Jeanette from her mother as they all began to walk back to the fort. Peter was of Albany Dutch descent, a hearty, bold fellow a little older than Mary, given to practical jokes and occasional brawling.

On this occasion, however, Ella noticed that both Mary and Peter were unusually reserved, almost grave. When she commented on it, both of them looked back over their shoulders toward another couple coming down the gangplank. Ella did not recognize this pair, and since they were garbed in flowing cloaks that concealed their faces, she presumed they were strangers.

"Passengers?" Ella asked. "Are they English?"

Mary seemed tense, and she glanced at Peter, then at several soldiers, including Colonel Campbell and Ensign Parker, standing close by. Mary drew Ella away and watched nervously as the strange couple moved quickly past the officers, taking care not to show their faces.

"Are they English?" Ella pressed again, curious now, as these two hurried by without being introduced.

Lee muttered, "Poor manners if they're English. Must be from Boston. Or maybe they're French, eh?"

Mary whispered to Ella, "Jacques and Angélique!" and her pretty face showed pain.

Ella did not want to believe it. Jacques Levesque and his wife Angélique should have been in Montreal. They handled French matters for the Frontier Company, hiring Canadian *voyageurs*—hardy canoemen who transported the company's goods and peltry in the rivers and lakes of the northwest—and arranging for trading permits and licenses. Out here Jacques was in mortal danger. Once he had been a renegade fighting for the Indians, and he had never been tried for this capital offense. Even though he had washed his hands of the Indian struggle against English domination, and had not been a wanton killer raiding settlements, Levesque was still liable to arrest and possible hanging if he were recognized here in Detroit. In crowded Montreal his past was not known. He was living a whole new life as an essential partner in the company, working to rejuvenate the French economy that had suffered so because of poor Bourbon colonial government and because of the British conquest. Ella found herself standing still, staring, as Jacques and Angélique passed in through the water gate.

Not having heard Mary's whisper, Lee was tickling Jeanette, who giggled and struggled as he carried her up the path to the gate. Ella and Mary stood together while Peter strode on to join the minister. Even Lee should not know that the Levesques were here, for a slip of the tongue might result in arrest.

When Ella's numbness eased, she asked, "Why, Mary? What's got into them? They were doing so well in Montreal! Why risk it all now?"

Mary took her friend's arm, and as they walked slowly along she said, "Because there will be *la crosse* in a couple of days."

Ella stopped walking again. She knew how incredibly important the frequent contests of *la crosse*—called *bagattaway* by the Indians—had been to the French and Indians before the British took control of the northwest, but she did not understand what the upcoming game had to do with Jacques.

Mary explained. "Jacques is a great player, Angélique told me, and for years he led the French against the Ottawa and Chippewa champions. But there hasn't been a championship game since we took this country; the last match was six years ago."

Ella grasped this much. She had marveled at the games played often in the fields beyond the fort, amazed at their brutality, ferocity, and astonishing skill. She also knew that to the victors went the bragging rights until the losers won. Pride—highly prized by French and Indians—was at stake in every match, and this match next week was the most important of all. For the coming year, this contest would mean more than any other, because the select players were the very best each race had to offer. Day after day for the past month she had watched the French competitors running, conditioning, practicing with their sticks—named for their resemblance to the bishop's crosier. These had small rawhide baskets on the crook at the end to catch and throw the hard ball used in the game. She had seen the players' intensity, determination, and grim purposefulness, but she had not imagined that anyone would risk imprisonment and even execution to play.

Again she asked Mary, "Why? It's just a game!"

"It's more than a game, Ella. You see, the French lost six years ago, and in all that time they have not been able to hold their heads up. Do you know what that means to someone like Jacques? Did you know he is said to be the finest French player in all America?"

Ella understood, though she shook her head in despair. If only Owen were home, he might be able to reason with Jacques, to persuade him to slip back to Montreal before someone found out he was here and alerted Colonel Campbell. The commander was a fine man, but he was a stickler for rules, and would never permit Levesque to go free without being sent down to Lower Canada for trial. That trial might result in Jacques's hanging.

Peter had let Lee go into the fort ahead of him, and he glanced over his shoulder at the approaching women. Aware that Mary had told Ella the news, he said, "We came to protect the madman!" Then he grinned. "And to cheer him on! Will Tamano play for the Injuns this year?"

Ella, shaking off confusion, said, "Tamano might not have the stamina, but he's just as strong as he was before the accident on the ice." Ella was referring to Tamano's nearly dying of exposure during a journey he made with Owen two winters earlier. Once the greatest of the Indian champions, the Chippewa was expected to compete, Ella said, if he and Owen came back in time.

Peter chuckled. "Then they'll be here quick. Tamano's as mad as Levesque when it comes to this redskin excuse for legalized rioting! Why, they spill more blood in *la crosse* than they do on the warpath. It oughta be fun to watch!"

"Peter!" Mary exclaimed. "You came out to help hide Jacques, not cheer him on for everybody to hear."

"Oh, that's all right, girl," he said as they went into the fort. "I won't shout his real name, an' he'll be so painted up like an Injun himself that nobody'll recognize him from any other crazy Frenchman out there. I'm gonna call him 'Frog,' 'cause he likes to eat frogs, an' he can jump like one! You'll see!"

Clearly Peter was not as concerned as Ella about their friend's being arrested for treason, but Ella was not so confident. She prayed Owen would get back soon. He would know what to do, and Jacques would listen to him.

Ella and the Defrieses followed the French couple toward the trading house of Jean Martine, the well-to-do father of Angélique, and also a member of the company. Peter took Jeanette from Reverend Lee, who returned to the converted barracks that served as his chapel and where he lived in two small rooms. Even before Ella reached the trading house, she noticed several Frenchmen talking to Jacques. They slapped him on the back and hurried off with a light in their eyes that could only be described as hope. The secret was already out. Ella wondered whether it would be kept among the French. It must be.

She went into the clapboard building, Mary at her side, Peter and the child following, and saw Jean Martine embracing his daughter. Angélique's hood had fallen back, revealing full, curled black hair piled high upon her head. Here was a woman who knew as much about the trade as any man, and could speak several Indian dialects and English, as did her husband and father. Angélique was alight with excitement to be home again. She was petite and delicate, with the sultry beauty of her Huron mother and the vivacious cheerfulness of her Norman father. Jean remarked on how chic she looked in her striking hairstyle and the fashionable crimson gown that reached almost to the floor—unlike most *habitant* women's dresses, which came only to the calf, like the Indians', and were overlaid with a short jacket. Angélique kissed her father's cheek and said the ladies of Montreal were not as brazen as the women of the frontier.

"At least not in public, Papa," she giggled. "Showing one's calf is a scandal, and everyone wears her hair up these days."

"English mode!" grumbled Jacques as he threw back his own hood and greeted his father-in-law, who apparently had been expecting them. No doubt, thought Ella, it had been Jean who told the Levesques about the *grand jeu de la crosse*.

Ella went to Jacques, intending at first to chide him for the insanity of coming back, but as he laughed and said she looked wonderful, she could only hug him and wish him well. A former *voyageur* and a knowledgeable trader, Jacques wore a full beard, which was unusual for most of his kind, who favored mustaches or were clean shaven. The Frenchman's courage and pride showed in his ruggedly handsome face. A bit shorter than Ella, like most French canoemen, he was proud to be small and therefore able to fit all the more cargo into his canoe. Also, like all *voyageurs,* he was incredibly strong, immense across his chest and shoulders. His narrow waist was swathed in a brilliant red sash that served as an adornment as well as a protection for his abdominal muscles, which were strained when he carried as much as three hundred pounds on his shoulders across portages of fifteen miles or more.

"Jacques, Jacques," Ella said, slowly shaking her head, then looking at Angélique, who kissed her on both cheeks. "How could you not stop him?"

Angélique smiled wistfully as her portly father shook hands with his son-in-law. "Stop him?" Angélique asked. "You have never seen the *grand jeu de la crosse,* Ella, but after you have seen it, you will understand. There is nothing like it . . . nothing save war itself."

Jacques laughed, his voice deep and strong, teeth showing white through his heavy beard. "When I learned the *grand jeu* was to be held once again, I could not cower in Montreal! It is for the glory of my people, do you not see? And in these times, my people hunger for honor, for glory! So if I no longer fight, then at least I can play!"

He gave a sweeping gesture with his hands, as though scooping up a ball in the stick of *la crosse,* spun across the room, and fired against an imaginary goalpost.

Jean Martine applauded and laughed with Jacques, just as excited, just as eager for victory. Jean took the long clay pipe from his teeth and said to Ella, "Do not worry, *chérie!* Only the French know the boy is here, and they'll never tell! Even those who might hold something against Jacques will not betray him at a time like this!"

Angélique was excited, too. "They want to win just as he does."

Jean added, "And no one will dare speak about Jacques,

or—" He made a squeaking sound and drew the pipe across his throat.

Jacques tossed his cape onto a chair and declared, "The sloop departs the morning after the match, and we'll be on it! We and sweet victory! Hah! It will almost make Montreal and those city-folk pork-eaters bearable!"

Ella thought a certain trouble came into Jacques's eyes at the mention of life in Montreal. She looked at Angélique, who smiled weakly and shrugged her shoulders.

Angélique said, "It is not easy for us, so far from Detroit . . ."

"City life and too many Englishmen," Jacques half-teased his friends, but they all knew he meant it. Peter laughed and said the French in Canada had never eaten so well now that British government had taken over from a corrupt French rule. Jacques did not disagree, for he knew Defries was right about that, though many Anglo merchants were profiteering and charging exorbitant prices for food.

Jean said, "Ah, my boy, there are as many if not more *Anglais* at Detroit, at Michilimackinac, yes, even at Vincennes and Kaskaskia these days!" He shook his head and shrugged in helpless resignation. "Times have changed! Times have changed." Then he put his arms about his daughter, who fondly laid her head on his chest. "But I'll say you both look well fed, indeed!"

Angélique asked her father's permission to open a bottle of brandy. He agreed, saying it was a good time for a toast to victory and to safe return for Owen and Tamano, who were "hunting for the most terrible killer this country has ever known!"

Jacques held up his glass and declared, "First, a toast to their safe return in time for the *grand jeu de la crosse!*" They all raised their brandy as Jacques went on. "Without Tamano, victory will not be so glorious, and our previous defeat will never be avenged in full!"

"To their immediate return!" Jean cried out.

Ella closed her eyes without meaning to. *Return soon, my Owen. Return safe.*

The next morning, word came to Ella in her house that another vessel was coming upriver, this one called *Helen*, belonging to the Montreal merchant Bradford Cullen. The message was brought by Lettie Morely, whose husband had been murdered by Jubal Swain last year. Lettie was a large, gray-haired woman, florid of face, with great hips and bosom. She had taken her man's place in the Frontier Company and, with her two growing boys, was running the trading house, which combined with Martine's house to supply Indian trappers and traders. Martine supplied the many French and half-breeds, who went out and traded company goods with the Indians, and also did some trapping themselves. Lettie had come to America ten years ago with her husband, and their house did business with the large number of Indian trappers who came in each season to trade their peltry.

"It be a spankin' new ship as fine as our *Trader!*" Lettie declared in her north-of-England accent. "Ooh, that there Cullen has a lot o' money, though! But that's the way it always is with the bad 'uns! They get rich an' the good get taken!"

Ella, who was washing breakfast dishes in a tub, dried the last cup, then poured the water out the kitchen window. She fetched Benjamin, lying on the rug next to Jeanette in front of a small fire in the hearth. Sitting near a sun-filled window, Mary Defries was stitching a torn shirt for Peter, who was visiting friends he had met at Detroit the year before. Having finished their work, they wrapped their infants in blankets and went out to watch the Cullen ship come in. Both knew that the rich, unscrupulous New Englander would have a cargo that would outdo their own in abundance, though not quality.

They decided not to give Cullen the satisfaction of seeing them ogle his wares, so they went to one of the southwestern ramparts and watched from there. Indeed, it was a fine ship. Unlike *Trader,* which was sleek and all black save for a white line running along her hull, the *Helen* was elegantly painted in red and gold. Even the ship's wheel was painted, mostly white and gold, with touches of red glistening in the sunlight. The deck was busy with laborers unloading an enormous cargo that made the ship ride low in the water, fat and smug, like the merchant himself. That cargo would be placed in Cullen's well-stocked warehouse at Detroit, eventually to be traded with the Indians of the region for their peltry. Acting as factor in charge of the warehouse was a Hampshireman named Caleb Soames, who distributed the goods on credit to the Indian trappers and kept the company's accounts. Soames's role as factor was like that of Lettie Morely or Jean Martine, the difference being that he was not a partner and had no say in company affairs.

"There he is!" said Mary, pointing with one hand while she held Jeanette with the other. "There's Cullen himself! Look how he tyrannizes his men!"

Cullen stood regally on the raised afterdeck, commanding his boatswain to get the most out of the landsmen swarming over the vessel and filling up the landing with cargo. Pacing about the deck as his swarthy boatswain growled at his men, Cullen looked every bit a pompous rascal who cared for no one but himself, and very little like a conservative New Englander. Dressed in a velvet frock coat of pinkish hue, with satin smallclothes and stockings, he stood out at rough-timbered Detroit like a peacock in a hayfield. His tricorn was so fine that it seemed to shine in the light reflecting off the river, and as he stamped about on the poop deck, his silver buckles caught the sun and gleamed like points of fire.

Mary was naturally the first one to recognize Cullen, for she had lived in his house for several months before meeting Peter and falling in love with him. Cullen had been in debt to Mary's deceased father, and in order to discharge that debt as cheaply as possible, he had taken the orphaned young woman into his household with the intention of repaying what he owed by supplying room and board.

But Cullen, his shrewish wife, Helen—the one after whom the sloop was named—and his homely daughter, Linda, were jealous of Mary's loveliness, and they made her life miserable until they finally drove her out. They held a grudge against Mary and Peter, particularly because the couple was in partnership with Sutherland's Frontier Company, now locked in a bitter duel with Cullen and Company to gain control of the northwestern fur trade.

"Look," Lettie said, "there be a crowd o' French an' half-breeds lookin' on, but they ain't got a chance o' gettin' work, I'll warrant."

Indeed, only Americans and British were working on Cullen's ship. He was typical of many Anglo merchants based in Montreal, who were trying to wrest control of the vast former French empire by monopolizing the trade in the region, purchasing all available goods, and bribing officials in order to prevent others from acquiring licenses and trading permits. Even though there were fifty thousand French in Canada and only a few hundred British merchants in Montreal, a British law forbade Catholics from voting, so the conquered French were not permitted to establish a free government. While the

British Parliament was laboring to resolve the sticky problem
of permitting French Canadians to elect political leaders, British
merchants in Montreal were maneuvering to create an assembly
of their own—one filled by their handpicked cronies. Such an
assembly, if allowed by Parliament, would determine the destiny of the great northwest as well as of Upper and Lower
Canada, without the French having a voice in their own government.

Mary said, "Cullen hates the French, just as much as he
hates Owen—" She caught herself too late, and said to Ella,
"I'm sorry; I didn't mean to bring that subject up again." She
felt bad because Cullen, with his political connections and great
wealth, was accumulating the power to destroy the Frontier
Company once and for all.

Ella patted her hand and watched the French at the landing,
about fifty yards off, drinking and laughing, obviously making
light of Cullen and his ship. Lettie clucked and said Cullen
must have pulled in favors from every supply house in the
colonies to have collected so many trade goods at a time when
a general economic crisis was afflicting America and Britain
alike.

A burst of derision arose from the French, who were angry
that Cullen so pointedly shut them out from work that meant
much to their livelihood. Cullen strode to the side of the ship
and shouted at them in language that would have disgraced any
other Boston Puritan—which was his bloodline and the lineage
of his wife. (She and the Cullens' daughter, Linda, were at
home, in Montreal.) But Cullen's anger only served to spur
the Frenchmen on, and another insult from one of them touched
off even louder laughter. That was too much for Cullen. He
called to his men, several of whom were pushing laden hand-
carts toward the fort. Some workers did not respond, but others
joined Cullen's crew in a rapid gathering on deck.

"What's he doing?" Mary asked.

"Handin' out belayin' pins an' clubs," Lettie replied, chewing her lower lip. "There be trouble a-comin'."

Ella looked from Cullen to the French and then to the Anglo
crewmen and laborers arming themselves. The taunting had
stopped, and the French were throwing off extra clothing, picking up stout sticks, and flexing muscles, eager for a fight.

"Oh!" cried Mary. "Oh, no! Not Peter!"

Peter Defries was at the water gate to the left of the rampart
where Ella and the women stood. He was rolling up his sleeves,

excitement in his eyes as he began to move toward the trouble. There was no question that Peter would relish a chance to crack a few of the heads employed by Bradford Cullen. Mary feared for him and called out. Peter waved to her and said he was going to pay his respects to Cullen.

By now the sailors and workers were leaping from the ship, advancing on the Frenchmen. The two groups were roughly equal in number, thirty or so on each side. Ella had to keep Mary from rushing off after Peter, but then Ella's heart leaped, for she saw Owen's canoe come in to shore near the sloop. She shouted to him as he stepped out. He saw her, followed her signals, and noticed the rapt Defries hurrying toward the trouble just as the two sides gave a roar of anger and attacked. Sutherland rushed for Defries, catching him in mid-charge. Glad to see Sutherland, Peter lifted him off the ground in a mighty bearhug, then clapped him on the shoulders.

Mary sighed in relief that Owen had halted her man. The sound of battle attracted attention in the fort, and in the next moment, other men rushed down to the fight, some to support the French, others to help the Anglos. Immediately, a squad of fifteen soldiers on guard duty trotted in two files out the fort's gate, though in no hurry to get mixed up in something that would be difficult to stop.

"Thank heavens Owen came just in time," Mary gasped as she saw the two friends happily talking, Defries pointing at the tumult, apparently explaining to Sutherland what had happened.

Ella had been smiling with joy to see Owen home safe and sound, but she suddenly caught her breath when Owen pulled off his buckskin shirt, removed his claymore, and barreled toward the fray. Whooping alongside Peter, they thundered upon Cullen's toughs with the fury of maddened grizzlies.

Ella did not even have a chance to shriek Owen's name. Instead, she whispered it helplessly, touching the silver pendant that he had given her, dangling at her neck. She hoped neither of them would be hurt too badly, for that would make it hard to be annoyed at them.

Lettie Morely giggled and swung her fists, hitting Ella accidentally on the shoulder. Apologizing, she turned her attention back to the fight.

"Give it to 'em, lads!" Lettie chortled, then tried to reassure her two friends. "Don't worry about thy men, lassies, there's no one there can match 'em! Oooh!" she winced. "Well, Mary, thee best be gettin' out them poultices an' comfrey." She winced again, and added, "Lobelia, too, an' some liniment, Ella. Thy lads be outa practice!"

At the Morely trading house late that afternoon, Owen and Peter nursed their cuts and bruises. Lettie busied herself boiling herbs and preparing a homemade remedy guaranteed to ease the pain of battered bodies and torn muscles. Each man sat in a rocking chair, holding against his face a wet cloth dipped in comfrey. Benjamin slept on Owen's lap, while Jeanette balanced on her father's knee. Nearby, Ella and Mary sat fuming at a long table, with nothing kind to say to their husbands.

Peter cackled, and Sutherland looked at him with his un-blackened eye. "What's so funny?" He was grinning himself, despite the annoyance of their wives.

Peter said, "Never thought that a sailor couldn't swim! An' a bos'n he was, too!" He laughed again, and his jaw hurt.

"He enjoyed your ducking him," Sutherland replied. "He just didn't want to admit it."

They laughed and felt the pain of a dozen welts and bruises. The fight had been worth it, however, ending with Cullen's entire crew being tossed into the drink, and the laborers soundly whipped. Only the reluctant appearance of Ensign Parker and additional soldiers had prevented Cullen from being thrown overboard along with his men. He had been frightened enough to climb the rigging, his frock coat flapping in the breeze, the ship swaying dizzyingly as he clung in terror to the mast. Yet no damage had been done to his property, and the soldiers were satisfied simply to stop the fight and threaten to arrest anyone who carried on further violence near the fort.

Cullen had demanded arrests, but there was no doubt that the merchant and his followers were as much to blame as anyone else.

Alongside the astonished Nate and Mel, Tamano had stood by and laughed to watch the fracas, then departed when it was over, and sought out his wife, Lela. As for the two greenhorn adventurers, Nate and Mel had kept out of trouble and were at this moment trying to arrange lodging with a family Sutherland knew that might take in boarders. He had offered them both occasional work, loading boats or baling furs, until they could either find steady employment or return east again.

Lettie laid a tray of cups and saucers on the table in front of Ella and Mary, declaring, "Come, come, ladies, no more poutin'! What's done is done, an' let it be. Come here, boys, by thy wives. Let's have a spot o' tea an' be friends, eh?" The women were not so sure. "Come, come! Get these knaves alone in bed tonight, an' do thy scoldin' private-like."

The men carried their children to the table and sat down across from Ella and Mary, who showed signs of relenting a bit.

"Ach, Ella, lass," Sutherland said softly. "Be gentle; I was just trying to keep Peter from hurting somebody—"

There was a knock at the door, and in came Jean Martine with Angélique and Jacques. Throwing back their hoods, they warmly greeted Owen, who immediately realized Levesque's peril. But he understood the importance of this contest of *la crosse,* and gave his friend the welcome news that Tamano was ready to play for the Indians. Just as he said that, in came the Chippewa and his pretty wife, Lela. Levesque and Tamano rushed to embrace one another, laughing and excited. Now the entire senior partnership in the Frontier Company was gathered in this room, and the door was locked to prevent anyone entering who should not see Levesque.

There was talk of the impending contest, but the main conversation concerned hunting Jubal Swain and his killers. Sutherland would see Colonel Campbell in the morning and suggest that soldiers be sent with civilian and Indian volunteers to wipe out the stronghold, which was surely somewhere in the eastern districts of the Wees-konsan. Everyone knew the damage Swain's force could do to the fragile balance of the fur trade. If he preyed upon Frontier Company traders, and was able to cut off routes linking Detroit with the fur grounds of the northern Mississippi, then the young partnership would be hurt severely enough to collapse.

Everything these people owned was tied up in trade goods and supplies. If the trading season was successful it would be the beginning of steady growth that promised prosperity a few years down the road. A failed season, however, or one disrupted even temporarily by Swain, would be disastrous, because none of the partners was wealthy like Bradford Cullen.

They were tense when Sutherland told what had to be done. The women in particular felt fear for their men until Sutherland insisted that neither Jean, Jacques, nor Defries could accompany this expedition—Jean was too old, Jacques was a wanted man in this country, and Defries was not a frontier fighter. Ella wished Owen, too, could stay behind for once, though she said nothing. Sitting quietly near Lela, who sat cross-legged on a chair, she took comfort in the woman's company. It would be their husbands who would lead the expedition, who would face death, with the odds on the side of a dangerous, cunning enemy.

chapter 3

THE CABIN WINDOW

As night descended on Fort Detroit, and the meeting of Frontier Company partners went on, Jeremy Bently and his friend Sally Cooper searched frantically through the fort for the pet otter. They had been looking all day for Sniffer, and with the coming of night, they were almost desperate, fearing that someone—perhaps the spiteful Farley Jones—might have snared the creature and harmed it. In this part of the fort, near the northwestern wall, shadows were long and it was difficult to see the children flitting along the palisade, softly calling the animal's name. Jeremy went first, slipping from house to house, crying out whenever they came to a box of trash awaiting disposal at the communal quicklime pit. They were concerned that Sniffer might suddenly bound from the garbage, his naughty face smeared with waste, and make so much noise that someone would look out and see the awful mess one greedy otter was able to make of a neat trash box.

Behind her friend, Sally hurried along, her auburn pigtails flying. A linsey petticoat, bodice, and drab apron covered her pudgy body. At nine years of age, Sally was like a younger sister to Jeremy, and the otter was as dear to her as to the boy. Every once in a while she whistled in a way that Sniffer would recognize, but so far there was no response. Sally had lived with Lettie Morely last year, after being rescued from the Indians by Jacques Levesque. Fleeing from Pontiac's camp, he had taken Sally along, narrowly preventing her murder. Shaken and suffering from seeing the massacre of her family in Pennsylvania, Sally was alone in the world until Lettie took her in. When the death of Garth Morely had made one extra mouth a burden to Lettie, Sally went to the Sutherlands. That was good for her because she could care for Sniffer and indulge her open admiration for absolutely anything Jeremy thought, said, or did.

As a rule, Sally preferred trousers and a shirt and bare feet, but today she was dressed like a girl for the company gathering—where she and Jeremy should have been having dinner just then. Yet even the thought of a reunion with Jacques Levesque could not keep Sally from hunting Sniffer. Like Jeremy, she was terrified that Farley Jones might have done something evil to the otter. He was nasty enough.

Without planning to, the children made straight for Jones's cabin, which stood alone near the palisade. One side of the house formed an alley with the palisade, the rest of the house was enclosed by a four-foot fence that also surrounded a poorly tended garden. Weeds were already rank, though it was not yet summer. The steep, thatched roof of the clerk's small cabin needed repair, but he was too stingy to have it done. His center chimney of clay and sticks, which supported the weight of the walls and roof of the house, was sadly eroded; within the garden fence was a mound of garbage that stank.

"Phew!" whispered Jeremy as they crept inside the low fence. "Sniffer would just love that smell."

Sally was shaking with nervousness. "Oh, Jer, I hope not! I hope he's not here at all."

"Don't call me Jer! It's Jeremy!"

Above, the reddish light of sunset glowed on the points of the palisade, splashed on the roof and chimney of the cabin. Below, all was cool shadow. Sally rubbed her arms, feeling chilly from the evening breeze as much as from worry. She followed Jeremy to a window, and both made sure no one was passing by on a stroll around the path that went along the base of the palisade protecting the fort's sixty buildings.

As the children came to the window, which was just above their heads, they heard voices within and smelled strong pipe smoke. Someone was speaking French, and there were English words as well. They looked hesitantly about the garden, but saw no sign of Sniffer rooting in garbage. Twice before, Jones had complained about the otter raiding his dump and even his kitchen. A third proven complaint would surely result in severe punishment for Sniffer. Jeremy and Sally quaked just a bit as she knitted her hands, took his foot, and helped boost him ever so slowly up the rough log wall of the house. He peeked into the room through a broken pane in the grimy window.

What he was looking for was some sign of the otter's having been caught. At the very worst he would see a bloody carcass.

Or he might see Sniffer caged. He hoped to see neither of these, but where else could the otter be? They had searched and searched for hours. In the dimness, Jeremy saw Jones standing with another man near the fireplace, where a small blaze crackled against the evening chill. Looking around, Jeremy saw no sign of the otter, and that gave him some relief. Then he recognized the other man as the overweight Bradford Cullen. Thinking little about it, he began to move away from the window.

When he heard the French voice, he thought it was familiar. He peered again into the room. Sitting with his back to Jeremy was a grizzled, skinny figure in the red cap and sash of a *voyageur*. Like the others, this one smoked a long white pipe, and mixed his languages, from English to French and back again, as he spoke to Jones and Cullen. Where had Jeremy heard that cackling laugh before? It was a greasy, uncouth chuckle, as though the man were sneering at life itself. Curious, Jeremy kept his eye at the break in the window just long enough to see the Frenchman lean over and knock the dottle from his pipe. The boy nearly fell backwards. It was the renegade Jean Dusten!

In 1763, Dusten, acting as guide, had betrayed the soldier-courier sent to warn Fort Michilimackinac, between lakes Michigan and Huron, of impending attack. This courier, named Duncan McEwan, was captured by Chippewas, who treacherously slaughtered the entire garrison at Michilimackinac. Later, McEwan met and fell in love with Mary Hamilton, when both were prisoners, neither sure of life or death. McEwan had escaped Dusten's cruel trickery, only to die in battle. Mary had been set free; it was McEwan's child she carried when compelled to go to Montreal for the help of Bradford Cullen.

In the meantime, Dusten had stayed with Pontiac's hostiles, and had a price on his head. Jeremy was not aware that the Frenchman was now one of Jubal Swain's men, but he knew that Dusten was dangerous. Why was he meeting in secret with Bradford Cullen and Farley Jones? Groaning to herself as she supported Jeremy, Sally whispered that he should come off, and Jeremy scraped down slowly.

Panting and blowing on her sore fingers, Sally listened as Jeremy told who was inside, but she did not grasp the importance of it.

"I've got to tell my father!" Jeremy said softly.

"What about Sniffer?" Sally asked, rubbing her hands together. "Did you see anything?"

Jeremy shook his head, but was listening to the muted conversation within, his smattering of French helping him understand what Dusten was saying.

"I can promise you, Monsieur Cullen, that my people in the Wees-konsan will cooperate with you for as long as it is profitable to us." Dusten's voice was slow and lazy, but with a haughty edge that obviously displeased Cullen.

"I want more than cooperation, Dusten," the merchant snapped. "I want results! If I'm going to hand out good money to you and your friends, I want the kind of results that will hurt Sutherland... hurt him badly. Make sure none of my canoe brigades are attacked, and you may have your way with anyone else's. Is that clear?"

Dusten cackled in that giddy falsetto that made him seem a fool. But he was no fool; he was quick to shed blood—as long as he did not endanger himself.

"Results I do promise you, monsieur, if it is well worth my master's trouble."

Jeremy could not resist urging Sally to cup her hands again and boost him up. She was trembling with the effort as Jeremy watched and listened to these three conspire to attack his stepfather in some way. Just how he could not yet tell.

Farley Jones said, "Mr. Cullen, I understand our friend Jean here has something for us already." The clerk's thin face was sly and cold, despite the color of the fire that lit his sunken eyes. "He says it'll cost you fifty pounds... sterling."

"Fifty?" Cullen blustered. "Why, that's outrageous, exorbitant, no matter what the information! Hah! Fifty pounds *sterling,* indeed! If you have something I can use against them, out with it, and I'll decide just what it's worth—in York currency, not sterling! Preposterous!"

Sally was wobbling. Jeremy tried to hold on to hear what was about to be said. Dusten was cackling and refilling his pipe.

"I'll compromise: Forty pounds sterling, monsieur, and I'll tell you all about Jacques Levesque."

Cullen looked up sharply. His agents in Montreal had pointed out Levesque to him, and he was also aware of the Frenchman from his run-ins with the Frontier Company. Yet he knew neither that Levesque was a wanted man, nor that he was hiding at Detroit. He made no sign of agreement until Dusten said, "You'll hurt Sutherland and the rest of them. I swear it."

"Speak up, then! If your secret is worth it, you'll get what you deserve."

Sally could hold Jeremy no longer, though he dug his toes into chinks between logs and clung with his fingers to the sill. Dusten cackled and took his time before he went on. Sally shoved her shoulder against Jeremy's legs. Dusten laughed and slapped his thigh, while Farley grinned, wiping his nose with a sleeve.

Sally whispered, "Jer, I can't...I..."

A voice startled them: "Hey, you two!" Jeremy fell onto Sally, both collapsing in a heap. They scrambled to their feet just as their friend, Tommy Morely, sauntered up, oblivious to what was going on. Sally and Jeremy ran, yanking Tom around and dragging him protesting along the darkened palisade.

Back at the cabin, Farley stuck his face against the glass, trying to see what all the commotion was about.

"Who is it?" Cullen asked from the door, ready to rush outside.

Farley snorted, shook his head, and walked back to the fireplace. "Just some damned kids runnin' through the alley. Kids! Oughta outlaw 'em!"

A little distance from the cabin, the children saw no one was chasing them, and they slowed down, breathless. Tom, who was the son of Lettie and best friends with Jeremy, panted for an explanation. Jeremy told him that they were trying to find Sniffer, but had learned that Cullen was conspiring with Dusten and Jones against the company.

Tom was a husky lad, with curly brown hair and freckles. A year younger than Jeremy but already a bit taller, Tommy was usually carefree, and had recovered from the loss of his father last year. As the eldest son he had taken on considerable responsibility helping his mother in the family business. Not as sharp-witted as Jeremy or Sally, he thought little about the Cullen matter. Instead, he shook his head and said:

"Tarnation! You doodle-brains won't find that otter 'round here! He's been with me all day, fishin'! Why, he'd rather catch fresh trout than grub in that skinflint's garbage! A mouse would starve in there!"

Jeremy and Sally sighed with relief when Tommy said Sniffer was safe at home, asleep with a full belly. But Jeremy insisted they had to hurry to tell the others what he had learned. Levesque's life might depend on it, and so might the welfare of the Frontier Company.

Breathlessly, Jeremy told all he knew. The friends in the Morely trading house were quiet until Sutherland said, "The *Trader*'s unloaded. We'll have men work all night to get her ready to sail, and Jacques can be on board—"

"No!" Levesque jumped up, anger in his eyes. "I will not run with my tail between my legs."

"*Chéri*," Angélique said, taking his hand, fear making her voice quiver. "If they know, then you are lost."

Levesque touched her cheek, held her eyes with his, then turned to Sutherland. "I can run no longer, my friend. If I am arrested, then so be it. I can run no longer."

Martine hurried to go out the door, saying, "We'll find Dusten, learn what he said; then we'll make an end to him!" He went out quickly, and the room was silent again.

Tamano got up and came to Levesque, putting a hand on his shoulder. "Frenchman, hear me. Open your heart and think of your woman." Levesque stared at Chippewa's somber face. "If you do not play, then Tamano does not play."

Levesque's face fell, and he looked at Angélique. Pursing his lips, he turned back to Tamano and took the Indian's forearms in his hands.

"Listen, Chippewa, when Jean rids us of Dusten, who is there to tell Cullen which French player is I? These are all new Englishmen, save for a few I know who will not turn me in. I have no fear." He laughed. "Bring me vermilion and ocher, and I'll paint myself like a demon. No man will know me, especially not the English commander."

Levesque glanced at Sutherland for support, but Tamano said, "In the *grand jeu*, no one will miss seeing Levesque."

The Frenchman was honored. "I will play," he said, and Angélique sat down, staring blankly at the floor. "Bring me the paint, Tamano, and remember it is I when a vermilion devil flies at you in the match."

The eyes of both men flared with the challenge, and they grinned fiercely, arms still fastened to each other.

• • •

Neither Ella nor Owen could sleep that night. He lay awake, while she sat downstairs by the fading embers of the fire. Sitting up in the darkness, he called her name. Above in the loft Sally stirred, and in one corner of the bedroom Jeremy mumbled and turned over. The infant Benjamin slumbered peacefully in his crib in another corner of the Sutherland chamber.

Owen pulled on his linen smock and went below, where Ella offered him some tea just made in a kettle over the fire. He accepted a hot cup and sat down opposite her, both thinking, each wondering what was on the other's mind, and knowing it was so hard to talk about the future.

He saw her eyes shining and sad in the firelight, and it pained him that they did not lead a simpler life—one that did not put their lives in such danger. But he would not be happy in the east, where life was more tranquil, more ordered. Out here a man fought hard for what he had, and death was always at hand, whether lurking behind a tree or in the form of an unexpected gale sweeping down on a canoe brigade on Lake Erie.

Yet it was not the daily danger that troubled Ella, and Sutherland knew it. It was the planned expedition for Swain. He was like the devil himself, and Ella feared for her husband. She knew Owen would pursue the renegade and murderer until one of them was killed, and Ella prayed the pursuit would end with Swain's demise, not Owen's.

As he knelt at the fire, plying it with pine kindling and building a bright blaze that lit the room, Ella spoke what was on her mind. "Owen, can't the army take care of this? After all, that's what Colonel Campbell is paid for; he's a professional . . ." She knew Owen would not agree, though it still caused an ache when he replied.

"The army can't beat Swain without help from men who know the woods, Ella." He tossed the last stick into the fire, then came to her side, resting on one knee and taking her hand. "We can't afford the slightest failure; if Campbell sends out an expedition but can't root out Swain, the outlaws will cut off trade and our company'll be ruined. You heard what Jeremy told us—Dusten and Swain are in with Cullen and Farley in some way, and I'd guess Swain could beat us where Cullen can't.

"Ella, if I capture Swain, or we can force Dusten to confess about an alliance with Cullen, then we'll bring charges against him that could drive him out of the trade, perhaps even get him jailed. After Jean Martine collars Dusten, what he can tell us about Swain will guarantee the expedition's success! Believe me, lass, I'll be very careful. We'll win, and then I'll settle down here for good."

Ella looked at him, her eyes moist, and kissed his hand. She had heard all this before. It was true, thank God, that Owen had always come home safely, once even rescuing Jeremy, who had been kidnapped by Swain. She could not help smiling at him. He kissed her.

"You will come back to me, Owen," Ella whispered, and he wiped a tear that had escaped onto her cheek.

"It won't be so long! Hey, we'll have this affair settled once and for all by winter." He grinned and stood, bringing her up, drawing her against him. "Then we'll rebuild Valenya, Ella, just the way you want, and whenever, wherever I go, you'll go, too."

Valenya! How Ella loved that place across the river, where great standing stones loomed above the shoreline and sandy beach. There Owen had lived with his Ottawa wife, who was buried in the shadow of those stones. Often Owen and Ella had spoken of building a fine house overlooking the straits at Valenya, raising a big family there, and running their company affairs from a trading warehouse on the site. For the present they would live in Detroit, though, because the expense of building at Valenya made it impossible. But once the company throve, their share of the profits would make possible the construction of a handsome clapboard house, painted white, with a real shingled roof and a veranda that gave a view of the wide Detroit River. Perhaps there would even be a few sash windows that opened and closed like those they had seen in Pennsylvania.

Just to think of it made Ella tingle, and she hugged Owen, held him close, and felt for the moment that she was the most fortunate woman on earth.

Without speaking, they went upstairs holding hands, and as they lay down, Benjamin gave a hint of awakening, softly whimpering. Ella caressed Owen, and he kissed her. Benjamin cried a bit louder.

Turning to the infant, Owen said, "Hush, Benjamin, you're all right; everything's all right. Go to sleep, laddie. That's it, son. Go to sleep."

The child was quiet, taking his thumb and becoming still.

"He's dreaming," Sutherland said, turning to Ella and kissing her throat and shoulders.

Ella smiled and closed her eyes. "So am I," she whispered to herself, so faintly that Owen did not hear her. "So am I."

Ella was planting roses in her small garden, which was surrounded by a new white picket fence, when Owen came in sight on his return from the interview with Colonel Campbell. Ella saw immediately that something was wrong. Wiping dirt from her hands on an apron, she stood up to watch her husband storm through the gate and into the house.

Hurrying behind him, Ella asked what had happened, and Owen roughly unbuckled his claymore and threw it on the settee.

"He won't do it!" Owen began pacing the floor. "He won't go after Swain. He says he doesn't have the men, and if he tries and fails, he'll be severely reprimanded for extravagance, recklessness, irresponsibility!" He was boiling with frustration. "Campbell doesn't have the funds to supply an expedition, doesn't have the supplies, doesn't have the ammunition, doesn't have the canoes—Damn!" He smashed his fist into his palm. "He won't gamble with his reputation, that's what it is!"

"Owen! He's a good man—"

"He doesn't want to be humiliated, not out here where his career can be damaged but never advanced!"

"Owen, not Colonel Campbell! Be fair!"

He walked to the mantel and leaned against it. Her hands twisted in the apron, and Ella wished she could say something better than defend the commander. In one way she was glad Owen would not be going off to fight again. In another, she worried for them, and for all who could be hurt by Swain's renegades.

She asked, "Did you tell him about Cullen and Dusten? About Farley Jones?"

Sutherland shook his head. "Not yet. I can't prove anything, and we won't be able to until someone confesses, either Jones or Dusten, if Martine has caught him." He went to the window and looked out, his chest rising and falling in fury. Little Benjamin crawled toward him and grabbed his leg, sliding down to the floor with a plop. Owen hardly noticed the child, and walked away so quickly that Benjamin was bowled over, banging his head on the floor.

"Owen!" Ella protested and picked up the wailing baby.

Sutherland turned, troubled, and took the boy, rubbing his

head and soothing him. To Ella he said, "Forgive me, lass, but I hadn't expected this."

He took Benjamin to the open door, bouncing him up and down until the crying stopped. Just then Jean Martine came into the garden, his face grave.

As he entered the door, Martine said, "Dusten has escaped."

"Where?" Sutherland handed Benjamin to his wife.

"We don't know for sure." Martine poured himself a glass of water from a pitcher on the table. "West, that's all we know. He had friends camped not far off, and they have three hours' start already."

"Is there anyone who can trail them? I'll go myself! Ella, can we get some grub together—"

"Hold on, *mon ami,*" Martine insisted, finishing his drink. "Indeed, we have the man to follow Dusten, and to find the exact location of Swain's stronghold. An old friend of yours: the Delaware named Niko-lota."

"Niko-lota? Here?" Sutherland was excited to hear that the young warrior who had helped him fight Swain a year ago had come to Detroit for *la crosse.* As another man who longed to wipe out Swain, the Delaware would make a perfect scout to prepare the way for an expedition. Then Sutherland realized bitterly there would be no expedition, and he told Martine that Campbell had refused.

Disappointed, Martine sat down heavily on the settee. Sutherland again paced the floor. Ella wanted no part of this. When the decision was made, they could tell her; she went outside to the garden again, her mind whirling. She needed air, distraction. Planting roses was something good, something creative. Planning a battle was something else.

In the living room, Sutherland said, "Jean, how many men can you get together who would go after Swain right away?"

Martine was surprised, and he answered, "I can get as many as we need, *mon ami,* but if the army says we cannot go, then who am I to defy them? We'll all be put in prison if we take an unauthorized military expedition into the woods, you know that."

Sutherland knew that, and the danger of arrest if he went without permission angered him all the more. Along with forty French and Indian allies and a few Anglos, he could make a quick dash through the forest, following Dusten. Using Niko-lota as an advance scout, Sutherland could launch the raid, destroy Swain's haven, and get back to Detroit before Campbell could send out a patrol to stop him. If everything was done in secrecy they might just succeed.

Martine spoke what was on Sutherland's mind. "Defying the government is no small thing. Armed whites are not permitted in the wild. What if the Indians think the wrong way and attack you?"

Sutherland waved that off. "We'll get word to them why we're out there, and with Tamano and Niko-lota along we'll have no trouble with other Indians." He was thinking, pacing, pacing. "We can do it!" He swung on his friend. "Jean, we have to do it! We have no choice but to defy Campbell, defy the army, defy Parliament itself if we have to! Times are changing, as you said last night, and those who can't change must expect to be defied."

Sutherland stared through the open door at Ella, who had heard him but was continuing with the planting. Benjamin played in the dirt at her side.

Martine got up, saying, "I'll see what I can arrange, and I'll send Niko-lota to you." He touched Sutherland on the shoulder and stared intently. "If you succeed, you'll be a hero, and even Parliament will go easy on such bold defiance." He paused and then said, "If you fail, you will be reviled from Philadelphia to London for being a hothead bent on burning up the frontier again."

Sutherland did not agree. "Those are killers in the Weeskonsan!"

Martine sighed. "They are, but until they attack many more white men or stir up Indians to another rising, the government will refuse to spend the money or risk the honor of its army to wipe them out."

Sutherland gave a laugh at the irony. "By then it'll be too late; the damage will be done."

Martine agreed but shrugged his shoulders. "I will do what I can to help you. But do not fail, *mon ami*."

As Jean left, Ella was watching, still crouched at her work. Sutherland caught her eye, and she looked at him a moment, then gave her hands to planting, though her heart and thoughts were elsewhere.

A little later, upon the arrival of Niko-lota, Sutherland forgot his restlessness and welcomed the Delaware. Standing in the cabin doorway, Niko-lota looked broader and more mature than he had last autumn, when he and Sutherland fought and defeated Swain's first band. At twenty, the young man was known as one of the wisest warriors of the Munsee, or wolf clan, and was also respected as a fighter. He chafed under British rule, but for all his repressed antagonism toward whites, Niko-lota knew where the hope of his race lay. Survival depended upon rapid transformation of the Indian way of life to resist white incursions, to survive the white culture, which could sweep away Indian civilization in a generation. Owen Sutherland was one of the few whites Niko-lota trusted, and that was a high honor, because the Lenni Lenape, as the Delaware called themselves, had good reason to despise whites.

A few decades past, they had been driven from their eastern homes by white trickery and legal deception; they were forced to travel into the northwest as wanderers relying on the kindness of other nations to help them. Since then, the Lenni Lenape thrived, but they had sworn to avenge their humiliation. The meaning of their name was "original people," and they were a proud folk who had led in the eastern uprising during Pontiac's rebellion. It was in this war that Niko-lota won fame as a fearless, intelligent war leader, and at the Battle of Bushy Run, Owen Sutherland had spared his life. As Sutherland looked him over, he saw how formidable Niko-lota had become with age and experience.

No longer on the warpath, Niko-lota was not hostile, but he hated Jubal Swain, the man who had caused much Indian persecution in Pennsylvania. Swain's evil ways had caused the death of Niko-lota's sister, a converted Christian who had tried faithfully to lead a peaceful life. Niko-lota had never believed in her dream of racial harmony, and had wanted her to return to the Delaware. He had failed, just as she had failed to convince him to bury the hatchet. Yet the young warrior had changed his attitude, having seen the awesome might of British guns. He knew the only hope for his people was to learn white ways and grow strong.

Yet to see Niko-lota, tattooed over his bare chest and up his neck and face—the story of his exploits, recently designed at his home in the country southeast of Detroit—no one would have taken him for a progressive, pragmatic man. Black hair hung down over his shoulders, his strong nose accentuated by the gleam in his eyes. He hardly smiled as he gripped Sutherland's forearms, but the Scotsman sensed the warrior's goodwill.

Niko-lota was in no mood to visit sociably and waste time, as was the pleasure of so many Indians. They sat down on the floor and shared a pipe of Sutherland's *kinnikinnick*—mixed tobacco and herbs—that formally opened their talk. Then the Delaware got right to the point.

"Martine has told me of Swain," he said in Algonquian. "I and my cousin Shamot will follow this Frenchman named Dusten to the ends of the earth, if we must. And we will return to tell the exact location of the devil."

Sutherland offered to supply food, ammunition, and any other gear needed for the long trip westward. He also made it clear that Swain's stronghold must be destroyed before winter, when the renegades could ravage the trade routes. Niko-lota understood. He smoked quietly for some time, thinking. Though he was not a member of the Frontier Company, this mission was one he longed to carry out. In return, he and Shamot would be paid in goods, including a share of the plunder from Swain's booty.

Ella brought them beer and bread, with smoked fish and boiled squash. Niko-lota hardly acknowledged her, as was common for male Indians in the presence of women; Ella was used to this custom and did not feel insulted. Their friend Tamano knew whites well enough to pay homage to their women in accordance with white manners, but Niko-lota understood little of such things, for it was seldom that he had dealt with any whites other than Sutherland.

Like the horde of Indians arriving at Fort Detroit, Niko-lota had come originally to watch *la crosse*. The scouting trip to Swain's lair, however, was more important. Later that afternoon, after appropriate good-luck ceremonies to the ancestors and spirits, Niko-lota would be on his way in a canoe offered by Sutherland. With the blessing of Kitshi Manitou, chief of the gods, Niko-lota and his cousin would carry out their tasks.

To symbolize the alliance between Niko-lota and himself, Sutherland took from a cabinet a small belt of wampum. The beads were painted black, and the pattern showed a red hatchet. This was a belt of war. By solemnly accepting this gift, Niko-lota promised to stand by Sutherland against Swain until the end. Niko-lota placed the belt into a deerskin sack that hung at his waist next to a small medicine bag of odd charms, sacred potions, and magic tokens. In presenting the wampum, Sutherland had given his own word to carry out their mutual aim.

As this ceremony was going on, Ella was in the garden with

the baby, thinking of Voltaire's *Candide*, the book that had of late so appealed to Sutherland. It was ironic that her husband should long to cultivate his own garden and live in harmony with the world, avoiding all conflict and discord. For all his readiness to do battle, Owen would prefer to live in peace. Why was the world made so, then, that when a man such as he tried to give up killing, he was dragged back into it again and again?

It was she who must cultivate the garden for both of them. At least for the time being. Was it not always the lot of the woman to wait, to raise the children, to go on no matter what her fear, what danger faced those she loved? The women cultivate the garden so that men might make war.

Ella did not understand, nor had she the desire to think and think and think again without an answer that satisfied her. She finished planting the roses, wiped away sweat with soiled hands, and called Benjamin to join her near the vegetable garden. She could cultivate—must cultivate—for all of them. She sighed, found the strength to go on, and closed her eyes for a moment.

Sally came into the garden, dressed in boy's clothes, pigtails pinned behind her head. She found Ella standing there, the sun in her face, eyes closed, spade in hand.

"Ella?" She approached carefully, wondering what was wrong.

Ella looked at her, blinking once or twice against the bright sun, but did not respond to the child's warm smile.

Sally asked, "Are you all right, Ella? You seem sick—"

Ella shook her head and went to the vegetable garden, which was partly spaded up for planting beans. Sally knew better, and she came to her foster mother's side and took her hand as she walked. Ella could not help smiling. So young, but Sally had seen much of what was evil in the world. Despite months of terror as an Indian captive—or because of that time—Sally had an abundant love of life, a special way of rising above sadness. Ella felt ashamed to let herself be so miserable when Sally could be so strong.

The girl beamed to see Ella come to herself again.

"I'll help in the garden." She picked up a spade and went at the heavy work of digging up the ground. "We're late this year, Ella. I kept hoping you wouldn't ask me to help, but then I felt guilty 'cause you hadn't planted very much. So, here I am!"

"Here we both are," Ella said. "Cultivating..."

As Sally worked, Ella paused and gazed at her. Benjamin toddled to the girl and got to laughing as she tickled his chin with a dandelion. This helped Ella shake off her melancholy, and she set to work with a purpose, enjoying Sally's cheerful company. While Owen and Niko-lota spoke of war, the woman and girl lived for the moment, bursting with a strength that most men took for granted in their women. Soon Ella and Sally were singing, and neither noticed when Niko-lota departed. In the doorway, Owen watched them for a little while, enjoying the scene. Then he removed his shirt and took up a hoe that leaned against the cabin.

Ella and Sally were singing a ballad called "The Gypsy Rover," and as they came to the chorus, Owen joined in, setting to work beside them. For a good hour they toiled and sang, talking of little else than planting, and it did them all good.

chapter **4**

A SOLDIER'S DAY

In the days before the match of *la crosse*, fields and woods around Detroit filled with Indians from every nation in the northwest. Word of the great competition between French and Indian champions had attracted five thousand Indians to the area, and many were packed into makeshift lodges thrown up for the duration of the festival surrounding the match. At least three hundred lodges of skin and bark were erected in meadows behind the fort, and many resident Ottawa, Chippewa, and Wyandot Huron families discovered they had more cousins and uncles than they had ever guessed.

Food was expensive, and on the day of the game some French *habitants* made the most of the opportunity, spreading plank tables with breads, pies, and sweetmeats, and taking up positions between the fort and the playing field.

The field was approximately two hundred yards long and lay a little distance from the northwestern bastion of the fort. Scythed short and fixed with two stout posts at opposite ends, the field was a traditional place for the game that meant so much to French and Indian pride. *La crosse*—or the Indian *bagattaway*—trained young men for war and for the hunt. It demanded the utmost in physical strength, courage, and spirit. For days the French and Indians crowding into the area had been excited, and that enthusiasm had quickly spread to the Anglos.

The entire event took on the atmosphere of a fair, as trading booths, stands for selling everything from books and pamphlets to pottery and clothing, opened wherever some entrepreneur hoped to make a profit. For a week before the bright, sunny morning of the game, Detroit rumbled with the noise of haggling, fighting over politics, and of one race trying to outsing and dance another. All work was suspended, and even Owen Sutherland, managing to rise above his determination to pursue

55

Swain, had fun with his family. Ella had never seen him so jolly and uninhibited.

He joined with the large Scottish contingent at Detroit in reels and sword dances, strathspeys, and even a sailor's hornpipe. The older children and Ella loved to see him this way, and for three days they stayed up late, got up late, and feasted on the food of Briton, American, French, and Indian until they were all stuffed and unable either to sing or dance.

In all Fort Detroit there were only two men not enjoying the day's festivities. Deep in the gloom of a dank public house, Nate Breed and Mel Webster sat at a table, too poor to get really drunk, and too drunk to overcome their self-pity. They had been here more than two hours, and that whole time they had argued in low voices about the lost treasure and their dismal future. Since the argument had failed to resolve itself in a concrete decision, they had fallen silent.

The dim room had a few tables, chairs, and a small counter in one corner where the young son of the innkeeper lunched on potpie and ale. The sawdust-covered floor was hardly disturbed this day, because all the activity was outside. Known as the Brave Wolfe, this spot was a favorite for soldiers and the humbler British or American civilians at the post. Each table had a tallow candle, and at the door was a rack with a collection of clay pipes for public use—each smoker simply nipped off the end to have a clean stem. The large hearth was unused now in the hot weather, but the guest could order cold soup or mush for fourpence—sixpence if a mug of beer were included.

Today, Mel and Nate had foregone the food for drink. Having failed to work out an agreeable plan, they were glum and getting glummer. When the door opened and a few soldiers strode in, noisy and in high spirits, Nate gave them a foul look and mumbled about "pushy Redcoats."

Mel sighed, sick and tired of all this unhappiness. He struck the tabletop and said, more loudly than he meant, "There's only one thing for it, cousin, we have to—" He caught himself and began to whisper, "—we have to join Owen Sutherland's expedition against this Swain fellow."

Nate was foggy, and the mention of fighting Swain's renegades caused him to squint at Mel, then shake his head to clear it. They had both heard from Sutherland about plans to send a private, volunteer force against the outlaws. Though Sutherland had not expected them to come along, he informed them in case they wanted to recover what had been lost in the Wees-konsan.

Nate grunted, "Join? Do ye think I'm daft, lad? I think ye be daft . . . no, mad!" His voice rose. "Doodle-brained! Touched!" Then he recovered, glancing around at the soldiers, who had sat down at a table nearby. They were not particularly interested in this conversation.

Nate leaned over, nearly spilling the last of his ale, and hissed, "Join?"

Mel sighed again and shrugged. "Is there any other way to get the map back?"

Nate slapped his own face, letting his hand slowly and dramatically slip down to his chin before saying, "Cousin, that there map ain't worth dyin' for." He held up a hand to prevent Mel speaking. "Now don't git me wrong; mebbe of late I ain't so sure that I ain't so sure it ain't a real"—he whispered—"treasure map. But whate'er it is, I ain't about to die for it!" He downed his ale and clicked the mug decisively on the table. "We ain't joinin'! That's that."

Mel had expected this response, but he was disappointed. He could not think of a better way to recover the map, but he suspected the same answer would come back from Nate time and again. He would have to go with Sutherland alone if he wanted the map. Indeed, he wanted it.

Nate queried, "That's that? Eh? Speak up, man."

Mel absently took a tin whistle from his pouch and began to pick out melodies. Nate sat back, examined his empty mug, and stared at the table.

Then Nate said, "How 'bout tellin' this Sutherland all about the map, havin' him git it back, an' splittin' the treasure with him after we find it?"

Mel stopped playing, thought for a moment, then shook his head. His voice was weak. "We can't depend on anyone but ourselves. If Mr. Sutherland burns the outlaws out, then—then the map surely goes up with the place." He felt a lightness in his stomach to think he had to fight the renegades. He began to play again to soothe his mind.

Nate was angry now. Through clenched teeth he said, "Gol-durn it, cousin, I can't let ye go alone! What will Granny Breed say if she finds out I let ye git sculped by renegades while ye was lookin' for—Hey, be ye listenin'? Stop playin' that damned song, anyway; ye know I hate it!"

Mel did stop, but he was annoyed, for it was a tune he

liked, despite Nate's objections. Written by a British military surgeon during the French and Indian War, it was titled "Yankee Doodle." Mel did not know the words, but he thought the tune a cheerful one. Also, it served well to trouble Nate when he was nettlesome and in need of harassment.

Mel asked, "Why do you hate that song·so? You've never told me why you turn blue every time I play it."

Nate grumbled and poked about his pockets for money to buy another drink. He had none, for their work with Sutherland's company would not begin until next week. He licked his lips and asked Mel to lend him sixpence.

Mel took out the coin, but when Nate reached for it, he drew it back, grinned, and asked again, "Tell me about 'Yankee Doodle' and why you hate it!"

Nate was growing angry. The very cheerfulness of the Redcoats at the next table antagonized him all the more. He scowled at Mel, saying, "If ye was a soldier in the last war ye'd know better than to ask about that damned poxy song!"

One of the Redcoats, a squat Irish corporal with a beefy face, looked over his shoulder and snickered, but Nate did not notice.

Mel had a twinkle of mischief in his eye. "Look cousin, I'll give you the coin, but first tell me the words. No? Well, then, I'll just have to play it until someone else sings them!"

Nate reached over and snatched away the flute, muttering, "If you'd been at Fort Oswego, like I was, an' seen a lot o' boys die 'cause of bad Redcoat leadership, you'd not be so glib about that tune, boy! Leave off, hear?"

"Oh, Nate, it's a delightful melody—"

"Delightful!" Nate was loud enough now to have the attention of all four soldiers, three of whom were laughing among themselves. "Keep yer damn sixpence! I won't sing them words!"

The florid Irish corporal leaned his chair back to Mel and said, "Give me sixpence, son, an' I'll give that ditty a warble." His friends chuckled.

But Nate was furious. Swinging around, he said, "Hold yer tongue, lobster—"

Mel leaped up to pin Nate's arms, and the Redcoats did the same to their friend, who was struggling to get loose. After a few moments of flurrying arms and fists, followed by reason and good-natured persuasion, both men sat down again. Like many regulars, the Irishman held a grudge against provincial militia, who so often were undependable in battle. For Nate's part, as a former militiaman, he despised the haughty regulars, who had scorned militia, though thousands of militiamen had fought bravely despite miserable equipment, supplies, and indifferent leadership from the regular army.

The Irish corporal was not to be denied his sport. He took a deep swig of ale, laid the mug on the table, and began to sing:

> ". . . Yankee doodle sold his cow
> To buy him a commission,
> Then he went to Canada
> To fight for the nation.
> But when Yankee, he got there,
> He proved an errant coward,
> He wouldn't fight the Frenchman there
> For fear of being devoured."

By the last line, Nate had thrown back his chair and leaped at the corporal, who nimbly skipped away, keeping the table between them. Two of the other three soldiers howled with laughter as their friend sang, and Nate, red in the face, pursued him.

> "Pumpkin pie is very good,
> And so is apple lantern,
> If you'd been whipped as oft as Yankees,
> You'd not be so wanton!"

Mel, too, became enraged, and he began to take off his coat. But there was one lone soldier who saw no humor in all this, and he rose to his immense height and bellowed in a voice that rattled the clay pipes, "Enough, damn you, Riley! Hold your temper there, Yankee!"

Though this man was the same rank as Corporal Pat Riley, his size and strength were enough to cause a sudden halt in the fray. Nate was at one side, the Irish corporal at the other side of the table. Mel was near to springing on Riley, but this big man, whose name was Jebediah Grey, was too imposing to disobey.

Corporal Grey's voice boomed around the room as he said, "I don't like that damned song, either! The next man that sings it or plays it or thinks it too loud will have his nose broken!" He glared at the Irishman.

Corporal Riley scuffed around the table and gave a wave of his hands. "Ah, Grey, we're jest funnin'! Don't be so fussy! Anyway, you're no Yankee, you're a Jerseyman, so what d'you care about 'Yankee Doodle'?"

Nate clenched his fists, but Mel stepped beside him and handed over the sixpence, insisting he buy them both an ale. Nate moved off, and Mel sat down.

Corporal Grey, a broad, well-proportioned man in his late thirties, looked darkly at Riley. Anger in his weathered face, his forehead knitting and eyes almost closing, he said, "That song was meant to insult more than just Yankees, and you know it. Any American can feel the prick of that song—and I do, too."

From the counter where the boy filled his mug, Nate spoke up, "I'm not going to let anyone sing that song an' not pay for it. I've seen too many brave friends die because of regular army glory-seekers thinkin' it their lobster-duty to git their lobster tails shot off while standin' on parade in the middle of the woods."

The corporal who had sung started in again. "At least we stood fast under fire! Plenty o' good lads died because gutless Yankees slipped away when the wind changed an' they thought they sniffed Frenchies."

Grey shut them up with a bang on the table. "By gad, you're both right, and you're both wrong! But those days are over, and I ain't about to see any more blood let because of it. I come in here for a drink and a smoke; now shut up, or this is one Jersey Yankee who'll do some fightin'!"

Corporal Riley sat down. "Hell, Grey, you ain't no Yankee so long as you're a soldier—Jerseyman, Yankee, none o' that's anythin' compared to bein' in the Royals!" The other two men raised their drinks to that.

But Corporal Grey said slowly, "Lads, it's time to tell you: My time's up next spring, an' I'm gettin' out for good."

Astonished, his friends gaped. Then genuine disappointment came over them, and Riley in particular looked dejected.

"After all we been through, Grey? It won't be the same without you. Why it's been almost ten years, man!"

Nate took all this in, and when he returned to the group, he placed an extra ale beside Corporal Grey.

"To your good health, Corp," Nate said, raising his own mug and handing one to Mel, who stood up. The soldiers also stood and toasted their friend, who seemed as sentimental as he was excited about leaving the army.

As he watched all this, Mel thought how glorious it must be to serve under arms. It would be an honor to fight alongside the likes of this soldier. In that moment he knew he would go with Owen Sutherland when the expedition against Jubal Swain departed. It would be a once-in-a-lifetime experience. He only hoped he would survive to record it in his journal, and to find the Indian burial mounds.

By the morning of the games, the Sutherlands and their friends were spent from the revelry. The French and Indian players had celebrated as hard as the rest of them, yet on this morning the teams paraded toward the field in two long columns, no one seeming the least tired.

Sutherland had been chosen as referee of the match, and in that role he walked at the head of the columns, which had fifty men in each. He carried the wooden ball used in the game and was dressed in a fine off-white linen smock that was bound at the waist with a scarlet sash. He wore buff knee breeches and his best silk stockings. Hatless, and striding rapidly at the forefront of the players, he was an extreme contrast to the men who would compete.

Sutherland glowed with civility and culture, but the Indians, right behind him, wore only feathers and breechcloths. For the rest they were stark naked, causing the more prudish white women to look away as they passed. Smeared with bear grease, painted for war, streaked with reds and yellows and blacks, the Indians chanted in husky voices as they paraded toward the field. Like the French, who were next, each carried a four-foot stick with a rawhide cradle fixed to a crook at one end. With this stick, they could catch or throw the ball, knock it from an opponent's stick, and even pound the opposing ballcarrier. The object was to score by striking the ball against the opponent's goalpost without using one's hands. The ball could be thrown or carried with the stick, or kicked, but not touched with the hand. It was understood that unnecessary roughness was dishonorable, but the game was always so fierce and hazardous that broken bones, bruises, cuts, and lumps were common— even desirable to those who judged courage by recklessness and the ability to take severe punishment while trying to score or defend.

Behind the chanting Indians pranced the French, many of them *métis*—half-breeds—who seemed even more savage than the Indians. Handsome, wild-looking young men, these players were the cream of the French community in the northwest. Though many *la crosse* heroes on both teams had died in the wars against the English, there were enough great ones here today to guarantee a most memorable contest.

At the head of the French was Jacques Levesque, his face and torso painted entirely in deep red, with white markings on his nose and broad chest. His head was unadorned, but around his neck was a small wooden crucifix—one of the best ways of telling whether a player was a Catholic Frenchman or a heathen Indian. Many French were painted as well as feathered, some *métis* also wearing only breechcloths.

Tamano led the Indians, his hair braided and knotted in back to prevent someone snatching it. He was the biggest man on either team, and when he broke into a trot, smoothly gliding onto the field, murmurs went up throughout the crowd. Many had doubted Tamano's strength because of his mishap on the ice two winters past. Yet as he loped ahead in a warm-up run, his men chanting behind, he looked every bit the champion he once was.

The mob of Indians howled and cheered as their side ran to the north end of the field. There were by far more Indian spectators than French or Anglos, who totaled fewer than fifteen hundred. The Indian din drowned out the cheers of the whites, Detroit's walls rocked with the roar of the crowd, and birds rose squawking in flocks from trees near the river. Weaving through the surging Indians, French songs lent a melody to the tumult, and the listener might follow the strains of a gay *voyageur* song or the beat of a hearty war chant as the thousands urged their combatants on to victory.

As players readied themselves at opposite ends of the field, stretching muscles, practicing stickwork, sprinting back and forth, the Sutherlands and their friends gathered at the midway point near the edge of the playing surface. Lying on blankets, seated in chairs and carriages, the Sutherlands, Defrieses, Morelys, and friends were accompanied by a veiled Angélique Levesque and her father Jean Martine. The children all were excited, and they scampered back and forth across the field. Jeremy and Tom raced one another, occasionally joining a mob of youngsters imitating *la crosse* players by pursuing a small ball in a wild melee that caused a few bloody noses and got angry shouts from some parents.

At first, Mel found it difficult to watch the game, for he

had seen a refined young woman in a handsome carriage; her plump, rosy face and black eyes enchanted him from the very first. Matilda Merriwether was in company with Reverend Lee, her mother, Claudia, and her father, Dawson Potts Merriwether, prosperous Virginians of good family, who recently had come to Detroit to investigate the potential for settlement on government land. Though some might have said Matilda was not a classic beauty, to Mel she was a queen, or at least a princess. She wore no face mask against the sun, as did most elegant women, and that assured him she favored the natural life, as did he. That further inspired him.

Curling out of her white cap, raven hair fell to her shoulders. Her lips were scarlet, her teeth, to Mel, sparkling. She was dressed in a stylish and tasteful yellow gown and cape that enhanced rather than revealed her ample figure; and from beneath the long over-petticoat that protected her gown from soil, Mel was sure, beyond doubt, he could see a shoe, and even a glimpse of ankle.

She looked toward him and smiled so faintly that anyone else might have denied she offered it at all. Mel's heart skipped, and he blushed, unsure whether to tip his hat in acknowledgment or to conceal the secret of what had passed between them. He simply coughed lightly. Matilda was distracted by the preparations, and she squealed with restraint, fanning herself so prettily that Mel felt weak in the knees. He swayed a bit, leaning against Nate, who did not mind, for he, too, was gazing at Matilda, a young woman of breeding and wealth, who had without a doubt smiled right at him.

The air crackled with excitement. A light breeze wafted colorful scarves and a host of parasols, making even the simplest of bonnets look elegant by blowing feathers or flapping brims. French and Anglos were in their Sunday clothes, some even in Christmas finery, though they were in hot June sunshine. Wine, ale, rum, beer, and cider were consumed in great quantities, with some vendors making a tidy profit in trade goods or colonial currency as thirst and hunger increased with the crowd's enthusiasm. There were strict rules against serving too strong an alcohol to Indians, and one unscrupulous trader was arrested by soldiers who caught him doling out a potent high wine on the sly to Indians.

All in all, however, the mood was generous and comradely, without the slightest hint that Jacques might be a marked man. Enjoying the tumultuous chaos was a sedate old Indian seated at the base of his people's goalpost. He was meditating, casting spells, with the contents of his medicine bag scattered on the ground before him: tufts of human and animal hair; the deformed leg of a raven; some powdered bear's gall in a skin pouch; a bullet that had miraculously appeared in the Indian's moccasin after a battle, though he had been unhurt. This was an important Ottawa chief, whose advanced age had made him something of a shaman to his people. Old Mawak had no doubt in his own supernatural powers, particularly since he also sang in the Christian Indian choir of Reverend Lee: Mawak assumed he had one leg in the realm of white spirits as well as a place beside the gods and ancestors of his own faith.

Though the din of the Indians overwhelmed his chant, Mawak invoked divine help in the contest that was intended to please the gods. By playing *bagattaway*, the Indians believed they won favor from the spirits, and the sport was part of sacred ceremonies meant to glorify ancestors and entertain them. Glistening with bear grease and rubbed with ashes of sacred fires, Mawak sent his offering up to the spirits, calling for victory. He made medicine guaranteed to confound French gods and magicians who might try to sway the outcome of the game.

Mawak was long past the playing days, but like every other Indian for miles around, he hungered for triumph. Sensing the game was about to begin, Mawak—whom whites had nicknamed the Prince of Wales—opened one bleary eye and saw Owen Sutherland at the center of the field, tossing the game ball in his hand. The old man made a quick end to his most powerful chant, and got up stiffly. Collecting his medicine bundle, he stood up as straight as he could and waited while a young woman, his fourth wife, hurried to him and threw a blanket over his sloping shoulders. It was done. He could do no more. Anyway, he needed a drink of the precious firewater he had bought the other day, anticipating that the army might forbid the selling of spirits to Indians during the match.

As Mawak stepped ponderously off the field, he was surrounded by Jeremy, Tom, and Sally, who were ever ready to hear the old man's tales and prophecy. As haughty and cranky as Mawak might be to some, he had a soft spot for these white youngsters. In the past year they had become like his own grandchildren—of whom he had uncounted numbers. Because the three favored him and his storytelling, he was indulgent with them, and unfailingly kind.

Mawak allowed Sally and Tom to walk at his side, while Jeremy carried the Ottawa's blanket as they went toward the Indian crowd near Ella and her friends.

Sally asked eagerly, "Tell us who will win, Mawak! What does your medicine bag tell you?"

Mawak nodded solemnly at Sally and stopped at the edge of the field before speaking. "It is not for Mawak to tell secrets of spirits."

Mawak noticed out of the corner of his eye that Sally was disappointed, but she was distracted by a shout from the Indian players, who were running toward midfield, forming a half-circle opposite the French. The start was at hand.

Not for years had Ella experienced so much noise and excitement. She felt the tension rise as Owen strolled near to where she sat and shouted for the teams to prepare. Sitting on a blanket near Ella, Angélique could not take her eyes from her own husband as he moved fluidly among his teammates, loosening up and talking strategy with them. Ella saw the concern in Angélique's eyes, and was about to reach out and squeeze her hand in reassurance when there was a flurry of movement across the field near the Frenchmen.

Owen, who had come to his friends, turned as Angélique gasped, her hand to her mouth. Jean Martine growled, but Sutherland said, "Stay here. Let me handle this."

To the dismay of the Sutherlands and their friends, Ensign Parker was walking straight toward Jacques, who had not yet seen him coming. Sutherland trotted over the field to cut off the young soldier, who hung his head a bit, as though ashamed. From where Parker had come stood Colonel Campbell with twenty armed men of the Royals. Campbell, too, seemed downcast, but resolved. Near him were Bradford Cullen and Farley Jones, both smug and pleasurably seated in a carriage, which had been unhitched from its horse.

There was no question about it: Parker was aimed for Levesque, who was doing knee-bends and exercising, holding his stick behind his back. As one man, the thousand French stopped singing; they seemed to have caught their breath as they watched Parker. Many of Levesque's teammates saw the officer and moved between him and Jacques, but Owen reached Parker first. With an eye on the unsuspecting Levesque, Sutherland got the soldier's attention.

"Ensign Parker, do you know what you're doing?" Sutherland walked at the man's shoulder.

Parker was tight-lipped but said, "I do, Mr. Sutherland. Unfortunately, I do."

"You'll cause a riot!" Sutherland warned, and Parker's head came up. "They're all watching you. They won't let you get away with this."

Parker slowed, then said, "Look beyond the crowd, Mr. Sutherland."

Parker indicated another seventy men with fixed bayonets, and even a fieldpiece that many had thought was brought out only to augment the celebration. The army meant business.

As they walked further, Levesque heard a teammate call his name, and he turned to face Parker, a few steps away. Noticing Sutherland at the officer's side, Levesque was confused but decided to bluff.

Parker came up, his expression glum. With a hoarse voice harried by the wind and the loud chanting of Indians far downfield, he said, "In the name of the king, you are under arrest, Monsieur Levesque, for the crime of treason and for being a renegade. I beg you, sir, do not resist."

Jacques winced, the muscles in his chest twitching. He looked from Sutherland to Parker and back again.

"Levesque?" he scoffed with a coarse laugh. "You are mistaken, Redcoat. I'm just here for the *jeu de la crosse.*"

By now, the entire French team had gathered round. Parker was not intimidated.

"Monsieur," Parker said gently, "you have been identified by Mr. Cullen, who had his way of learning your identity. Please, understand I requested that Colonel Campbell permit me to reason with you . . . to avoid confrontation and unnecessary bloodshed. Arrest is unavoidable. Trouble for your people can be avoided. Come quietly. Think, man, I beg of you, before you act."

The brawny Levesque seethed, his men awaiting a signal to fight.

Sutherland's heart pounded. "Ensign, hold on, just a moment." He looked at Jacques, whose face could be seen to have blanched, even under the paint. Like a stag ready to spring, Jacques was barely restrained by Sutherland's intervention. The Scotsman took in the surly, keyed-up *voyageur.*

"Jacques," Sutherland said with feeling, "we cannot prevent this; the entire garrison is turned out, with cannon. But we'll stand by you! We'll defend you any way we can. You've proven yourself to us. Don't waste all you've done."

Levesque made no reply, but he gripped his stick until his arms shook and his knuckles were white.

Sutherland said to Parker, "Wait with this, Ensign. Wait until the game is finished, and then..." He looked right at Levesque, whose expression now was blank, as though he heard and saw nothing. "Then I give you my word, Monsieur Levesque will go quietly."

The other Frenchmen voiced their wrath. Levesque stared at Sutherland, who awaited his promise. After a tense moment, Levesque spat, then turned to Parker. "When it's done, soldier, I am yours."

At first Parker was unsure. His eyes narrowed as he thought what to do.

Levesque helped him decide. "If you will not permit me to play, then you'll have to fight me." He raised the stick across his chest, and the mass of Frenchmen pressed a bit closer into the center, where Sutherland, Parker, and Levesque stood in confrontation.

Parker was cool. He stared at Levesque, unafraid. Levesque saw this and relented slightly, letting the stick come down to his waist. Parker said sharply, "Very well, monsieur!"

Levesque held out a hand, and the ensign took it, saying, "I am sorry. I will request permission to accompany you down to Montreal for trial. I'll do what I can, monsieur."

The players made way for Parker to return to his commander. Levesque called to the ensign, "You'll find me at the Indian goalpost!"

Parker looked over his shoulder and nodded. Sutherland stood downcast as the French gave a shout of encouragement to one another and to their anxious friends and families. They trotted into position, leaving Sutherland staring at Cullen, who seemed somewhat annoyed that Parker had come back empty-handed. The ensign spoke to Campbell, who nodded, folded his arms, and took a chair to watch the contest. As Sutherland walked to the middle of the field, he saw Jones jump from the carriage to complain at Campbell's shoulder. The colonel made a disdainful movement of his hand and sent the clerk scurrying back to Cullen, who was livid at the reply.

Levesque also saw Cullen's reaction. He stared deliberately at the merchant, purposefully studying him as if to fathom what he was made of. Cullen realized Levesque's eyes were on him and turned his head, squirming in his seat, attempting to con-

verse with Jones. The clerk, too, felt the heat of the Frenchman's stare, and he fidgeted a little. Then Cullen flourished a
bottle of claret, urged Jones to find the glasses in their picnic
basket, and they set to drinking with exaggerated gestures and
a forced air of good cheer.

Levesque had turned away before they knew it, the Frenchman lost in thought for the moment. To anyone watching
Jacques, he was simply contemplating his stick, tightening the
rawhide thongs of the cradle, preparing his mind for combat.
But within he raged. He had no regrets; he was simply furious
at having been captured. His strong hands trembled as they
worked, and he found himself gazing past the thongs, across
the field, to where Angélique sat. He saw her make a furtive
sign of the cross, head bowed in prayer. In that moment, anger
left him. An unexpected serenity poured through him. He would
not have said it was religious exaltation, but rather something
else, something he could not name, above anger. He felt calm,
though his heart pounded so that he could almost hear it. Angélique looked up, and he smiled at her. She would not weep.
Lightly she touched her lips to him, and he strode away.

Coming to Sutherland, he said, "Do not tell Tamano."

Sutherland nodded. Jacques called to his teammates. He
was ready.

chapter 5

THE CONTEST

Oblivious to Levesque's fate, the Indians were working up to a fever pitch in mock play, wielding sticks like clubs, sprinting and whirling around one another, pretending to carry the ball on bursting runs between. Poling, swinging, dashing, eluding, chanting, and whooping the battle cry, the warriors were eager and frenzied.

As he observed the field, Sutherland thought that many French spectators were also unaware of the trouble, for they renewed their cheering. By contrast with the crowd, Sutherland was gloomy, his pent-up anger about to burst. But he shook off the bitterness, for he had a task ahead: As referee, it was his job to control the game, to rule on illegal play, to assure that balls thrown out of the field were returned to play by the correct team, and to judge scores. It would be a difficult and taxing job, for the match lasted four hours or until one team made twenty points, whichever came first.

The Indians sang and shouted against the swelling roar of the French supporters. The players tensed as Jacques and Tamano confronted each other, both fierce and braced to leap. Sutherland was between them, ready to throw the fist-sized ball high to start the game. The Scotsman looked from one side to the other, then hurled the ball into the air.

As Tamano and Levesque went up to snare the ball, the spectators exploded in a joyous clamor. The teams surged forward into a vortex of humanity, and to the surprise of all who thought Tamano past his prime, the Chippewa came down with the ball. As he landed he whipped it toward his own men, where it was caught and thrown back and forth among them until a runner spurted forward, trying to run through the French team. The Indian flew like a darting swallow between defenders, taking savage blows from their sticks as they tried to knock him down or to bat the ball from his cradle. He protected the ball and cradle with his body, shifting it from side to side as he ran. The Indian crowd howled in excitement, and the French shouted out for their men to stop the runner any way they could.

But the warrior broke into the open behind the French team and raced for the undefended goal seventy yards away. The onlookers clamored in deafening pandemonium. The Indian was nearly within shooting range when, from out of the mob of pursuers, bolted Jacques Levesque, leaving the rest behind as though they were standing still. At the last moment he dived at the warrior with his stick outstretched, jabbing it between the Indian's legs, just managing to trip him. The man went down with a crunch, the ball sailed into the air, and the French crowd shrieked with delight—a delight that dissolved as an Indian blurred past and snatched the ball out of the air. From twenty yards he whipped a perfect shot that whacked off the post for a one-to-nothing lead.

Ella clapped and cried out, "Tamano! That was Tamano!" She saw Lela, alight with happiness, holding her face in her hands. Angélique was shaking her head, for this game meant so much to Jacques, more than they had ever imagined.

Tamano trotted back to the cheers of his people, his teammates tapping him with their sticks as he passed on his way to midfield. Levesque appeared there, anger in his face, ready to compete for the next toss-up.

Sutherland took the ball, waited until both teams were positioned in half-circles, and threw the ball high. He ran backwards to get clear before he was swarmed over. This time Levesque outjumped the Chippewa, setting the ball in motion by passing quickly to a teammate, who hurled himself against the Indians, attempting to break through on a lone run that would even the tally. But Tamano smacked the ball away. Levesque dug it out, shouldering a burly warrior aside, and again passed the ball to a teammate.

But the French team lost its composure and charged recklessly through the enemy without passing the ball. Levesque tried to restrain his men, but they were so anxious for a goal that the ball was lost to warriors who inundated the carrier. The Indians scooped up the ball and hurtled toward the French goal. Driven backward, caught with too many players up on attack, the French were again scored upon—once more by Tamano, who made a brilliant run around the post, then leaped high to shoot from behind it.

Sutherland whooped to see his friend in such top form. To Ella, who sat nearby, he said, "Tamano always could do that! But can he run for a whole game?"

Jacques then steadied his teammates, who overcame their frantic urge to score and played more carefully, and much better. The struggle went back and forth for half an hour, with neither team able to score. This was unusual in *la crosse,* which saw numerous goals, but both teams were so evenly matched that they were stalemated. Furthermore, Tamano was conserving his strength and playing indomitable defense against the French.

Then, out of a battering, bloody melee, Levesque emerged with the ball in his stick, flitting this way and that, eluding opponents, and running backwards to get away from the opposition. Surprising everyone, Jacques suddenly changed his cautious tempo and rushed forward into a mass of Indians. He seemed to lose his balance, and as he went down, he whipped his stick at the trailing Frenchman who apparently caught the ball and set off around the Indian right wing, the entire multitude in wild pursuit.

For some reason, Sutherland was doubled over, laughing. The Indians caught the Frenchman, knocked him down, and tried to get the ball from his stick. But there was no ball. The man was a decoy. Jacques was dashing around a couple of dismayed defenders, having outwitted the entire Indian team by keeping the ball after faking a pass that fooled his opponents. He scored easily, making the score two to one in favor of the Indians. The French supporters sang with glee, and Peter Defries blared at the top of his voice, "Come on, Frog!"

When the game began again, it wore on without another score, the crowd sensing it was witnessing a marvelous spectacle. Never before had anyone seen so brutal yet skillful a match with so little scoring. Excitement rose to an incredible pitch, and the yelling and chanting went on hour after hour, until thousands were hoarse and exhausted from shouting. At last, a strange silence came over the crowd, as it watched this magical contest.

Two to one, in favor of the Indians, and shadows were lengthening. Even the cynical Farley Jones and the aloof Bradford Cullen were caught up in the struggle. Neglecting a fine picnic Cullen had ordered for them, they followed every attack and counterattack as closely as anyone in the partisan crowd. How long could Tamano and the Indians keep up their defense before they cracked? Levesque was a genius with the ball, a master on the field. His men played cleverly, always dangerously, and would have scored many times against less worthy opponents.

Twenty minutes before time, the Indians finally cracked under the relentless pressure of the French. Levesque stole the ball and seemed impervious to pain as he drove along the right wing. He held the ball high in its cradle, impossible to knock away, though a few weakened Indians made desperate lunges and missed. The French cut straight through them, passing the ball swiftly, the final pass going to Levesque, who leaped and fired a shot right against the post. Crashing full-force into the post himself, he collapsed, stunned.

The French were delirious for the goal, but when they saw Levesque lying unconscious, they became quiet. Tamano and Sutherland went to Jacques, but a moment later, he was on his feet, and the crowd on both sides clapped and stamped their feet in his honor.

Levesque's eyes were glazed with exhaustion and strain. His chest heaved, the muscles in his legs trembling, almost cramped. It was two to two. Time was gone, but because it was a tie, the game would continue until someone scored. If it grew dark before it was over, they would continue tomorrow. Where would Jacques Levesque be tomorrow? In a British jail?

It began. Summoning all his raw power, Levesque caught Sutherland's toss. He called up an inner fire that even he did not know he possessed, and tried one last time, with all he had. Indian chanting and French cheers drowned all sense of reality. For the moment, Jacques felt no pain, hardly saw things distinctly. He acted, he attacked, purely with animal instinct and with utter determination.

He ran back a little, and the Indians pursued him, as he wanted. Again the defenders were spread out, and Jacques feinted right, spun to elude one defender, and began to run. And what a run it was—up the left sideline, past the thundering crowd, taking the entire Indian team—those who could still move—with him. All but Tamano, that is, who drifted into midfield, keeping abreast of the dodging, slippery Levesque.

Kneeling side by side, completely caught up in the game, Lela and Angélique held hands tightly, voices hoarse and shrill as they shouted. The meadow reverberated with pandemonium, as Jacques tore past. The two women leaped to their feet, still holding hands, no longer shouting, to gape in wonder and fascination at this supreme moment.

With the din of the people pounding in his head, Levesque sensed where Tamano was, guessing the Chippewa expected him to change directions, cut across the field, and race for the post through the fewest number of defenders.

Perhaps the other Indians anticipated the same thing. Perhaps at that moment they were counting on Levesque's having to confront Tamano once again; but Levesque did not change directions.

Instead, he made as though to run inside, then dashed like a rabbit up the left sideline, past everyone, taking desperate whacks and chops with sticks, leaping over a man who dived headlong to trip him. He twisted and turned, then galloped for the post, a run of fifty terrible, agonizing yards. It was as though he ran through water, and even the wind was a cruel hindrance. He eluded the Indians as though they were children. He outran helpless defenders until he came to the last, just a few feet from the post. This one he bowled over with the violence of his charge, and with a bellow of agony, slammed the ball against the goalpost.

Amazingly keeping on his feet, Jacques ran right past the post, legs churning, off balance, the jubilation of the French echoing far off. He felt himself falling, tumbling, but then was lifted into the clouds, blue and fluffy and beautiful. Somewhere his people were singing the *voyageur* song "En Roulant Ma Boule," and it had never before sounded so glorious!

The next morning, Jacques Levesque woke up in a dark, damp prison, alone with his triumph and physical pain. It was with a mingling of pride and anger that he awoke, still painted for *la crosse*. Listening to rain patter on the shingled roof of the tiny, one-room jail, he gazed at a small window high above that let in gray light. He heard a faint rumble of distant thunder. Within the thunder and behind it, he heard the sound of the French crowd singing, though all Fort Detroit now slumbered. For all his misery, aching body, and dismal future, Jacques closed his eyes and sang "En Roulant Ma Boule," about a rolling ball and three pretty ducks. He would have laughed had it not hurt so much.

For Sutherland, the expedition against Jubal Swain must wait until he returned from Montreal, where he would try to win a favorable decision from the judges. But a fair trial was unlikely, for Levesque would be judged by Anglo merchants, men who would find Cullen twisting their arms and using his influence to have Levesque hanged. Cullen had departed on his ship, *Helen*, a week ago. By the time Sutherland's party reached the city, Cullen would have begun to muster his forces so that the outcome of the trial would be a foregone conclusion. The prospects of anything less than a long, soul-crushing prison term were bleak. At the very best, Levesque would be locked up for years; at worst, executed.

Along with the Levesques, Sutherland's *Trader* carried Ella, Jeremy, Sally, and little Benjamin, and four guards under Ensign Parker. Also returning to Montreal, Peter and Mary Defries would handle all company affairs there. It was dreary on that journey of two weeks to Fort Schlosser. From there the party traveled overland by horse and wagon to Fort Niagara, and then set off in whaleboats for Montreal. Levesque was confined the whole way, though allowed to share a cabin with his wife. Parker treated him well and with respect.

Sutherland had one hope, and that was to appeal to the British governor, James Murray. As a respected soldier and a man who had high regard for Canadian French, Governor Murray might be able to reduce Levesque's sentence. Surely Murray was well aware of the good work Levesque had done in the economically suffering French community. Jacques had employed men who could not find work with merchants like Cullen; he had helped organize public bakeries to feed people, and had arranged for the reestablishment of commerce between farmers and city folk. His endless hard work had encouraged the *habitants* to repair roads and bridges at their own cost in labor and materials, because the British government had no funds to do so. Further, he had instilled a new sense of pride in many French of Montreal, making relations between the military government and civilians much better then they had been just after the war.

Also on Sutherland's mind, beyond the immediate peril to Levesque, was the mission being carried out by Niko-lota and his cousin, Shamot. It was dangerous to follow Jean Dusten to Swain's base, but if anyone could enter that country, penetrate to the very heart of the outlaw domain, and get out safely, it was Niko-lota.

chapter 6

THE PLACE OF ONIONS

Moving light and fast, Jean Dusten and two companions led Niko-lota and Shamot on a grueling trek through the vast forest between Detroit and Lake Michigan. It was not difficult to follow the renegades, and the Indians were careful not to be detected, often managing to observe them unseen at portages.

Day after day they journeyed, as Dusten took a familiar trade route that passed through some small villages. At these communities of Miami or Pottawattami, Niko-lota learned about his quarry's apparent plans. Dusten was known in these villages, though no one realized he was with Swain's outlaws or he surely would have been murdered. Being well received by many people he knew, Dusten felt secure enough to ask questions about his intended route: Where was the water low, or was a certain tribe friendly to whites these days? By asking their own questions, Niko-lota and Shamot pieced together that the Frenchman was apparently heading for the southerly edge of Lake Michigan.

Two weeks of hard traveling brought Niko-lota to the cold springs known as Kalamazoo, meaning "beautiful water," where flatlands were flooded by crystal pools that fed a westward-flowing river. Down this river they went, passing through dense pine forests until they reached the wide expanse of Lake Michigan.

As Niko-lota and Shamot hid in a thicket above the river's mouth, they saw Dusten and his friends push off southbound along the shoreline. The canoe was held fairly close to land, avoiding the danger of a sudden windstorm catching them far out on the lake. By now Niko-lota had learned where the Frenchman was going. Some passing Indians had said the renegades lived at the mouth of a small river across the lake. Called Eschicagou, this place was the former home of a Pottawattami village that had been taken over by Swain's people, the Indians having been killed, driven out, or kept as slaves.

It would have been quicker for Dusten to shoot across open water, straight for Eschicagou, but it was more prudent to take the shore route, because of storms. As Niko-lota set off after Dusten, it did not occur to him that there might be renegade outposts along the south shore, where sentries would be on the alert for potential prey or for a government expedition headed to the outlaw settlement. The young Delaware was anxious to spy out Swain's habitation and then to return to Owen Sutherland with information about the stronghold and suggestions on how to take it. Staying within sight of Dusten, the two Indians kept near the shore so they would be difficult to spot if their prey looked back. It was a gamble to follow this way, for they might be seen, but Niko-lota could not let Dusten get too far ahead and vanish.

The crafty *voyageur* might put into a cove and watch for any pursuit. If he did that, Niko-lota wanted to see it, and then to head for cover until the Frenchman set out again. It was a long way to Eschicagou, generally pronounced Chicagou, meaning "place of wild onions" and known for its swamps and sand dunes. Niko-lota had to be patient and careful if he wanted to get there and back to Detroit again.

Just before dawn on a cool, clear morning, Niko-lota and Shamot concealed their canoe among scrubby pines that clustered against the base of dunes within sight of the sandy Eschicagou River to the south. The evening before, they had seen Dusten pull into the river mouth, and they had gone ashore to wait until early morning to paddle to a spot north of the river, where the high dunes would give them a good view of the renegade camp. They were tense and excited to be here at last, and as Shamot slashed some branches to cover up their craft, Niko-lota stood guard, rifle at the ready. In the faint light the Delaware could see far down the white beach, and he watched the crests of the line of dunes that rose high above him.

When Shamot was ready, he joined Niko-lota and they hurried up the slippery slope through dimness that was giving way to an eastern glow from across the lake. Neither man talked as they scurried along the top of the dunes, keeping below the skyline lest they be seen. Niko-lota appreciated the company of his sturdy, brash cousin, who also had a reason to pursue Jubal Swain. Last year, Shamot's brother had been killed in the fighting against Swain, and like Niko-lota, the warrior had sworn revenge. As light came into the sky, the two Indians reached the end of the sand dunes and saw a hundred yards away the campfires of the settlement.

They lay down, concealed by brush, to await full dawn, when they could assess the place, count the enemy, and reconnoiter for the best means of penetrating with Sutherland's force. As they lay in semidarkness, Shamot dug from a pouch a handful of sweet corn mixed with maple sugar. He handed the pouch to Niko-lota, saying he should eat, for they might need the strength to flee later that day.

"I don't like to be chased when I'm hungry," Shamot said, greedily munching the fistful of corn, then taking more when Niko-lota had done with it. "Cousin, we should take care now; in my bones I feel it was too easy to follow this Dusten."

Niko-lota ate in silence, thinking of all his cousin meant with those few words. It *had* been too easy. The Frenchman had never wavered in his path, had made no effort to cover his tracks. The three days of following the Lake Michigan shoreline had gone smoothly, with Dusten behaving as though he was in no hurry to get back.

Shamot was known for his intuition. He had a sharp mind and was an extremely skilled hunter. Though not warlike or boastful like many his age, he was a good fighter, whose powerful body had won victory in several hand-to-hand fights. When he expressed his uneasiness, Niko-lota listened. They drank some water from a nearby rivulet, careful not to expose themselves, for a collection of outlaw canoes could be seen drawn up on the beach beyond the river mouth, and partway upstream. They hardly talked after that, lying on top of the dune, taking in the sight as morning reached the settlement.

The Indians were on a hill that rose fifty feet in the air. The settlement across the sluggish river was composed of a half-finished palisade erected around a clutter of thirty bark-and-skin lodges, tents, and lean-tos. Niko-lota saw immediately that the settlement was vulnerable to attack from the river mouth, where pickets had not yet been erected. There were a few canoes over there, on racks near scaffolding, ropes, pulleys, and tools for digging and for hauling up timbers to finish this gap in the palisade of about sixty yards along the water.

As the Indians watched, a gang of black and red slaves was driven out of a hovel by men with bullwhips. These twenty dejected prisoners were set to work on the palisade, moving to the crack of the whips and the curses of six vicious overseers.

In other parts of the settlement, men collected in little knots to have breakfast, to smoke or drink, or to gamble at cards or dominoes.

It was too early in the day for these lazy vagabonds to depart for a foray or a raid. They seemed satisfied to ramble about the community, visiting, joking, wasting time, and even teaching a dozen or so children the rudiments of guns and knives. From where the Indians lay, the settlement might have been any other sprouting community on the frontier, save that the men were exceedingly listless. No one took a team and plow to the nearby grassy meadows, or drove cows in for milking. There was work being done, but it was mainly by slaves or women. Gardens were hoed and planted, women came and went at a washing place on the river, and children played with hoops and sticks, much as they would at any other settlement in the northwest. Niko-lota found it strange to think that this ragged band had been responsible for so much cruelty and robbery, harming people who had not wronged them or even known they existed until attacked.

Near the river was the only large building, perhaps forty feet long and thirty wide. It seemed to be a storehouse, because goods, furs, and equipment were steadily brought in or taken out. A guard there spoke to those who came and went, and it did not take long for Niko-lota to guess that this was where booty was held. Off to the left was a small stone building similar to military powder magazines. Considering the amount of gunpowder known to have been stolen by these outlaws, this undoubtedly was where it was kept, a safe distance from the dwellings. Niko-lota marked these and other strategic considerations, and by midday he had seen enough to give a daring assault every chance of success.

The two Delawares would depart later, under cover of darkness, and hurry back to Detroit. Though excited, they showed good sense, taking turns sleeping so they would be fresh that night for the arduous journey eastward.

By the time Niko-lota fell asleep, he knew the location of Jubal Swain's lodge, having watched the giant redbeard leave and enter it several times. Even if the Delaware had never seen the man before, there was no doubt that this was indeed Swain. No one in all the settlement carried himself so pompously through the compound, and he was always trailed by a few lackeys—including Jean Dusten. Niko-lota dozed off, thinking how much he would like to take a shot at Swain, but realizing the chances of killing him from that distance were slim.

The sun felt good, warm and soothing after so many days of nonstop travel. They were surrounded by low pine, but above them the sky was a brilliant blue, cloudless and crowded with birds that roosted in the sandy marshlands or on the high dunes that followed the shoreline. A little inland, the Eschicagou River twisted sharply, part of it forking north, the other branch south, within easy portaging distance of a Mississippi River tributary. This was certainly a wise choice for a base camp, for it afforded access to the Father of Waters, where it was said Swain shipped stolen goods to trade with the French and Spanish.

Also, being on the shore of Lake Michigan made it simple for Swain to send his men in canoes to attack trappers and traders en route to and from the main British trading posts. Yet the site was far enough from garrisons to be safe from anything but a major military expedition.

Niko-lota thought Shamot said something and opened his eyes, lifting his head and blinking against the bright sunlight.

"What is it, cousin?" he asked sleepily.

He got no answer, but there was movement all around, and Niko-lota sprang to his feet. He found himself staring at Jean Dusten's rifle. There were others, at least eight of them, all surly characters who seemed eager to kill him. Then he saw his cousin writhing on the ground, a throwing knife in his belly. Fear for Shamot coursed through the Delaware, and he dropped to his cousin's side, yanking the bloody knife out and angrily tossing it on the ground.

Someone kicked him in the kidney, and Niko-lota groaned in pain, collapsing near Shamot. The outlaws laughed, and Niko-lota was kicked again, this time in the face.

"Hold there, Thrower," said Jean Dusten, gently easing back a tall young man, who was dressed in a well-made homespun hunting shirt and doeskin breeches. Dusten cackled to the one he called Thrower, who backed off reluctantly, a scowl on his face. He was sinewy, like a whip, and darkly handsome, though something in his eyes was haunting, as though his fine body were possessed by evil.

"The boss wants one alive," Dusten said. "You showed us your art already, and we are impressed, *mon ami*." Niko-lota looked up at him, a grizzled, aging man with an unlit pipe stuck in his mouth.

Jim "Thrower" Simpson picked up his bloody knife and wiped it purposefully on Niko-lota's leggins. "Red bastard scratched my knife!" He faked a lunge at Niko-lota, who did not flinch. That made him angrier, and he lunged again, perhaps to stab the Indian if Dusten had not moved nimbly in his way.

"I say the boss wants to question 'im, *mon ami;* he be mad if you rub 'im out."

Thrower grunted and spoke in a mocking accent to the others, who were standing around, leaning on rifles. "He be mad at me, says this Frenchy shit!" Then, with a snarl: "Nobody gits mad at Thrower Simpson, you frogeater, not even Jube Swain, understand?"

Dusten beckoned for Niko-lota to get up. "You ain't been with Swain very long, Thrower—"

"Long enough!" the man shouted, his voice breaking, almost hysterically. A native Virginian, he was wanted for murder at home and had fled to the northwest last winter, joining Swain's gang two months ago.

Dusten said no more and, shifting his pipe from one side of his mouth to the other, gave a high-pitched laugh, but otherwise did not dare agitate the big man further. He suspected Thrower was deranged, and he had seen him behave like a mad dog more than once. The Virginian's eyes were pale, almost white in color, always open wide and alert for the slightest movement.

As Thrower walked behind the prisoner, he was about to give the wounded Shamot a cruel kick when another man picked up the bleeding Indian and tossed him over one shoulder. Thrower sneered at that, but the man said, "We'll have some fun with him if he lives; don't be in such a rush, boy. Ye'll git yer chance."

Niko-lota would have bolted if his cousin were not so helpless. He would have tried to fight his way out, had he been alone. For now, however, he had to wait. His side hurt, and he was disgusted at being caught so easily.

They crossed the river in three canoes, and on the other side, Niko-lota was allowed to help Shamot, who was weakening, on the verge of passing out. His cousin was Niko-lota's worst concern, but there was no way to tend to him, and he feared the young man might die in his arms.

A crowd gathered as the group came through the unfinished palisade. The Delaware got a close look at these killers, who were worse than he had imagined. Even the women were as cruel and vulgar as their men. Dirty children threw rocks and sticks at the prisoners, and Niko-lota was kicked and punched by the jeering crowd that took every chance to hurt him. He shielded Shamot from the blows, taking most himself, though a few struck the wounded man, who dragged his feet, stumbling and delirious.

In that moment Niko-lota knew he was finished: Either he would die later under torture, or he could fight to the death now. A hatchet hung from Dusten's belt. Niko-lota could reach it easily. One blow would spare Shamot a horrible death, and then Niko-lota would kill Thrower, too. Never mind Niko-lota's hatred of Swain; that was a vengeance he could not take. More fists and rifle butts cracked down on him and Shamot, and Niko-lota readied to spring for the Frenchman's hatchet.

Then someone leaped into the crowd, driving them back from the Indians. It was a young woman, slender and seeming older than her years, but one still pretty, with long black hair that hung down over her shoulders. She shrieked and kicked and punched anyone who tried to hurt the Delawares, and frail as she was, Lucy Swain was not to be crossed. She was the leader's wife.

"Git your hands off, scum! Leave 'em be! Git back! Git back!"

They gave her room, though many grumbled at having the fun stopped. Niko-lota stood before this fiery woman with the beautiful eyes—eyes that were profoundly sad. She looked at him for just an instant, then went to support the other side of Shamot.

She cried out, "Dusten! Git somebody to help this Injun to the sick-lodge, hear? Help me!"

Niko-lota was amazed that a woman had so much influence among this riffraff. Lucy Swain was obeyed, and Shamot was carried away to a nearby lodge; then Niko-lota was shoved roughly ahead, to the center of the village. He thought he had seen this woman before, and then recalled that she had been with Swain last year when the renegade and some followers had been wiped out by Owen Sutherland and a combination of Indians from several tribes. The woman and Swain had escaped by fleeing through a raging grass fire that made pursuit impossible.

Niko-lota passed the slave work gang, and when a few

paused to stare at him they were lashed. Up ahead a large tree shaded a group of men. Sitting in a rocking chair was Jubal Swain.

Niko-lota stopped before him. Swain grinned like a death's-head, his vast beard and flaming eyes making him seem a devil. He wore a brown linsey tunic that would have dwarfed an average man. Around his waist he had a bright green sash, and his leggins and moccasins were of Chippewa make, no doubt stolen from some victim. He wore a string of bear's teeth around his thick neck, and his arms bulged inside a light cotton shirt that underlay the tunic. The rocker was a throne, and Swain a barbarian prince. He looked Niko-lota up and down as though trying to recall something. He rubbed the leather gauntlet that covered his left forearm and wrist, concealing the iron hook that had replaced his hand—the hand that Niko-lota himself had chopped off in that other battle.

Fear and defiance fused in the Delaware. He longed to spit in Swain's face and declare that it was he who had taken the hand. Hanging at the Indian's side was his medicine pouch, which every Indian male owned. In it was Swain's severed forefinger, a magic talisman, a charm the Delaware believed had led him to the man responsible for his sister's death. What would Swain do if he searched that medicine bag and found his own shriveled, dried flesh?

"I know you?" Swain asked, closing one eye, his bushy red brows coming together as though they had a will of their own.

Niko-lota looked above Swain's head and said, "No talk white talk."

"He lie!" someone cried out in a croaking voice. When Niko-lota turned to see who it was, he reeled, struck in the face by another Indian.

It was the Illinois called Spide-toah, a coward and an outcast. He had seen Niko-lota many times in Pontiac's camp at Kaskaskia. The Delaware restrained himself, but if Spide-toah tried to hit him again, he would surely lose control.

"Speak up, Spider," said Swain, whose voice was gravelly and slow. "Yuh know this shit?"

"Spider" was a good nickname for this gangly, scarred Illinois, who was dressed more like a white man than an Indian, and a poor one at that. With a battered tricorn, several colorful trade shirts one upon the other, and worn buckskin leggins that were too short for his bony legs, Spider was a miserable-looking wretch. His narrow face constantly twitched, and he moved hunched over, as though his arms were not part of his body, the elbows swaying out and in as he went to Swain's side. Bending down, pointing at Niko-lota and snickering, he told of the Delaware's friendship with Owen Sutherland, who had visited Pontiac last year. It was fortunate for Niko-lota that Spider did not know who had taken Swain's left hand.

"He be spy, boss," Spider insisted, shuffling a bit toward Niko-lota and shaking his fist at him. "He be spy, this shit. Be spy for big white son of beetch. Kill 'im slow. Git 'im—aargh!"

Niko-lota had spit in his face, hitting him in the mouth as he was speaking. Swain and his men howled with laughter. Spider recoiled, vicious and full of hate, yet clearly unwilling to challenge even a doomed man surrounded by enemies. Spider cursed and wiped his mouth.

Swain slapped the arm of his chair with the sheathed hook and said to Niko-lota, "Damn, Injun, yuh put on a good show! When we git yuh on the stake I'll be expectin' some laughs!"

A man shouted, "Let's flay 'im first, Jube!"

"Right," yelled another. "I need a new tabaccy pouch! This here Ottaway skin's done dried right up!"

"Delaware's real slimy, like every red nigger from back east! It's the greasy muskrat they eat!"

Swain held up his hand for silence and asked Dusten whether he knew anything about Niko-lota. Before Dusten could reply, Thrower Simpson shouldered to the front and declared, "'Course he knows this nigger! The French monkey told me he comes from Detroit! He's a spy, all right, an' this French son of a bitch led 'im right to us!"

"Shut up, Thrower," Swain commanded and looked at Dusten for an answer.

Once again Dusten had no chance to speak, for Thrower loomed over Swain and snarled, "Who'll shut me up? Anyone listens to French shits is just as big a—"

The sound of Swain crunching into Thrower was like a mule kicking his stall. The mob parted as Thrower was driven backward and smashed to the ground. He tried to fight to his feet, but Swain forced him down, kicking and struggling. Swain's hand was throttling the challenger. In a moment, Thrower's face was blue, his neck bent at an awkward angle, as though about to snap. But Swain did not kill him. He cursed and lifted the man off the ground, then hurled him face down, like a rag doll. While Thrower was choking for air, Swain pressed a knee

on his spine, slipped the leather from the iron hook, and used
it to twist Thrower's right arm cruelly up his back.

Thrower grunted in pain. Swain said, "Yuh'll learn to throw
with yer other hand now, son." He gave a wicked wrench, and
Thrower's arm broke near the shoulder. Thrower squealed a
bit but fought the agony, groaning and huddling on the ground
as Swain stood up.

Turning back to his chair, Swain heard a cry of warning
from Dusten, and he turned to see Thrower on his knees, knife
in his left palm, ready to fight. Swain looked the man right in
the eye.

"Jimmy, boy, yuh ready to head up this outfit?" He let those
words sink in. No one doubted Thrower was good with either
hand. "Go ahead, son; put that picker 'tween my eyes, as I
know yuh kin. This hoss ain't lookin' at death for the first
time—or the last. So let fly. But don't miss . . ."

Thrower's eyes were wider than ever, but the moment of
decision, of madness and recklessness, had passed. Thrower
lost heart. His face covered with dirt and sweat, his body
wracked with pain, he shuddered once and stood up. The knife
was ready in case Swain should come at him again.

But Swain said, "Go home an' patch that hurt, son. Bygones
is bygones." He smiled with a charm that could not be denied,
the same charm that had won him Lucy, the wife of his dead
brother. Unknown to Lucy, he had murdered her husband to
win her, claiming that it was an act of the Indians. She was
passionately wild about Jubal, though she did not approve of
the uncivilized life they were living. That magnificent, unfet-
tered strength that set Jubal Swain off from every other man
she had ever met overwhelmed Lucy, though she was not sure
it was love. She stood at the edge of the crowd watching her
man, seeing Thrower retreat in humiliation.

To Lucy, Jubal was a kind of untamed thing that brought
out a hunger in her, a hunger that kept her with him in this
isolated refuge for homeless rabble and criminals. Combining
with that hunger was the longing to find her two boys, who
had been stolen by Indians. Often, during her frequent fits of
bewildered depression, Jubal swore to help her find Willie and
Joe, boys of nine and six. Willie's birthday was three days
earlier, and she had not left her lodge from sunrise to sundown
that day. The boys had been the joy of her hard life, and since
her youth as a farmer's child in western New York Province—
the same home neighborhood as Jubal—she had never enjoyed

happiness as that which her children had given. Now they were gone, and Lucy's obsession made her irrational and unpredictable.

With Jubal she had hope of finding the boys again; without him there was no hope. Thus Lucy Swain was here, in a virgin, lovely land where she would like nothing more than to put down roots, to plant, to build, and to make a new life—if only she had the boys at her side.

Lucy saw the Delaware prisoner staring at her. He seemed confused. Niko-lota could see that Lucy did not belong with these people. Swain stepped between them, calmly sheathing his hook as he stared at Niko-lota.

"Boy, when I git together with yuh later on, yuh'll do some talkin'." He grinned that cold, lifeless grin. Niko-lota did not waver. Swain looked to Dusten and said they had much to discuss before questioning Niko-lota. The outlaw did not want to kill his prisoner before he learned all he could about Owen Sutherland and Detroit.

As the crowd dispersed, disappointed not to have seen more violence, Swain noticed Lucy gazing at Niko-lota, sadness in her eyes, pity. That bothered him, for he worried about her mental balance.

"Yuh sorry for this red varmint, girl?" He hated to see weakness in his woman, and he saw this kind of weakness all too often. "Yuh oughta hate 'im; he's Delaware, same as 'em what done fer my brother Matt!" Swain became agitated. "Understand, girl? This snake's pals shot yer husband! Don't pity 'im!"

Swain ordered Niko-lota to be taken to the lodge where Shamot lay, and tied up. As the Delaware was led away, he recalled an incident a year and a half ago, when he saw Jubal Swain slay a man who might have been his own brother. The dead man was also big, and redheaded, and from the start, the Indian had presumed they were related. It could be that Swain had killed the man who was this woman's husband—his very own blood.

Niko-lota glanced back and saw Swain and Lucy walking toward their lodge. Niko-lota was surprised to see Swain affectionately draw Lucy close to him as they walked. The Delaware never imagined such tenderness possible in that man.

In the dim light of the lodge, Niko-lota bathed his cousin's injury. Shamot had not regained consciousness during the hour

Niko-lota had been with him. Sorrow came over Niko-lota for having failed so miserably. He swabbed Shamot's purple, oozing stomach wound, and swore he would assault Swain when the man came for him. His hands had been bound behind his back, but he had found a pointed stick in the lodge and used it to cut the hemp rope. Now concealed up his sleeve, the stick was sharp enough to take out an eye—one hand and an eye in exchange for the lives of his sister and two cousins. Not enough!

He would die soon, that was certain. Shamot mumbled in delirium, his face drenched in sweat. It was not right that his cousin be kept alive only to be tortured to death, as surely he would be after Niko-lota wounded Swain. There was only one thing to do for Shamot. He let the pointed stick slide down into his hand. It would pierce Shamot's jugular . . . a sorry way for an Indian warrior to die, but better than what was in store for him. Taking a deep breath, knowing awful despair, Niko-lota struggled with himself. Shamot lay still, as though ready for death. Niko-lota brought the stick's point against the vein at Shamot's neck, and sobbed within. He could hardly breathe. . . .

Suddenly, the flap of the lodge was thrown back, momentarily letting in bright daylight, then closing. Niko-lota sprang around, poised to strike. It was Lucy. So then, Swain would lose his wife. Niko-lota tensed like a wildcat as Lucy's eyes adjusted to the darkness. Niko-lota hesitated. She was carrying a tray of food, with wooden bowls and a pitcher of water. Their eyes met and held. Niko-lota was shaking with excitement.

Lucy hardly noticed the stick in his hand, and she laid down the food, then knelt at Shamot's side. It did not occur to her that Niko-lota was not tied up. To the Delaware's surprise, Lucy had bandages and some clean water to bathe Shamot's wound.

Without looking around, Lucy said, "Eat this if you want. In a minute you kin help lift him so I kin get bandages 'round him." She glanced at Niko-lota, her eyes slow and sad. "You understand what I'm sayin'?"

Niko-lota nodded. She began to clean Shamot's wound, babbling to Niko-lota, unaware of how close she was to death.

"I don't know why I care anythin' 'bout an Injun . . . but for once I gotta do somethin' about all the sufferin' 'round here! Love thy enemies, the Good Book says. Well, I don't love the Injuns what—what stole my babies. But . . ." She was trying not to cry and bravely succeeded, taking deep breaths. "But I can't stand to let even an Injun suffer like this."

Niko-lota had been thinking about what Swain had said earlier, and now he recalled seeing two redheaded boys in a Shawnee village last year. They must be her kidnapped children. Though many prisoners had been returned to the whites after the failure of Pontiac's uprising, it was possible these two were still deep in the forest at a remote Shawnee town on the Ohio River.

Thinking all the while, he tucked the stick inside his shirt and hungrily ate the pemmican and cabbage Lucy had brought. He was not yet prepared to die, so he ate for strength. He did not respond to the woman's maundering about her boys, but listened carefully. A plan was taking form in his mind, though it was not yet the moment to tell Lucy that Jubal Swain had murdered her husband. That would wait for a better time. For now, he knew the boys meant more to her.

Lucy bathed Shamot's face, and he seemed to rest easier. Niko-lota came to her side and lifted his cousin's body at the middle so she could bandage him. For all his hatred of whites, Niko-lota could not hate this woman, even though she was the wife of his mortal enemy, and killing her would inflict severe pain to her husband.

Haltingly, Niko-lota said, "This Injun thank lady."

Lucy had not expected that, and she paused a moment, then tied up the wound. She froze when Niko-lota said, "This Injun know where boys are."

Lucy shuddered. She tried to speak, but they heard someone coming. Heavy footsteps approached, then the flap was thrown back. Swain pushed into the lodge. Niko-lota had just enough time to sit down, putting his hands behind his back, as though still tied up.

"What the hell! Lucy! What the hell yuh doin' with these red niggers? Why, the whole settlement'll think yer a' Injun lover, Lucy!"

Almost venomously, Lucy shrilled, "Leave me alone!" She was floundering to grasp what Niko-lota had said. Jubal was dark with anger, but Lucy did not waver. "Leave me, Jube! Leave me do what's right!" She could not find words. She could not tell him that Niko-lota had almost driven her mad with what he had said. She wanted to find out what the Indian knew before Jubal spoiled it all and Niko-lota fell silent forever.

Swain growled at Niko-lota and lifted his hand to hit him, but Lucy begged, "Jube . . . Jube, please, just give me this—

this one pleasure, please. I had enough killin'! Don't deny me this chance to—to be Christian."

Though confused and close to rage, Swain never could deny Lucy anything. Sometimes it infuriated him, but he always gave in. Almost all his life he had loved her, then lusted for her when she married his brother. Now she was his alone, and even the power to rule a vast country did not satisfy him the way Lucy could. It might have been her very goodness that hypnotized him and combined with her physical beauty to reduce him to meekness.

She put her hands on his chest. "Jube, it makes me so sad to see this. Let me alone for jest a little. I'll be all right." She was trembling, and that made Swain all the more anxious for her.

"Lucy, girl, don't let scum like this make yuh sad." He scowled at Niko-lota, who stared blankly at the ground.

"Jube," Lucy said warmly, and kissed his cheek. "Jest give me a minute. Then I'll come to you. Wait fer me in the lodge. Alone . . ."

Swain softened, then grumbled at Niko-lota and left. As soon as he was gone, Lucy lost her composure and begged Niko-lota to tell where the boys were.

"If you have any honor at all, don't lie to me . . . Oh, God, please don't."

"Niko-lota no lie." He described Willie and Joe, and she almost fainted, sitting back on her heels, hands to her face. "Lady have good heart; trust Niko-lota. Niko-lota get boys back."

Lucy was pallid, her lip quivering, hands locked against her breast. "What do you want from me?"

"Help Injuns escape, now. Niko-lota go to boys in Shawnee country. Bring boys to you. Can lady come for 'em?"

Lucy sighed and said in a quavering voice, "I'll do anythin' to get my babies back! Anythin'."

"Your man take you?"

Lucy hardened. "He'll do anythin' I want if I want it bad enough. If he won't, he'll lose me. He knows he'll lose me!" She began to weep and buried her face in the bandage roll.

A chilling thought hit her. "Are they well? Are my boys well? Are they safe?"

Niko-lota nodded. He did not say that Willie had taken to Indian ways and was regarded as a good hunter and a courageous boy; but he did tell enough to convince her that her sons were with the Shawnee.

Outside, Swain bellowed, "Lucy!"

Hesitating, she wiped her tears and called, "Be—be right out, Jube. I'm comin'."

They heard Swain say, "Hell! She's cryin'! Kin ye believe it, Dusten? She's cryin' over some godrottin' redskin bucks what ain't worth the skin they're wrapped in!"

Dusten cackled and said something, but inside they did not hear, for Lucy was agreeing to help the Delawares get away. At the last moment, as Swain shouted again, she whispered, "I trust you . . . please don't let me down! Please!"

When she went away, Niko-lota was encouraged. They had the faintest chance of escape, and if they succeeded, he would keep his word to Lucy and help find her sons. He was still sworn to kill her husband, and it was possible that in reuniting Lucy and her boys, he would lure Swain into a trap. Yes, there was a chance. He looked at Shamot, who was still asleep. He prayed there was a chance for him.

An hour later, at suppertime, Lucy came out of her lodge carrying a bundle of food and a sharp knife wrapped in two old blankets. Her heart beat wildly as she listened for Jubal, but he slept, sated and pleased. She had known exactly how to distract him. He would likely stay in the lodge for the time it would take to release the Delawares.

The settlement was quiet, with most people at supper or sleeping. No one noticed Lucy enter the unguarded lodge of the Indians. The sort of folk who had joined Swain out here were not industrious or responsible to anyone but themselves. There were few guards at night, and there was no volunteer to sit at the lodge of the prisoners, for Niko-lota was thought to be tied and unable to get away. These people had left society because they hated rules and authority, and they wanted as soft a life as possible. Even though they obeyed Swain, it was mainly because he was a capable leader who terrorized them. Fear they understood, but otherwise they were slothful, sedentary, and given only to satisfying lust, hunger, and a taste for strong drink.

Niko-lota was ready, with Shamot sitting up, only half-conscious, leaning against the side of the structure.

"We ain't got much time," Lucy said hurriedly and began

to slit through the sewn hides to make a hole in the back of the lodge. The Indians would slip through, coming out close to the gap in the palisade, which was always unwatched, because the outlaws had no fear of surprise attack. Since virtually all the inhabitants of the place would be in their lodges, the way would be clear along the thickets of the riverbank. After creeping upstream they would come to a ford. Then they would slip over the dunes, recover their canoe, and paddle all night and all the next day and night to elude pursuit.

"You have an hour before my husband will come for you," Lucy told Niko-lota, handing him the food and giving him the blankets so they could disguise themselves to leave the settlement.

Niko-lota said, "One day I send word of boys. I find boys and tell 'em about mother. One day, you come for 'em."

Lucy went to the front door, wondering whether she was making a mistake. If anyone knew she had helped these two, she would suffer for it. Hesitating, she looked back to see Niko-lota drag Shamot to the slit in the back of the lodge. It might be foolish, but she would risk anything to recover her boys. She went outside, where there was not a soul close by. As she had guessed, they were all at the evening meal or getting drunk preparatory to the torture planned for that night.

Across the grounds a few men were throwing firewood around a post planted in the ground. It was there the Delawares were to be burned alive. Lucy slipped back to her lodge, to her relief meeting no one on the way, and went inside. Jubal was snoring, lying naked on their pallet. Lucy took off her clothes and lay against him, thinking of what she had done, and fearing her husband's wrath. She wanted to sleep, to forget, to dream of happier days. Life with Jubal was seldom happy.

It might make things better for her if she bore a child. Jubal wanted it, as he had told her enough times, but she had miscarried last spring.

With her mind so often wandering in the past, lost in melancholy and heartache, Lucy had not let herself go in a way that would enable her to be with child again. Yes, she thought, a baby would do her good, and Jubal, too. She put her arm over his massive shoulder, and he stirred, muttering her name. He took her in his arms. Now he would never know she had left him.

• • •

Lucy awoke with a start, her mind groggy, body throbbing with dread. Had she been dreaming? Jubal was sitting up, smacking his lips and burping. Lucy came alert, and saw it was still light outside. A French clock on their pine table chimed seven o'clock. It was an hour and a half since she had let the Indians escape.

Stifling fright, Lucy got out of bed to put on her clothes as Swain sat contentedly, admiring her body. For all of her years as a settler's wife, Lucy was still shapely, the way Jubal liked her. She played him false with a smile and fetched a bottle of rum and a mug. No one dared waken Swain when he lay with his wife, but there were sounds of many people collecting outside, craving for the torture to begin.

It was not until Swain had dressed and downed a large mug of watered rum that the cry went up in the settlement. The alarm chilled Lucy's bones, though she pretended surprise. Swain rumbled out the door and into the meeting ground, where the lowering sun cast soft, reddish shadows on trees and lodges.

"The Injuns're gone," Dusten croaked.

Swain screeched like a wounded bear and set everyone into motion; but before the outlaws began the search, there came a strange, haunting call from the dunes across the river. A hush came over the mob. They looked toward the top of a dune, where a silhouette stood, solitary and contemptuous. "That's him!" someone said. "Let's go!" cried another.

Niko-lota's voice carried on the wind off the lake, and Swain heard his own name.

"Shut up!" Swain commanded. "Listen!"

"You lower than dog, Swain! It is no honor to slay you! I will burn your heart on a dung pile!"

"Go for 'im!" Swain yelled, but as the men started for their canoes to cross the river, Niko-lota shouted, "Swain, I Niko-lota, hand taker! I took hand. One day I take your head!"

At first Swain was lost. The color left his face, and he became a ghastly gray. Then his body shook violently. He went mad with fury and rushed for the river, his only weapon a skinning knife. Diving into the water, he swam strongly for the other side as the others hurried to their canoes and pushed them off. They did not know that Niko-lota had already prepared his own canoe. The Indian vanished from the top of the dune. On the other side he bounded down the sandy slope, skidding most of the way to the bottom. His feet churning, he dashed to his waiting craft.

He dragged it across the sand, careful not to puncture the frail birchbark hull; but Niko-lota had not counted on Swain being as swift or as obsessed as he was. Before the canoe was in the water, there came a wild, hellish shriek as Swain, drenched and brutish, barreled down the slope. Sading, Niko-lota heaved the canoe into the water. Swain raced at him. Swain's arms were raised, hook and skinning knife ready as he ran across the sand.

Niko-lota used all his strength to push the canoe away from shore, then leaped aboard, grabbing for the paddle that lay across a thwart. Swain dived ahead, clawing at the canoe, splashing headfirst into the shallow water, his hook striking and holding the stern. The canoe reared like a frightened horse, and Niko-lota nearly went overboard. He pounded at Swain with the paddle, smashing at his head as the renegade wallowed in the water, struggling for a footing. Swain's men were on the dune and running down to the beach. The canoe tipped dangerously. Niko-lota fought for balance, then snatched out the sharp stick he had found earlier and dug it with a cry of fury into Swain's hooked wrist.

The outlaw bellowed in agony, the hook ripped free of the boat, and Niko-lota barely kept his canoe from capsizing.

As Swain battled to stand up, his outlaws fired at the Delaware, but Niko-lota thrust his craft quickly across the lake. Head down, he paddled furiously, pulling away from shore, where the outlaws lumbered Swain out of the water. He blared at them to go back for their canoes and follow the Indian, and they obeyed like frightened children.

Swain stood panting as Niko-lota fled. The Delaware had a good start, for the renegades would lose precious time by paddling downstream to the mouth of the river. If the Indian kept ahead of them, at nightfall he would be safe, shrouded by darkness.

Knowing this, Swain howled at the sky, shaking his fist and his unsheathed hook. The man who had deformed him had been his helpless prisoner, and now was gone. How Niko-lota had escaped Swain did not guess, but he could never have suspected Lucy. That was unthinkable. What mattered was revenge, the quenching of his terrible bloodlust. If this Delaware eluded him, other Indians would pay.

He went to the edge of the sand dune and yelled for his men, who were scrambling up the slope, to follow the river and catch the canoe. Swain had not noticed that Niko-Iota was alone. Concealed by brush, not far from where he stood, the soft earth had been freshly turned. Beneath lay Shamot.

chapter **7**

THE TRIAL

Montreal had changed, even in the months since Sutherland had been there last. The French were the same, spirited and good-natured as always, but there was another mood in the city, one of resignation. Sutherland sensed it in British soldiers and French civilians alike. He soon witnessed how Anglo merchants led by Bradford Cullen had the city's economic life in a brutal grip. They wrung high prices from the ordinary man for whatever essential goods they shipped into the new British province. Furthermore, they were determined to force the removal of the popular governor, James Murray, because he sympathized with the French.

In spite of the growing oppression by these few greedy men, the French population and the soldiers made do, relying on their remarkable ability to be merry even in difficult times. Proud and disdainful, the Anglo merchants went through the streets of the city like lords on a personal estate. Though many were new-rich, uncouth, and poorly mannered, they treated the French and the soldiers like so much unworthy trash. Despised by natives and soldiers alike, the merchants sometimes were harassed. More than once there had been outbreaks of violence resulting in small mobs of soldiers destroying a rapacious merchant's house or thrashing him senseless in his own living room.

Sutherland had learned all this from Jacques and Angélique on the journey to Montreal. When he reached the sprawling city set on an island in the Saint Lawrence River, he further noted the despotic attitude of these merchants with regard to the Catholic French.

Formerly ruled by a corrupt colonial government, the French residents of Montreal were not especially eager to win the right to vote—a right they had never before exercised, for they were not democratic like the British. But they chafed at the bigotry and oppression from many British and American businessmen—all Protestants who hated the Catholic Church. The Canadian bishop had died soon after the fall of New France, but to the dismay of the populace, the British had not permitted another to be invested. It was rumored that Governor Murray secretly labored to arrange for a replacement, making him more obnoxious to the merchants.

Sutherland knew the French would not take too much of this. It was one thing to milk the inhabitants, to keep them under an economic bootheel, but it was another to jeopardize their faith.

After a period of military rule, civil law had been reinstituted in Canada, with the French allowed to resolve their own legal matters as they had in the past, using militia captains as judges. When Britons or Americans were involved in cases, however, merchant justices of the peace made decisions that invariably supported their own kind, whether against French or poor soldiers.

The trial would likely go hard on Jacques because he would be tried by merchant justices who were influenced by Cullen. Sutherland decided immediately to call upon Governor Murray, himself Scottish, and ask him to intervene and see that a fair verdict was reached.

It was a cloudy, hot day in early July when Sutherland walked through the busy city. Dressed fashionably in a dark blue coat, with gray smallclothes, breeches, and stockings, Sutherland looked as though he belonged there. He doffed his new tricorn to a priest strolling in the gardens of the Jesuit seminary on the rue Notre Dame, and knew he was close to Murray's home. This street had some of the finest buildings in all America. Most had been bought recently by merchants from poverty-stricken French *seigneurs* who had lost their wealth in the new order.

Rue Notre Dame had a view of the harbor and broad river, where ships were anchored against an approaching storm darkening the western sky. The street was dirt, but there was a cobbled sidewalk, which Sutherland used to hurry to his appointment at the magnificent Château de Ramezay. Of all the handsome buildings on the street, and even by comparison with the Jesuit seminary, the governor's residence was the most imposing.

While another house was being prepared for him in the south part of the city, Murray had chosen for his temporary residence a home that once had been the seat of genius for all French

America. Constructed of gray and white native granite that
matched the grandeur of thunderclouds overhead, the château
had sheltered the greatest heroes of New France. Military campaigns, explorations, trading expeditions, and deeds that brought
glory to the *fleur de lis* were born, planned, discussed, debated,
and approved here since it was built by a royal governor in
1705.

Sutherland approached the building slowly, admiring the
massive turret that anchored the right corner near the street. It
had been built in an age when the danger of Indian attack
required strong defenses even in the center of a city. There
was a fairly steep roof, with several second-story dormer windows, and the château was separated from the street by a low
stone wall set with a wrought-iron fence.

Imposing, functional, unadorned, this relic of French power
was unpretentious in comparison with the merchant residences.
These had been renovated, the wooden trim painted brightly,
and many had new shingled roofs. To Sutherland, the Château
de Ramezay was no place for a British colonial governor to
reside, but better Murray than someone like Cullen, who lived
a few doors down the street. Better a man who respected French-
Canadian culture than someone who scorned the heritage and
plundered what was left.

Raindrops began to fall, and the wind picked up. Sutherland
nodded to a Redcoat sentry who brought his musket to present
arms, then opened the door. A dapper English butler greeted
Sutherland and showed him through the gracious, immaculate
house. Windows let in little light because the day was so dark,
yet the fine French, English, and American furnishings had a
sheen that lent warmth to the place.

On one wall was a full-length portrait of King George III.
Garbed in blue satin, with purple robes, kingly accoutrements,
and a benign expression, His Majesty gave the governor's residence a bit of color and humanity. Sutherland expected the
château to be more lively and busy on this Tuesday afternoon,
but the office of the governor was empty as Sutherland walked
past, no sign of business at all.

Saying Murray had refused to see anyone in order to receive
Sutherland, the butler knocked at a brightly polished door, then
opened it. He announced Sutherland, who went into a large
room with ceiling and deep-set windows. His attention was
immediately taken by a grand view of the river, where the ships
were bobbing in the squall. Though wind whistled at the win-

dows, the house otherwise was impervious to weather. The tick of a tall, upright pendulum clock dominated the chamber, which was enhanced by a colorful Persian rug set with Chippendale chairs at the edges.

Then Sutherland saw Governor Murray rise from a leather chair near the windows that faced the south and the river. Murray was a tall, slender gentleman, graceful and well dressed in a splendid brown frock coat over a yellow waistcoat and blouse, with matching breeches and brown stockings. Like Sutherland's, Murray's hair was his own, powdered and clubbed in the back, but with none of the curls and puffs that appealed to the more picturesque men of the day.

From the start, Murray and Sutherland liked one another. The governor was thoughtful and sensitive, not given to glib talk or quick replies. Sutherland saw the burden of a difficult office in his eyes, which were almost melancholy at times. There was intelligence in his face; it was fair, with a high forehead and aquiline nose. They talked over a glass of brandy, and Murray often seemed deep in thought. There were frequent prolonged silences as he pondered what Sutherland told him about Jacques Levesque.

After listening closely, Murray stared out the window at the rainstorm sweeping the city and river. His fingers were tented at his lips, elbows resting on the arms of the chair. It took some time before he said he knew of Levesque's work with the French community.

"Though I had never guessed at his background as a renegade. Who could have? Levesque seemed an honest, responsible partner in your company, Mr. Sutherland. He has always been prepared to foster a harmonious relationship between his people and ours."

His eyes seemed shadowed when he said, "It's a terrible pity that this should have happened, or that he did not give himself up a year ago. A year ago I might have done more for him, but today, as you well know, there are powerful and malevolent forces at work in Canada, forces that will make the most of any chance to discredit your company, the French, and, yes, even the governor—particularly the governor."

He looked directly at Sutherland. "There are a number of other men in the city who hope, as you do, that I will step into this case and intervene in the trial. They would like nothing more than to accuse me of favoritism, of succoring French rebels, of acting against the interests of England . . ."

Silence. The clock ticked loudly, and wind and rain harried the windows. Sutherland understood the dilemma, but he hoped Murray would indeed step in before Jacques was tried and sentenced to death. His friend was being held in the military jail pending trial, the date for which had not yet been set.

Murray looked out the window for a while before saying, "Their hopes will come to pass, Mr. Sutherland. I will help him."

The frontiersman knew now that Jacques had a chance to survive. He felt profound relief, and was grinning. He lightly tapped the arm of his chair. "You will be helping a fine man, and I couldn't have asked for more."

Murray raised a hand to qualify himself. "However, Mr. Sutherland, this matter will take a full official investigation. I cannot make such a decision final without at least giving the impression of responsibility, restraint, and careful scrutiny of the facts." He smiled. "Mr. Sutherland, I believe all you have told me today, largely because I know much about you—both your military prowess and your poetry."

Sutherland inclined his head in acknowledgment, adding, "I, sir, have heard much about you." The servant poured them more brandy as Sutherland asked, "I wonder, Governor Murray, if I might ask something personal—about a rumor, about a question that you have never publicly answered."

Murray raised his glass to Sutherland, and said, "You may ask, sir, but just how and whether I answer will, of course, depend."

"I've heard it said that it was you who planned the scaling of the heights to capture Quebec."

Murray sipped, peered over his glass, and gave the hint of a smile. The fall of Quebec City, the capital of New France and a powerful fortress once deemed impregnable, had been the beginning of the end for French Canada. The glory and credit had gone to the young British General James Wolfe, who died in the battle and to whom Murray was a subordinate. Nevertheless, there were a few among the more thoughtful, less hero-worshiping military minds who insisted that acclaim for victory belonged to Murray.

The governor laid his glass on a side table and said pointedly, "That is in the past, Mr. Sutherland, and it does neither of us any good to bring it up again; but if you insist on discussing my past, then I must insist on hearing about your valor at Bushy Run with Bouquet. Or perhaps about your aid to Benjamin

Franklin during the trouble at Philadelphia last year!" Sutherland squirmed, and Murray grinned. "I am honored to know
you, sir, and proud that you are a Scot."

Sutherland replied, "Again we talk about the past. I believe
I am more American than Scottish now, though I'm not quite
sure just what being American means."

Murray nodded. "Few, from the king to the Bostonian,
really know what it means to be an American, but I daresay
your clever Doctor Franklin knows, and so do many others,
who are agitating for political change in the colonies."

"Do you think the agitators are wrong, sir? I think they have
a good case against being taxed by a Parliament that doesn't
represent them. It may be brazen to say this, and it isn't intended
as disloyal to the king, but Americans, whatever else they are,
must be granted the same rights as Englishmen."

Murray thought a moment before replying. "And what about
Catholic French in Canada? They are part of the empire. Do
they have the same rights as Englishmen, as Americans, under
British law?"

"Certainly."

Murray sat forward, picked up his glass, and said, "Per-
plexing, isn't it, that liberty-loving Boston Americans such as
Bradford Cullen do not agree with you. To him, Protestants
deserve liberty, but Catholics do not. If Cullen has his way, a
hundred heavy-handed Protestants would tyrannize fifty thousand Catholic French, stamp out their religion, destroy their
culture, outlaw their language..." He fell silent.

The clock ticked. The storm had passed, and sunshine was
filtering through the clouds. Golden light shimmered on wet
rooftops, fell upon the river, and found a ship letting out sail
for a journey downstream to the sea and the distant land even
native-born Americans referred to as home.

Sutherland asked, "Will Catholics in Canada ever be given
a vote?"

"That is my deepest hope, Mr. Sutherland. But before it
happens, men such as Bradford Cullen will raise the devil about
it, will accuse Parliament of creating a papist colony on their
borders, and will say the government is trying to hem in the
English colonies, just as the French before hemmed them in."

Both men knew it would be a travesty of liberty to permit
the establishment of a Canadian assembly that could accept
only Protestants as delegates. The sole way of preventing an
all-Protestant assembly under present British law was to have

no assembly at all—at least until Parliament permitted Canadian Catholics to vote.

Sutherland asked, "What if Parliament doesn't allow an assembly to be elected in Canada?"

Murray replied, seemingly weary to recall all the haggling and in-fighting over this very question. "If no assembly is elected in Canada, Cullen will declare that Parliament is establishing a permanent tyrannical rule in this colony and the northwest. There will be accusations in the lower colonies that Parliament intends to dissolve their elected assemblies, too, ultimately turning all the colonies into private plantations for the benefit of a few wealthy men at home."

Clearly there was no simple answer to ruling Canada and the northwest. Yet if Cullen and his cronies were influential enough to establish a wholly Protestant assembly, Canada and the interior would be exploited by his clique—the one that cared only for personal enrichment no matter what the cost to the people. In the middle of this gathering storm was James Murray. Sutherland knew well that pardoning Jacques, an admitted French renegade, meant peril for Murray's career. Though moved by the man's nobility and unselfishness, Sutherland feared the worst. Nevertheless, Jacques and Angélique and the rest of the French in Canada were fortunate to have James Murray as their royal governor.

When Sutherland gave the news of Murray's support to the others, he brought joy where before there had been despair. He found them all with the children and even Sniffer in the airy, well-furnished apartment of Dr. Michel Devalier and his wife, Marie, close friends of Mary and Peter. The Devaliers, an elderly French couple, were also members of the Frontier Company, though primarily as investors. Both spry and energetic, the Devaliers were a happy pair—she was bent but alert; he was rotund and vigorous. Marie was placid, while Michel was excitable. Dr. Devalier wore a white goatee that lent a certain flair to complement his active nature.

Also in the apartment was Emmy Cole, the middle-aged black household servant of Bradford Cullen. The warm and outgoing woman had been a close friend during Mary's difficult and lonely time as a lodger in the Cullen household. Also, Emmy had been present at the birth of Mary's daughter, and it was as though Jeanette were the woman's own granddaughter, for she lavished affection upon her whenever she could slip away from her house and secretly visit the Defries family.

Everyone was full of cheer as they discussed how long it would take before Jacques and Angélique would be back at work for the company in Montreal. Though Angélique tried, she found it hard to be happy until her husband was really at her side once again. The others tried to encourage her, and Mrs. Devalier brought out a raisin cake with maple-sugar icing, making the announcement in French and English that they had to celebrate Sutherland's success and Angélique's birthday.

Applause and birthday songs lifted Angélique's spirits somewhat, and in a little while, the adults crowded around a long table to drink coffee, brandy, or cider. In another room, the children and Sniffer had their own party, with Emmy as supervisor.

Sitting next to Sutherland, Peter Defries was somewhat restrained, and his friend noticed it. While the others were chattering and making most of the fun, Sutherland poured Peter some cider and asked what was wrong.

The Dutchman thought for a moment, then said quietly, "When will the governor give his formal pardon?"

Sutherland replied, "As soon as he comes back from an official journey down to Quebec. I imagine that will be in two or three weeks. He's sailing to Quebec today, and he'll be back after the official investigation here in Montreal is completed."

Defries drank some cider, then asked, "Who's in charge of the investigation?"

Sutherland said the office of the governor would undertake the work, which would likely begin in a few days. The trial, said the Scotsman, would have been held in civil court, so it was fortunate for Levesque that Murray had thrown his support to him.

"From what I've seen of this city, Jacques couldn't get a lawyer, because the merchants control what few British lawyers there are in the city."

French lawyers were not permitted to plead in British courts unless they, too, were Protestants. Levesque would have had to accept a lawyer linked to the merchants or would have been obliged to represent himself. All these things were considered, and by the time the women cleared the tables and went to the kitchen or to the children, Defries was still worried.

"Cullen won't let Murray beat 'im so easy."

Sutherland was surprised, saying no one but the king and Parliament could stand up to a royal governor's wishes. Defries disagreed, explaining that the merchant clique was ruthless, willing to go to any lengths to humiliate Murray and force him out. To avoid distressing Angélique, they did not discuss these things for others to hear. Dr. Devalier came to sit near them, with the women out of the room, and he was told how Peter felt.

The old man nodded slowly, the light in his blue eyes losing its sparkle. "I am of the same mind, my friends. Jacques is not out of danger yet . . . no, not at all."

Bad news came the following afternoon: While Murray was away in Quebec, and before the official investigation into the case could get underway, the civil authorities had called for an immediate trial. The entire city was distressed, but even protesting officers such as Ensign Parker, who was staying in the city on furlough, were ignored. Civil government was corrupt and powerful, and the subordinates of the governor were obliged to obey the legal system controlled by Cullen's cronies. With James Murray on board ship and virtually unreachable until he put in at Quebec in a few days, the merchants had the run of the city.

Sutherland and Defries hurried to the garrison commander, but they were rebuffed, told the army was no more than a police force. Now that Levesque was in prison, it would stay out of the entire affair. Though the commander refused to cooperate with the merchants, he did not have custody of the prisoner, who was now housed in a municipal jail. Furthermore, with the growing, intense hostility between regular troops and local officials in so many colonies, he was reluctant to stand up to the merchants. If violence erupted, he might be accused of denying colonials the right to rule themselves.

Furious, Sutherland went to the chief justice of the peace himself—a sour, lean Yorker whose business was haberdashery—and demanded that the trial be put off until Murray returned. That did little good. No formal papers had been filed with the chief justice to delay the trial. Of course not, Sutherland exclaimed—Jacques did not have a lawyer to do that, for no one had expected a trial to be so speedily arranged. The entire court calendar had been swept aside for this case, which the chief justice insisted must be resolved "to teach these French a lesson in loyalty to the king!"

If Defries had not been nearby, Sutherland would have leaped over the desk and taught the man a lesson of his own. Thanks to the immense strength of the Dutchman, Sutherland was restrained, held back while the justice cowered in his chair.

To Sutherland's dismay, the trial was set for the next day. An effort to find a lawyer failed, but it made no difference, for Angélique visited Jacques and was told he would accept no English attorney.

The trial began at ten the following morning, with a fat, seedy lawyer from Liverpool as the prosecutor. Evidence was swiftly presented, accusing Levesque of rising with the Indians in 1763 and of remaining a fugitive from justice until captured at Detroit.

The audience in the large room was mostly well-dressed Anglo merchants, who filled virtually every seat in the place. High windows let in plenty of light, and the room was gracious, with new plaster, freshly painted woodwork, and good tables and chairs for the justices. Levesque was required to stand off to the right, inside a dock. Angélique, the Sutherlands, and the rest sat close to him, though he did not look at them during the entire argument of the prosecutor.

Next to Angélique sat Sally Cooper in her best brocade dress. She alone of the children was present, for she might be called up as a witness. Teary-eyed, Sally was overawed by the grandeur of the courtroom. Before being brought to Montreal, the girl's only contact with civilization had been limited to Fort Detroit. The splendor—for so it seemed to her childish, frontier consciousness—was overwhelming. Afraid for Jacques, Sally gripped Angélique's hand, squeezing it each time he was falsely accused of some terrible deed.

It was close to lunchtime when the prosecution rested its case, and, as the lawyer sat down cumbersomely, the chief justice asked Jacques whether he would like to wait until afternoon to defend himself.

The justice stretched his arms. "It's rather near lunch, and I don't fancy listening to your tale on an empty stomach, what?" He looked at the other two judges, got their assent, and began to rise.

Levesque interrupted, saying loudly, "My rebuttal will not take long, gentlemen."

The merchants and judges grumbled and took their seats again. Someone shouted that the court should adjourn and to hell with the Frenchman's wishes. The chief justice banged the gavel and called for silence. Then he looked sternly at Jacques and said, "We shall adjourn for a meal in fifteen minutes, sir. You may continue after that, at two of the clock. Begin. Call your first witness."

Wearing clothes Angélique had brought him, Jacques looked handsome and proud as he stood there, dressed in the finery of the *voyageur*—a scarlet sash about his waist, a good satin shirt of rose color, and brown corduroy breeches. Compared to the justices, who were garbed in black robes and periwigs that were too big for them, Jacques was an eagle among crows.

"I do not deny my past," he said in a voice that rang out clearly. "But my past is gone, and I have made a new beginning. Judge me on who I am today, if you desire to be just. I have fought for my country"—it pained him to say this—"and I have been defeated."

Bradford Cullen nudged someone sitting next to him who jeered, "You should've surrendered when your country surrendered!" The gavel rapped for silence, but the same fellow pointed with his hat and shouted, "You're a traitor and a murderer, and you deserve nothing less than hanging, like any common criminal!"

The merchants in the audience shouted in agreement, applauding so raucously that the gavel was not to be heard. At last, with Levesque unperturbed, the audience grew quiet, and the chief justice got silence, though he did not warn Cullen's accomplice to be still.

Levesque was told to go on, but he simply said, "I am finished."

"No!" shrieked Sally Cooper, standing up, her hands to her face. "No, Jacques, tell them how you saved me from the Indians!"

The gavel and cries of the merchants obscured Sally's words, and when a man reached over to pull her to her seat, Dr. Devalier rapped his knuckles with a cane. A few others got up to harry the old man, but Peter Defries rose and pointed at them, and they sat down immediately. After a little while, the chief justice managed to still the outburst and asked Levesque whether he had anything to say about this child. Had he, in fact, saved her from the Indians?

"I did," the Frenchman answered.

"And do you wish to call a mere child as a witness?" The justice was scornful, for Sally's testimony meant little to him.

Jacques looked at Sally, seeing she was intimidated and

extremely upset. "I do not," Jacques said. "It makes no difference to what I have done, or to what I am."

Angélique whispered, "Oh, Jacques, don't be so stubborn." No one heard her but Ella, who was on the other side from Sally.

Sutherland knew Jacques was too proud to bow or to show the least respect for these men. It was the same fighting spirit that had driven him to join Pontiac in a lost cause. The Frenchman's courage and gallant defiance were qualities that had made him a remarkable force in the northwest. But here, where law was bigger than a man and was controlled by a handful of corrupt rascals, his finest qualities were his doom. No matter what Sally said, it would change nothing.

Sutherland stood up and declared, "This court is a travesty of justice! There has been no time to prepare a case or to seek proper counsel!"

The uproar began again, with Cullen's lackey the loudest of all. The gavel and the shouts of the judge did little good to restore order until Sutherland sat down. He knew the case was lost. On the frontier, scoundrels such as these soon would be broken by adversity. In the wild, not one would have dared scorn the likes of Levesque or Sutherland. In Montreal, however, they were princes, with life and death in their hands. Sutherland was already thinking what he would do next.

The justice cleared his throat loudly. "Have you anything more to say, prisoner?"

Levesque simply glared, giving no reply.

"Very well. Let it be recorded that the prisoner has presented his case in full, called no supporting witnesses, has neither denied nor repudiated his past life . . . Ah, correct that please: has not repudiated his life as an admitted renegade guilty of the crime of treason against His Majesty's government . . . et cetera, et cetera . . . You know how it should read, clerk."

With that, the court agreed to adjourn for a verdict.

"What about our lunch?" someone shouted, and the spectators favoring a guilty judgment laughed. Cullen's companion said they should send out an order to the public house and have no fears, for the soup would not get cold before the verdict was in. The justices departed, and Jacques was also led out.

Ella was almost in tears, and she marveled that Angélique could be so strong. Unlike Ella, Mary, Mrs. Devalier, and Sally, Angélique refused to break down, though she knew her husband would be found guilty and imprisoned. She sat gazing at the empty dock, where Jacques had stood, then Ella and Sally took her hands.

The court returned after five minutes of deliberation. Jacques was brought out. They pronounced him guilty as charged. To the stunned horror of his friends—though apparently not to him, for he did not flinch—the penalty was death by hanging. He would die the following morning just after dawn.

chapter 8

MARKET DAY

The sun was just up when Owen Sutherland entered the deserted cobblestone marketplace near a gate in the city's southeastern wall. It was Saturday, market day, and the courtyard should have been bustling with shoppers and farmers squabbling over prices, passersby carrying bundles and baskets of food, and friends sharing gossip from the past week. But the square was desolate, save for Sutherland and a burly hangman who was testing the drop for a high pine gallows erected overnight.

There was not another soul in sight. Every window of the stone row houses facing the market was shuttered against what was about to happen. The market gate had been opened in expectation of a crowd, and a lone guard was stationed outside in a sentry box; but the crowd had not materialized. The farmers and shoppers had stayed away. All of Montreal was silent, save for swallows flitting and diving about the gallows tree.

Presumably a convicted felon condemned to die, the hangman was hooded in a black cloth with holes for his eyes and mouth. Hangmen were spared death as long as they carried out their grisly task, but it was likely he would eventually swing himself, and his place be taken by a younger man.

Sutherland stood across the way from the gallows and was studiously ignored by the executioner, who grabbed the noose and then released the trapdoor. He hung onto the rope with his full weight to see that it would not break.

The executioner was ready, and he leaned back against the railing, arms folded. Sutherland was staring right at him. From the distance came the sound of raucous laughter and the grinding of iron-rimmed cartwheels on cobblestones. Sutherland and the executioner tensed in that moment. The hangman stood up, waiting. The approaching sound meant the prisoner was being brought to his death.

Sutherland watched the rue Saint Paul at the opposite side of the square from the gate. He listened to the loud laughter and talking that echoed down the street. There must be a hundred militiamen accompanying Jacques, he thought. Though there were no soldiers parading to guard the marketplace—because the commander would not cooperate—the merchants would be sure to have a stout escort of loyal followers along to prevent trouble from sympathizers of the prisoner. The air was cold as the sun clouded over. A sharp gust of wind scattered leaves and debris across the courtyard. It did not seem like July at all. It seemed summer had withdrawn, leaving Montreal dreary and forlorn.

The hangman faced Sutherland as the crowd of merchants and their henchmen swung around the corner of rue Saint Paul. They were a cheerful bunch, many drunk. Joking and bantering, they were noisy enough to drown out the tap, tap of a snare drum being played slowly by a man who walked in front of the execution cart. Drawn by a single black horse, the two-wheeled cart swayed from side to side, making it hard for Jacques to keep his balance as he stood with hands tied behind his back.

Sutherland's heart leaped. He longed to unsheath his sword and have done with these blackguards. Not yet. It would be rash and fatal to act too soon, for half the men walking before and behind the cart were armed with muskets or pistols, and others had swords and clubs. These merchants intended to finish what they had started. They would insult Murray with this execution and dare him to retaliate with charges of an unfair trial. Once Murray took on the powerful merchants in this way, he would be wide open to accusations of being a Francophile, and perhaps even a secret ally of with papists.

Yet if Murray did nothing to challenge the high-handed behavior of the justices, he would be humiliated in Canada and would lose the initiative to those Anglos who hungered for absolute power. At any rate, what might or might not happen in the future meant nothing to Owen Sutherland. His friend was about to die, and whether Murray won or lost in his struggle with Cullen's party mattered little this morning.

As the insolent procession passed the Scotsman, he felt guilty for having permitted this to happen. Perhaps he should have stood by Levesque that day when Ensign Parker arrested him, and they should have fought it out there and then.

Drunken laughter attracted his attention to the forefront of the group. There he saw the chief justice, dressed elegantly, with a cudgel at his side. Chatting with the justice was Bradford Cullen, who carried a heavy cane. As Cullen went by, he saw Sutherland, smirked, and touched his tricorn with the cane. Sutherland, to the merchant's surprise, took off his own felt hat, as though in greeting, and held it against his chest.

That confused Cullen, but it was clearly understood by Dr. Devalier, who watched at the square's only unshuttered window, on the other side of the gallows. Devalier in turn signaled to Sutherland that all was ready, and he left the window.

As the cart jounced toward the gallows, Levesque looked down at Sutherland, both of them impassive. In Levesque's face was tranquillity, not the slightest trace of fear or doubt. A priest waited for him at the foot of the thirteen steps leading up to the platform. Two militia guards were ready as the cart drew up and stopped. The tapping drum continued. The onlookers crowded close around the gallows, and Levesque climbed down from the cart. The rollicking merchants quieted somewhat, a thrill of anticipation coming over them. One drunken Anglo began to sing the *voyageur* song, "En Roulant Ma Boule," and the crowd sniggered. A few, unable to stifle their amusement, guffawed. Levesque gave no response. The priest made the sign of the cross before the condemned man.

Jacques began to walk up the steps. As he ascended, his tread on each plank clicked hollowly. The monotone chant of the priest haunted the marketplace. Even the Anglos fell silent.

When a deep rumbling, as of thunder, rose from beyond the city wall, few paid it any attention. Jacques was almost up to the platform now. Some in the crowd were betting how long he would kick before he died. Others were passing bottles and wishing they had a chair. The thunder rolled closer. It came from the south, not the west, where the clouds were darkest.

A couple of men in the mob were uneasy at the rumbling. They peered at the market gate, where the Redcoat sentry was standing, a grin on his face. Owen Sutherland was well back from the crowd, looking toward rue Saint Paul as if expecting to see something. He was eager and aroused. The thunder beyond the gate then mingled with the sound of many voices singing. Jacques had reached the platform, the priest close behind, and the hangman brought forth a black blindfold. Bradford Cullen shouted for the hangman to get on with it, but the man took his time, snapping the blindfold, even talking to the prisoner.

It was obvious a large mob was approaching from the city.
A spirited French battle song rang out in a treble to the bass
of the rolling thunder. Toughs among the Anglo mob moved
to form a ring on the perimeter of the group, ready to ward off
attack. The merchants and their followers seemed less brazen
and warlike now. As they shrank in upon the gallows at their
center, they appeared fewer in number and increasingly anxious.

"Hang 'im!"

"String the French bastard up, hangman, or we'll string you
up instead!"

The poor priest was troubled. He no longer chanted. This
unseemly conduct at such a solemn occasion caused him to
call for order, but he was shouted down. The rumbling was
close to the city gates now, the singing just around the corner.
Cullen's assistant ran to the rue Saint Paul to take a look. No
sooner had he reached the corner than he skidded to a stop and
scampered back to his friends.

"Frenchies! Hundreds of 'em!"

The merchant group was vile but not cowardly. They readied
themselves, slapping clubs into palms and checking the priming
of their guns. They had been confident that if trouble
started they would have the city guard on their side, but now they
were uneasy that soldiers were nowhere in sight. Even the
sentry at the market gate had gone.

When a couple of merchants ran to close the gate against
whatever was approaching from there, they were distressed to
see the soldier had made off with the heavy bar that held it
shut. This discovery was immediately followed by retreat, as
into the gate rolled farm wagon after farm wagon. Big draft
horses hauled four-wheeled carts, all loaded with hay. Hay was
not commonly sold at the city market, and that caused some
confusion among the merchants.

At a few signs from Sutherland, the drivers divided into two
lines, forming a circle around the entire courtyard. The merchant crowd was trapped. The marketplace resounded with the
clatter of hooves and the roll of thirty heavy wagons—a din
that was louder than the singing coming from rue Saint Paul.
Furious, and determined not to be intimidated, Cullen himself
rushed to the foot of the scaffold and demanded the hangman
execute the prisoner. Levesque had not even been blindfolded
yet, let alone placed into the noose.

The executioner seemed not to understand. "Fool!" Cullen

blared over the uproar. To several companions he commanded, "Get up there and make an end to it! Throw the hangman down!"

Two brawny militiamen bounded up the steps, shoving the priest aside and grabbing Levesque. That was as far as they got. The executioner went at these two and literally collared them, crashing their heads together with a crack that sounded above the chaos in the marketplace. They were heaved back down the steps. The black hood was whipped off, revealing a blond head of hair and the exultant, angry face of Peter Defries. The priest staggered backward. Defries drew a knife and cut Levesque free. A couple of Anglos raised their rifles, but at a mighty shout from Owen Sutherland, the loads of hay flew apart, and the wagons became in an instant ramparts for a hundred armed men, who stood up, rifles at the ready.

At the same moment, a host of Montrealers, men and women, pounded around the corner, no longer singing, ready for a fight. Though armed only with pitchforks and clubs for the most part, these folk yearned to take on the merchant gang. They had a score to settle.

Sutherland leaped onto a wagon, claymore drawn, to call for the surrender of the merchants. Levesque's sympathizers—among them a number of British soldiers in civilian garb—surged around the embattled group of Anglos. In all, there were at least a thousand against Cullen's hundred. But the merchants were well armed, and in the center of the square they had some advantage. They were tough, willing to fight, most of them former soldiers who knew their business. Some dropped to one knee, and others stepped alongside them, in volley position. A militia captain prepared them to fire. The Montrealers growled, ready to surge forward.

Matters were moving swiftly. Sutherland did not want it to go too far. He raised his sword and again called for surrender. But Bradford Cullen scorned him and was about to give the order to decimate the crowd by firing first. In the instant that followed, the entire multitude fell silent. To Sutherland's dismay, he saw Ella and the children among the people who had come through the street. For that moment, he was shaken, sword above his head. The moment swelled to bursting. There was no way back. Then a trumpet blast, sharp and piercing, startled them all. The ear-splitting sound was followed by a voice that roared, "Stand fast! In the name of the king, stand fast!"

In the market gate was James Murray astride a blown and sweating charger, his sword flashing in a light that broke through the clouds. His horse plunged and reared as Murray forced the animal toward the scaffold through the mob. The people of the city cried out for joy at Murray's arrival, but the merchants grew surly, fiercely belligerent, still dangerous. It was not over yet.

Behind Murray came twenty dragoons and officers, all on big, nervous horses that lumbered like ships through the sea of people, separating the two sides by forming a ring around the Anglos. Alongside Murray rode a grim Ensign Parker, who looked harrowed and exhausted, as though he had been riding for many hours.

Sutherland lowered his sword. He realized that Parker must have galloped downriver to intercept the governor's vessel on its way to Quebec. The full-speed return to Montreal had been a grueling ride, apparent in the tired horses and in the dust that covered every rider, head to foot.

For all his weariness, Governor Murray had fire in his eyes as he addressed Bradford Cullen and the others in that crowd.

"You, Cullen, are fortunate not to be the next upon that gallows tree! I have decided to pardon this man!" Cullen sputtered, growing nearly purple with rage, but before the man could reply, the governor declared, "The hanging of a pardoned man is a crime, Mr. Cullen. I would have charged you and your accomplices with murder! Now call off your dogs and get out of my sight before I allow Mr. Sutherland to finish what he has begun!"

Cullen continued to bluster, but none of his gang were willing to oppose the royal governor and so much armed force. Sullen, cursing, and burning with hatred, the Anglos lowered their weapons. Some muttered oaths of revenge; others, such as Cullen, were too mortified and infuriated to speak. At Parker's direction a passageway was made in the crowd for them, and slowly they moved away.

Murray and Sutherland looked at one another, both men aware how dangerous it was for the governor to pardon the Frenchman before the investigating committee had filed its report. But it was worth taking such risks to see scoundrels like Cullen thwarted. The crowd erupted in triumphant cheering, waving hats and kerchiefs, shaking guns and sticks above their heads. Levesque was carried from the scaffold, laughing, hailing friends. He leaped down to embrace Angélique, who

was weeping in relief and happiness. Nearby, Sally kissed
Jeremy hard on the cheek, much to the boy's distress.

The jubilant French began to sing again, then poured out
of the square, rejoicing through the streets. Tonight there would
be boundless revelry in the city and the countryside, for the
hated Anglo merchants had been defeated for the first time in
five years.

After Jacques thanked Governor Murray, he and Angélique
slipped away home, leaving their friends to bask in the fleeting
glow of victory. In the midst of the tumult, Murray pressed
his mount toward Sutherland and reached down to shake hands.
Somehow, Ella managed to reach her husband's side, little
Benjamin wailing in her arms because of all the racket.

Murray said the formal pardon would be drawn up in a few
days, and he gave much credit to Ensign Parker for having
given so completely of himself to see justice done.

"I should say *Lieutenant* Parker now, after his promotion!"
Murray beamed, as though his bold action had not jeopardized
his own future in Canada. Elated, despite his beleaguered position, Murray leaned forward to the Sutherlands and asked
them to join him for dinner that night. Then he touched his hat
to Ella and added, "That is, madam, if you will not object to
our discussing some official matters related to an expedition I
have authorized for the destruction of a certain renegade stronghold out in the Wees-konsan."

Dumbfounded, Sutherland wondered if he had heard correctly. Murray saluted, swung his horse's head, and rode back
to his waiting troop. The riders trotted away down rue Saint
Paul, leaving the market square almost silent. His eyes alight,
Owen turned to Ella. She took his hand and kissed him.

In the distance, the French were singing a song Sutherland
knew well.

> The river runs free,
> The west wind is clear,
> And my love is calling to me.
> There is a good wind,
> There is a free tide,
> And my love is waiting for me.

He kissed Ella and held Benjamin, who laughed with him.
Soon they all would go back to the wilderness, back to silence,

the west wind, and rivers running free. First, however, came Jubal Swain.

As in Montreal, it was cloudy in the upper Mississippi country. There Tamano and Lela, with ten half-breed and two Chippewa canoemen, had made camp weeks earlier in the hope of establishing trade with Plains tribes. A few Indians had come and gone, mostly Ottagamie and Kickapoo, peoples with whom the Frontier Company were already doing business. When a lone Sac had passed through heading north, Tamano had hoped he would tell those he met about the trading camp. It was the western tribes Tamano wanted to reach, in the expectation that they would bring buffalo pelts and pemmican, both valued articles of exchange in commerce with tribes of the lakes.

Essential in the northwest, pemmican was a staple, eaten when other foods were scarce or when folk were on the move. It was made laboriously, from meat beaten to a soft consistency, mixed with melted fat and sometimes berries, then dried. It could be stored for long periods; therefore, hunters, traders, war parties, travelers, all depended on pemmican for survival. In some areas, a skin bag of pemmican was a better item of trade than British sterling; it was said that seventy men could eat more than four hundred and fifty pounds of pemmican a day.

In exchange for hides and pemmican, Tamano had brought trade guns, black powder, lead, and bullet molds, as well as bolts of cloth, trade blankets of various weights, and a vast assortment of trinkets, mirrors, body paints, jewelry, ready-made clothing, and tools. One of his half-breeds was a skilled gunsmith whose trade would be welcome here, far from white trading or military posts. On this trip, Tamano intended to make a good impression with the more remote tribes. He would start an annual trade fair at this location, thus guaranteeing a source of exchange to bolster the company's northern trade in peltry.

By opening a flow of Plains Indian goods, the Frontier Company would make a good profit. Plains Indians would gladly pay high prices for Tamano's manufactured articles, because so far away from civilization, such things were extremely scarce. This camp on a windy bluff on the western bank of the Mississippi made it possible for Plains tribes to trade without making the long journey down to the French settlements or up to Fort Michilimackinac. Later, Tamano would take the buffalo hides and pemmican up to Lake Superior and then to Fort Michilimackinac, to be traded for furs that were then shipped east and abroad.

In the first weeks of waiting, Tamano's party had built three pole lodges covered with skins, and had set up a large canvas army tent to serve as the warehouse.

From this bluff, the world fell away on every side in a rolling grassland. The Mississippi was broad here, winding lazily between ridges and through swamps, where clumps of trees collected, offering firewood and small game to Tamano's party. A steady wind swept in from the stormy northwest, but it had not yet rained. The ground was dry, the grasslands brown and in need of a good soaking.

For two hours Tamano had been observing the approach of a dust cloud from the northwest. A large group was coming toward his camp, but he did not know who they were. Against the dark sky, the dust was whitish brown, and it seemed to move very slowly. Yet advance it did, and Tamano alternately worried and hoped. These might be enemies, raiders—or they might be coming to trade. He had made a point of giving favorable trades to all those who had come in during the past weeks, sure that word soon would spread that the Frontier Company was offering high prices for hides and pemmican.

The closer the dust cloud came, the more excited he grew. Since the group approaching was not traveling by the river— which farther north forked westward to drain those plains and hills—he knew they had to be a tribe of the grasslands who used horses and seldom canoes. By noon, he learned he had been correct.

From out of the long grass rode several young warriors, painted and feathered, with wooden breast armor, hide shields, and coup sticks—a pole curved at the end and decorated to tell the history of its owner's career as a warrior. Their horses were fast and sure-footed, tirelessly galloping at full speed for more than a mile. This was the advance party of the main body, which was still five miles behind.

Tamano stood on the bluff watching the antics and tricks of these Plains Indians, who put on a show for the traders. Gathered around him, their guns close at hand, Tamano's followers were astounded by the acrobatic riders, who lay flat on their mounts, hung under their necks and bellies, and even raced along while standing on their animals' backs.

Impressed as he was, Tamano was also concerned. These

were Santee Sioux, blood enemies of Chippewa, who generations before had driven them from their lands just west of Lake Superior. Because of Chippewa attacks, the Sioux—or Dacotah, as they called themselves—had migrated to the Plains and learned the art of riding. They no longer fished or harvested wild rice, for now they were Plains hunters, slaughterers of the enormous buffalo, and dangerous enemies to those who were caught on the grasslands and could not ride like them.

Others in Tamano's party were anxious, but none showed fear or doubt. When the vanguard of the Sioux rode up, feathers flying, spears and muskets raised in salute, Tamano lifted his right hand, palm open, in the sign of peace. It was with sign language that Tamano communicated, for he had traveled far and wide and had learned this skill. The Sioux recognized the Chippewa, but they showed no anger. This was a trading venture, important to their people, who valued the guns and equipment they would receive. From the first it was made clear there would be no animosity between Chippewa and Sioux.

A little while later, the main body of Indians approached, twenty-five of them in four families. There were two venerable old men, four full warriors, and six boys able to fight. The rest were women and children. With them were twenty packhorses, carrying hides and hauling travoises laden with pemmican and additional hides. The travois was made with two long poles lashed together and fastened over the horse's back. The other two ends of the poles were dragged along on the ground behind the animal and loaded with goods.

Tamano could not have asked for better customers. The Sioux were excited to have traders so near to their home, which was ten days' travel away. During a formal ceremony, they sat around a council fire with the strangers, and Tamano's gifts of wampum and tobacco opened their hearts. Their leader, a man in his forties, could speak the common Algonquian tongue known to the Chippewa.

This warrior's eldest son, a boy of eleven, was also familiar with Algonquian, saying his grandmother had been a captured Chippewa and had taught him and his father much. The boy's name was Little Hawk, and he was a tall, strong lad, friendly and intelligent. Tamano admired Little Hawk's hunger to learn everything he could about all the traders had brought. When the time came for barter, the boy brought a horse dragging a travois with two elk hides, which he had taken alone. In exchange, he asked for a trade rifle, and chose one with a carved maple stock but of a light caliber.

Tamano liked Little Hawk so much that he took the rifle back and said, "To hunt buffalo, a stronger gun is needed," and he brought out a weapon that was almost too heavy for the youth.

Determined not to admit he was still too young for the heavier gun, Little Hawk politely thanked the Chippewa, accepted ammunition and powder, and lugged the weapon away. Seeing the uncertainty in Little Hawk's eyes, Tamano called him back, then held out the lighter gun and said it was a gift.

"When you and your people come back next year, I expect you to have become a master with the small gun," Tamano said warmly. "Then I will teach you to use the big one. When the trading is done for today, I and my men will take you and your hunters to the river and teach you how to shoot true."

Excited, Little Hawk whooped and ran off to his friends, who were just as enthusiastic as he. Indeed, Tamano had made a good beginning with the warlike Sioux, and the company did well in the days of trading that followed.

Three days after the Sioux arrived, the young men put on a remarkable show, demonstrating their riding prowess, attempting daredevil stunts that delighted the half-breed and Chippewa canoeists. A good deal of firewater was consumed all around, but not enough to cause drunkenness and the inevitable mayhem that would have followed. Cheerful and satisfied, both traders and Sioux enjoyed the thrilling exhibition.

Lela and Tamano spoke about Little Hawk, their favorite, and undeniably the finest rider of all. Lela said he was the kind of boy they would have someday, and Tamano smiled at her.

"One day," he said, and touched her cheek, "we will have many fine sons and daughters."

Lela loved Tamano deeply. After four years of marriage, she had borne him no living children. Two had been lost, one a miscarriage, the other stillborn—both boys. By all rights, Tamano could have declared her barren and taken a second wife. But she meant everything to him, and he would never hurt her that way.

Sitting beside her husband, Lela watched Little Hawk perform, her eyes glowing. She was a strong woman, not given to much talking. In her heart she knew she would have children, and the sorrow of losing her first was not so profound that she despaired. As the wife of an important trader, life was exciting, and Lela was a close companion in Tamano's work. She could not have been happier at that moment, as she saw Little Hawk ride alone far from the camp, standing on the back of his pony.

The boy's proud father sat cross-legged nearby, eating raisins and pheasant supplied by Tamano. His coup stick, adorned with beads and feathers, lay across his knees. Little Hawk's rotund mother was also enjoying herself, as were the other Sioux and traders. Ancestral hatred was completely forgotten, and there was no doubt that next year many more Sioux would come here for a rendezvous. A whole new world was opening for Tamano and the company, and a bountiful country lay at their feet.

Tamano was amazed to see Little Hawk bound from side to side over the back of his moving horse, now riding toward the camp. The Chippewa leaned to congratulate the father, when a woman screamed in terror. Leaping to his feet, Tamano felt a bullet zip past, and then the long grass behind the camp burst into a wall of gunfire and smoke. Sioux and traders fell on every side. Wounded horses were screaming, and frightened dogs bolted through the camp. Men shouted and scrambled for weapons. But the Sioux had little skill with their new guns, and the traders were either shot down or so overwhelmed by the heavy fire that they could not get to their own weapons to shoot back.

The horrible turmoil in the camp had been caused by men firing from a half-circle of cover, not one attacker showing himself. Men, women, and children fell in the first minute, and the camp was covered with bodies. Tamano braved withering fire and got a rifle and ammunition from his lodge. He tried to retreat down to the river, which was not yet occupied by the enemy. With three or four other men shooting back, Tamano hurried the stricken folk through the grass, dragging their wounded, and trying to keep down as bullets flew among them. There were few left, and with every few paces, more fell.

Smoke rose thick and gray into the gloomy sky. Horses hobbled nearby had fled or were caught by Indians desperately trying to escape. But no one got away on horseback. The attackers easily cut down three Indians who tried to ride off.

Tamano and the others with guns formed a frail rear guard as Lela led three wailing Sioux women down to the canoes. They were about sixty yards from the campsite when the first of the enemy appeared. They were white men, who ran into the lodges and tent to pillage and scalp. Tamano knew immediately these were Swain's renegades. He guessed there were at least twenty of them, only these few becoming bold enough to show themselves in the campsite.

Furious, Tamano ran back toward them and shot a man down. The rest scattered in fright, thinking this was a counterattack. Then, out of the corner of his eye, the Chippewa saw a horseman pound into the campsite. It was Little Hawk, who leaped from his wounded mount and fired an arrow at a man who had been cutting away a scalp. The outlaw screeched and staggered for the brush, the arrow stuck in his side. As Tamano reloaded, he realized the boy was kneeling by his father's body. The outlaws were momentarily disorganized because of the sudden loss of two men, but in a moment they would surely kill Little Hawk.

Tamano felt someone at his side and turned to see Lela. Her face blackened with powder, she carried a loaded rifle. Without a word, they rushed back, calling for Little Hawk to flee. The boy was overwhelmed by sadness. His father was dead. Tamano dragged him away. The outlaws were returning. Little Hawk struggled to go back to his father. Bullets sang past.

Lela yelled that the boy's mother was going to the canoes. "She lives!" Lela shouted. "Go to her while you also live! Go!"

Tamano fired and reloaded. Gunfire broke out more heavily, and a bullet struck Lela's rifle butt. She became furious, raised her weapon, but held her fire rather than waste a shot. Little Hawk came to his senses and snatched up his father's coup stick. With bullets whizzing all around, the three of them fled. Sounds of exultant howling came from the camp as the killers broke out and pillaged. Little Hawk ran through the grass, not looking back.

Ahead, approaching the canoes, the three Sioux women were fleeing with two of Tamano's men running alongside. Other traders were at the canoes, thirty yards beyond the women.

Then, out of the grass on the right, the Illinois Indian named Spider and Jean Dusten rose along with two others. They fired point-blank at the fugitives, hitting a trader and all three women. Little Hawk's mother struggled to her feet, then collapsed. The other trader fired back but missed. Little Hawk, Tamano, and Lela yelled in fury and charged. The renegades tried to take cover to reload, but Tamano and Lela shot two of them.

Spider and Dusten retreated through the grass, Little Hawk pursuing them, though all he carried was his father's decorated coup stick, no weapon against rifles. As Dusten ran, he reloaded, and when he saw it was only a boy chasing them, he called to Spider, who turned. Spider laughed, whipped out his tomahawk, and went for Little Hawk, who was just a few paces away and closing fast.

But when Spider saw the big Chippewa racing in behind Little Hawk, he spun around and fled, for his rifle was unloaded, his courage not enough to use the tomahawk. Dusten took careful aim at Tamano. The Frenchman, however, had not counted on Little Hawk's courage. Thinking the boy too young to trouble him, he let Little Hawk come closer than was prudent. The boy threw the coup stick, hitting Dusten in the left eye, and he fired wildly, missing his target.

Dusten, whose eye was bleeding, did not dare stay and fight Tamano. He swung his rifle at Little Hawk, sending the boy sprawling, then ran away himself, not looking back until he was over a grassy rise and had rejoined more of his companions.

Tamano picked up the coup stick and the unconscious boy, whose scalp had been split by the blow; he carried Little Hawk back to the waiting canoes. In one craft Lela cradled Little Hawk's wounded mother, who, breathing hard, was delirious. Little Hawk was laid in the same canoe, and the survivors launched two more. Only three canoes were enough to hold those who had escaped. Paddling upstream, Tamano looked back at the campsite, which swarmed with renegades looting and taking trophies of war.

Heartsick, Tamano counted five of his people dead, four wounded. Only he, Lela, and three others had been unhurt. All the Sioux were dead, save for Little Hawk and his badly wounded mother. The shock, the remorse overwhelmed Tamano, who silently paddled away.

In a little while, Lela began to sound the death chant. The Sioux squaw had died. Only Little Hawk was left. They would take him with them until he was well enough to go home— though there was no one waiting for him.

chapter 9

INTO DANGER

It was early September when the Sutherlands returned to Detroit. The weather was dry, the sumac turning scarlet in the waning summer. It would not be long before autumn gave way to winter, and all hope of attacking Jubal Swain would be lost for this year. The ship *Trader* was greeted by many friends of the Sutherlands, who offered congratulations upon the success of Levesque's ordeal. Owen and Ella had sent letters to Jean Martine and Lettie Morely to explain what had happened, also telling Jean the news that Governor Murray had authorized military support of Sutherland's expedition.

With these things to be happy about, it seemed strange to Sutherland that Jean and Tamano were not more enthusiastic when they greeted him at the landing. Immediately, he learned why, for they told him what had taken place: the recent massacre on the Mississippi and, earlier, Niko-lota's perilous journey to Swain's camp, with Shamot dying. Sutherland's high spirits subsided, and buoyant hope became grim resolution. The loss of life and the capture of so much in trade goods were severe blows to the Frontier Company. A little while later, he and the others, including Niko-lota, met at Martine's trading house to make plans. At the end of the day, Sutherland called on Colonel Campbell with the letter from Murray instructing the commander to lend Sutherland assistance.

For the sake of speed, Sutherland wanted, in addition to his force of civilians, only a dozen regulars—men with wilderness training and experience—and a few Rangers. Campbell would supply and arm the expedition, which would probably require three months of wilderness marching and fighting before it was done. It could take no more than three months, for winter was too close for a longer campaign.

Details were arranged quickly. Campbell was glad to be authorized to support Sutherland, for he agreed with the purpose of the attack. When Sutherland had first requested military aid, Campbell had not had the power to give it on his own authority. Now Murray's direct orders made it all possible, and the responsibility would not be Campbell's if the mission failed.

To Sutherland's surprise, Campbell said he had already been informed about the expedition by Lieutenant Parker, who had returned from Montreal a week ahead of the *Trader*. Campbell said Parker had volunteered to command the regulars if Sutherland had no objections. This, too, was good news. Parker, like his entire regiment of Royals, was a veteran wilderness fighter, seasoned in several major battles of the last war against French and Indians.

Thus, Sutherland went homeward feeling there was every possibility that the campaign would succeed, though it would be difficult, because Swain was cunning, and his followers were tough. In all, Sutherland would take fifty men; except for the soldiers, most would be frontiersmen, with a dozen Indians and French also along. He was striding through the fort when Mel Webster called to him.

Mel was standing with Nate at a corner of the parade ground when he spotted Sutherland and waved. During the summer, the two cousins had continued to work for the Frontier Company, taking odd jobs under Lettie Morely's direction, just managing to make ends meet. But Mel was not willing to return East yet, and Nate, feeling responsible for him, was unwilling to let him remain in Detroit alone.

The Scotsman paused and saw Mel push his journal into Nate's hands and run toward him. It was apparent that Nate had no interest in talking with Sutherland at the moment. Moodily, he walked away, head down, carrying Mel's writing book, which contained poems, notes on botany, and diary.

"Mr. Sutherland, I'm so glad you're back!" Mel exclaimed and pumped Sutherland's hand. "I haven't forgotten your offer to take us on the expedition after Jubal Swain—"

Sutherland shushed him, because the plans were to be kept secret as long as possible. In particular, Farley Jones was not to be told, though that would be tricky because of the clerk's closeness to military affairs. At first Campbell had been skeptical at Sutherland's insistence on utter secrecy, but the commander promised Jones would hear nothing from anyone in the army.

Sutherland said, "From now on, no one talks about that expedition—not if you want your goods returned."

Mel agreed, saying, "Since you've been away I've had time to think about your offer, and I . . . I want to go!"

Sutherland looked closely at the young fellow. Certainly he was brave enough, for all his naïveté, but this was a campaign for experienced men. He told Mel so, adding, "Understand, my friend, that I made the offer out of simple politeness, but I never expected you would actually want to go out after Swain! Do you know what you're saying?"

Mel nodded, looking determined and resolute. "I do, sir. Don't you see? It's not fair for me to ask you to bring back our possessions if I don't go along and share the inconvenience and danger."

Sutherland thought for a moment as the hubbub of the fort swirled around them. "Well, it's possible we could use you as one of the guards to stay with our cache of supplies. We'll leave them halfway there—"

"No! No!" Mel insisted. "I want to go! I want to be there when you attack. I want to be sure I get back everything, and I'm afraid you won't know all that's mine . . . I mean, there are personal papers and such, which . . . well, you must get my meaning, being a writer and poet yourself."

Sutherland smiled with understanding. "I like to compose verse now and then, but nothing I've done is worth risking my hair for it! Is your work that good, then?"

Mel laughed with embarrassment. "It's not that; it's just . . . well, I really think it would all be a jolly stimulating adventure!"

Mel was grinning broadly. Sutherland, thinking about Voltaire's innocent Candide, who had to learn about life the most painful way, was not smiling.

Mel asked, "May I go, Mr. Sutherland? I'll pull my own weight; I've even been taking canoeing lessons from that old Ottawa named Mawak! You won't be sorry!"

Sutherland softened. "I hope not, laddie. Aye, you'll be with us. And your friend?"

Mel shook his head.

Sutherland said, "Smart man! We'll find some more work for him here if he stays. A good number of company lads are going out, and he can fill in somewhere."

Grateful and wrought up, Mel hurried off to catch Nate. He dashed around a corner onto rue Saint Jacques, ran past log and clapboard trading houses, and saw Nate in the distance. His cousin was stopped at the intersection with rue Saint Honoré. Mel's excitement waned when he saw Nate conversing with none other than Matilda Merriwether. Mel slowed down and began to walk. Shyness overcame him. The street was busy, with fast-moving French *calèches*—two-wheeled pony carts—rattling by.

How had Nate managed to meet this wonderful young woman? For the past two months Mel had strained every nerve to contrive some way of meeting the girl. Just as he had been too nervous to push himself at her on other occasions, he was unable to approach the pair, and his legs felt like lead. He did not realize Matilda was taking a look at his very own journal, which Nate had opened before her. All Mel was aware of was Matilda's sparkling eyes, her lustrous hair that curled from under her cap, the white parasol and how she twirled it so charmingly. He leaned against a porch post and gazed from thirty yards away, seeing Matilda smile; she had such perfect red lips, such lovely, full cheeks. He did not notice what she was wearing. He did not consider why she was smiling so warmly at Nate. In that moment, all Mel thought about was a woman like none other he had ever seen before. This was the perfect opportunity to walk right up and have Nate introduce him.

Could he do it? Could he not do it? He straightened up and absently brushed the front of his coat. How scuffed his shoes were! No matter. Such as she would not care. Even though the sun was bright, Matilda still wore no mask, as any refined and civilized woman did. She understood the higher beauty of natural things; she comprehended divine laws, which ruled a man and a woman just as they governed nations and kings.

He would go to them. He would bow and make his presence known, once and for all. He removed his tricorn and dusted it off. Straightening it on his head, he swallowed a few times to get rid of the lump—which would have gone if there had been time to swallow once or twice more. But there was no time, for it seemed Nate was bidding her good day. Mel had to act, and act now!

He strode into the street and was nearly run over by a racing *calèche,* whose shocked and rowdy driver had no respect for young men in love. Ignoring French curses, Mel regained his balance and struggled to keep sight of the girl through the crowd.

To his dismay, he saw her getting into another carriage, where her father and mother sat in the presence of Reverend

Lee. He had missed his chance. Mel kicked the ground for being an indecisive fool! The Merriwethers and Lee drove away toward the northwestern gate, no doubt to enjoy the September evening on a drive along the river. Ah, fate! But Mel had been closer than ever to meeting Matilda, and now, with Nate as the intermediary, he was bound to do so properly before long.

Nate, too, was gone from the street, and Mel rushed off to catch him before he reached their lodging on rue Neuve Saint Germain. When he found Nate, Mel immediately asked how his friend had come to know Matilda.

Nate, apparently reluctant to talk, kept on walking and mumbled, "I jest sorta bumped into her, is all."

"Is all! Just bumped—Nate, man, you met Matilda Merriwether right on the street! Right on Saint Jacques, there! How can you make light of that?"

Nate shrugged. They returned onto Saint Germain. On their left were vegetable gardens and a stable for officer's mounts. Several young officers were taking their horses for a ride, cantering out of the fort to enjoy the rest of a perfect late summer's day. Neither Nate nor Mel paid much attention to these dashing fellows, whose horses were galloping even before they reached the gate.

Mel said, "I was watching you both—"

Nate looked somewhat guilty. "Ye was? What did ye see, then?"

"Why, Matilda, of course! I certainly wasn't looking at you! Isn't she beautiful?"

Nate muttered that she was. They came to their cabin, a ramshackle place of one small room, with a steep thatched roof. In the back was a communal waste pit and an outhouse shared by twenty such shacks. It was fortunate that the prevailing breeze off the river kept the stench downwind of their humble home—at least the breeze prevailed all but early morning, when it changed briefly. Invariably, the stench awakened them too soon if the window had not been closed the previous night.

Inside the dark cabin, Nate laid Mel's journal on a stool near his own bed. Mel picked it up to put it back in the usual place on a shelf above a small table in one corner.

Nate said gruffly, "Give me that!"

Startled, Mel stepped back. Nate rudely took the journal away, then recovered and grinned in apology.

Hemming and hawing, Nate said, "It's jest that, ah, this

here writin' ye done is, ah, quite nice, see? That's right, I like yer poems."

"Nice? Like them? You?" Mel was astonished. Nate had never before admired one line of his poetry. "You think—?"

Nate nodded and sat down on his bed, the notebook in his lap. "That's right, that's right. Don't be so surprised, neither. A man kin change his likes an' dislikes, can't he? Eh? Look here, ain't ye all hot to go out an' git shot up by renegades? Ye never woulda done such a fool thing afore, now would ye?"

"Why, of course not, but before there was no treasure map to recover—"

"Exactly, see? That's what I mean. Ye be changed, an'—an' I be changed."

"What's changed you, then?" Mel sat down on his bed, genuinely flattered that his down-to-earth, barrel-maker cousin would actually take an interest in his poetry. And Mel's own poems, at that—though not all the poems in the journal were his own; a few were by Owen Sutherland, whom Mel admired. He had copied Sutherland's work from back issues of the *Pennsylvania Gazette*, intending one day to spend some time discussing literature with the Scotsman. If Mel was to be here all winter, occasional visits with Owen Sutherland and conversations about higher matters would be thoroughly enjoyable, and would make the time pass.

As he thought these things, Mel realized Nate had not said just what had changed him so drastically from a scornful critic to an enlightened dabbler.

"Well?" he asked Nate, who looked up, that same, strangely guilty look on his face.

Nate sought an answer. He thought hard, cleared his throat, waved his hands in small circles, and finally said in exasperation, "'Swounds, Mel Webster, if I ever asked ye such a question about why ye like poetry, ye'd be up in arms declaimin' an' exclaimin' about art an' muses an' the Greeks! Ye'd be danged sore at me if I persisted in pokin' my nose into yer own literary tastes and whatnot! Wouldn't ye? Admit it! Yer danged persnickety about yer own revylations, ain't ye?"

Mel was taken aback. Nate was right. One really never could explain such elusive things. Art was beyond cold dissection, beyond intellect. Besides, it did not really matter to Mel exactly what had changed his cousin's outlook on life. It was a change for the better, and Mel Webster was not one to question the mysterious ways of Apollo.

Nate interrupted Mel's thoughts by asking, "And what did Sutherland say? Did he talk ye out o' yer fool notions an' tell ye to stay here outa trouble, where ye belong?"

Mel sighed and sat up a little rigidly. "Cousin, Mr. Sutherland has accepted me for his expedition."

"Arrgh!" Nate clapped his hand on his face and slowly shook his head. "What's Granny Breed goin' to say when she hears I couldn't keep ye from gittin' killed? She'll be boilin' to whip me!" He peered at Mel as though to find some chink in his confidence. But it was all true. Mel was going to fight renegades. Nate was sick at heart. Sadly, he asked, "When does it start?"

Mel replied, "I don't know yet, but if I did, I'm afraid I couldn't say. Military secrets, you understand."

Nate groaned. He lay back on the bed, forearm to his head. The journal was beside him, but he had no interest in it now. Once he had been a soldier. Mel had not. Nate well knew what his cousin was going into, but Mel did not. Nate had no clear idea of what he should do to stop Mel, but he feared for him.

After a long and exasperated sigh, Nate muttered, "Danged doodle-brain!"

A few days later, all was in readiness for the small force to slip away from Detroit, with Niko-lota as guide. After canoeing down the Detroit River to the River Raisin, the force would split up—half the men, under Parker and Niko-lota, going up the Raisin, the rest with Sutherland and Tamano heading for the Maumee. Parker's group would eventually portage their canoes overland to the headwaters of the westward-flowing Saint Joseph River. Sutherland's men would paddle up the Maumee to that river's northerly tributaries. Eventually, both divisions would reunite on the shore of Lake Michigan, at the mouth of the Saint Joseph.

Dividing the force was meant to make the most of the element of surprise. Renegade scouts might encounter one group or the other, but twenty-five men were less likely to worry the outlaws than the full force of fifty with regulars in uniform. By the time the expedition joined at Lake Michigan, there would be less chance of the renegades organizing a strong defense or fleeing into the interior in the face of such a stout body of men. In this assault, days were of the essence, and the longer Swain's renegades were kept uncertain of what was about to happen, the better the chance for success.

Sutherland wanted to recover as much of the stolen trade goods as possible, for what Swain had already captured was a severe loss to the company. If the renegades fled instead of standing to fight, they would undoubtedly take their loot with them, and the victory would be only partial. The wealth Swain would realize from the sale of all he had stolen would finance another outlaw settlement in the northwest next year, and this campaign would have failed to root out the renegades once and for all.

The afternoon before he was to depart, these thoughts tumbled in Sutherland's mind as he and his family canoed across the wide river to Valenya. This grove of birch and oak was where he had once lived with his Ottawa wife, Mayla. Two years earlier she had been buried near seven huge standing stones. Since that time Sutherland had replaced the first rude cross marking the grave with another of cedar, and he intended one day to place a granite headstone there. Though Ella had not known the young woman, she had seen Sutherland at the height of his grief, and had sympathized with his loss. She felt no jealousy, for she knew such deep wounds took time to heal. Further, she owed her life to Mayla, who had warned the garrison at Detroit of an impending Indian attack that would otherwise have wiped them out.

While the children played nearby on the pebbly beach, Ella and Owen went to the grave, and there placed sprigs of lavender. Knowing of Owen's wish to mark the grave with granite, Ella said she would write her brother at home in England to arrange for a headstone to be shipped over. At that, he put his arm over Ella's shoulders, and they turned away from the grave and standing stones to watch Sally and Jeremy laughing and running along the beach. Little Benjamin was crawling nearby, playing with Sniffer.

For a brief moment Sutherland thought of the unborn child that had been within Mayla at the end. It all seemed so far away now. His remorse had faded. He and Ella strolled along the riverbank, and he noticed the sun glinting on the silver, cylindrical pendant that dangled prettily from her neck. That had been Mayla's once.

For all the pain of the past, he was happy now, and had rebuilt his life. With Ella, their future was sure to be generous and joyful, no matter what happened with the trading company.

They would be content to end their days out here. As he often did, he let his thoughts wander to the fine house they would build on this site.

Valenya was named for the seven stones—"the singing stones," Indians called them, for when the wind was in the north, they gave a haunting, echoing sound that seemed like far-off chanting. He would build the house on a rise in sight of the stones and the small dwellings that still stood there. The structures were unused now, save for Tamano's lodge, which was the Chippewa's summer home. In winter, Tamano roved to the north and traded. Today, he and Lela were staying at the fort, for the expedition would leave in the middle of the night. Also at the fort was the fully recovered Little Hawk, who had chosen to remain with Tamano and his wife for a time, rather than return to his own people.

While Sutherland thought of the future, Ella thought of the past. Arm about his waist, she carried her moccasins as they ambled along the shore, water lapping at her feet. Ella's mind was back in Philadelphia two winters past, when she had refrained from telling Owen she was pregnant with Benjamin. Worried that he would not take her back to Detroit on a hard winter's journey, Ella had not told him of her condition until they were almost home.

Now, with Owen about to depart on a perilous campaign, she again knew she was with child. To tell him now would trouble his mind, she knew, and his mind must be clear to carry out the mission. Yet not to tell him would be much worse, for both of them. There would never be a perfect time—at least none more perfect than this.

With the sound of the children enjoying themselves nearby, Ella turned to Owen and put her hands on his arms. They looked at one another until she said, "We'll have another baby in the spring."

Without hesitation, he hugged her close and laughed. As he held Ella, the wind gusted about them, swinging into the north, but it was not cold. He pushed her back a little and kissed her gently. She was trembling with excitement and fear for him.

He said, "So," and kissed her forehead. "You make me happy again and again." She pressed against him, head on his chest, and, anxiety gave way to peace. There were no tears at parting; no terrible sadness engulfed her. She had chosen this world, this life, and she wanted none other. One day he would no longer take up his rifle and claymore and go away. One day he would stay, and here on this shore they would realize their dream, with the timeless river, the wind, and their children.

She whispered, "I love you so, Owen."

He passed his fingers through her hair as he said, "You give me too many good reasons to come back to you. Never be afraid, my lass. Never be afraid."

The children were coming, Sally lugging Benjamin, Jeremy pursuing Sniffer, whose tail stood up straight as he scampered along. Ella and Owen gazed at one another. For just the briefest of instants, she had a premonition of evil, of death and defeat. There was a flaming tomb, an inferno of heat and smoke, and she winced so sharply that Owen asked what was wrong.

Then it was gone, and the wind and sunshine and noisy children took its place. She closed her eyes and shook her head, not speaking. Owen's arms were strong, his face beautiful as she never imagined a man's could be. She turned to Sally, who had all she could manage to stump along with Benjamin in her arms. The baby was getting big and husky. He was dark like Owen, and always happy. Ella took him, but Owen lifted the infant up onto his shoulders, and off they went, back down the beach to have the picnic they had come here for.

That evening, Mel Webster could not sleep. In their small cabin he had gone over his gear again and again to be sure he had included everything Owen had told him to bring. He had a buckskin shirt and breeches, several pairs of stockings, two pairs of moccasins, a blanket rolled up—in this he had wrapped a few unrequired but essential things such as a magnifying glass, a book on practical science, one on botany, and his tin whistle. Also in his haversack was a durable tow shirt, a jack-knife, tomahawk, rifle wadding, six flints, greased cartridge paper, a pound of powder in a horn, a cartridge box with fifteen cartridges already made, and a pouch with forty lead balls. Nate had suggested taking a wooden bottle to hold a quart of water, and added that he might have an extra shirt, some jerked beef for an emergency, and a scissors mold with bar lead for making more bullets in case they had a few extra fights for the fun of it.

As Mel sorted through his gear, Nate sat on his bed, smoking a pipe of strong tobacco; the wind was in the wrong direction for the river and the right direction for the outhouse. Nate was completely bald; his deteriorating wig hung on a makeshift wig stand. Mel sensed a change in Nate, who was exceedingly grim and businesslike as he helped Mel outfit himself. Mel never before had seen the soldier side of his paunchy cousin, but in the course of preparing for this trip, it became apparent that Nate was experienced and no-nonsense when it came to warfare.

Nate gave Mel a small cloth sack, saying, "These be medicaments for this an' that: some comfrey powder, a bit o' cinchona bark, olive oil fer snakebites, an' some cure-all that ye kin mix with straight rum an' ye'll feel better right off, at least fer a while." Also, he handed over a leather bag of needles, thread, fishhooks, line, tweezers, and a pointed tool he said was good for picking teeth or getting lead out of a wound.

Mel stashed all these things into his haversack, and Nate asked, "Ye got a spoon? No? Well, 'swounds, man, ye gotta eat to fight an' paddle an' tramp, an' ye'll do more paddlin' an' trampin' than eatin' or fightin', believe me, so get a spoon— a big one. Sometimes ye'll have to eat quick-like. An' remember, join up with a few Yankee lads fer mess; they're decent an' they'll have small spoons, I guarantee it! Keep away from reg'lars at mealtime; they don't know what good food is, an' when they git on the trail an' eat fresh game, they'll think it's Christmas an' gobble up everythin' but the finger bowls. The big spoons they got is surprisin' when ye think soldiers git such bad food as a rule!"

Nate went on like that for some time, even after Mel was equipped, had oiled the rifle Sutherland had loaned him, and was writing a poem in his journal.

It was a poem about Matilda, as were most of the poems he had composed of late. It was short, but he was happy with it. Nate asked about it, and when Mel told him, his cousin seemed uneasy—and again, for some reason, guilty.

"You want to read it?" Mel asked cheerfully, but Nate waved him off. That was surprising, for Nate had been so very interested in Mel's poems, often borrowing the journal for days at a time. "You seem awful down in the mouth, cousin. Don't worry about me."

"About ye? It ain't ye I be worried about, it's me an' what Granny Breed'll do when she learns I let ye git et up by renegades! She'll whale me if ever I go back to White Plains without ye safe an' sound. She always liked ye best, but that's the way with grandmas an' doodle-brains!"

Mel laughed and told him not to trouble himself so. "I'll be back before the snow flies, with the map, and maybe with Jubal Swain's scalp!"

Nate did not think that was funny and warned against over-confidence.

Then Mel closed the journal and asked, "If something should happen to me, Nate, will you see that this gets home? Maybe some publisher would find it interesting, and you might even earn a few shillings with it."

Nate paled, his face sallow in the candlelight. Then he stirred and said hoarsely, "How ye gonna make all them notations an' calceelations without yer book?"

Mel showed a smaller notebook in the pouch of his haversack, where a bottle of ink and a few quills were tucked away. "That'll do me fine. We won't be gone long, but, listen, there's one more thing . . . Nate, you know how I've been such a coward when it comes to telling Matilda Merriwether how I—"

Nate grimaced and made a sound of exasperation.

Mel went on, "If something happens, which of course it won't, I'd like you to give Matilda the poems about her. Just say I meant to present them in person, and—well, that I intended to do it when I returned from the campaign."

To Mel's distress, he saw a tear in Nate's eye. Nate cleared his throat, sniffed, and scratched his bald head; then, with forced anger, he said, "Listen here, man, if ye intend comin' back, then go out thinkin' ye'll come back! 'Tis true a poet's writin' seems better when he's dead, 'specially when he gits killed fightin' outlaws, but don't talk to me about such things! Come back an'—an' give 'em to the girl yerself!"

Nate was very upset. Mel could not understand just why, though he presumed it was because Nate was so dead set against this campaign and chasing the treasure map. Mel felt affection for his irascible cousin and tried to cheer him up. They talked the rest of that night until four o'clock, when the rendezvous was planned for a cove downstream, just out of sight of the fort.

Mel sighed and stood up. He felt slightly queasy. Nate rose, too, and they shook hands firmly. Without another word, Mel shouldered his haversack—which was heavier than he had expected—picked up his rifle, and went outside. Several other men were moving silently through the darkened fort. The sky was starry and clear, an ideal morning for the start of an expedition. Mel turned as Nate wished him Godspeed, and left him standing there at the door.

A few minutes later, he was tramping alongside Lieutenant Parker with a crowd of men marching through the water gate. They filed along the riverbank trail, where they were enveloped by a low mist that hung there sleepily. A faint light in the eastern sky filtered through the fog. Mel breathed deeply, and felt fine with the rifle on his shoulder, tomahawk handle slapping against his thigh. He wanted to sing, but this was not the moment for that, even though he was off to battle for the first time in his life. He was grateful the queasiness had left him.

In the foggy semidarkness, Owen Sutherland and Lieutenant Parker directed the manning of fifteen big master canoes, some with supplies and gear, others carrying mostly men. Mel was put in the middle of Parker's craft, along with Corporal Jeb Grey and a French canoeist. Colonel Campbell, wrapped in a cape, stood to one side as the preparations went ahead.

On the shore a few women bade farewell to the men, among them Ella, Lela, and Lettie Morely. Lettie had her apron full of fresh rolls, baked during the night and still steaming. She bustled from man to man, canoe to canoe, even wading into the cold water, to hand out her gifts. Men thanked her kindly, joked with her about her pretty knees, and told her to have a panful of rolls waiting when they came back.

Jeb Grey accepted the rolls for the men in his canoe, and when Lettie went away he asked Mel who she was. "Fine woman, that," he said to the Irish corporal, Riley, who was in another bark boat. Grey passed the rolls about, and took a bite of one. "Good baker, too!"

Lettie gave Campbell her last roll, and he thanked her before wishing Sutherland and Parker good luck.

Just before the canoes were all manned, the young Sioux, Little Hawk, appeared, standing alone in the half-light, head hanging. Tamano, in the bow of a canoe, noticed the boy, who had begged to be taken along on this mission against the murderers of his family. In Algonquian, Tamano said quietly, "Wish us luck, Little Hawk."

The slender youth looked at Tamano, and Lela moved to the disappointed boy's side. Little Hawk stepped to Tamano's canoe, and from where it was held against his side, produced his father's coup stick. Tamano accepted it as Little Hawk said, "Carry it to battle in memory of my people." The Sioux returned to Lela while other good-byes were said.

Of the expedition, only Sutherland remained on shore, next to Ella. Several canoes began to drift into the current, like shadows against a deeper darkness. The sound of paddles clattering and men talking softly to one another mingled with the rhythmic slapping of water against bark hulls. The sentries had come in, including the man assigned to watch the cabin of Farley Jones. The clerk was still fast asleep.

Sutherland took Ella's hands and kissed her. She was about to say something to him—anything, she knew not what—when there was a commotion on the trail from the fort. Parker, whose canoe had not yet pushed away from the shallows, challenged whoever was approaching so hurriedly. Out of the morning mist came Nate Breed, a rifle on his shoulder, knapsack and blanket on his back. He stumbled, puffing and complaining, along the shore until he reached Owen and Ella. Mel nearly fell from the canoe to see him.

"Volunteer reportin', Mr. Sutherland!" Nate panted. "Equipped, supplied, deloused, an' recently fed!"

Sutherland chuckled, slapped Nate on the shoulder, and motioned for him to join Mel in Parker's canoe. Nate splashed through the water and climbed clumsily into the craft. Sutherland felt Ella move close, rubbing her arms against the chill.

He held her a moment.

Patting her tummy, he said, "Don't catch cold. Take care of the children. I'll be back for Christmas."

He kissed her hard, then waded to his canoe. The mist yielded to a puff of wind; weak stars glittered their last before morning light snuffed them out. Ella stood by herself, shivering, watching the vague image of Owen's canoe drift away. Water lapped near her feet; the mist returned, shrouding her, the beach, the river. Owen was gone, and it seemed it never would be dawn at all.

Paddling downriver was easy, and the men were in high spirits. Mel asked Nate why he had come if he hated campaigning so.

"Granny Breed!" he declared. "I hate to have her sore at me! Rather fight renegades and git ye home safe! Let's paddle!"

As they traveled, Sutherland considered again the plans they had laid for the assault on the settlement. Using Niko-lota's knowledge, they had mapped the layout of the place, and it was obvious that the unfinished palisade on the bank of the Eschicagou River was the best way to penetrate the defenses. First the enemy canoes would be tomahawked to make them unusable. Then a party would enter the settlement before dawn and torch the lodges as quickly as they could. At the same time, the stock would be driven right through the settlement to cause confusion when the inhabitants rushed out of their homes. While this was going on, others would free the twenty or so slaves. By tomahawking the renegades' canoes, Sutherland intended to trap the enemy. He would allow them to retreat to the beach, where they would be caught in the open without canoes, and would either surrender or die.

It would all happen fast, and everything depended on secrecy and surprise. If the outlaws got wind of them, the attack would fail. Either Swain would flee or he would ambush the expedition at a place of his own choosing.

First came the long and taxing journey of three weeks to Lake Michigan. They arrived at the River Raisin the next day, and, as planned, the force divided. Parker and the regulars with a few guides and frontiersmen headed west; Sutherland's group hurried south to the Maumee. For the first few days, the weather was good but noticeably colder. Winter was closing in sooner than Sutherland had expected. Within two months ice would be on the lakes, and it would be treacherous getting home.

Day after day passed on that arduous journey into winter. Sutherland's men were hardy, uncomplaining, though the air grew sharper, especially at night. By the time they crossed the higher ground at the Maumee portage—where the bones of Sutherland's friend, Garth Morely, lay—the hours before dawn had a bite to them that made a man grumble in his sleep. Ice crept into the edges of quiet water, though it was only early October; and Sutherland hoped for an Indian summer to temper the onrush of winter.

Weeks passed, counted out by the steady beat of the paddles, and by strides across portages, carrying gear, supplies, and canoes. So far, Sutherland's scouts had found no sign of renegades; in the few villages they passed through, nothing was known of Swain's marauders. Sutherland thought the triumph over Tamano's party and the vast haul of trade goods and hides taken then might have sated the outlaws for a while. Either that or they had already abandoned the northwest and gone south down the Mississippi to sell their booty and sit out winter.

Rapids, shallows, swamps, bluffs, rockfalls, and tangled undergrowth impeded and bedeviled the party, but they made good time. Three weeks after setting out, they reached the mouth of the Saint Joseph on the southeast side of Lake Michigan. It was mid-October, and Sutherland's party was on schedule. There was, however, no sign of Parker's group, which had taken a shorter route and should have been here by now. Sutherland settled down to wait on the north side of the river mouth. He hid his canoes and made a concealed camp on a wooded bluff set back from the lakeshore. Scouts went out in every direction on that first day, and each day thereafter for almost a week. Still there was no hint of Parker or renegades. The weather worsened, turning stormy and cold, with a wind that lashed waters and shook trees. The lake was so choppy that a canoe could not float upon it.

During the wait for Parker, the wind howled without relent. Not a bird was to be seen all that dreary, gloomy time, and the sun was no more than a pale glow in a gray sky. Waves battered the shore, wind tormented pines along the bluffs, and Sutherland became uneasy. He could not throw away these days; he worried about Parker's group. His own men were restless and anxious to get on with their bloody work, but they were too few and the lake too savage to attempt it.

It was not until ten days after first arriving at the river's mouth that they saw the sun come up to shine on a calm lake. The wind had died, and the weather turned milder, though cloudy. This year there would be no glory of autumn in the country, because most of the leaves had been blown from maples and aspens. Only dark evergreens offered any color; for the rest, the world was dull, the color of stone.

At noon, Sutherland was called by Tamano to come up to the lookout on top of the bluff. Good news! There, below, canoeing into the mouth of the river, was Parker's force. Sutherland wanted to shout for joy. Then he realized the lieutenant should have made for a sheltered cove rather than so imprudently expose his men to spies who might be watching from trees along the banks.

He was surprised at Parker's laxness, because the man was a professional who knew the woods. In the next moment, Sutherland realized that something was wrong. Parker had three canoes more than he started with—ten of them, with three smaller half-canoes in front. The half-canoes were far out in front of Parker's flotilla, their paddlers stroking furiously toward the lake. As they came closer, Sutherland realized these were not Parker's men, and whoever they were, they were trying to flee.

Parker's canoemen drove fast in pursuit, but the fugitives

had less weight and smaller canoes, and they were sure to escape when they reached the lake. Sutherland knew these had to be renegades. He called for his men to uncover their own canoes and cut these three off before they escaped and warned Swain. Working quickly, Sutherland's followers shoved their birch craft into the water.

Chased by Parker's master canoes, the three half-canoes were like rabbits eluding bears. Four paddlers were in each, and the heavier canoes of the expedition could not keep up with them. There was nothing they could do but get close enough and open fire to keep them from getting away.

Sutherland was in the bow of the first canoe, and he led his group in a course that cut across the path of the prey. They were spotted by the renegades, who swung sharply left, to the south. Sutherland's canoes were within forty yards of the renegades as they began to turn south and pull away. He took aim with his long rifle. Accounting for the leap of the canoe and the wind, he fired. A paddler slumped in the last craft. Ten others of Sutherland's group also fired, and the fusillade shattered this lagging canoe, as nearly every bullet struck it or its passengers. Floating helplessly in the water, the canoe turned broadside to the waves and heeled over. As Sutherland's canoe flashed past, he saw no one was left alive to save.

Now for the other two, which were increasing their lead. Again the expedition's riflemen opened fire on the trailing canoe, which was sixty yards off. The concentrated fire once more had a terrible effect, and three of the four renegades were hit. The fourth, who was the sternman and closest to the gunfire, miraculously was unhurt. He threw his hands into the air, and the attackers closed swiftly.

Sutherland called to Tamano, who was his own sternman, to keep on going, while other canoes got control of the prisoner. It was urgent that no one escape to warn Swain, but the fleeing canoe was darting over the water, its paddlers impelled by fear of death. Sutherland called to Tamano to paddle faster. They raced stroke for stroke with the enemy, making one thrust a second. As the canoe flew along, the Scotsman leveled his rifle. Their quarry was seventy yards off and seemed unable to widen the gap. Perhaps if one of the paddlers were hit, their prey would lose heart. It was a long shot.

By now, most of his own canoes had fallen back. Parker's force, apparently exhausted from a prolonged pursuit of the renegades, had turned aside and were putting in at Sutherland's camp. One other heavy canoe, far behind, kept up the chase. Sutherland knew they could catch the outlaws only if he fired true. His rifle banged, and when the smoke cleared, he peered ahead, hoping to see someone go down. He had missed.

Another rifle was handed him. Tamano cried out a cadence, and his men redoubled their incredible effort. It actually seemed as if his canoe was closing. They had gone four brutal miles, and the following heavy canoe had dropped off the pace. Sutherland did not want to miss again. He encouraged his men, called on them to bring him just a little closer. They cried out, and Tamano began to sing a Chippewa racing song. The canoe seemed to spring ahead. Sutherland whooped and cried out that they were gaining.

Sixty yards became fifty. Fifty became forty. Forty closed to thirty, and Sutherland had good range. Still, there was no certainty a shot from a bounding canoe would ever hit its target. He sighted carefully at the sternman, who was paddling furiously. This was obviously a *voyageur;* he wore a scarlet sash and stocking cap. He was an expert canoeman, who knew how to handle his craft. Kill him, and they were finished. Sutherland sighted. Just another five yards closer . . .

Then, to Sutherland's surprise, the *voyageur* abruptly swung the canoe around, neatly jerking it completely toward his pursuers. That maneuver spoiled Sutherland's aim, and before he could fire, the front three renegades raised rifles and blasted away from less than twenty yards off. A bullet nicked Sutherland's waist and struck the chest of one of his men. Another knocked the paddle from Tamano's hands. A third ripped a gash in the canoe below the waterline.

Sutherland fired back quickly, and a figure clad in buckskin cried out and pitched overboard. The renegades had other loaded rifles at hand, and the three survivors put another vicious hail of lead into Sutherland's crew. A bullet ricocheting from the canoe's bowsprit imbedded itself in Sutherland's thigh. He went down. Another of his men was shot in the head, and his canoe lurched broadside to the renegades, with only Tamano and a French canoeman unhurt.

Tamano snatched up his own rifle, and Sutherland found another on the bottom of the craft. The enemy had begun to flee.

Tamano's shot hit one man, who vanished from sight; Sutherland shot the stocking cap from the *voyageur* sternman's head, revealing sparse gray hair. As the fellow turned to curse and shake his fist, Sutherland saw he was Jean Dusten. With him in the canoe was an Indian, by the looks of him an Illinois. Tamano, too, knew them, and he was enraged at their escape.

There was no way to catch them now. The wounded in Sutherland's craft—including Sutherland himself, for he was bleeding heavily from his thigh—had to be tended to. The canoe itself was taking on water rapidly. When the following canoe came alongside, Sutherland labored with Tamano and the Frenchman to get the two injured men into the other craft. Bailing bloody water, Sutherland, Tamano, and the Frenchman brought their own canoe back to camp. Dejected and angry, Sutherland was also in severe pain. The bullet had not gone deep, and could be removed by Parker with a forceps.

During the operation, Sutherland and the lieutenant recast their plans. Parker had run into Dusten's force upstream, in a Miami village they had destroyed and pillaged. Parker still showed the effects of that fierce battle, his face black with sweat and powder, eyes hollow from lack of sleep. He sat at a campfire, where the forceps were heating for the repair to Sutherland's leg.

"There were twenty of them, Owen," he said. "They put up a stiff fight, but we managed to force them into a small defensive circle. We fought them for three days until they offered to surrender at dawn today..."

Parker used a cloth to protect his hands, and took the hot forceps from the fire. Tamano was on his knees behind Sutherland, and Mel Webster was at hand with a cup of strong rum.

Parker came close, forceps ready to draw out the bullet. Sutherland's wound had been cut open further with a clean knife, and he was in considerable discomfort.

"Keep talking, Lieutenant," he said. "It'll keep your mind off your work."

Parker aimed the forceps at the wound. The ball could just be seen; it had lodged against the bone. Had the force of the shot not been taken by the wood of the canoe, Sutherland's thigh would have been broken, and he would have been left here to wait until the attack was finished.

Parker said, "One of them told us, before he died, that they were mostly new recruits learning their trade under Dusten. They were brave enough, but our men outfought them."

The instrument penetrated the wound, and Sutherland bit into a piece of leather Tamano stuck in his mouth. Parker grunted, "Now I've got it..." But the forceps slipped off, and the officer grumbled with annoyance. Sutherland gasped and looked away, his eyes glazed, face pale.

Parker continued talking as he prepared to try once more. "We were caught . . . off-guard, thinking they were coming out, and most escaped to their canoes. When I set out with a detachment after them, the rest of the swine opened fire on us. We lost three dead and four wounded. We killed them all, much to my chagrin, for I wanted a prisoner who would tell us more." He stuck his tongue out in concentration, and Sutherland, sweating from the pain, found it hard to take a breath.

One last tug, and Sutherland sat up, moaned in agony, then fell back. Tamano caught him. Breathing deeply, Sutherland looked at Parker, who was pleased with himself, holding the flattened bullet proudly in his forceps.

"Think I'll keep this as a memento of our acquaintance, Owen, my boy."

Sutherland took a swig of rum, and the rest was used to swab out the wound. His leg burned, and he could not get comfortable. Mel bandaged him, after using a little comfrey powder to help the healing. Parker sat down, exhausted, and drank his own rum before finishing the story of Dusten's escape. Parker's group had followed him for six straight hours, and he would surely have escaped unscathed had Sutherland not joined in the pursuit.

The lone prisoner, who had been taken by Sutherland's force, would be interrogated before they set off for the outlaw settlement. But there was the larger problem of getting to Swain's lair before the renegades could be too well prepared. There was no time to lose now, because if Dusten followed the lakeshore he would reach Swain in less than three days. It was too late for Swain to flee with his booty, for Sutherland's force would surely catch up with him. Swain would fight, and would be an even more dangerous enemy. The element of surprise was lost to Sutherland's expedition. Or was it? He had an idea.

Looking up at the sky, he saw it was clear to the northwest. To Parker and Tamano, he said, "If we go straight across the lake, we'll get there a day before Dusten."

Parker and Tamano glanced at one another. Nearby, Nikolota was cleaning and oiling his rifle, which had been soaked in the wild chase. For Parker's benefit, he spoke in English:

"This Injun do same to get away from renegades." He nodded thoughtfully, saying, "Long way over big water; if bad wind come up, boats finished. No can get back."

Then, in Algonquian, he said, "Yet I believe it is the only way to do it, brothers; Swain is too strong for us if we cannot surprise him. These men we defeated upriver were not his main body. There are many more. We must go now, if we want to do it. It is dangerous, but there is no other way. I am willing, Donoway."

chapter **10**

WATER, WIND, AND FIRE

Within the hour, they were crossing the lake, heading for the western horizon. If they were fortunate, they would reach Eschicagou in two days and two nights. If they were unfortunate, and the weather changed, they would all be lost.

His thigh bound up, Sutherland paddled in the middle of the lead canoe, with Parker's craft skimming alongside. Extra food and equipment had been left at the Saint Joseph camp, along with their wounded men and a guard of two others. There were about forty of them in ten lightly loaded canoes, with rations for four days. They had plenty of ammunition, and pine torches for burning the settlement; the prisoner was with Parker. Though they would fire the place, Sutherland was determined to save the storage building Niko-lota had told him about. It held a tremendous fortune in goods, part of which would be divided up—as was customary with spoils of war—among the members of the expedition; the rest, where possible, would be returned to those who had lost it.

In addition, he would free the slaves and take back those who wished to go to Detroit. As for the women and children known to be in Swain's camp, Sutherland had given instructions to save them, though he knew the burning and the attack would jeopardize their lives. Niko-lota had told Sutherland about Lucy Swain and about his promise to her. They agreed that Niko-lota's first task was to get Lucy clear of the fighting. At the same time, Sutherland would go after Swain.

Using an old French military chart and a compass, Parker headed the tiny flotilla toward the west. That first day, under rapidly clouding skies, was harrowing. The waves were strong, the wind unmerciful. Driving against the starboard beam, wind and water compelled them to set a course that veered partially into the approaching waves. This slowed progress but made it less likely the canoes would be swamped and founder.

Gradually, land disappeared, and there was only gray sky

142

and grayer water. By the time night fell, men were tense and weary. Lanterns were lit and placed on the stern of each canoe, with Lieutenant Parker's light often covered and uncovered to indicate which craft was his. Throughout the long, tossing, black night, the lieutenant hardly slept. In the dim lantern glow he constantly checked the compass bearings to make sure they were going generally right. In the darkness, they compelled themselves to head into the wind. It was dismally wearying. Canoes leaped and fell awkwardly, jarring sleeping men awake, and making more than one seasick.

Hour after hour they paddled, alternating labor and sleep with their mates. They sang every *voyageur* and soldier song they knew, and then sang them again. Corporal Pat Riley's tenor gave them a few Irish tunes, lifting spirits. It was reassuring to hear voices from other canoes, and to know one was not alone in this pitching, dizzying hell of darkness. There were no stars for guidance, only the compass that was held near the lantern. Progress was impossible to determine. Where they were with regard to the distant western shore could not be guessed, for they had no navigating instruments, and Parker knew nothing at all of that art.

On they went, until the sun rose behind them, red and smoldering on the horizon. At least, Sutherland thought, they were still aimed in the right direction, though there was no sight of land on any side. He looked from one man to the other in his canoe; even Tamano seemed tired, his eyes slow and deep in shadow. Sutherland knew he must appear just as worn.

They had been almost eighteen hours on the water, paddling without rest save for a turbulent hour snatched here and there. For all the monotonous tedium, no one complained. Food and a jug of watered rum were passed around. With full light came renewed boldness; men's spirits rose with the sun, and several jaunty *voyageurs* challenged an all-English boat to a race. Tireless, of great heart, the *voyageurs* urged their own Anglo mates to paddle ferociously, and they handily defeated the competition.

So it went, hour after hour. Sutherland was glad for the choice of men. He could have asked for none better. They combined the finest qualities of every people on the frontier, each with something different and valuable to contribute to the whole. It would go hard on Swain if they reached the settlement before Dusten—if they reached it at all.

Gradually, the clouds cleared away, turning the sky and water blue. Gusts were stronger during the first hours of the morning, but gradually lessened to a steady breeze from the north.

Parker was exhausted. He asked whether anyone else knew how to read a compass. Mel Webster offered, saying he had some familiarity with navigating and would take over if the lieutenant liked. Dubious at first because of Mel's apparent inexperience with military affairs, Parker relented only because he was so utterly spent, and no one else volunteered. He told Mel to keep them headed northwest as long as the wind was from the north, and to call him if the wind or weather changed. Obediently, Mel took the officer's place in the bow. Parker moved to a second thwart, huddled in a blanket, and fell asleep immediately.

Sitting in the lurching bow of the canoe, Mel felt sick to his stomach. Not only did the rough passage distress him, but the memory of battle was fresh in his mind. He had been in the thick of the original fight with Dusten's party, though for the most part he had been useless to his own side, disoriented by the rapid flow of the struggle, and forced to keep his head down whenever the enemy poured lead into his position. For the entire first day of conflict with Dusten's group Mel had not even fired a shot. He had jammed his ramrod in the muzzle of his rifle, and for hours alternately attempted to wrench it free or was compelled to crawl back and forth with the movement of his own companions.

He had seen dead and wounded, smelled blood, and known cold fear. Defenseless save for his pistol, he had been confused and inept, always a few steps behind the rest as they attacked or withdrew, covered one another, or advanced. In the end, he had acquitted himself well enough, expending twenty precious bullets and a good deal of powder—though this last was largely spilled on the ground.

The fight had not been a total failure as far as his soldierly bearing was concerned; but by the time it was finished and the renegades beaten, he was used up, light-headed from exertion and emotional strain. He had been impressed by Nate, who had stayed near him most of the time. Cool and cautious, Nate had guided him through the worst of it right up to the final assault, when they overwhelmed the renegades who had not reached their canoes. It was then that Mel saw how dreadful and heartless war could be. Nate's transformation into a killer, almost an animal, had shocked him. It was one thing to see a stranger's battle-madness, but it was appalling to see savagery and bloodlust consume a cousin known always to be humane and decent.

These thoughts combined with nausea continued to afflict Mel, so that it took considerable willpower to pay attention to their course. Now and again he directed the sternman to bear this way or that, and the rest of the canoes followed, strung out for a hundred yards or so behind. After some time, he wondered what would happen if they became lost or if the elements drove them too far south of the Eschicagou. Dusten, who was following the shoreline, would have no difficulty maintaining his own route. He might get there first if the expedition did not follow the most direct line to the settlement.

An idea came to Mel, and he took Parker's chart from its leather case and unfolded it. Nate, paddling steadily in the middle of the canoe, gave him a look of warning, for the map was an officer's, not the affair of a volunteer. But Mel hardly noticed him. On the map, he saw the latitude and longitude of the Eschicagou, then dug into his own pack for the book on science, mathematics, and rudimentary practical skills.

Nate whispered, "What in the name o' hell are ye doin', man? Yer supposed to follow orders, not browse through books."

Mel hurriedly assured Nate everything was fine. He checked the compass bearing and called for the sternman to head more to starboard. Then he pored through the book, found what he was after, and declared, "Eureka!"

"My what?" Nate demanded. "What in the—"

"Your chronometer, cousin!" Mel reached over the sleeping Parker to pull Nate's timepiece from his vest, chain and all. Nate protested, lost the stroke, and as the canoe wobbled in response, he got a sharp rebuke from Corporal Jeb Grey.

Mel was fumbling through both his gear and Nate's, coming up with such things as a mirror, tow, a vent-pick normally used to clear a flintlock touchhole, and the cardboard cover of his small notebook, which he tore off with gusto. Whatever Mel was doing, Nate could not fathom it. He dreaded what would happen if Parker awoke to find his bowman fumbling with playthings, but he could not stop Mel for fear of waking the officer, who lay between them.

Time passed. Mel stuck things together with string, then took out an almanac to read something else. His enthusiasm had overcome weakness, and he read feverishly.

Nate was not quite sure, but he had the feeling that the line of canoes behind was forming a sort of curve, and the curve was becoming more pronounced with every passing minute.

"Mel!" he hissed, but he was waved off, for Mel was flipping pages and scanning the almanac. Others in the canoe began to mutter that their course seemed to be edging too far to port. It was not for them to ask questions, so they thrust and thrust, presuming Mel knew their bearing. Even Sutherland, in the second craft, tried to puzzle out why their course was turning southerly in the extreme.

"Aha! Got it!" Mel cried out, then reached down for the telescope, which was on Parker's lap. The officer awoke and sat up suddenly, looking around, still groggy.

Parker saw Mel grinning and holding up some contraption upon which his telescope was propped, his compass tied down, and a mirror positioned for a reason that he could not fathom.

Rubbing his eyes in the bright sun, Parker croaked, "What in the name of Harry are you about, then?" But before Mel could reply, the officer nearly leaped from the canoe. In front of him was the tail end of the flotilla. His craft had turned right around, forming a wide circle with the others. Parker gasped in astonishment and fury. Sutherland's canoe pulled alongside at that moment, the Scotsman asking what was wrong.

"Wrong?" Parker shouted and turned on the gasping Mel. "What's wrong is this man has been derelict in his duty—either that or he lied to me when he claimed he could read a compass! Speak up, fellow, which is it?"

Mel was pale, embarrassed to have neglected the compass while he was so busy constructing a crude sextant. He gulped, looked to Sutherland, who was not quite as grim as the officer, then held up his makeshift navigational instrument and said sheepishly, "I was just trying to help."

Parker was steaming, but Sutherland recognized what Mel had done, for he had served on merchant ships, though not as an officer.

Promptly excited, Sutherland asked, "Can you use that thing? Will it work?"

Mel cleared his throat. "I don't see why not. I have the necessary tables in my natural science book, and my almanac gives enough information about the position of the Polestar tonight, and some other stars. I'm reasonably certain it will work, for I've done some elementary things with a real sextant."

Mel looked from Sutherland to Parker and back again. By now, the canoes were bunching up, the men confused at this indecision. Parker did not know what to say.

Sutherland said, "Lieutenant, if this lad can do it, I'll wager we'll reach the Eschicagou tomorrow morning. We've been only guessing until now, but—if Mel's right—we'll set a course that will get us there like homing pigeons!"

Away they went, reorganizing and pushing off against choppy water and a strong breeze. By late afternoon every man was dead tired, arms and back aching. All but Sutherland and Mel seemed worried, for still they were far out on the water with no comforting mass of land to be seen. Night approached, the sun sinking in a magnificent glare of orange and lavender, and the men became more and more uneasy. Darkness on the lake was perilous and lonely to these men. Even their most experienced canoeists would never have taken a risk such as this under normal conditions.

In the bow of his craft, Mel was anxious for the stars to pop out above the velvet haze of twilight. One after the other they appeared, and he identified constellations—Orion's belt, the Great Bear, the Little Bear . . . and there it was—the Polestar. His makeshift contraption was bulky and hard to maneuver, but he worked it until the telescope was aimed at Polaris. In the light of the lantern, he calculated degrees with the circular compass, and struggled to take bearings despite the canoe's rising and falling irregularly.

Close by, Sutherland waited until Mel looked up, eyes glittering even in the dimness of dusk, and cried out, "Head west-southwest, and we can't miss it!" The sextant worked. Knowing the latitude of Eschicagou, and employing published tables and the almanac, he had estimated where they were.

Sutherland congratulated him, and the flotilla altered course. How long it would take was still a question, for distance traveled was dependent on wind, waves, and strength of arm. Throughout that night, Mel calculated and recalculated until he said they must be close to land. Though the night was clear and starry, there was no sign of shore. Sutherland passed the word that lanterns be shielded on the side facing west, so only following craft could see their light. Thus they would stay together but not be seen from the western shore.

Weary and anxious, they paddled on, hoping land was not far away. Soon heavy clouds rolled in from the northwest, and stars were obscured. The wind picked up, and the lake became more choppy. It was heavy going, with paddling more difficult, and the canoes rose and fell like so much driftwood.

Each craft was on its own now. To stay afloat they headed into the wind, thrusting hard against chilling spray and towering waves. Men swore, stroking with all they had left. Sutherland knew they could not last much longer. Morning was a few hours off, and there was danger of the force being split up and scattered like chaff. If that happened, they could never find one another in time, and the expedition would collapse.

Both hands on his own lantern, Sutherland swung it back and forth so the others could see, and know it was his. He counted all nine lights still in sight. Their covers had been removed, the better to shine toward each other. Lanterns on the other canoes bobbed wildly, as though tossed by ghostly jugglers. The wind gusted and rocked Sutherland's canoe. His leg aching, he almost lost balance as the craft lurched. Barely keeping hold of the lantern, he heard Tamano shouting to him over the wind. It was no use; he could not understand what the Indian was saying.

For some reason, the canoe had heeled over and would not right itself. He could hardly believe the canoe was tipped by wind alone. In the next moment, Tamano was at the bow of the canoe, standing in the water, the windstorm blowing his hair and feathers. To Sutherland's amazement, Tamano held up his hands and did not sink. They had run aground.

Shouting, "We are beached, and look, others are, too," Tamano pointed to the lights, some of which were not moving at all. Indeed, many canoes had been cast by waves against a sandy shore. They were safe, but where they had landed they would not know until morning.

Hopping out of the canoe, Sutherland stood in icy water up to his waist and struggled in pain to shore. There he swung the lantern to signal those still afloat to come toward him. Obeying against the wind was not easy, but within half an hour, the birchbarks were beached, men lying exhausted and grateful on the sand. Sutherland ordered all lanterns snuffed in case they were seen by a sentinel. The tempest raged more viciously down the lake, as though vexed that they had escaped.

Among the men on shore was the prisoner, a nondescript Yorker of forty named Bailey. Lying unbound on the sand, he found himself, for the moment, unwatched. In the darkness, he edged away from his captors, who were drained from their ordeal. Slowly, he moved back, not making a sound, and, when far enough from them, scrambled to his feet and bolted.

Bailey never saw the paddle that struck full force on his forehead, stunning him, and he crumpled. Jeb Grey shifted the paddle to his left hand, and with his right lifted the man by the back of the shirt and dragged him to the others, where he was laid at Sutherland's feet.

Grey commented, "This one ain't got permission to piss by himself, does he?"

Sutherland looked Bailey over, then said, "Go easy on that paddle, Corp; it's on loan to the army from my company."

Soon, a vague light came into the sky, though it was not yet dawn. Looking up, Sutherland saw the clouds were passing, with them the wind, and the lake became more calm. Hardly a drop of rain had fallen, though the storm was already departing. As the sky cleared, stars shone, sharp and bright. The outlines of bluffs and the lake's horizon took form.

Before dawn, the canoes were hauled far from the waterline. Under Niko-lota, Tamano, and a Ranger sergeant, scouting parties were formed, and the three separate groups slipped away, moving up and down the beach, with one heading inland over the sand dunes.

Mel leaned on his rifle, guarding the outlaw prisoner. Nearby sat Sutherland, talking quietly to Lieutenant Parker. The Scotsman's throbbing leg had been bandaged again, and now he sat on the sloping side of a high sand dune, taking in every aspect of the shoreline as light filtered gradually upon the world. They were on a long beach, and soon they would have to find cover behind or among the dunes.

Parker began to interrogate Bailey, who was surly and uncommunicative, saying this place did not look familiar. After a little while, scouts under Tamano, who had gone southward, came running back to report the settlement lay no more than half a mile off. Parker slapped Mel hard on the back, gleefully congratulating him for such masterful navigation.

Mel smiled shyly, shrugged, and looked out at the lake. He felt wonderful but still unsoldierly. Sutherland laughed and said to Mel, "You don't need to fight to be of service to us, laddie. Don't waste your talents throwing lead when you should be chief navigator in our little army."

Even more self-conscious, Mel smirked, and put his hand up to rub his chin. He fumbled his rifle, nearly dropping it. The prisoner gave a snort of derision and spat.

Sutherland looked at Bailey and said, "Now you'll tell us

about outposts, lookouts, scouts—and make no mistake."

Bailey was not impressed at all until Tamano loomed over him. In the early light, the Chippewa looked fiendish. Toying with a scalping knife, he knelt before Bailey, whose teeth abruptly chattered. Grey said with a wink to Parker, "Please, sir, I got a squeamish stomach afore breakfast, an' I'd rather not watch this if you don't mind."

Parker said Grey was excused. Bailey quaked with terror. Before the corporal departed, he whispered something in Tamano's ear, then walked off. From a little distance, he called, "Hold on; make that the left one. I cut off a right one back at the first fight with these bastards . . . And do me the favor of washing it off first; as I said, I get squeamish."

Tamano gazed coldly at Bailey, who was sweating profusely. Sutherland said, "If you want to live for a fair trial, man, you'll tell us what we want to know. Do so, and I give my word, we'll spare you and bring you back—in one piece."

Bailey clutched his own arms, whimpering, "I'll tell you what you want . . . anything! Just keep that red devil away from me!"

Bailey warned them of a lookout post set atop the dunes to observe the north shore of the river and the main lake. It was from here that Niko-lota and Shamot had been seen before being captured.

The other scouts came in, and, as the first glow of morning began to wipe away the night and stars, an attack was set in motion. Canoes were dragged up a sandy defile and concealed with slashed brush. Sutherland hobbled along, Bailey at his side, and led the men southward across the dunes through dissolving darkness. There was hardly a sound from anyone, nothing more than the squeak of feet on the sand. The outpost was nearby.

Bailey hailed the two sleepy guards, and they were lured out to be jumped and knocked unconscious, then tied up along with their companion. One guard was Thrower Simpson, his bad right arm in a sling, still aching from Swain's breaking it. The sky was lighter, the eastern horizon illuminated by a sun that was almost up. Sutherland was troubled because he had wanted to strike in darkness, to torch the sleeping settlement, cause confusion, and drive the renegades down to their beached canoes.

Hurrying on, Niko-lota guided Sutherland across the river's ford, then downstream to the settlement. Approaching the un-

finished stockade, the force divided. Five men dashed around
the palisade and down to the beach, where thirty canoes, bateaux, and whaleboats were suspended on racks, most upside-
down. Sutherland assembled his attackers, passing unlit torches
to several who would be the first to rush in. From the beach
came the thunk and crackle of tomahawks biting through birch
and wood as the boats were disabled.

Already there was movement to be seen through the unfinished section of rough palisade. A few women were lighting
fires and hauling water. So far not a man was in sight.

Sunlight was on the high clouds, and the heavens were
turning blue. It was past time. The raiders were in position,
and everyone knew his duty. At the last minute, Sutherland
wanted to tell Mel Webster to stay behind, but he could not
find him. The shadowed faces of his fighters were visible among
the trees. They responded to his directions and advanced. At
the edge of the woods, they lit pine torches with the flash from
unloaded rifles, and that was the final signal to assault.

Without a battle cry, they rushed forward, thirty-five tough
men, white and red, American, French, and British. With Sutherland and Niko-lota in the lead, they raced along the base of
the palisade, turned the corner of the gap, and erupted into the
clutter of lodges like angry bees swarming from the hive.

Women screamed, and cooking pots were overturned.
Torches flared. Smoke burst from ignited roofs and walls.
Within their corral, stock bellowed and whinnied. For a full
thirty seconds not a shot was fired. The few women shrieked
and fled; dogs snarled, snapping, barking. Flames, whipped
by the morning breeze, turned into a crackling roar. Then
renegades staggered from their homes, wild and reckless, brav-
ing hot lead to find their comrades. Bullets cut down the first
few, but it was only seconds before the defenders began to
reach cover with their guns and ammunition. Thick smoke
covered the settlement, fires raging on all sides. During these
first moments, Sutherland and Niko-lota ran to the low reed
door of Swain's lodge. The Delaware torched the roof, then
took one side of the door, Sutherland the other, claymore and
tomahawk ready.

The first one out was Lucy, stumbling and coughing. She
pitched forward, and Niko-lota caught her, dragging her away
to safety. Sword raised, Sutherland looked for Swain to come
next. Again the reed door was thrown open. It was Swain. He
hesitated, and Sutherland reached for him, clutching a handful

of hair and dragging him forward.

But Swain was a powerful brute, and he yanked backwards. His sheathed hook cracked down on Sutherland's wrist, breaking the hold. In spite of the black, acrid smoke pouring out, Swain vanished into his lodge. Wasting not a moment, Sutherland leaped forward, kicking the door clear. The blast of a pistol drove him back, the bullet so close that he felt it pass his face. He drew his own pistol and prepared for whatever Swain would do next. The lodge was in flames. Swain had to come out soon or be burned alive.

Sutherland looked over the courtyard of the settlement where his men were advancing, firing, reloading, and a few dropping, shot down. Screaming horses and terrified goats burst through flame and smoke, running among his men, who had come up against surprisingly stiff resistance. Clearly the renegades had not been forewarned, or the assault would never have come this far; nevertheless, there were far more of them than expected, and they were tough. The embattled renegades were now collected in a strong body at the far end of the settlement, and they were well armed. Desperate men, every one of them, they returned fire as well as they took. Their losses were heavy, but they were numerous, and at least forty stood their ground behind a hastily built barricade of carts, barrels, and dead stock.

For a full minute Sutherland lingered at Swain's door, waiting for his enemy to spring out. No doubt the man suspected that several raiders were waiting to shoot him down, and he was not about to die so easily. Sutherland checked the back of the burning lodge to see that Swain was not trying to cut through that way. The noise of battle grew, the smoke making his eyes and nose run. His wounded leg was painful, but he ignored it for this chance to finish Swain.

He had to step back from the left side of the lodge because the flames were hot and blinding there. Above, a towering cloud of smoke rose from the village straight up into a blue sky. Sutherland stood in a hellish cauldron, sword in one hand, pistol in the other. Though the main fight was being waged with increasing ferocity, he was alone—he and his hidden adversary.

From out of the smoke, Lieutenant Parker emerged, coughing and spitting, his face black from gunpowder and sweat.

"Owen! We can't hold them back any longer!"

"What? We should drive them to the beach!" He eyed the door where at any moment Swain might suddenly appear.

Parker shook his head. "No! They're too strong, and we've lost heavily. They're outflanking us along the river side. We're holding the main gate, but if we don't retreat quickly, we'll be trapped here."

"Swain's inside there!" Sutherland snarled, and gripped his sword. He could not leave Swain now! He would not go until he had done for him.

Parker touched his arm. "I'm going to make a fighting withdrawal toward the gate! You have to go! There's no choice. We'll come back and hit them again. Leave off, man!"

Parker rushed back into the smoke toward his battle line. He had to think of his men. Sutherland saw him go, and noticed two of his followers lying dead. Another man, dazed and wounded, knelt with his head on his chest, half-conscious.

Bullets zipped past Sutherland, who ached in body and soul. His men began to appear out of the billowing smoke, backing up as they fired and reloaded. The enemy was advancing, driving them back. In a moment he would have to flee with the rest of them, or be cut off. Lead dropped and ricocheted all around. Swain's lodge burned, part of it about to fall in. How could the man stand it? Sutherland's men were almost abreast of where he waited so maddeningly for the outlaw leader.

Parker again was near at hand. He waved his sword at Sutherland, calling for him to withdraw at once. Sutherland would not do it. In anger he struck his claymore against the lodge doorway. No response. He had hoped to make Swain fire his pistol again, and then he would have barged in, no matter what. He slashed again with his sword and shouted Swain's name. He kicked the door and the side of the lodge, but it would not cave in yet. His raiders were behind him now. Through the dense smoke, enemy fighters were in sight, flitting here and there. The flash of their rifles revealed they were just a few yards away.

"Come on, Owen!" Parker blared, trying to hold his men, who were falling all around him. Sutherland's companions were trying to protect him, but they paid for their loyalty in blood.

Sutherland had to go in. He crashed his shoulder against the lodgepoles framing the door, and dropped to the ground in the next instant. His tactics worked perfectly. Swain took the bait and fired too high, missing Sutherland, who burst ahead, the Highland war cry in his throat, and broke into the reddish glow of the lodge interior.

But Swain had another pistol.

Sutherland charged into a blast of fire and gunsmoke that erupted point-blank. He pitched sideways, stunned, searing pain overcoming him. As he hit the ground, he instinctively swung his claymore, feeling it bite flesh, and heard an angry oath. His pistol went off on its own as he tried to get up. He could not. In the depths of that inferno, he saw Swain's terrible eyes, more fiery than the flames. Sutherland tried to strike at them with his claymore, but his arms would not obey his numbed mind.

Then the roof sagged and dropped smoldering embers, and the face of Swain vanished with a howling bellow of sheer savagery. The lodge was caving in. Lying on his side, Sutherland shielded his head with his arms. He could not get up. The fire was falling on him, and he was too stunned to save himself. Heat scorched his clothes and hair. The sound of fire roaring and the harsh searing of the flames swallowed him. He felt helplessly afloat in some tormenting nightmare that would never end.

He must get out. The roof of the lodge gave way. Flaming poles clattered next to him, embers scorching his buckskin. He kicked them away. He found the strength to poke his claymore against a pole about to drop on him. For just this moment he could delay death. For this last instant he could hold back fate. But no longer. He closed his eyes and saw Ella, fresh and beautiful. He heard something: a voice.

Was someone else in the blaze? Could it be Swain struggling to escape? Swain was fighting for his life, ripping back sections of crumbling lodge. Sutherland would not let him get out. He screamed the Highland yell and fought to his knees. With every bit of his being, he lurched forward to the figure, who caught him up. Sutherland tried to cut at him with his sword, but he was too groggy. Suddenly he felt himself being dragged bodily forward by more than one man. He struggled mightily, shaking them off, and collapsing on the ground.

Miraculously, he was outside the lodge. The heat was gone. He was clear of the flames, though everything was black with smoke. Once more he was being roughly pulled to his feet. Someone was shouting into his ear, shouting his own name. Through smoke and sweat and blood he saw the face of Mel Webster, filthy with muck and blood. Supporting Sutherland's right side, Webster had a warlike light in his eye. On the other side was Nate Breed, his wig stuffed into his shirt, and his bald pate bleeding from a slight wound.

Sutherland tried to master his wobbly legs, and he stumbled, but they held him up. From within the smoke, men were shouting—not their own men, for they had been beaten off. The three of them would be discovered any minute now. Sutherland felt like a babe, so weak that he could barely stand.

"Save yourselves," he groaned, knowing they were surrounded, with only the heavy smoke keeping them from a quick death. "Save yourselves—"

"We will, don't worry!" Nate replied coolly.

On his side, Mel saw something he did not like and shoved them off to the right. But Nate saw something else and pushed in the opposite direction. They ran forward, Sutherland at last getting a lungful of clear air. They had broken out of the smoke. Able to breathe, Sutherland felt stronger.

Then the outlaws loomed like shadows from the screen of smoke. Easy targets, Sutherland, Mel, and Nate turned to defend themselves.

"Down!" Sutherland cried, and they fell to the ground just as a burst of firing erupted, sending lead over them.

The Scotsman was regaining his senses, blood running down his cheek from the gash on his head where Swain's bullet had grazed and stunned him. Twenty yards away, the outlaws at the edge of the smothering cloud were reloading. They had fired a futile volley, trying to cut down Sutherland and the others. Nate and Mel frantically reloaded their rifles, and Sutherland took Mel's empty pistol, for he had dropped his own. Just a few paces apart, a dozen renegades and the three raiders confronted one another, laboring to be the first to fire.

The outlaws were almost finished loading, most of them ramming home bullets while Sutherland and his friends were just pouring the powder down the barrel.

"Ready to duck again," Sutherland said, but he reckoned they would rush in close to finish them off. His claymore would be their only defense.

Then the outlaws yelped in terror, and tried to get their guns up to shoot. They were too late. With Parker at their head, six howling Redcoats rushed at them, long bayonets gleaming. They covered the short distance in a few seconds, though one or two of the renegades got off shots—shots fired in haste and in mortal fear of the murderous bayonet. A bullet hit Pat Riley's foot, but he kept charging at the enemy. Those who did not flee back into the smoke were run through like so many speared fish. The whack of steel against flesh and the shrieks of stricken outlaws dismayed the rest, who retreated for the moment.

Parker ordered withdrawal, and his grim soldiers trotted back to the remnants of their force. As Nate, propping up Riley, and Mel—who was carrying a large leather satchel—hurried back with them, Sutherland limped alongside Lieutenant Parker.

"Provincials never could take a bayonet charge," the Scotsman muttered in complaint. "That was the biggest little counterattack I've ever seen."

Parker saw Sutherland wince in pain, and he said, "We have to see to the wounded, all of you. Swain'll regroup soon, and I'd guess they've got thirty effectives yet."

The soldiers, Nate, Mel, Parker, and Sutherland rejoined their own men, who were passing through the settlement's gate, making for the bluffs to the southwest, where they would reorganize. Carrying their wounded—of whom there were ten—only fifteen raiders could still fight, including their leaders. Sutherland was relieved to see Tamano without a serious wound. Niko-lota was lugging an injured provincial, and Jeb Grey commanded the rear guard in case the renegades came on again. Sutherland asked Niko-lota what had happened to Lucy Swain, and he was told she had escaped.

Sutherland had burns on his hands and neck. Save for the head wound and his injured leg, however, he was otherwise able to fight. He resisted the pain as best he could and, with Parker, organized a withdrawal into the bracken-covered hills, where low pines grew in clumps. Behind them, the entire settlement was in flames, smoke blowing across the lake and staining the sky black. The column paused on the bluff to assess more exactly how much damage they had done. Sutherland saw a dozen renegades and their women desperately trying to pour water on buildings near the large storehouse, which held all their booty and valuables. He was relieved they would probably save that building, for he was not finished yet. Somehow, his battered force would strike again; he must utterly defeat Swain's men, and had to regain all that had been lost.

On that bluff, which was south of the burning settlement and across the river from their own canoes, they held another council of war. As they talked, men ate what little food they had with them, and drank stream water. Though they were sorrowed at the loss of so many friends, no one else died or seemed about to, and that was something.

Nate bandaged Riley's foot and told him to keep it out of his mouth for a while; the Irishman asked what was the doctoring fee, for no Yankee ever gave anything for nothing.

"A rum at the Brave Wolfe," Nate replied, "though ye'll have to water it down considerable extra to make the exchange fair."

Riley chuckled and said, "I'll teach you a verse or two of 'Yankee Doodle' I 'eard come from the garrison at Boston! Those boyo's got more gripes an' more verses about beaneatin' Yankees than anybody else!"

Sutherland moved through the men, checking wounded and seeing who could still carry a gun. As he passed Riley, the corporal said, "I can't dance, Mr. Sutherland, but I can escort the more serious wounded back to the Injun boats if you like."

Sutherland said, "We can't divide up, lads. But if you're willing, I think we can draw Swain after us and then hit them again. If you're willing."

Without hesitation, they replied as one that they could not flee. Gratified, Sutherland explained his plan to all of them. It was tricky and dangerous, but if Swain was as headstrong as Sutherland thought, he might just be finished off.

As the group readied to push off for the ford farther upstream, Sutherland saw Mel sitting dreamily, the heavy leather satchel in his lap, rifle leaning against his shoulder. Next to him lay Nate, with a bandage around his bald head. Sutherland approached and thanked them for rescuing him. Nate sat up and replied that they owed it to him.

Sutherland indicated Mel's partly charred satchel, and asked what it was. "It looks heavy to carry along with you before we're out of this, lad."

Smiling, Mel patted the satchel. "It's mine, Mr. Sutherland; it's got all the papers Swain stole from me. Everything."

Sutherland thought about that. "You're a fanatical poet, Mel, jumping into a fire to save your work."

Mel said, "We wanted to get you out, too, Mr. Sutherland. We saw you go in, and were coming to help when Swain broke past us and got away to his own men. When you didn't come out, we feared the worst, so . . ."

As Sutherland departed, he said, "One day I'd like to read what's in there; it helped save my life."

$\bullet \quad \bullet \quad \bullet$

The Yorker named Bailey could hardly believe he was free and running through the bracken on dunes near the burning settlement. He often looked back to make sure the raiders were not after him, especially their Indians. They had released him to take a message and a small deerskin pouch to Jubal Swain. The message had been verbal, and easy to memorize, though its meaning was unclear to him. Sutherland had given him the small pouch, with the warning not to open it before Swain did, or the outlaw leader surely would punish him.

The Scotsman had beckoned for Niko-lota to come forward, and the Delaware had said, "Tell Swain this: The hand-taker will return again."

With that, Sutherland had cut the prisoner's bonds and let him go. Bailey had fearfully rushed into the turbulent stream and waded across, anxious to get back to Swain and safety. The pouch was suspended on his neck, and as he scrambled out of the water, something inside rattled dryly. Giving one last look across the surging river, he saw Sutherland assembling his men, apparently pulling out. The other two prisoners— Thrower and the other man captured at the start—had been left tied, sitting on the ground on the north side of the river-crossing. There they could be seen easily from the south bank a hundred yards away.

Ahead of Bailey rose a column of smoke, black and dense. He crested the dune and saw the devastated settlement. Bitterness filled him, and he wanted revenge. Making for the stockade, he bounded down the sandy slope and was met by a few others, who brought him to Swain. Assembling his fighters after having saved the storehouse, Swain was seeing to last-minute details to defend against another attack.

Nearby, Lucy sat with the other women and the children, all dejected and downcast. Most of the lodges had been burned to ashes, and all their possessions, except for what had been preserved in the storehouse, were lost.

When Bailey was brought in, Swain swung around on him, hungry for news of the enemy. Swain was suspicious of a trick, asking Bailey how he got away. The weary man said he had been released to bring the message and small bag.

"Out with it then," Swain ordered. "Give me whatever it is!"

Bailey said, "They told me to say, 'The hand-taker will come again,' but I don't—"

He stopped talking, cowed by the ugly look that overcame

Swain as he peered into the pouch. The battered, sulking survivors of the raid saw madness in their leader, and they drew back. Swain was shaking, his face purple. He could not take his eyes from whatever was in the pouch. He was transfixed, as though about to blow up. Then slowly he became icy calm, and that was even more frightening. A strange look of humor came into his eyes. He glanced around at his men, gave a dry, harsh laugh, and held up the contents of the pouch: a shriveled forefinger, his very own, taken by Niko-lota a year ago.

Lucy shuddered when she saw it and looked away with a gasp of revulsion. Swain's good hand trembled as he carefully returned the severed finger to the pouch. He was like a volcano, simmering, exploding within, but on the outside, he was very cold. His eyes were slitted as he spoke in a soft voice to Bailey.

"Tell me where they went an' how long ago. They think Jube Swain's a fool who'll walk into a ambush 'cause he's a little het up, but they're dead wrong. Speak, man, an' we'll make a end to 'em in time fer dinner."

Half an hour later, before the sun reached noon, twenty-five ill-tempered renegades led by Swain and Bailey moved in cautious skirmish order through low growth near the river-crossing. They had sent out scouts, and when they reached the edge of the water, found them hunched down, waiting for the main body. Moving with stealth, Swain joined his scouts, who told him two of their men were tied up across the river.

Swain saw them, and suspected a trap. Hallooing the two prisoners, he cried, "Where be they swine, boys? They got yuh covered?"

Thrower, bound hand and foot, called back that Sutherland's rear guard had gone less than five minutes earlier, making for their canoes up the lakeshore. Swain and his scouts surveyed the landscape, which was for the most part scrubby trees and bracken, with no especially good cover for an ambush. Following closer inspection of the surroundings, Swain sent two scouts across. They waded with difficulty through the swift, waist-deep water and, on the other side, cut their friends free and took to cover. These four moved around the far bank, and after a search, found no sign of their enemy.

Swain decided that Sutherland and Niko-lota must really be attempting to escape. Making quick decisions, he ordered his men across the river. They went into the rushing water holding rifles and powder horns over their heads. The ford was hazardous and the going slow. Swain was last in line, keeping watch on the near riverbank in case of some trickery that would end with Sutherland appearing from behind to surprise them.

Swain's men were strung out across the river, toiling to keep their balance, when someone yelled a warning. Confused, the renegades looked around, but there was no enemy in sight. Not a shot had been fired. The man cried out to look upstream. It took a moment to see a pounding line of driftwood bound by rope in the form of a raft half the width of the river. Men shrieked with terror, trying to scramble out of the water and escape the hurtling mass. Just before the driftwood bore down on them, some made it out of the water. Others ducked under the surface, but when the full might of the wood smashed into them, they were dragged away, kicking and screaming. The raft hit the ragged line of men with tremendous force, though a few renegades bobbed up after it passed.

Swain was the only one who escaped back to the near bank. Before he could even shout to the handful of survivors on the other side, gunfire erupted from upstream. Close behind the raft raced four canoes of raiders, whose bullets flew among the men struggling in the water and on the opposite shore. Swain was beaten. His force was crushed, most of the men swept downstream, if not to drown, then at best to be out of the fight for a long time.

Swain's men on the opposite side were throwing up their hands in surrender. He stood alone on the southern shore, the canoes closing fast. A few shots were aimed at him but missed. Boiling for vengeance, he dropped to one knee and took careful aim at Niko-lota, whose canoe bobbed wildly in the current. He would have Niko-lota. That would take the sting out of defeat.

He squeezed the trigger. At that moment, Niko-lota leaned over for his powder horn. Behind the Delaware, Corporal Riley grabbed his chest and fell backwards, the bullet meant for Niko-lota killing him instantly.

Swain cursed the Indian, but there was no time to reload. Already, another canoe with Owen Sutherland and Tamano was slicing toward him, and he had to fly. With bullets pursuing him, Swain zig-zagged away through the dunes, making for the settlement and Lucy. Somehow he would get away with her, though he knew not how, since his canoes were all damaged. Either he would escape, or he would die fighting. Owen Sutherland and Niko-lota would be his first targets.

Back at the riverbank, Sutherland and Tamano leaped from their canoe, which also had Mel and Nate aboard. Niko-lota's craft slid alongside. These five rushed after Jubal Swain. They knew that at any moment he might ambush them, but there was no time to lose. They could not let him escape, so on they ran, reckless and determined to get at him. Slung over Mel's back, his leather satchel with the treasure map and his writings bounced clumsily. He was unwilling to part with it again, no matter what the effort. Fourth in line, he trotted behind Niko-lota, with Nate bringing up the rear; Sutherland was first in the file, Tamano right after him.

They ran to the end of the dunes, heading for the smoldering settlement. Since there was no sign that others were joining Swain, they presumed he would not make his stand until he reached the place. His tracks made directly for the main gate. From the dune, they saw the women and children huddled together in the courtyard. And there was Swain! He had Lucy with him, running through the settlement. It was too far off to try a shot. They had to go down there now.

Sutherland and his men skidded down the slope and rushed forward, searching the top of the palisade for any concealed sniper. Reaching the gate, they slowed. They must be more cautious, for they did not know how many were still alive and willing to fight. Passing through the main gate, they saw no sign of life until by rounding a charred building they brought the crowd of women and children into view. In company with these sorry folk were three wounded renegades, who raised a hand if they could, to surrender.

There was no sign of Swain or Lucy. The fires had mostly died down, the lodges almost all ruined. Sutherland and his men spread out to hunt through the ashes. The storehouse was still intact, but as Sutherland moved cautiously around it, there was a tremendous explosion. He and his men fell to the ground, with rocky debris from the renegade's powder magazine raining down. Sutherland ran to the rubble of the magazine, expecting to see Swain getting away. But there was no sign of him anywhere. A charred black line led to the ruins, where powder had been trickled, then ignited to serve as a fuse. Swain was close, but where?

"Donoway!" Tamano shouted, and Sutherland whirled to see another line of black powder—this one hissing with flame and smoke that rushed straight for the storehouse. Mel rushed to it, using his hat in an attempt to beat out the ignition before it reached whatever explosives Swain had put in the building.

Sutherland caught movement near the main gate. As he turned, a rifle cracked. Mel went down. Sutherland fired, but the figure vanished out the gate. The fuse kept sizzling, then disappeared into the back door of the storehouse. A heavy explosion followed, blowing out a wall, igniting the roof, and starting a raging fire. Sutherland and the others quickly recovered from the concussion. He and Nate hurried to Mel, while the Indians ran to the main gate.

Mel was lying on his face. Anxiously, they turned him over. There was no sign of blood. Pale with fright, Nate put his ear to Mel's chest.

"Still beatin'! Where's the wound? Where's the wound?"

Sutherland dragged off the leather satchel. Lifting Mel's tunic, they found a nasty bruise on the back of his rib cage, but no blood. Mel groaned and blinked open his eyes. Looking around, he spoke in a choked voice, for his breath had been taken away by the impact of the bullet.

"Am I shot?"

Sutherland tossed the satchel to him, and said, "There's a slug in there along with your poems. Stay here and guard him, Nate. We'll get Swain."

Tamano and Niko-lota were already through the gate, where Swain had last been seen. Sutherland joined them, and they crept out to the cleared ground and a path that led down to the river. Swain had gone this way, Tamano said, noting Swain's and Lucy's fresh tracks leading along the palisade. They went after him, Sutherland first, Niko-lota behind.

Mainly meadow and saplings, the ground was not thickly wooded here. They ran fast, knowing Swain was just beyond the next rise, which would reveal the lake to them when they reached it. When they came to the crest, they looked down at the vast Lake Michigan, blue and whitecapped, stretching to the horizon. Immediately they moved a little below the ridgeline, to make less of a target, then took shelter in a clump of birch trees. Their quarry's tracks went to the shore, a hundred yards off.

"He's ours now," Sutherland said, and they moved downhill.

"No," Niko-lota replied, taking the front. "He's mine."

They had not gone far, however, when Sutherland saw a dismaying sight: Darting away from the wooded shoreline, a white canoe was fleeing across the lake. With an angry shout, the three men raced to the waterline. When they got there, they knew Jean Dusten had arrived, just in time to rescue Swain. Out on the water, Dusten and Spider paddled hard as Swain and Lucy hunched in the center of the craft.

The three pursuers opened fire, attracting Swain's attention, but the outlaw did not reply with gunfire. He did not even shake his hook in defiance. He simply sat staring at his conquerors, gazing at them as though fascinated, while his canoe bore him away.

Sutherland and his companions said nothing at all. They knelt dejectedly on the sand, watching Swain's canoe shrink until it was far out of sight.

He was free, once more. Though his settlement was destroyed, his army shattered, he lived on, just as dangerous as ever. In defeat, Swain had inflicted a crippling blow to the Frontier Company, which could not replace the destroyed goods in the burning storehouse.

Niko-lota tossed a stone into the lake, then said, "Perhaps it was wrong to send him back his finger; it was a magic token, and now it is gone. It will be hard to find him again."

Sutherland thought about that, and answered, "Next time, my friend, it may be that Jubal Swain will come looking for us."

Niko-lota considered Lucy and her compelling need to find her sons. He knew he would have to return East, to Shawnee country, and there search out the boys. Once he had located them, he would get word to Lucy, wherever she was. Then, as Donoway had said, Lucy Swain would surely come to him; so would Jubal. And Niko-lota would be ready.

PART TWO

Father of Waters

Indian Peace Council

chapter **11**

WINTER

The winter of 1765–66 was a lean one for the Frontier Company. If Swain had not torched his settlement's storage shed, destroying great quantities of stolen company goods, there would have been every prospect for success. Without the lost goods and furs, it required all Sutherland's Scottish mercantile skills to avoid financial disaster that winter.

The season was not a total failure, thanks to the close relations Sutherland had with scores of Indian trappers. They came to him with their harvest, trading at the Morely and Martine warehouses for the goods that had come out on the *Trader* when the Sutherlands returned from Montreal last September. These—which included the heavy goods in barrels and bales ordered by the military—were not plentiful, but there were still some valuable items, including tobacco and blanket coats that Peter Defries had managed to acquire at favorable prices. The *Trader* had stayed at Detroit throughout most of the fall, making one trip up to Fort Michilimackinac to bring goods to the company's agents there, then returning with the peltry they had purchased. Now the ship was back in Montreal, having taken the furs to be shipped abroad, and bringing to Levesque and Defries the bad news about the loss of company goods in the fire at Swain's camp. Owen urgently requested Peter to find new sources of credit.

The Indians might have received more for their furs by trading with Bradford Cullen's new chief factor at Detroit, Farley Jones, who replaced the former factor, the Hampshireman Caleb Soames, but kept him as a trader for the company. Jones had been fired from his post as clerk to Lieutenant Parker after coming under suspicion as an ally of the defeated renegades. Since there was no hard proof against the man, he was not charged with any crime. Indeed, there was no hard proof that Cullen had been working with the renegades, either. Colonel

Campbell, talking to Sutherland, had been emphatic on that point, and even Lieutenant Parker—who that winter continued to oversee the fur trade—told Owen it was hopeless to try to implicate Cullen. Meanwhile, Campbell enthusiastically expressed his pleasure with the outcome of Sutherland's expedition. Now the colonel's chief preoccupation was commanding the fort and getting through another winter, looking forward to the time when he would be given command of a more prestigious post in the empire. For Campbell, Detroit was merely a stepping stone in his career.

As for Jubal Swain, it was rumored that he and his wife had gone down the Mississippi with Jean Dusten, perhaps even as far as New Orleans. Harried by hostile tribes who had heard of his crimes against Indians, Swain was virtually driven from one stopping place to another. He was recognized by those who knew of his hook and flaming red hair. It was some satisfaction to Sutherland that the outlaw would be unable to return without a strong group of fighters at his back. How long Swain would be kept out of the region was another matter, however, because there were many men who objected to government restrictions on colonial migration and settlement. The worst of them would do anything for the promise of land or booty.

No doubt Swain could assemble a group of such men as were willing to venture into the interior. If Bradford Cullen chose to continue his secret cooperation with Swain, then there would be a ready source of funds to finance a new band of marauders.

Métis and *voyageur* minor partners in the Frontier Company remained loyal throughout that difficult winter, even when Cullen had attempted to lure many away by promises of good pay and less work. What Cullen did not offer was a partnership in his firm's profits; and because the Frontier Company took on partners and few employees, the French, half-breeds, and Indians felt pride allied with Sutherland. That was one reason they took goods out into the Indian villages for the Frontier Company, even though they made no more than a subsistence living that season.

Throughout the winter, Detroit was busy with the comings and goings of Indian and half-breed trappers. The poverty caused by Pontiac's 1763–64 rebellion and subsequent British cutoffs in trade had somewhat abated by late January. Indians had turned to trapping and trading instead of war, and their health had been restored after the smallpox epidemics that had swept through their villages during the hostilities and soon after. Renewed trade meant better supplies and equipment, easier hunting, and an improved way of life for the Indians. The natural result of an invigorated Indian population was a bountiful harvest of pelts and a rebirth of optimism, neither of which had been enjoyed at Detroit in five long years.

Tamano and Lela were at Valenya, and Little Hawk was with them. Tamano was occupied that winter doing some trading and trapping, and spending time with the young Sioux, teaching him the ways of the Ottawa. When conditions permitted, Little Hawk in turn taught Tamano how to ride a horse. Meanwhile, Niko-lota had headed south to join his relatives and friends living in Pontiac's village. Next summer, the famous chief would attend the big Oswego conference in the east, and Niko-lota would accompany him. At that time, he would also locate Lucy Swain's boys in Shawnee country; he would keep his promise to their mother—and take his revenge on Jubal Swain.

For the Sutherlands, the winter was pleasurable in spite of the uncertain trade. Benjamin took to walking, and Sally—who was almost like a daughter, though still not adopted—showed signs of approaching adolescence that no one had anticipated in such a tomboy. She turned nine in January, and as if by magic, seemed to lose her pudginess. Her face had a delicate, sensitive quality, and she became quite pretty, though the boys did not notice.

Jeremy was stretching physically and expanding mentally, as eager to learn about books and science as he was to develop his physical strength and skills. He and Tom Morely became fast friends with the Sioux Little Hawk. Although it was expected Little Hawk would go back to his home country that spring, he made friendships that were both firm and deep.

There was little riding to be done in the snowdrifts surrounding the fort, but there was plenty of hunting, snowshoeing, and dogsled racing to keep the boys busy. Mawak, the old Ottawa, taught the youths to train dogs, care for them, and drive them. Though Sally was simply tagging on at the end as far as the boys were concerned, Mawak took a special liking to her, and found her a quicker learner than any of the males.

Heera, the great lead dog who two winters earlier had taken Sutherland to Montreal on a disastrous journey, had been brought back to Detroit to be cared for by the Ottawa elder. Though Mawak was far ahead of his own people in the use and training of these dogs, the Ottawa's abilities were not generally understood. To most, a dog or two sufficed to haul a sled in that country; but from more northerly tribes Mawak had learned that as many as nine dogs could be harnessed to a sled. It was said that Mawak had the right charms in his medicine bag, for he stood alone in this country as a master of sled dogs.

When the boys were not racing or training dogs, they were competing against one another in hunting, tracking, running, wrestling—especially wrestling—shooting, and climbing. There was no end to their competition. For the most part, it was Little Hawk who triumphed, because he was older and bigger. The younger boys learned quickly from him, and practiced what he taught by pitting themselves against one another. Jeremy and Tom were a close match.

There was a fourth boy, though he was seldom with them. Tom Morely's younger brother, James, was a sickly child, hardly ever out of doors. Studious and sober at the age of nine—a year younger than Tom—James was already better than his brother in school and in the family's business affairs. That suited Tom just fine, for he was happiest outside and not at all enthusiastic about clerking and cleaning and weighing and storing trade goods or peltry.

Jeremy was friendly enough with James, for like him, the younger brother took great interest in book learning. Jeremy, for all his cleverness, was not as sharp with sums or figuring as James. On the other hand, James had little curiosity about anything other than factual matters, practical and commercial things. He was mildly entertained by Defoe and Swift, but found *Goody Two Shoes* frivolous. He was at his best when devouring all his mother could teach about financial transactions and trading business.

So it was that James seldom joined the others, and was scarcely more than a shadow on their lives, although not an unpleasant one. For Tom's part, the energy James spent in the family business relieved the pressure on him, who, as the eldest male in the family, was responsible for taking the lead in as many things as possible. Tom was known as an aspiring trader, with a canny eye for furs—just like his late father.

The other three boys grew extremely strong and fast for their ages, while James throve in business and schoolwork. Jeremy could not get enough fiction and drama, and Tom never overcame his frustration at being defeated in wrestling time and again by the smug Little Hawk. Though stronger than Jeremy, Tom did not have his friend's ability to learn from books. Already Tom was the toughest of the community's white children, even up to the age of twelve.

Ella and Owen took close interest in the development of Jeremy and Benjamin, and they found themselves wrapped up with concern for Sally Cooper. It was clear by now that she would never go back to Pennsylvania, and often they sensed a certain wistfulness about the child that spoke of uncertainty and loneliness in the world. Sally was quite happy with the Sutherlands, and had only a vague memory of her past—a past destroyed so savagely and abruptly that she had blotted out much of it.

In February, Ella and Owen resolved to adopt the girl, if she would like it. They brought the subject up one morning, after Jeremy had gone out snowshoeing with the boys. Much to Sally's disappointment, she had not been asked to go along. Sitting by the window, the sunlight pouring in, she had on her lap the little polished rosewood music box she had been given by a friend of Jacques Levesque's at Pontiac's village two years ago. When Jacques had saved Sally from Pontiac's cruel treatment and had brought her to Fort Detroit, he had taken her music box, too. She was listening to the pretty *voyageur* song tinkling from the box, as she absently touched her pigtails and looked through the window at her three friends striding away toward the fort's gate. Snowshoes over their shoulders, they laughed and joked together, and Sally sat alone, thinking.

Ella left Owen at the table, a cup of coffee in his hands, and went to join Sally on the window bench. They listened to the music box for a while, and when the song had finished, Sally closed the lid and put the box beside her. Ella said, "Being a girl isn't always easy, is it?"

Sally looked around at Ella, who was big after seven months of pregnancy. The girl forced a small smile. "I guess being a boy has its difficulties, too." Ella took her hands and held them.

"Sally, dear, Owen and I have been thinking about you, and how you need a family . . ."

Sally glanced from Ella to Owen, and then at her hands, still held by Ella. She did not look up.

Ella continued, "And we would like it very, very much if you would accept us."

As she stared at Ella, Sally's eyes were like points of light, intense and questioning, unsure, yet perhaps she had expected this moment all along.

Ella tightened her hold on the girl's hands. Owen, who was smiling, thought Sally must feel a great melancholy lifted from her young shoulders.

He said, "We'd like to adopt you as our daughter, lass."

Sally flushed, her lip trembling, and looked out the window. Ella saw tears welling, and took Sally's shoulders, drawing her close. Often the child had restrained any truly powerful love she might have felt for the family, as though she had buried such a vulnerable emotion, never again to allow it injury. It would take time for Sally to forget, to let herself love the Sutherlands as only a daughter could. One day, she would be happy as their daughter; she would change, and would heal.

Sally looked from Owen to Ella to the window to her hands, but she gave no answer, no sign of joy or relief or gratitude.

Ella asked, "What do you think, Sally? We love you so very much—"

With more force than any of them expected, Sally burst out, "Oh, Ella! I can't! You mustn't! I—I don't want to be your daughter! Not this way!"

Ella was shocked, Owen concerned and surprised. Sally stood up and threw herself into Ella's arms, sobbing, trying to speak. Ella caressed her hair to calm her, then at last pushed the girl back, handing over a handkerchief to wipe away the tears.

"There, there, Sally," Ella said softly. "We understand how difficult all this is, and how much you've been hurt. We know, and we don't want to force you too soon—"

"Oh, Ella, it isn't that!" She turned to Owen, who was listening intently. "Please understand me, I love you both, and I'd be so happy to be your daughter. It's just—" She pressed the handkerchief against her mouth. She could not say what she thought.

Owen came over to crouch next to her. Holding her hand, he asked, "Would you like us to take you back to someone in Pennsylvania?"

Sally was almost frantic. Shaking her head, she cried, "Oh, no, no! I want to stay here, with you! I never want to leave Detroit! I want to live with you, but just don't adopt me. Please? I'll be anything you want, just like a real daughter. I'll even say ma and pa, if you like, but you can't adopt me!"

Ella and Owen exchanged glances. Then Ella said to her, "Perhaps we can become your guardians, then. Shall we make that legal?"

Sally was unsure, and blurted, "Does it mean I couldn't marry—?" She cut herself off, wrenching her head away and staring at the window, seeing nothing. After a moment, she said carefully, "Does that mean I'm not—I mean, I wouldn't be able to . . ."

Still she could not say it. Ella was confused, but Owen knew. He said, "Marry Jeremy?"

Both Ella and Sally whipped around to face him, one startled to hear this, the other dismayed at her innermost secret being revealed. Owen was smiling.

Sally mouthed some words, but nothing came out. Ella cleared her throat, thought a moment, and then realized that it was not so very serious after all. They were just children. Yet she was confused, not knowing what to say next.

Owen said, "You don't intend to marry Jeremy within the next few days, do you?"

Sally shook her head. "Oh, no, no, no! Why, he doesn't even know that I lo—I mean, he doesn't even know I'm alive!" She was about to say more, then hesitated before asking carefully, "You wouldn't object, would you?"

Lightly, Ella said, "Of course not, Sally! Not if you wait a few years or so."

Owen added, "You know, child—I mean, lass—the boy has plans to go abroad in two or three years, or at least to Philadelphia for his education. What will you do if he goes far away?"

Sally was pained, but she had thought this through already. "I'll wait for him."

Ella and Owen nodded. Ella said, "It might be a long wait."

"I'll wait for him, if he'll have me."

Owen stood up and said, "Well, lassie, just remember that soon there'll be lots of boys knocking on the door." He winked at her. "Maybe in a couple of years Jeremy won't matter at all to you."

Sally became distressed. "Oh, that won't happen; I just know it, Owen! There's nobody in all the world like him."

Ella smiled, "Even though he doesn't want you to come along when the boys go out together?"

Sally shrugged and appeared undeniably sad at that.

Owen said, "Ach, don't let that trouble you, lass. They're

just afraid you'll show them up. Mawak says you're the best of all at handling the dogs and sled."

"He does?" Sally beamed. "How wonderful!" Then she became serious. "Do you think Jeremy minds?"

Ella patted her hand and touched a braid, saying, "If he minds, then he won't make much of a man, will he? Don't you worry whether he likes it or not; he'll learn to accept and admire you. I didn't raise the boy to be resentful of those who can do something better than he can." Ella leaned over and whispered, "Even if it's his future wife."

So there would be no adoption, but Sally Cooper would be formally placed in the guardianship of the Sutherlands. The necessary papers had to be signed and sent to Montreal, the seat of government. In a few months, it would be official, and Ella and Owen assumed that in a year or two Sally would lose her infatuation with Jeremy. Then they would offer Sally adoption again. As Owen had said, she soon would have many a young man to court her; and those boys would be more charming to her than Jeremy, who hardly even knew she was a girl.

That winter there was much talk of the colonial political and economic situation, and the steadily deteriorating relationship with Mother England. There were more immediate and intriguing matters to be discussed, however, among them a number of romantic liaisons, the more obscure ones naturally being of most interest to gossips. There was talk of the charming giddiness that had of late come over Lettie Morely ever since the soldier Jeb Grey had made a point of praising her baking; Lettie had become more cheerful and enthusiastic about everything. It seemed Grey had a soft spot for Lettie's fresh rolls, and she apparently took pity on the provincial regular stationed so far from his home in New Jersey. Whether their friendship was anything more than a harmony of affections—he for rolls and she for lonely soldiers—was a subject of much debate at Detroit.

There were those who insisted that no long-term relationship could ever come out of it, because Tom, Lettie's eldest, was set against any other man's taking his father's place. Indeed, the boy changed somewhat over that winter. With the development of warmth between his mother and the corporal, Tom had become more serious, his carefree nature subdued a bit. It was said he longed to prove to his mother that the Morely partnership in the Frontier Company could be borne by Morelys alone.

Tom and Jeb were not hostile to one another, and Owen once observed to Ella that they would make a good pair if only the boy would give the man a chance. It was an interesting source of speculation, this affair, but it held none of the high drama that another relationship offered. This was the favor of the wealthy Matilda Merriwether for Nate Breed.

Even Mel Webster had seen, at last, the flickering glow of passion between his cousin and the woman of his own fantasies. It hurt at first, whenever Nate departed for Matilda's house to make a courtesy call. To Mel, the first weeks of winter had been as desolate and cold as any young man could ever know. He wrote sad poetry, observed the graying, dying season with utmost melancholy, and saw the hand of death and loss in everything.

Just before he learned of Nate's romance with Matilda, Mel had traded some odds and ends for an old fiddle that needed considerable work to make it playable. He had labored over it day after day. When not writing or working as a tutor of languages, sciences, and metaphysics for boys of the wealthier families in the vicinity, he could be found at the fort's cabinetmaker shop, borrowing tools, sanding, refinishing, glueing, or minutely adjusting the instrument. When the news of Matilda's affection for Nate crashed down on Mel, he lost heart in everything but poetry—poetry which in its despair was disheartening—and set aside the fiddle.

Owen Sutherland took note of this, and because of his liking for Mel, encouraged the fellow to finish his work on the instrument, then to join Ella at her spinet in the council house for duets. This proved effective in relieving Mel's sadness, and he turned out to be quite an accomplished musician. Though his inclinations lay more to folk music and dance tunes, Mel knew enough to follow Couperin or Handel when Ella supplied the scores.

It was his love of playing the fiddle that kept Mel sane that winter—that and his plans to renew his quest for the treasure next spring. Never bitter toward Nate, he accepted his cousin's good fortune as an act of fate. It was still his way to be shy with attractive unwed women; and he saw his shortcomings in a fatalistic light, something that had to be accepted and lived with.

For Nate's part, he felt pity for Mel, but his interest in Matilda—and interest it was, more than simple love—was strongly rooted within him. As hearty as was Nate's liking for the young woman, so was his attraction to her family's prosperity and high place in the world. Certainly Nate felt a bit guilty to have taken advantage of poor Mel, but he was a practical man who knew where his own prosperity lay. It never occurred to Mel that Nate so often borrowed the writing journal for anything more than personal pleasure. Mel did not guess that Nate had won the better part of Matilda's heart by the false pretense that these poems were his own.

It was early March when Nate's courtship gave promise of bearing fruit. The Merriwethers were impressed with Nate's allusions to family links in Massachusetts and New York, which spoke of formidable bloodlines and considerable social status. Further, the Virginians accepted Nate's oblique hints that he was an adventurer traveling more or less incognito as an agent of fabulously wealthy New England speculators who sought land that might be purchased. In addition, Nate made it clear he was far more interested in pursuing a career under the guidance of someone like Dawson Merriwether; this confession opened the merchant's dusty heart.

One night Nate came home to tell his cousin, "Lad, it appears yer kin is on the brink of wedlock!"

Mel's face would have fallen had it not months ago dropped as low as it could drop. He took a moderate breath, sighed, and generously congratulated Nate.

Nate saw the dullness in Mel's eyes and clapped him on the shoulder. "Come, come, son, don't be so glum! There's many a fish out there for yer own hook! Jest cast yer line—"

"Don't use that metaphor when speaking of Matilda!" Mel was harsh, and meant to be.

Nate shrugged and took off his wig—a new one purchased after the expedition—and placed it on its stand. "Mel, my boy, ye've much to learn about life and love! They don't always mix so sweetly or so clearly. As Granny Breed says, 'Livin' don't always guarantee a love, an' love don't always guarantee a livin'.' Now listen to yer cousin, an' I'll give ye some encouragin' advice: When me an' Matty ties the knot, there'll be funds aplenty from old Dawson, an' ye an' me'll open our own firm with the blessin' o' Matty's family—uncles, cousins, brothers, grandfathers, in-laws, an' outlaws, an' all of them richer 'n lords—"

Mel got up and paced, his hands opening and closing, as though he did not know what to do with them. Finally he rammed them into his pockets and stood moodily at the window.

He said, "Rich! Money! Business! Nate, how on earth can you tell me you're about to marry the most wonderful blossom of the American colonies, perhaps of the whole British Empire, and then defile such sacred words with talk of money, mercantilism—"

"And Matty!" Nate spun on his heel, determined not to let Mel's misery further aggravate his own already troubled soul. "Money, mercantilism, and Matty Merriwether! That's real poetry, lad! Can't you hear it? Aw, Mel, cheer up an' compose somethin' with them words: money, mercantilism, an'—"

"Matilda!" Mel shouted and waved his hands in the air, knocking them painfully against the low ceiling. "What kind of name is 'Matty' for a child of the sun? Nate Breed, how can you so act the rascal, the scoundrel? Don't you want a poem about love, about bliss, about unfathomable, incomprehensible yearning? Doesn't Matilda deserve such   y?"

Thoughtfully, and with some uneasiness, Nate mumbled, "Well, I guess she's had some of that, too." He looked at his cousin, though not in the eyes. "I do care for her well enough, Mel. Matty's a peach all right, but that's only part of it, don't ye know? In weddin', ye got to consider the financial aspects—"

"Enough! Silence! Silence, I say!" Mel covered his ears and closed his eyes. "No more talk of lucre or profit in the same breath that you utter the name of Matilda!"

Nate felt sympathy and patted Mel on the back. "There, there, now. Look, why don't ye spill out some of them emotions in a poem . . . a nice little one about, say, a caterpillar that becomes a butterfly an' then gits happy as a lark?"

Exasperated, Mel sat down heavily at his crude table. There the writing journal lay open at a poem of Owen Sutherland's, which he had been copying from the *Pennsylvania Gazette* that morning. Gloomily, he replied, "Larks eat butterflies. Nate, tell me no more about what I should write."

Then he fought off this depression and stood up, bravely offering his hand and best wishes. "I pray you have all the fortune and happiness . . . I mean happiness and fortune in the world. Promise me you'll always be good to her."

Nate shook hands vigorously, grinning as he said, "That's more like it, lad! An' I'll expect ye to be the best man at the weddin'. Now that's worth a poem, too, ain't it?"

The next day, Ella received a visit from Matilda, who often came by, since she had considerable interest in the latest news and fashions of England. Ella's letters from her brother, Major Henry Gladwin, always included a page or two from Henry's wife, with descriptions of gowns and hats, colors and designs. Though Ella, who cared nothing for fashions, took only a passing interest in these things, young Matilda was forever eager to hear it all. A skillful seamstress, Matilda no sooner had made careful notes from Ella's letters than she was off ordering cloth, thread, and feathers to execute the style of the London gentry—though it was likely ten months out of date because letters traveled so slowly.

With the impressionable Sally sitting nearby—attempting to learn the flighty movements of Matilda's chubby hands, and imitating that sophisticated, refined way Matilda had—Ella and the Virginia woman had tea in the living room near the stove Ben Franklin had sent as a gift from Philadelphia. Ella enjoyed the young woman, who spoke in a slow, deliberate manner, every word pronounced and rounded with delicacy. It was a wonder to Ella what Matilda saw in the rough Nate Breed. He was an amiable, though ungenteel fellow, wholly different from Matilda, who was soft and sheltered, if somewhat excitable.

The same question about Matilda's apparent choice of suitor had puzzled every woman in Detroit, and Ella could keep it in no longer, though she asked discreetly.

"Well, Matilda," she began, and poured three cups of tea, "Detroit certainly hasn't been the same since you and your family came out; I think half the eligible bachelors in the fort have become like puppy dogs panting after you wherever you go. Doesn't it exhaust you, all that attention?"

Matilda tittered and fluttered a hand to her chin. "They are such dears, are they not? La! Why the beaux back in Virginia were never so sweet, and certainly never so enthusiastic."

As Ella listened and Sally sat in awe, Matilda told how no fewer than three of her dropped handkerchiefs had been torn to pieces by young men who had fought over them.

"It seems," she went on coyly, "these strong fellows out in

the wilderness think it more important to return even a piece of the handkerchief than to rescue it intact; why I've been obliged to choose less valuable kerchiefs when I go walking, for fear of having my finest silk ruined." She giggled again, and Sally mimicked her, though not very naturally.

Sally contributed her best effort to the conversation. "It's true, Mistress Merriwether, I saw two private soldiers fighting over your handkerchief one day, and you hadn't even dropped it for them. You let it fall in front of Lieutenant Parker, but he was too busy with his thoughts to even see it. Those two lummocky privates were all black and blue by the time they tore your handkerchief apart."

"La, child," Matilda said, "you do have sharp eyes! But what makes you think I wanted that grumpy Lieutenant Parker to retrieve my handkerchief, anyway? He's much too severe and soldierly, it seems to me."

Sally thought about that as Matilda drank her tea, little pinky high, lips rounded, and not a slurp to be heard, though the tea was quite hot. Sally tried the same, but a pinky out was not easy, for the cup was too heavy for her. She tried to sip like Matilda, but burned her lip and gasped, "La! That's hot, I'll say. La!"

Ella asked Matilda whether there was any beau she favored above all the rest. Matilda became just a bit dreamy and sighed almost imperceptibly. Sally gave that a try, too, and thought she did it well enough.

After a moment, Matilda replied, "There is one gentleman different from them all, though he's not as refined outwardly as some; yet his soul is the soul of a poet, his heart the heart of a gallant knight. He writes sonnets that wound me with their poignancy, and composes verse that ignite me with—with unrequited passion."

"La!" Sally whispered.

Matilda sighed deeply, and Ella asked, "This gentleman must be wonderful. And do your parents approve of him?"

Matilda recovered and said, "They are learning to, though he is not, at first glance, the usual match for one of my blood. But times are changing, are they not? And he is of good family. Though they be Yorkers and Bostonians, they are the cream of those colonies." She tittered. "La! I never had imagined anything good could come out of those rude places, but my Nathaniel is the flower of them all."

"Flower?" Sally asked bluntly.

Matilda did not reply, but went on about Nate's wonderful poetry, saying they spoke volumes about his noble, innermost being.

"Oh, he has much to learn about our ways," Matilda admitted kindly, "but he'll soon be one of us, more or less. Anyway, we intend to dwell at Detroit, where a gentleman is not judged solely on good manners." She paused a moment and then said with a blissful smile, "I shall be married one day to the poet laureate of the northwest."

Ella and Sally both blurted, "Married?"

Matilda flushed and her hand went to her lips. "Now I've gone and let out our secret! Oh, I beg of you both, breathe not a word of this to anyone! Promise me, please, if you have any regard for an engaged woman whose parents have not yet bestowed their blessing! Promise me!"

To Matilda's relief, they swore to tell no one. Sally felt absolutely wonderful to know such a fabulous secret, and to share it with Ella, whom she so admired. Further, it was Matilda Merriwether's secret, and Matilda, to Sally, was undoubtedly the most sophisticated, most worldly lady she had ever met.

The conversation went on a bit longer, and by the time it was done, Matilda had told much about Nate's poems—actually the poems of Mel and Owen, though she knew nothing about that. Mel's poems had touched her the deepest, for they had, in truth, been written about her. The subject of Mel's longing was a butterfly princess, a wildflower, queen of the fairies, even a muse in more classical verse. Not even the debonair beaux of Virginia had suggested that Matilda might be so described.

Whenever Nate recited the poems from Mel's journal, he managed to keep Matilda from reading it and inadvertently discovering it belonged to Mel. After all, he told her, a poet could not reveal all his work at random and without considered reflection!

Week after week he had read to her, until the heart in her ample bosom burst with emotion. It was only a day or two earlier that Nate had proposed, and she had accepted with the reservation that her parents give their consent.

"La!" gasped Sally, astonished at such a romantic courtship.

Ella said with care, "So you love him for his poetry as much as for his goodness and strength?"

"I love him and his poetry, Ella. Can you understand that?"

Ella said she could, but did not speak of Owen's poems to her. Yes, she could understand Matilda's passion for a poet, but she hoped the young woman had enough in common with Nate that she would still love him when the poems lost their glory, his courtship its rapture.

It was Sally who brought up Owen's poems, saying once she had been the subject of a ditty he wrote. The girl recited it:

> "Where Sally's wandering I don't know,
> She's such a rover,
> Roves the world over.
> Thoughts flying o'er the wide lakes, so
> Fleet o'er the water,
> Like the wind's daughter,
> With her I'd like to go."

Matilda thought the poem quite dear, and Sally pressed home this opportunity to elevate herself in the young woman's estimation.

"Owen has been published lots of times. La! Every newspaper in the colonies is after him to give them his work. He won't give all of it to them, of course. My poem is private, you know."

Ella gently protested that Sally should not be so proud and boastful about Owen. Matilda, however, was interested, and asked which publications had taken Owen's poetry.

Sally could not resist answering first, and said Dr. Benjamin Franklin's *Pennsylvania Gazette* printed a poem or two every month. Matilda was indeed impressed; before long she had asked Ella all about Philadelphia and learned of Owen's fame among the better classes in that great city. Finally Sally jumped up and got a few spare issues of the *Gazette* to lend to Matilda.

Without looking closely at the poems, Matilda said she had other copies of the *Gazette* at home and would make a point of looking through them that very night to find Owen's work.

As Sally and Matilda talked, Ella gazed into the fire and thought about Owen, who had not written much poetry in the past year. He had been too overwhelmed with the work of the company, but more than that, he seemed to have lost interest in poems. She smiled to herself, recalling the night he had told her there was no reason to write poetry these days. He had said his life was fulfilled with her and the children. Somehow, the urgency had faded. Being with Ella was enough for him, and poetry paled by comparison.

Ella hid her inner contentment by sipping tea and watching the fire. To Owen she was no muse, no fairy princess. She was his woman.

The Sunday following Matilda's visit, the ice began breaking up on the river. The smell of earth filled the air as snow melted, and spring erupted at the straits. That afternoon Ella and Owen strolled through the fort on their way to the council house, where she would play her spinet with a few others, including Mel Webster, who had joined their chamber group. As usual, a number of residents would be in attendance to enjoy the music, for these gatherings were bright spots in the lonely humdrum of a remote outpost.

Ella wore a dark woolen cloak, and her pregnancy filled it. Owen walked at her side and thought how lovely she looked, her face glowing with the happiness and radiance of an expectant mother. They walked close together but did not hold hands, for to do so on Sunday would have caused a minor scandal. The fort was busy with folk enjoying the first sunny day of the month, and it seemed new life had been breathed into Detroit. It was awkward to walk in the mire of thawing ground, but Ella and Owen did not care as they savored the freshness of approaching springtime. Tramping along, they were hailed by Reverend Angus Lee, who stepped from his doorway and joined them on the stroll to the council house.

Lee asked what Ella would play that day. He was delighted when he heard it was a Handel sonata.

As they walked through the thickening mud, they saw Nate Breed standing at Matilda's door. Having pulled the bell-rope, he unbuttoned his soiled spatterdashes. They greeted Nate, who waved gaily back, removing his hat to Ella. He would have fared better had he kept the hat on his head, for a bundle of *Gazettes* thrown from Matilda's second-floor window struck with considerable force, knocking his wig off, and staggering him.

In the window above was Matilda, teary-eyed, and red in the face. Trying not to scandalize herself in front of the Sutherlands and Lee, Matilda barely refrained from screaming aloud at the astonished Nate, who stood stupidly, holding the newspapers.

Losing a battle with the urge to weep, Matilda squeaked, "Fraud! Faker! Never come back! Fraud! Seducer! Liar! Fraud!"

She gave a brief look of agony at the Sutherlands and Lee, then slammed the shutters closed, leaving Nate ashamed and helpless below. Ella and Owen discreetly passed on, allowing Lee to pursue his earthly calling. The minister approached the distressed Nate, who was staring at the papers, scenting the smells of ink and sulphur mingled with Matilda's unmistakable fragrance. Nate looked up as Lee put a hand gently on his arm.

Lee said, "Come to the council house and hear some music, my friend; take your mind off this little spat."

Nate could not reply. He was too astounded by what he saw circled in rouge on the first page of a recent *Gazette*.

Lee adjusted his thick spectacles, cleared his throat, and urged, "Really, Mr. Breed, the young lady will surely get over all this before very long. Perhaps if I put a word in with her on your behalf . . ."

Nate was shaking his head slowly. "No, Reverend, I guess she'll never git over this."

To Nate's profound distress, he recognized a poem from Mel's journal. It was a poem he had read many times to Matilda during their budding romance—in fact, it was one she always asked him to read at the outset of each interlude. Nate was stunned to see the poem was by Owen Sutherland. There were others circled in rouge, all of them works he had thought were Mel's—and Matilda had thought were his.

Lee was talking again, insisting Matilda would forget whatever it was that had provoked her so. Nate simply shook his head and wandered away, carrying the *Gazettes*. His romance with Matilda Merriwether and his flirtation with the Merriwether fortune were over once and for all. In his heart, Nate knew he had got just what was coming to him. At least, Granny Breed would have said so.

chapter 12

A STORM

In the days that followed her shocking awakening to Nate Breed's duplicity, Matilda seemed to take to religion for solace. It did her and the elder Merriwethers good to have the frequent company of Reverend Lee, whose sensitivity and kindness eased the pain of their embarrassment. Pompous and stern, Dawson Merriwether might have challenged Nate to a duel had Lee not stepped between them and soothed the Virginian's bruised honor.

Nate, too, had paid a price for his overzealous ambition. His confession to Mel had created a rupture between them, and although neither of them could afford to move out of their hovel to live alone, there was scarcely a word between them all the month of March and into early April. Both continued to work as laborers for the Frontier Company from time to time and so kept body and soul together. Also, Mel tutored, and added music lessons to his inventory; he accepted Sally as a student of the violin. When Mel could, he continued to research the site of the treasure by poring through military maps and charts made available by Lieutenant Parker. The officer knew nothing of the quest, but after Mel's artful navigation on the Swain expedition, Parker was happy to provide any chart in the army files.

At first Mel was too upset with Nate's wrongdoing to consider approaching Matilda with the truth of who, other than Sutherland, had authored the poems she liked so much. When finally he had ventured to go to Matilda's house and ask for an interview with the young woman, Dawson Merriwether met him on the garden path and commanded his immediate departure. A friend and relative of Nate Breed's was not welcome at the Merriwether house, and this further deepened the hurt Nate had inflicted on his cousin.

By the end of April, Mel could stand it no longer. He

determined to write Matilda a letter, enclosing a poem that she would recognize from the journal Nate so often had read to her. In the letter Mel would ask for the briefest of interviews with her to reveal his heart—a direct assault where caution had failed. Thus, while all Detroit was excited about the news that Parliament had repealed a despised stamp tax on colonial documents, Mel Webster cared or knew nothing of politics or social unrest.

Even forgetting his obsessive research about the Indian treasure, he stayed up one whole night in balmy April weather, writing and rewriting his letter, succumbing to the urge to recast the poem's end. By dawn, a second candle guttering, he knew he could do no better with the poem. Though tired, he was emboldened by the decision to cast all to the winds. He washed carefully, changed into his best nankeen smallclothes, shined his shoes, donned a frock coat borrowed from Reverend Lee for the occasion, and spent an hour brushing his faded tricorn.

Lying in bed, Nate watched all this with one eye open. Knowing what his cousin was up to, he made no comment until the very last moment, when Mel was looking into a grimy bit of mirror set on the table, leaning against the wall.

Nate moved onto his back and spoke up. "I wish ye all the best, cousin."

Mel turned to him and realized that the resentment had gone. He no longer bore a grudge against Nate. Whatever had been done was past and dead; Matilda had no right to hate Mel for it. Once she read this letter and poem, it would be up to her to decide the next course of action. If she refused Mel, though she knew full well he was the one whose writing had captured her heart, then there was nothing else for it. Then Mel's romance with Matilda was simply not written in the stars—as he knew such things must be.

Mel gave Nate a polite nod and said softly, "Thank you." He went outside, where the people were beginning to go about their business in the first light of dawn. It was much too early to go calling, so he would wait. As he placed the letter with care in his coat pocket, his hands were sweating unreasonably. To calm his nerves he would stroll through the commandant's flower garden, watch morning touch the daffodils, and see the tulips heavy with dew.

Taking a deep breath, Mel felt more relaxed now that the uncertainty had left him, and knew this lovely new day was a turning point in his life. As he walked, he planned how to tell Matilda of his love.

The commandant's garden in a western enclave of the fort was a quiet place, filled with color, and rich with the scent of blossoms, cut grass, and turned ground. Mel found Ella working there, singing to herself. Ever since her brother, Henry Gladwin, had been Detroit's commander, Ella had taken special interest in the flowers planted along the wooden walkways and between the vegetables. She looked as happy as the morning was bright, and Mel greeted her with a jaunty doff of his hat.

By now Ella had heard the entire story of Matilda's aborted courtship and Mel's misappropriated poems. She stopped singing when Mel strolled up to her. It had been some time since Ella had seen him, and she wondered whether his recent heartbreak had passed. She was relieved that Mel was smiling and whistling "Yankee Doodle."

She nodded to him. "Good morning, Mel. You look cheerful today!" She went on weeding around some pansies recently transplanted.

"And you, Mistress Sutherland, look very well, I must say."

Indeed, for a woman on the verge of giving birth, Ella had a glow of beauty and contentment that a single man like Mel might not expect. She carried big, but she was careful about working in the garden. Getting up and kneeling down were intricate and precise movements calculated to avoid strain on her body. So far she had not changed her daily routine much. This, her third child, was a normal pregnancy, and Ella was determined to be outdoors as much as possible and avoid the self-pity and depression that swallowed up some women in the tedious late stages of childbearing.

For a little while, they talked of this and that, and Mel made as though he had come to the garden to reflect and read a book on botany by a Quaker scientist. After pleasantries with Ella, he sat down on a bench in the sun and tried to read. It was not easy, for he was too tense with anticipation of his imminent confrontation with Matilda—or perhaps with her father. But at least he would drop off the letter and poem.

Ella busied herself with the garden, finding that today she had far less strength than she realized. Her legs were like jelly, her breath hard to catch. She had been in the garden for less than an hour but felt spent and a little light-headed. Standing up, she wiped her brow, knowing she could not work in that kneeling position anymore. It was a pity, for the garden needed considerable weeding, and if she was unable to do it for however long it took until the baby was born, the flowers would be swarmed under.

After a few deep breaths, Ella felt better, and thought that later she would take a walk outside the fort. The day was absolutely beautiful, the sky cloudless, and the air already warm. She often strolled a mile or two from the palisade to some high ground near a pasture and a small clump of woods. Perhaps Lettie Morely would like to go along, as she sometimes did.

About to bid good day to Mel, Ella stopped short when Lettie herself came bounding into the garden, face alight in the way that meant she had some juicy gossip to relate. Lettie was so excited that she did not notice Mel awkwardly pretending to read, and Ella had no chance to mention the fellow's presence.

"Ella, Ella!" Lettie exclaimed, clapping her hands with glee. "Thee'll never guess what's happenin' next! Yon Matilda Merriwether's always the center of some delightful adventure!"

Ella glanced around at Mel, who was peering, having heard Matilda's name. Though Ella tried to hush Lettie until they could walk away, she failed, and Lettie enthusiastically spilled over, "Yon girlie's gone an' hooked Reverend Lee hisself! The dears! Believe it? They're engaged! I just heard it from the Merriwethers' maid! Now they'll make a happy pair, I'll warrant! What fun, eh—?"

It was then that Lettie noted the distress in Ella's eyes, and in the next moment saw Mel, sitting stiff as a statue, staring right through them. Lettie exclaimed, and her hand clapped over her mouth. Mel seemed not to notice.

With an unnaturally sweet voice, Lettie cried, "Mornin', Mr. Webster. Nice day, isn't it?"

Mel gave no response. He sat with the book in his lap, face numb. Lettie felt simply awful. She whispered to Ella, "Shall I apologize?"

Ella was sad. "There's nothing to apologize for. Come, you can keep me company while I do a few things in the house, and then we'll go for a walk. I need some time away from the fort and all these poor folk with their troubles."

Then Ella said to Mel, "Won't you come and visit us tonight, Mel? Owen said just yesterday he'd like to talk about, ah, writing matters and such with you. And he hears you're quite a chess player. Mel?"

The stricken young man gazed at her like a cow might look at a milkmaid. Ella said she looked forward to playing a duet at the council house on Sunday. Mel blinked once, reached into his frock coat, and took out the letter to Matilda. As Ella and Lettie turned away to leave the garden, he crumpled the letter slowly with one hand, until it was no more than a small wad of junk, good for nothing but to be thrown away.

Ella and Lettie left Mel there, and went to the Sutherland home, where Lettie helped Ella do wash and housecleaning. Then they prepared some food and packed a picnic. No one had been at home all morning, and Benjamin was being looked after by a neighbor, so Ella and Lettie departed without telling anyone where they were going. As they went through the fort's northwestern gate, Ella sensed a twinge of discomfort, as though she had eaten something wrong. She let this sensation pass and walked peacefully along with Lettie, who carried their basket.

Field workers, travelers, and loggers were going out with them, through the meadows and bracken, past long strip fields where toiling French and *métis* farmers handled plow and hoe. The lands close to the fort were alive with the labor of spring, and it took another twenty minutes walking down a grassy, little-used path to find a comforting silence.

Entering a grove of trees, where sunshine turned small clearings into glades of light, they paused for a while. They often came here, and usually talked all the way to and from this sanctuary. Today, however, both Lettie and Ella were lost in thought. Ella was contemplating her body and how it had changed so in the past two weeks. The baby had dropped, and pressure was almost constant on her pelvis, suggesting that the birth was not far off. It would be good to have it done with, and to make a new start at life. She would like a girl, and so would Owen. They even had a name: Susannah Gabriel. It sounded good, and Ella whispered it as she leaned against a fallen log. Close by, Lettie sat down on a stump near a brook.

Referring to Mel, Lettie said, "'Tis a sorry sight when young 'uns make life so hard for themselves."

Ella nodded agreement.

Lettie sighed and plucked a purple wildflower, touching it to her lips before she said, "But then, us old folks make trouble, too. Maybe we get notions about things we should know better than to. I mean, thee expect them youngsters to make mistakes and break hearts, but when it comes to the foolishness o' old hens the like o' me..."

Ella began to realize that Lettie was beating around the bush. She forgot all about the discomfort of her body and asked Lettie what she was getting at.

Lettie blushed a little and sighed again. "Thee have enough worries to addle thy mind, Ella, an' I be sorry to have brought up somethin' that oughtn't to be thy concern." She gave Ella a sidelong glance, then continued. "But—but it seems this old hen needs some advice from a friend, an' thee be..." Lettie tossed the flower weakly into the water. In a voice just audible, she said, "Ella, Jebediah Grey has asked for my hand in marriage."

Ella was astounded, filled with joy. She hurried to Lettie and hugged her until they both got to weeping. "What's so troubling about that?" Ella asked. "Jeb is a fine man!"

Lettie dried her eyes, half-crying and half-laughing. "A particular fine man! But it's only a year and a half since poor Garth..." She could not say it. "I'm just not sure it's quite right, Ella."

Holding Lettie by the shoulders, Ella said with an encouraging smile, "I understand, Lettie, but life must go on. You have to think of your boys, and—"

"That's just it! Tommy's dead set against Jebediah! Dead set! James likes Jebediah, but Tommy won't hear o' it at all."

"Have you put it all to him?"

Lettie shook her head. "Not yet, not in any final way. I'm afeared he'll blow up like a tinder box. Tommy never talks much to Jebediah when he visits, an' sometimes the lad seems so closed up tight these days! Ella, I just don't know what to do!"

Ella felt the baby stir and kick. It was a dull, prolonged pressure that made her want to sit down, but she stayed at Lettie's side and asked, "Do you love Jeb?"

"Oh, Ella, I do that! As much as an old hen can do!" Lettie's face took on a glow like that which Ella had seen come over Matilda during a conversation about young love. "He ain't Garth, but I don't ask him to be! How I miss my Garth, an' the boys do, too."

They spoke further about Lettie's situation, then walked on. Ella could not ignore the discomfort she felt. It was considerably more insistent now, but she put it aside, hoping to help ease her friend's troubled heart. They rambled from the coppice of trees across a farther meadow where swarthy men were cutting grass for stock. The time passed swiftly, talk changing from Lettie to Ella's children, to the future, and back again to Jeb Grey.

"He'd make a lovin' father to the boys, an' both James an' Tommy like him, 'tis sure, never mind Tommy's show o' independence when Jebediah's a-visitin'."

Lettie said Jeb once had two children of his own, but they and his wife were killed in an Indian raid on the Pennsylvania frontier, where he was stationed during the French and Indian War.

"Jebediah don't talk about it, for it hurts too deep; an' for all his loss, he don't hate Injuns the way some do when they suffer at their hands."

Ella knew Jeb well enough by now to think highly of him. He was thoughtful and, though uneducated, wise in a practical, down-to-earth way. Unlike many men in this country, Jeb desired to work the land, to farm while others wanted to trade, get rich fast, and leave. He intended to put down roots, and already was searching out land to buy so he could start a farm after his discharge. He was the first of a new wave of Americans filtering into the farther reaches of the northwest, a man who had come to stay, to plant, and to make the foundations of a new civilization.

As Ella and Lettie walked, they even discussed politics, because all Detroit was attentive to the ups and downs of the stormy relationship between colonial America and Mother England. Both women knew there was considerable opposition in the east to the expensive British military establishment, which had ten thousand regulars in a number of scattered outposts like Detroit, though there was no longer a French enemy to oppose. The stamp tax had originally been imposed in order to finance this army, but the colonists firmly believed they could organize their own militia and defend themselves. In the East, there had been severe rioting in protest against the stamp tax, and that was why Parliament finally gave in to colonial pressure and repealed the act.

By midafternoon, Ella's discomfort had passed, and they sat down near a stream and an old hayshed to eat rolls and cheese.

Lettie said, "Now that Parliament has repealed the stamp tax, things'll change in America! I never saw so many folk out here brimmin' over with optimism to think that they won their point with old England."

The point Lettie meant was the assertion that Parliament had no legal right to tax American Englishmen without granting them representation at home. Only American colonial assemblies could legally tax Americans, Lettie declared, and if Parliament tried to, it would be tyranny.

"How do you know all about political affairs, Lettie?" Ella asked, leaning over to fill her hands with streamwater.

"Jebediah an' I talk about it all the time. We're too old to talk about romance an' sweet nothin's an' such-like!" She giggled, and Ella laughed, saying she did not believe that. Lettie added, "Jebediah is a real Son of Liberty—you know, one o' them lads what speaks out against taxation an' tyranny. When he gets out o' the army next month, he's plannin' to stay here, 'cause he says the hand o' government—be it colonial *or* British—don't pinch so tight in the northwest."

There was even more news, Lettie said. "With all my worries over Tommy, I forgot to tell thee that yon friend o' thine, Governor James Murray, has been recalled home on account o' pressure from his enemies in Montreal."

Ella had been leaning over to the stream when Lettie said this, and the shock made her move awkwardly. The discomfort felt earlier became a breathtaking ache, and it showed on her face, which was wan and beaded with sweat.

Lettie scrambled to Ella's side. "What is it, darlin'? Oh, my . . ." Ella got hold of herself, and said faintly it was nothing and would pass soon.

Both women waited for half a minute before the sensation subsided. Then Lettie insisted, "We best head home! Ella, darlin', I fear thy time has come."

Ella shook her head, though the effort to rise made her slightly dizzy. "It'll pass, Lettie. Just give me a moment to rest, and then we'll go right back."

Lettie glanced at the sky, where clouds were gathering, dark and swift. The wind had picked up, and the weather had changed while they picnicked. They had not seen the powerful rainstorm coming on fast.

Lettie hurried Ella. "We have to go now, afore yonder rain comes down. It's gettin' cold, an' thee should be home restin'. Oh, I am a biddy of a fool to take thee so far from home at a time like this!"

Ella got up ponderously and said, "No, really, Lettie, I'm

fine; it's just the sadness I felt that such a good man as Governor Murray has to suffer because of evil people. He deserves better, and so does Canada."

Ella knew that Murray's efforts to help Jacques Levesque must have stirred up tremendous hostility to him among wealthy British merchants at home and in Montreal. They had wielded all that vast power to have him recalled, and no doubt removed as governor.

They began to walk but had gone only a few steps when thunder rumbled close by, and a chill wind found them in need of cloaks. They had been deceived by the warm day, and before they had crossed the near meadow, the cloudburst poured down. The men with scythes, running from the fields, called for them to take shelter. Laughing like young maidens, they scampered to the hayshed. Their shelter was a three-sided affair with some old cuttings from last year piled up, and it did well enough to keep off the downpour.

Ella was relieved to sit down, for the pressure of hastening had been considerable on her lower body. She also felt the familiar discomfort of past pregnancies that had put stress on her spine, creating an ache that would not go away. Secretly anxious that she was in the first stages of labor, she said nothing to Lettie for fear of worrying her. They were two miles from the fort, but could cover that in an hour after the rain let up. It would be muddy going back, and their clothes would pay for it.

From where they sat, they faced a broad field lined with trees and undergrowth. Thunder and lightning caused a terrific din overhead, and rain came down in sheets. The old shed swayed with the force of the wind; water dripped from several gaps in the shingles above. When the wind gusted they got a heavy spray of cold rain, but otherwise they were cozy enough crawling under the hay, scaring off a fieldmouse, which shivered and watched them before finding another hiding place.

After they had been here for some time, Ella realized Lettie had not said a word. She looked at her friend, who was peering back out of the corner of her eye. Ella smiled, then felt the constricting pain again, but tried not to let on to Lettie. Yet Lettie saw well enough what Ella was undergoing.

"Ella Sutherland, this be no place to have thy babe, so don't go gettin' any silly ideas, hear?" Ella smiled bravely but had to look away when the pressure on her abdomen became too great. Lettie took her hand, saying, "Shall I run back to the fort an' get some help?"

The rain cascaded in gray curtains, too miserable for Lettie to venture through it. Ella shook her head, took a breath, and indicated the sky, where there were faint but promising patches of blue. "It'll be clearing up soon. We'll be home in an hour. I can wait that—" She gasped; another pain was coming on, surprisingly soon.

With that, a tremendous crack of lightning struck a tree close at hand, startling them both. Ella had to lie back to relieve her growing distress. Lettie was nervous. She put her light jacket behind Ella's head. Ella, eased somewhat, told her not to worry; Lettie said she would worry for both of them.

The rain came down harder, and with it deafening blasts of lightning and howling wind. The storm swept in over the straits with renewed strength, the clouds so black that it seemed almost night. They could not leave while the downpour was so fierce, lest Ella catch a cold. They had to stay under shelter, even though it was agonizing, because Ella's contractions seemed about to begin in earnest. An hour passed, but the storm did not abate. Rivulets became streams, and streams became torrents washing out paths leading from the hayshed.

Ella had mastery of herself, but she could not will away the contractions that were so demanding, so insistent, and so obstinate to have come upon her out here, far from home and her own bed. She thought herself foolish to have wandered here, but this kind of thinking was useless now, a waste of the strength that was already being drained from her with every contraction. Still ten minutes or so apart, the contractions were very strong now, and it became difficult to think rationally, let alone speak coherently. Lettie hovered over her as lightning crashed and flashed in Ella's foggy senses. At one point, she almost forgot where she was and felt next to her for Owen, coming to when she realized with a jolt he was not there.

Lettie was as afraid to leave her alone as she was to delay any longer. She had scoured the woods nearby for some sign of the cutters who had been in the fields. They had all gone home, however; the weather was not letting up, and the grass was too wet to work. They were alone out here, remote from any farmhouse and the fort; with the fury of the storm shaking the world as though to shatter it, they could not leave. It was increasingly apparent, too, that Ella could no longer walk home without help. Lettie prayed that someone would come looking for them—if only they knew just where to look. She wiped Ella's sweating, flushed face. Ella's eyes closed, rolling back as a powerful contraction heaved through her body, and she groaned.

"Please, dear Lord," Lettie prayed. "Let them come. Let them come soon!"

Sutherland had waited long enough. In the cozy living room of their cabin, where a fire crackled cheerfully, he and Jeremy donned oilskins and went out into the storm. They left Sally behind to care for little Benjamin, who had come home from the neighbors', and though she longed to go with them, she did not protest. Sutherland hurried through the swampy streets, Jeremy splashing along behind, as they went from house to house in search of Ella. They did not find out she was with Lettie until they checked the Morely home.

Tommy and James joined in the search through the fort, which was flooded with rainwater that gushed from steep roofs and from ramparts in scores of waterfalls. The sky was leaden; lightning and thunder blasted and boomed without relent. Normally, Ella and Lettie being delayed by a rainstorm would have caused little concern, but Ella's condition worried Owen. After they had searched half an hour longer, and had been joined by Jeb Grey and Mel Webster, they knew the women must be outside the fort. But where?

Night was coming on sooner than expected, and Owen became genuinely afraid. By now, even a storm such as this should not have prevented Ella and Lettie from getting home before dark. Fighting their way through a howling, cold wind, the searchers went to Sutherland's cabin to make plans and fetch lanterns. When they got there, Sally was ready with tea and a pot of soup. More searchers had to be enlisted and the hunt must be widened to places beyond the palisades. While they talked, Sally slipped away, a cape thrown hurriedly over her head, and ran to the kennel where Heera was kept when not being worked by Mawak. Desperate to get back to the cabin before her absence caused a problem—they might want to leave, but no one would be there to watch Benjamin—Sally rushed heedlessly through deep puddles and sloshing mud. She was spattered with muck that covered her legs and dress by the time she reached the pen where the massive white sled dog yowled in greeting. Other than Mawak, who lived outside the fort, Sally knew Heera best, and they had a remarkable understanding.

She opened the gate, spoke to Heera, then ran with him back to the cabin. Sniffer scooted under a chair at the sight of the dog. Indeed, Sally had been missed, and the others were annoyed that she was holding them up. Sally was not to be put off from her plans, however, and she declared, "Heera can find Ella if we tell him to!"

Sutherland thought a moment, looked at the wet dog and wetter girl, then fetched a scarf of Ella's to let Heera sniff.

"Tell him what to do, Sally," Sutherland said, knowing the girl's rapport with the animal.

Sally bent to Heera and said clearly, "Find Ella, Heera! Find Ella now! Go!"

The dog sniffed and whimpered, went out the door, and stood in the rain, nostrils flaring.

Jeremy said, "It's too wet! He'll never scent Ma in this."

Sally protested, "It's more than scent he'll follow! He knows something already! Look!"

Heera was not trailing Ella's spoor by sniffing along the ground. Instead, the animal was sensing where she was. He howled, like all huskies, his tail curled up, ears pointed, then set off for the gate Ella had used earlier in the day.

"Come on!" Owen called out, and the group—carrying lanterns, covered blankets, and food—ran through the downpour that clattered on their rain gear. "You, too, Sally, we need you to work Heera!"

Sally started off, but skidded to a halt, calling, "I can't! Benjamin's inside!"

Sutherland thought for just an instant, then ordered Jeremy to stay behind instead. Astounded and insulted, Jeremy stopped in his tracks. Sally gave him a furtive glance, then followed Owen and the others who were running after Heera. They all vanished out the gate, leaving Jeremy standing in the heavy rainfall, sullen and angry that a girl should go while he must watch a baby. From inside, Benjamin made a cooing sound, and Jeremy ignored it, cold rainwater dripping from his hat and running down his neck.

"Easy does it, Ella! There, there, don't fight it, darlin'." Lettie had midwifed scores of times, and more than once in difficult situations. But this was more than difficult; it was frightening. With a raging spring storm beating down about them, and nothing at hand with which to deliver Ella's vulnerable child, Lettie fought against nervousness. She had seen too many new-borns die, and twice had witnessed the mother lost. Giving birth was dangerous in the best circumstances: with a fire, hot water, blankets, medicines, and catgut and needles for stitching. There were none of these, only her hands and Ella's strength. Lettie did not even have the will to pray anymore. The birth was at hand, and Lettie felt very lonely.

In the dimness, Ella lay on her side, half-covered with hay. From time to time, when a contraction abated, she spoke lucidly with Lettie, insisting her friend go back to the fort for help.

"I fear you'll have to go," Ella said. "I'll be all right for now, if you're not too long . . . not too—"

Another powerful contraction took hold, and Ella tried to listen to Lettie's soothing voice; she tried to go with the pressure, to yield rather than resist, and not to be afraid. Yet she was afraid—afraid for the baby, not herself. She wanted the child—a daughter, she was sure of it—she wanted Susannah to be safe, to be warm. How her mind circled round and round that name: Susannah Gabriel Sutherland. She would be safe. Susannah would be safe. *Lettie, take care of Susannah. Keep her warm!*

"Everything will be fine," Lettie said, all the while firmly massaging Ella's back to relieve the pressure. "Just fine, darlin'. Don't worry."

Nine months Ella had carried the child. She had thought about her hour after hour and from moment to moment, with increasing intensity, until Susannah was already a member of the family. She was not born, but she was with Ella in every other way. It was time. It was cold. It was frightening. *Lettie, keep her warm.*

Rain drummed on the hayshed roof. Thunder grumbled from farther off, as though the storm was receding. Lightning flashes were fewer and farther between, but Ella could not go back. She could not walk, and Lettie could not carry her. Nor would Lettie leave Ella alone out here, where she might bring forth the babe at any minute. Ella previously had gone through two labors, and this one would likely be over soon.

When the contraction passed, Ella breathed deeply, Lettie wiping her face with a bit of torn frock. Ella smiled and said, "Born in the hay? That's romantic."

Lettie said, "Perhaps we should name her Christine, after our Lord, born in a manger." Lettie chuckled, then looked

anxiously about. There was no one in sight. By now she could
barely see the far end of the fields. The wind had lessened,
and the rain had let up a bit. She turned back when Ella moaned,
"It's anytime now, Lettie. Any . . . time . . ."

Shivering from cold, Lettie helped Ella turn on her back
and, looking closely, saw that her time was certainly near. A
few more strong contractions and the child would be born. She
wanted to cry and pray all at the same time, and beg Ella not
to deliver yet, but she controlled herself for the good of her
friend, and patted Ella's hand. Lettie thought about what must
be done to protect the babe from the cold, then began tearing
up her petticoat. She did not have much, but what there was
would have to do. The hay would help, too, so she prepared
a place in it for the child to nestle close to the mother.

For all her own fears, Ella did not lose courage. Between
contractions she kept up a light banter with Lettie, who soothed
her with diverting conversation and singing. At times, when it
all seemed too much for Ella, too impossible to finish and too
overwhelming to escape, Lettie encouraged her as she might
an unhappy child.

The storm grew strong again. Lightning still broke over
them, illuminating the deeper darkness of the treeline. While
Ella was too far gone into a drifting world of dreams to flinch
at the blasts, Lettie was rattled with every flash and clap. By
now, Lettie had given up searching the gloom for some sign
of help. She was prepared to deliver this child here and now,
but her main concern was for Ella's safety, even if it meant
losing the infant. It made Lettie cringe to think so, but Ella
came first, no matter what.

Ella's eyes were closed. Barely conscious of where she was,
she turned her entire will inward to the successive pains and
driving urgency of contractions, one upon the other. It was not
new or unfamiliar to her, but it was so powerful and absorbing
that she thought it would not end. She might never in her life
have been anywhere else but upon this bed of hay, swallowed
up by a black storm. All of her being, all her life experiences
had brought her to this ultimate moment.

Ella thought only of the unborn child, not of herself; nothing
but the child, a great, relentless pressure within that pushed
out into the world. "Go with it," she heard Lettie say, and she
tried—oh, how she tried, but whether or not she succeeded
she did not know. How could she know? She knew nothing,
understood nothing, cared for nothing; not cold, nor thunder,

nor even pain. Only the demanding contraction that meant life to someone else, someone of her own flesh and blood and soul.

"Give it now, Ella." Lettie was an eternity away. "That's it! Now . . . thee can do it! That's it, darlin'."

Lightning flashed, and thunder rumbled. Lettie spoke Ella's mind, but Ella's inner heart cried out, *Can I? Oh, I can't, I can't! Lettie! Where's Owen? Owen! Lettie! The baby's coming . . .*

"That's my girl! It is comin', Ella!"

"I can't!"

"Thee can! It's comin' now . . . give it to me. I'm ready, Ella! Let it come now! Push! Push!"

Ella screamed with the effort, called for all the strength of her body, of her life. She pushed and pushed in an unthinking surge of need and force.

"Owen!" she cried to the thunder, her voice giving the ultimate power to deliver. "Owen! Owen!"

And then there was a great release, a vast, numb, and weightless floating. It was done. It was over. Ella wept softly. "Owen."

"I'm here, Ella. I'm here."

In her dream world she saw his face through a haze lit by lanterns, close, remote, near, distant. He was smiling, and a baby was crying.

Was she dreaming? "Owen!"

"It's Susannah Gabriel," he said and moved aside while Lettie, grinning, laid the newborn infant on Ella's breast. There were warm blankets and light, other faces and low voices. The storm lessened, the hayshed was luminous with the glow of lanterns. Ella felt vast relief. Joy filled her, and she laughed.

Owen was beside her. He kissed her forehead, and gazed at Susannah, who was so small and beautiful.

"She cries like a sergeant major!" he said. "She's strong, like her mother."

Ella could feel the warm baby against her breast, but sensed little else of her body. Was she still dreaming, still adrift? No, it was all real. Susannah, happily, did wail loudly; and that was wonderful. Her baby was there, furious, beautiful, glorious, and safe.

Sally was there, too, thoroughly splashed with mud, holding back a little, but excited to see the baby. Ella put a hand out to her, and the girl came close. Behind Sally was Heera, lying in the lantern light like some giant dog of an ancient god. His coat shimmered with rain as he lay calmly and licked his paws.

Near Heera stood Tommy Morely. His mother, who trembled with exhaustion, leaned against Jeb Grey. Jeb smiled, put a blanket over Lettie's shoulders, and held her close to his side. Neither noticed Tommy move just out of the lantern light, a look of gloom and confusion on his face. He found it hard to watch his mother and Jeb display such affection, so he turned away to walk on home through the rain, alone.

Susannah Sutherland was fair, like her mother. Robust and untroubled by the hazards of her birth, she was incredibly lovely from the very first; it seemed she could see almost immediately. Her presence brightened up the world of the Sutherlands and their close circle of friends. Nothing could detract from the household's joy in those early weeks of Susannah's life.

Both Jeremy and Sally took close interest in the child, and even Benjamin, who was toddling about, was not jealous of his sister. He gave Susannah more attention than everyone else combined, and the baby became his very own pride and treasure. It was true, though, that Ella seldom nursed Susannah without Benjamin climbing up alongside, cuddling, and sucking his left thumb in a way he had never done before.

chapter **13**

CHIEFTAINS

Late that spring the impending grand peace council planned for Oswego on Lake Ontario was the talk of Fort Detroit. This council was to be the final settlement of Pontiac's rebellion, and the great war chief himself had promised to attend. With the culmination of the meeting, the Indians of the northwest would at last have the terms they wanted from their British conquerors; restrictions on trade and white travel would be eased, and it was hoped a new era of peace and prosperity would dawn on the frontier.

In attendance at the council, representing thousands of warriors from the Hudson River in the east to the western reaches of the Mississippi, would be all the most powerful chiefs of the Ottawa, Chippewa, Huron, Iroquois, Shawnee, Delaware, Mingo, Miami, and Illinois. Owen Sutherland would be there as counselor to Chief Pontiac, who trusted him above all whites. Sutherland was disappointed that the new acting governor of Canada and the northwest, Guy Carleton, would not yet have arrived in North America to oversee this important council. Governor Murray would have left Canada for England by the time the council began in July, so the highest British official present would be Sir William Johnson, the Irish-born Indian superintendent for the northern tribes.

Sutherland had mixed feelings about Johnson, whose power was growing steadily in the northwest. It was Johnson who had proposed to Parliament a new system of controlling the Indian trade, and Sutherland was opposed to some of the baronet's ideas. Under Johnson's plan, each important trading post would have a civilian commissary answerable only to Johnson and appointed by him, thus replacing men like Lieutenant Parker, who worked for the military. This civilian commissary would have as much official power over Indian and trade matters as would the post commander himself, and in most cases, he

would have the final say, including who received a license and
where they could travel.

Sutherland and other traders thought this plan left open too
many possibilities for corruption. It was well known that Johnson and other officials governing Indian affairs had considerable interest in acquiring Indian land for themselves and their
secret partners. They intended to sell the land to settlers or to
land speculation firms, although private land purchases from
Indians had been ruled illegal by Parliament. Johnson had claims
on Indian grants of hundreds of thousands of acres given him
as gifts before regulations prohibiting private acquisitions had
gone into effect. He would surely press his case with any person
of political influence to gain government approval of those
grants.

If Johnson dominated the post commissaries—men who
could have great power among the tribes because of their influence on the trade—then he had the potential for becoming
a virtual emperor over the northwest, answerable only to the
king. This trade and commissary plan proposed by Johnson
had not yet been approved by Parliament, but British military
authorities in America favored it, especially General Thomas
Gage, commander of all forces in North America.

By taking the high cost of managing Indian affairs and the
trade away from the military—soldiers were the sole police
force in the northwest—then Gage could reduce his expendi-
tures, which were constantly under attack by colonial governments and Parliament. As part of his trade plan, William Johnson
promised to finance commercial and Indian management from
trade license fees, custom taxes, and other income, which would
cost the traders and merchants dearly but government very little.
Thus Gage was willing to give Johnson a free hand in Indian
country, and the superintendent was determined to put his plan
into operation, even though the government at home had not
yet officially sanctioned it.

This shadow over the northwest of potential political corruption and official greed might eventually lead to hostilities.
The Indians had to be alert for duping and the gradual eating
away of their lands by treaties. For these reasons, Sutherland
was glad to attend the council as Pontiac's advisor, though he
knew his own influence was miniscule compared with the
sweeping powers of Johnson and other officials of the Indian
Department.

Despite his inner doubts about the long-term benefit of the

council to anyone but Sir William Johnson, Sutherland was able to accept these things philosophically and with a certain amount of hope. At least the fur trade would be given new stimulus, and he was confident his own company would profit as long as it could procure credit and goods from eastern suppliers.

These matters concerned Sutherland as he prepared to receive Chief Pontiac at Detroit that June. The chief and his retinue would gather at the post before traveling eastward to Niagara and then Oswego. Meanwhile, Sutherland's *Trader* would take the Scotsman's entire family to the council meeting.

Upon learning the whole story of how Matilda's impending marriage had hurt her friend and teacher, Mel Webster, Sally took it upon herself to cheer him up.

In those days, the young man appreciated Sally's friendship, and more than once they went for strolls by the river after the violin lessons. They learned from one another, though their ages were far apart. Mel taught Sally much through conversation about literature, music, and history. For Sally, he unfolded the outer layers of a whole new world, sparking an interest that burned brighter as she discovered a realm beyond her life as a child of the frontier.

Mel, in turn, saw that happiness need not be so brittle nor so dependent upon the whims of others. Through Sally he saw how adversity must be overcome in time. This girl had lost everything to the savagery of war, yet she was unselfish, outgoing, and considerate. Their friendship was free and easy, completely spontaneous and without demands upon one another. In this way, Sally helped Mel's wound to heal, and soon he was once again engrossed in his secret studies of the Indian burial mounds.

As Mel and Sally walked near the landing one morning, he told the girl about these mounds, though he said nothing about his search for them. Sally was fascinated. Quick and alert, she asked questions he had never thought of, and stimulated him to go back to his resources for the answers. They were about to return to the fort's water gate when there was a tremendous fusillade of musketry out on the river. They turned to see three hundred canoes paddling against the current, gray smoke rising above them. Each craft was filled with Indian families who had saluted Detroit with the traditional "fire of joy," always given by an approaching canoe brigade.

There were at least six hundred fully adorned warriors and
chiefs in these canoes, along with several hundred squaws and
children. Mel was excited by the spectacle, but when he turned
to Sally, he saw she was pale and breathing hard.

"What is it, Sal?"

"Ottawa," she whispered. "Pontiac's people."

At first, Mel did not really grasp the gravity of Sally's
enslavement to this chief for an entire winter, when she had
been under the sentence of death before Jacques Levesque saved
her. Looking from the Indians to Sally, Mel tried to shake her
out of this fright by chuckling that all was well, and she should
not worry anymore. Then, as though struck by lightning, Mel
realized why Sally was so mortified. In the first canoe, just
yards away, he saw a burly, aging man bedecked with feathers
and painted hideously in whites and yellows that streaked his
face from forehead to chin.

Weakly, Sally murmured, "Pontiac."

The chief's canoe glided to shore, and with great pomp, he
climbed out, wading through the shallows toward Sally and
Mel. Sally was trembling, and she edged close to Mel, who
put his arm around her shoulders.

She whimpered, "I've got to get away. I've got to go."

She wanted to flee but could not move. It was as though
Pontiac hypnotized her. He was coming toward them, with no
one else on the beach. Everything Mel had heard of her imprisonment with Pontiac came into his mind, and he felt a
brutish anger rise within.

Pontiac took hardly any notice of Sally as he passed, not
aware who she was. Mel glared at him with tremendous hatred.
Poor Sally, he thought. This must be like a nightmare come
true. It would have been better had she never seen this man
again.

"Pontiac."

To Mel's shock, Sally had spoken to the chief.

The Indian stopped, heard her say his name again, and
slowly turned around. His eyes narrowed. Recognition came
into his devilishly painted face, and he was cold, heartless as
he stared at her. Sally did not flinch, though her long gown
was slightly shivering as her legs betrayed emotions.

There was a pause, in which all the other Indians stopped
where they were in deference to their chief. Pontiac turned his
back on her without saying a word. Then soldiers and post
dignitaries poured down the slope to welcome this most im-

portant of all northwestern Indians. They greeted him with
solemn handshakes and kind words, and led him up to the fort,
where he would be treated with utmost respect and honor.

Owen Sutherland saw Sally standing with Mel, and had not
missed her encounter with Pontiac. He came to her side and
crouched down to look in her eyes. Mel said softly that he and
Sally had not yet finished their morning's walk.

For all her unexpected confrontation with Pontiac, Sally's
face was clear, untroubled, as though the past somehow had
lost its sting. Owen wanted to ask her again to become his
adopted daughter, but this was not the right moment. He kissed
Sally's cheek and stood up. She took his hand and Mel's.

"I would like it," she said with a faint smile, "if you would
both go with me for a walk, since this is such a special day
for me."

In Montreal, the approaching Indian council at Oswego was
cause for much excitement in the Defries household. Peter and
Mary were looking forward to leaving the city for a while and
joining the Sutherlands at the council. In company with them
would go Angélique and Jacques Levesque, who had been
laboring hard for the Frontier Company in Montreal. The tasks
of both couples had been heavy, for there was still a shortage
of trade goods with which to supply the western establishment.
Cullen was growing in power, buying up shiploads of wares
even before they reached the Quebec docks far downriver.

Thanks to Peter's contacts in Albany, the Frontier Company
was still able to purchase goods on credit from New York and
New England merchants and brokers. It was increasingly apparent that Montreal was Bradford Cullen's domain, and the
company was steadily losing ground there. Though their work
organizing *voyageur* canoe brigades to travel westward with
trade goods had been a great success, Angélique and Jacques
were tired of the city. The network of French canoemen and
laborers was so firmly established that it could run itself without
Levesque's supervision, and that was what he wanted, for his
heart was in the wilderness.

Each spring the canoemen started out from Lachine, paddled
up the Ottawa River, portaged across to the French River, and
then journeyed down to Georgian Bay and eventually the lakes.
After taking this northern route to Detroit, these hardy fellows
stayed out there shuttling back and forth to Michilimackinac

or down to Vincennes with trade goods—particularly light-weight, expensive items like clothing and jewelry that were easily transported by canoe. On their homeward journey in late autumn, they were laden with peltry to be shipped eastward.

Peter, too, had done well as the head of the company's procurement office. Though hard-pressed by Cullen's intrigues and by a shortage of available credit in economically strapped America, he had always been able to find enough to get through the winter trading season and thus keep the company going. Summer was a welcome respite for him, and in the days before departing for the Oswego rendezvous, he rested. What next autumn would bring in terms of supervising cargo shipments west and fur shipments east remained to be seen, but June was Peter's time for relaxing. That was appropriate in Montreal, hot and muggy in that month.

He made the most of a sunny Saturday morning lying in a hammock, listening to bees buzzing in his wife's flower garden. Shut out from the city by a high stone wall, the Defries house was private and comfortable. Often it was a center of activity for those connected with the Frontier Company, but on this particular morning, Peter savored the quiet. So did their brown, flop-eared mongrel Toby, who was asleep under her master's hammock.

Mary's voice drew him from a light slumber. He squinted around to see her approaching, a slate and chalk in one hand, Jeanette tramping along at her side, carrying a reader and speller.

Peter closed his eyes quickly, hoping they would think him asleep. Mary, however, knew he was playacting, and said, "Peter, it's time for your lessons."

No response. Jeanette, pretty and petite, with raven hair and fair skin, shook her father's hammock. "Papa! Papa, you have to read! Mama says wake up."

Peter looked out of one eye, groaned, and turned over, mumbling that this was a day off. For the past six months, four times a week, Peter, who had never learned how to read, had endured elementary lessons in numbers and letters. He had progressed quite well, but it was always a painful process that took all Mary's patience, just as it required all Peter's brain-power.

Jeanette crawled under the hammock, clambered over patient Toby, and came up at the other side to tickle her father's nose. "Wake up, Papa."

Defries grumbled and turned over, but Mary was on that side, a fair image of her dark, blue-eyed daughter. Peter was trapped.

"Aw, ladies, it's too nice a day to be readin' an' cipherin'!" He had to sit up when Jeanette hopped onto his lap. "Anyway, bein' it's Saturday, don't Emmy come over today to visit?"

Mary replied, "Emmy should have been here long ago, but she hasn't come by yet. I hope the poor thing isn't sick, because if I know those Cullens they'll be furious with her if she misses her market-day shopping."

Ever since Jeanette's birth two and a half years earlier, the Cullen's black maid had passed by the Defries home on her way to market. Each Saturday Emmy spent an hour with Jeanette, the real joy of her life. Her own children long gone, dead or sold to other masters, Emmy was alone in the world, with only Peter and Mary as true friends.

"Perhaps," Mary said, "Emmy will come by later on. But first, Peter, your lessons."

Defries flexed the fingers of his right hand. "Aw, Mary, sweetheart, I can't do no writin' today; I got a sore hand, don't you know? Why, it's still cramped up from the last lesson."

Mary was unsympathetic. "Then you can read. Your brain hasn't had much exercise lately. Come on!" The three of them squeezed into the hammock, swaying placidly, while Mary shoved a book into her husband's hands.

Peter licked his lips and peered at the book. *"Mo–ther— Goose's—S–Songs of the Nur–s–ery.* Mother Goose's Nursery Songs! Nursery songs! Why, what'n the name o' Jupiter do you think I am, wife? Readin' nursery songs?" He glanced over at the wooden door in the garden wall. "Anybody hears me readin' Mother Goose'll think me a lunatic! I'm too old—"

"Read, Papa!" Jeanette, dressed like her mother in a yellow cotton dress, with a blue bow on her head, clasped her hands together and waited. "Do you know how?"

"Know how? Me? Nursery songs? Why, child, of course I do! These are kids' words!"

He licked his lips again and opened the book. Clearing his throat, he mumbled something about needing spectacles, then cast one more quick glance at the garden gate. No one was there, so he brought the book quite close to his face.

"Mother Goose's Songs." He smiled at Jeanette. "Just till Emmy comes, an' then I'm gettin' forty winks, all right? Fine. Now listen here, little lady, an' I'll learn you somethin' . . ."

"Teach," Mary said.

"Teach," Jeanette echoed.

Peter glowered a little into the book, turning pages and looking more at the illustrations than at the words. He recognized black sheep, babies in cradles, little boys eating pies and sleeping in hay. Finally he found what he wanted. Mary watched closely and saw he was hardly looking at the words at all:

> "Rockabye baby, your cradle is green,
> Your father's a nobleman, mother's a queen!"

Proud of himself, he grinned at Mary, who said, "Very good, Peter! One would think you'd been practicing, or might have learned that one by memory."

Peter's blond eyebrows knitted, but he made no reply. He read the entire poem—or seemed to—with Jeanette rocking her arms as though a baby were in them.

After a couple more, recited perfectly, Mary announced, "That was so good, Peter, that we'll have a go at your hornbook!" Peter was not enthusiastic, but he did not complain when Mary brought out the thin piece of wood, about five inches long, two inches wide, with a handle at the bottom. It had affixed to it a piece of paper containing the alphabet and simple syllables. This printed page, which also contained the Lord's Prayer, was covered with a transparent sheet of yellowish horn material that permitted the letters to be read, and also protected them.

Peter went through all the letters perfectly, gaining enthusiasm and confidence as he did so. To cap his performance, Peter read the rhyme at the bottom of the board: "All the letters are digested, hateful ignorance detested!" Jeanette applauded.

Mary complimented him once again, then brought out her *New England Primer*. Peter groaned. This book was as boring as it was taxing, but he went on with it, struggling through such pious rhymes as "In Adam's fall, we sinned all" and "Zaccheus he did climb a tree, his Lord to see."

Peter tried hard, and Mary turned to more appealing subjects: arithmetic and measures. Peter's natural affinity for commerce and trade made learning numbers easy, and he positively shone. He could read and figure with everything from firkins to tuns, butts to anchors to kilderkins. He knew all the dry measures by heart, reciting the relationship between pottles, weys, and lasts. Though her father's interest waxed, Jeanette's diminished, and she wandered off to play on the grass with her rag doll.

Peter was struggling through a problem when Toby yipped and Jeanette gave a cry of surprise and delight. Coming in the gate was Emmy, but she was not carrying her market basket, and her face was streaked with tears.

Mary ran to Emmy, who declared, "I mustn't stay, Missy. I got to go afore they find me here and punish you for hidin' me!"

"What is it, Emmy?" Mary asked. "Have you run away?"

The slave shook her head and buried her face in her friend's shoulder. "I can't run, I got nowhere to go! I hate them folk, Missy! I can't go, but they treat me so bad!"

Peter was at Emmy's side, and he led her to a garden chair while Mary shooed Jeanette into the house. Emmy told them Linda Cullen, the daughter of the merchant, had seen her approaching the Defries house that morning, then had intercepted her and commanded she go home. There Emmy was beaten with a cane by Bradford Cullen, and had fled from him in terror.

"Linda's been watchin' me lately," Emmy said, weeping. "She suspected I came here, and she took me home and told Mr. Cullen. He . . . he . . . struck me so hard!"

Peter was boiling, but no matter how angry they might be with Cullen for his treatment of Emmy, there was nothing they could do. She was the man's property, to dispose of as he saw fit. As long as he did not kill or torture his slaves outright, there was little the law would do to forbid mistreatment. It hurt the couple deeply to see Emmy so sad, for the slave had been Mary's closest companion during the lonely time when she was a lodger in the Cullen house.

Mary looked at Peter, frustration and despair in her face. Emmy was a godmother to Jeanette and a dear friend. They could not stand by and see her suffer.

Just then there was a commotion at the gate, and in barged Bradford Cullen in company with a city constable, who carried a club. Peter barred their way as Cullen shouted for Emmy to come to him. Toby growled, her tail up, in warning.

"There!" Cullen roared to the constable. "See that? Harboring a runaway! I ought to have you arrested, Defries! Come here, girl, or I'll have you beaten properly like the disobedient wench you—"

Peter took a menacing step toward Cullen, who cringed behind the constable—himself a big fellow but no match for Defries. Mary held Toby by the collar.

"Now hold on thar," the constable said, his Adam's apple bobbing, eyes blinking. "Let's cure all this peaceably, or I'll git the city guard on ye, lad."

Peter answered, "Tell that oaf to mind his manners on my property. Unless you have a warrant, get out or I'll toss you over the wall."

Emmy protested, "Oh, please, Mr. Peter, don't get yourself in trouble." She ran to Peter's side and appealed to Cullen, "It's not their fault, sir, I just came to . . . to visit, is all. I was afraid you'd hurt me more . . ."

"Enough!" Cullen commanded. A crowd was gathering at the gate to watch, and Cullen wanted no one to know that he had abused a slave. He composed himself and said, "Constable, if my servant returns immediately without troubling us further, I'll press no charges against this fellow."

The constable, his beetling brow rising and falling, nodded and said, "Come along, woman. And you, Defries, let it lay as it is; don't make no trouble now."

Peter wanted to go for both scoundrels, and as Emmy passed, he almost reached out to hold her back.

"Wait!" Mary shouted, and gave the dog to Peter. She rushed to Emmy, taking her by the shoulders, and looking at Cullen, she said, "Let us buy Emmy from you! Sell her to us for any price you ask . . . if we can afford it, and we'll assume responsibility for her."

Cullen thought about that, his face dark, mouth working. He could hardly resist a profit, and here one could be made at the expense of enemies. He rubbed his mouth and sneered, "Any price, eh?"

Peter said, "Name your price, though she means nothing to you."

Cullen chuckled to himself, still rubbing his face, rocking on his heels. "She means considerable to me, my man. Why do you think I've chased her all the way here? My daughter and wife depend on Emmy for cooking, sewing, and she's an excellent companion to them on long journeys—never gets sick, strong like her kind always are. Yes, Emmy here's worth quite a lot to me." He lifted his chin, and his eyes half closed. "In fact, she's worth two hundred pounds."

Peter and Mary did not show the dismay they felt. Neither

had any way to come up with that much money in less than a year's time. Emmy's anticipation vanished. Her head bowed.

Cullen said, "I didn't think so—"

Mary pleaded, "Let us pay it every month until—"

Cullen was shaking his head, still sneering. Emmy did not look at her friends. She stepped toward Cullen and went docilely through the gate, the constable close behind. Cullen went, too, leaving the gate open, and laughing as he strolled away.

In the next few weeks, Emmy did not appear again at the Defries residence. They asked the other Cullen servants about her, and were told she was well enough, but miserable. At first she had been relieved of her duties as chambermaid to Linda, and required to do endless laundry and scullery work. Then Cullen's daughter had complained that no one else could wait on her quite like Emmy; furthermore, Helen Cullen favored Emmy's cooking. Before long, the servant was allowed to forgo the heavy labor and was returned to her former role.

Peter and Mary felt terribly guilty at having been partly the cause of Emmy's misery. Yet there was some solace in the knowledge—as one of the other household servants had said— that Emmy was not beaten again. This servant, a young indentured Irishwoman, said Helen Cullen had been overheard warning her husband not to strike Emmy lest "that villain Defries lose his head and break into the house" to punish the merchant.

The final days of preparation for the trip to Oswego were tainted by the unpleasantness of Emmy's situation. When Mary learned that the Cullens, too, were going to the council, she hoped to see Emmy there, if only briefly, to offer her another chance to escape if she really wanted to.

In the back of Mary's mind was the knowledge that Jacques and Angélique were sick and tired of Montreal and favored moving to the far northwest to settle. If all went well, it was remotely possible that Emmy might flee with them, and no one would be the wiser. This was a faint hope, a distant possibility that Mary nurtured as they set out by carriage for the western extreme of the thunderous Lachine rapids. By the time she and her family were aboard a small sloop and headed up the Saint Lawrence for Lake Ontario and Oswego, Mary knew that somehow she had to free Emmy, and do it soon.

• • •

From the moment his sailing ship anchored in the harbor before
Fort Oswego one July afternoon, Jeremy Bently was fascinated
at the sight of five thousand Indians swarming over the grassy
vale that lay between two army fortifications. As the vessel's
crewmen clambered down from the rigging, and Sutherland's
party prepared to disembark by jolly boat, Jeremy stood as if
glued to the rail, eyes taking in more than his young mind
could comprehend. The racket, colors, movement, and smells
of so much savage humanity crammed into a seething city of
lodges and tents intoxicated his senses and delighted his mind.

Ella, carrying Susannah to the ship's rail, where a sailor
took the child down to the boat, called to Jeremy, but he wanted
to watch a moment longer. The panoramic view from the ship
in the harbor was as perfect as any boy could ask. From where
he stood, he could see the two forts: one up on the right,
bristling with cannon; the other on the left, an earthworks no
longer in use. It was on the left knoll that most Indian dwellings
had been pitched or erected. The neat, orderly lines of an
abandoned military structure, carpeted with new-mown grass,
were overlaid with every size and shape of skin and bark Indian
lodge.

As colorful as a living kaleidescope, the crowds of temporary inhabitants of this makeshift community moved endlessly among one another, spilling down the slope to the vale
and river below. There was such a diverse mingling of bright
colors, furs, deerskins, civilized clothing, feathers, and paint
that Jeremy let his eyes go slowly out of focus, and he soaked
in the dazzling profusion of light and color.

Owen came to his side and saw Jeremy's enchantment. In
a moment he identified a dozen tribes for the boy, described
as many nations, and had pointed out individual warriors and
chiefs known personally to him. By contrast with the lodges
of the Indians, the efficient, clean ramparts of the fortification
still in use by the army was a tranquil setting where one or two
scarlet-coated soldiers walked sentry duty, muskets on their
shoulders. The fort, with its flapping Union Jack, commanded
the wild and raucous array of milling Indians. The general
scene was more of a festival than a solemn council, a vast fair
rather than a political conference.

"Those tents there," Sutherland said, pointing to a village
of billowing white canvas near the lakeshore, "are where the
traders have set up to do business and keep the Indians happy."

Sutherland's company had chosen not to open a shop here because the trade would mostly be in food, trinkets, and ornaments in exchange for some poor-quality skins and perhaps pemmican. The merchants collected here were local Albany and Montreal shopkeepers out for a quick, small profit. Asking high prices, they were hoping to take advantage of western Indians who would pay dearly for whatever they got.

"There," Sutherland said, and indicated a group of British regulars and green-coated Rangers, "do you see Major Rogers? The big one in green with the black infantry cap. Remember him? He brought the reinforcement to Detroit in sixty-three when no one else could get through."

Jeremy remembered the arrival of Rogers, the unofficial leader of soldiers who had slipped past fifteen hundred warriors to relieve beleaguered Detroit. The most famous Indian fighter in America, Rogers was renowned in Britain as the leader of Rangers who were second to none in forest fighting. Relaxed and regal in bearing, he stood out among the others. He was dressed in the uniform of the Rangers, who had also been crucial to the British victory in the French and Indian War.

Sutherland said, "Rogers has been named lieutenant governor up at Michilimackinac, in charge of all civil and military affairs in the upper lakes, outranking even the commander of the post. He'll be the most important man in the northwest in a few years. Nobody can handle the former French-Indian allies better then he can, not even William Johnson."

"Not even you?" Jeremy asked.

Sutherland just smiled and said that such special rapport with northwestern Indians caused others to be jealous of Rogers. Johnson was one who saw Rogers as a threat to his own influence in the northwest, where the superintendent was notorious as a patron of the hated Iroquois. Jeremy and Owen climbed down the ladder to join Ella and the children in the boat for the short trip to the landing, and the boy learned more about Rogers, who was said to be seeking the fabled Northwest Passage to the Orient.

"At Michilimackinac," Sutherland remarked, "he'll be closer to the passage, if there is one, than any other official in the British Empire; but if Johnson has his way, Rogers will be watched closely by whoever's the commissary up there, and he'll be limited in his powers of office."

Ella said, "He's a lieutenant governor, Owen. How can a civilian commissary have any power over him?" She held Susannah, and Benjamin sat next to her on the seat, thumb in his mouth.

Sutherland replied, "According to the proposed new trade regulations, Johnson's commissary will have the final word on whatever is done at Michilimackinac; even a lieutenant governor of Roger's stature will be hard put to act independently of Johnson's wishes." He thought a moment while the two seamen guided the boat close to a wooden landing, where dozens of Indians and a few soldiers were watching them approach.

Then Sutherland said, "From what I've heard, Rogers has his own ambitions, but if his ambitions conflict with Sir William Johnson's, there'll be sparks flying, and perhaps worse. They both can't hold total sway over the northwest, though I reckon they'll both try."

The Indians on shore applauded and yelled in welcome as they recognized Sutherland, the one they called Donoway. Admiring him and his family, scores of Ottawa, Chippewa, Miami, and Piankashaw collected to shake his hand and clap him on the back. Watching the tumult from a little distance off, Major Rogers grinned to see Sutherland arrive. He strode through the Indians, who parted in deference to him, and heartily took Owen's hand.

Rogers said, "So, Mr. Sutherland, I'm told you're here as the advisor to Pontiac, eh? Well, then, best keep a weather eye on old Johnson; he'll skin these Indians and tell 'em it's for their own good. He'll dance with 'em, drink with 'em, an'—" He noticed Ella and hesitated. "—An' cuddle up to their daughters, an' all the while be makin' secret deals with land speculators to rob 'em blind."

Sutherland agreed it would be a difficult task to keep Pontiac aware of all that was said. He was not the one who would translate for the chief but would talk later on, after speeches were made. As Rogers spoke critically of Johnson, Sutherland noticed a short, square fellow he knew to be a confidant of Johnson's. William Butler of Johnson's Mohawk Valley domain had obviously listened to everything Rogers had said about Johnson, and when Sutherland stared directly at him, the man became self-conscious and moved away. Rogers also knew Butler was at hand but seemed not to care. Bluff and friendly, the lieutenant governor took great interest in Ella and the children, giving Jeremy special attention that made the boy feel very important and honored.

Then Rogers asked Sutherland, "Where's Chief Pontiac? I heard he was comin' east with you."

The Scotsman grinned and said, "He came behind the sloop with his people in canoes, and they made as much distance as we did, despite our sail. But when we came to a point a few miles west of here, Pontiac and his whole mob put in to shore to get themselves painted and decorated for a proper entrance. They'll be along tomorrow, after they drink the last of the rum they brought with them."

"Good thing," Rogers said. "Drunk Indians around here'd touch off another war." He smacked his lips and said, "Too bad I didn't know aforehand about the old boy's plans; I'd have enjoyed droppin' by and helpin' him waste that rum."

Rogers touched his hat to Ella, apologizing for such rough talk, adding that his own wife, Elizabeth, was also at the fort and forever being embarrassed by naked Indians and loose tongues.

Ella replied, "After three years at Detroit, I've learned not to see or hear some things, Governor Rogers; I'm sure Mrs. Rogers will learn to do the same in time."

Rogers grinned, but there was something uneasy about him as he thought of his Maine-born wife, a civilized, difficult woman with high hopes for her husband's new career.

He said, "I hope you an' Betsy'll meet durin' this council, Mrs. Sutherland, but that won't be easy, seein' as she's not feelin' well most of the time. Doesn't like the smell of bear grease and sweaty soldiers. She's dinin' mostly with the wives of officers. . . . Ah, you understand."

Ella understood well enough, for Betsy Rogers was known to be snooty, to consider herself too good for anyone not stamped with the mark of high society or political influence. That was just as well as far as Ella was concerned; she was anxious to be reunited with Mary and Angélique, who were probably already quartered in tents pitched on the right-hand slope of the shallow valley. They parted with Rogers, but not before Jeremy asked the man about a play he wrote about Chief Pontiac, titled *Ponteach*.

Rogers had a gleam in his eye as he said, "So you're that sharp a lad, eh? Well, then, if you like, I'll fish a copy of the play out of my kit and send it to you."

Jeremy wished Rogers had invited him to come to his lodgings in the fort and fetch the play in person, but that was too much to ask of such an important man. As it was, the boy reveled at Rogers offering him the loan of the play that had delighted London and evoked great interest among the British in American Indian affairs. The controversial play severely criticized government Indian policy, saying the red man was misunderstood and mistreated by British and colonials alike. As a result of his heroic reputation and literary triumph, Rogers was gaining in prestige at home, and this redoubled the resentment of men like Johnson, who considered him a distasteful rival.

The next day, while Jeremy alternately wandered dreamily about Oswego or lay on his cot reading *Ponteach,* the others in Sutherland's party congregated for a cheerful celebration of their own. They had raised three tents on high ground overlooking the vale, where they shared meals and old news. There was much admiring of children and new clothes, as well as the exchange of opinions about the present and the future. Jacques Levesque made it clear to Sutherland that he and Angélique had lost interest in Montreal and preferred to go west. They talked about the possibility of the Levesques becoming company factors up at Michilimackinac, where Jacques had many acquaintances among the tribes there.

It was also apparent to their friends that the Levesques were a bit disappointed at not having children yet, though they tried hard enough. The vivacious Angélique was enthralled by Ella's children, and Mary Defries said in private that Angélique longed to be a mother. Sally floated about from couple to couple, feeling very independent and pleased to be at Oswego for such a momentous occasion. She also found herself less afraid than usual in the presence of strange Indians. The effects of her imprisonment with Pontiac had not yet worn off, however, and she was reluctant to accept Jeremy's suggestions they wander through the Indian area. She resolved to avoid Pontiac during the council, despite her earlier boldness with the chief when he first came into Detroit.

Plans were made that Jacques, too, would make a point of keeping away from Pontiac, lest either man lose his temper and a quarrel begin. The Frenchman and Sally were happy to be reunited, but after word came that Pontiac had arrived at Oswego, they remembered the darker days, and their lightheartedness diminished.

Yet there was much for Sally to do at Oswego, and she was Jeremy's frequent companion as they explored the place. Sniffer had been left behind at Detroit in Tom's care, and they were relatively free to come and go as they pleased. Now and again Jeremy teased Sally about her reluctance to go near the Indian section, for he did not know much about the hardship and terror she had endured when a prisoner among them.

As for Sutherland, he had no abiding love for Pontiac, but he bore the influential leader much respect. Though Pontiac was in his waning days as a chief, there were many tribes who still looked to him for guidance and advice. Without Pontiac's agreement, there could never be peace on the frontier.

The next morning Sutherland went to Pontiac's camp. There he was greeted by Niko-lota, who had come out with Pontiac and whom Sutherland had last seen when the chief and his retinue had stopped at Detroit last month. Niko-lota said he intended to leave at the conclusion of the council meeting to search out Lucy Swain's children in Shawnee country. Then, when he found them, he would draw out the Swains from wherever they now were, and see to it that Jubal Swain would never again trouble the northwest. For Sutherland this was good news. He had had enough of going out on chases, and would be content if he could just stay at home and see the Frontier Company prosper.

When Pontiac and Sutherland met in private council, there was much to discuss. Sutherland knew Pontiac had no illusions about the diminished strength of the red man. The chief was here to do whatever he could to prevent the ultimate success of whites who sought his people's land.

In a morning council with a few other chiefs present, Sutherland and Pontiac smoked and talked outside the Ottawa's skin lodge, while a council fire spat and crackled before them. Pontiac made it clear that even though his people were losing their land and power, they might still make a great defense if they united. Black eyes glittering with some far-off dream, he spoke of a mass rising, of French or Spanish support, and of the Great Spirit's aid. Pontiac believed the Great Spirit knew the heart of pure Indians and ultimately could bring them victory.

Sutherland thought these words hollow, but to look at Pontiac, it was apparent he was still formidable, a spiritual chief with the warlike soul of his nation coursing like a fire through his blood. Pontiac was a massive figure, even seated with legs crossed, shoulders covered by a fine white French trade blanket. His raven hair fell past his shoulders and was fitted in the back with eagle feathers showing his distinguished rank. From his large nose a white bone crescent dangled, moving as he spoke slowly and with conviction.

"The Creek and Chickasaw in the south are preparing for war, and the French traders want to arm them; not far from here the Delaware and Shawnee still burn for revenge against the British, and against the settlers who steal their lands and murder them without being punished by white government.

"There are surveyors everywhere in our country, measuring, asking questions, counting trees, and preparing the way for soldiers and plowmen who will come after and say the land is theirs, no longer the land of my fathers and my sons. Donoway, for all the blood that has been spilled, and for all the treaties we make here or will make in the days to come, I know what your white leaders have in store for us."

He gazed at Sutherland, eyes lit by a passion that could be stilled only by death. Pontiac went on. "I have not come to surrender, but to make peace with the Great White Father across the seas, the one you call king. But I know that peace will not last.

"I have come here to bend my knee and swear allegiance to the White Father only because my people must have time to recover from the last war, to recover and regain strength. Not strength for an attack, but for defense. We will need all our young men, and great reserves of powder and ball, and we must learn the skills of the gunsmith. Stores of food should be placed in every village, for when the whites march against us again, they will march without stopping, into the very depths of Indian country, and there they will tear out our heart. So it will come to pass if we do not unite against them, and to that end I have advised my people."

Sutherland knew there had been many secret conferences here between tribes and among nations, to discuss what might happen if the colonies of England burst their western bonds and invaded Indian lands in force. In generations past, Indians had cleverly played French against British, keeping a balance of power in America to prevent one or the other white side from becoming too strong. But now the British were rulers of the entire eastern half of the continent, and the Indians were too feeble to stop them from expanding unless all the tribes stood together.

Pontiac said, "The ancient hatred between tribes is gradually being put aside, Donoway, and the more this white peril looms over us, the more we are willing to join and defend ourselves.

All the chiefs know the white men would take our lands tomorrow if the Great White Father did not prevent them."

Pontiac leaned forward and said unexpectedly, "What will happen, Donoway, when your king no longer rules the colonies?"

Sutherland was surprised. Despite all the conflicts between American and Britisher, there had been no real talk of open fighting or a serious break between the colonies and the mother country.

He replied carefully, "The king and Parliament rule us for the good of America—yes, and for the good of the Indians. Do not the soldiers drive out white settlers who take Indian lands without permission? Now the trade, too, is closely regulated by the royal government to prevent the cheating of Indians. The king has declared that no whites may purchase Indian lands by private treaty, or even by permission of individual colonies. Only the king and Parliament can approve treaties. Your lands are safe, Pontiac. You have fought hard, and whites know that you will always fight hard if anyone tries to take your country."

Pontiac was impassive. After some thought he said, "I swear allegiance to the king, not to the colonies, because the king will protect us, not the colonies. Yet I know well of the widening gap between Americans and English. It may be that the Indian will have to choose a side, as he has done in the past."

Thinking, pondering a memory that was painful to call up, Pontiac knew Indians like himself, who had chosen the French, had chosen wrongly. Yet there had been no other choice, for the French traded with the Ottawa, Chippewa, Algonquin, Huron, Delaware, Seneca, and Shawnee, and those folk had depended upon French goods to survive. Most of the Iroquois League—including Johnson's adopted Mohawk, the Oneida, Cayuga, Tuscarora, and Onondaga—had chosen the British, and were now haughty allies of the victors.

Sutherland said, "Chief Pontiac talks of civil war in America; that will never be. Britain is our homeland, our mother country. She supplies us with goods, and we give back raw materials for her to manufacture into what we and Indians need." As he spoke, Sutherland had the unsettling feeling that his own words rang emptily. Perhaps it was the skeptical look on Pontiac's face. Perhaps it was the knowledge that Pontiac was well known for having second sight.

For all the friction between the colonies and Mother England, there was no thought in Sutherland's mind that war would ever break out. That was too cruel to contemplate. Besides, Britain and America had so many things in common. They were civilized countries with close family ties on both sides of the ocean, and would surely work out all difficulties with reason and mutual affection.

A little while later, Pontiac said quietly, "I have seen much in a dream, Donoway, much that you will not now believe, so I will not tell you. But hear this: I have seen false treaties with false leaders, red and white. I have seen men like wolves who consume our land. I have seen soldiers without uniforms or flags attack our villages and drive us deeper into the forest, and then blame us as first aggressors. I have seen these things and more, Donoway, and they make my blood run cold.

"No longer can I lead in battle, for I have admitted defeat; soon I will buy time for my people by giving my allegiance to your king. But I tell you now, one who was once my brother, that the time will come when every man in the country you call America must make a choice and fight for what he believes is right."

Pontiac's eyes bored through Sutherland, who attempted to be as impassive as the chief; but he was troubled by the Indian's predictions.

Pontiac said, "In the past, Donoway, you too have made choices, and have chosen the victorious side. When the time comes to choose one last time, this Indian wonders where you will be, and whether, then, you will choose correctly."

Sutherland took Pontiac's words to heart, though he could not begin to imagine the catastrophe the chief foresaw taking place in America. He took a slow, long breath, and replied, "If that time comes, Chief Pontiac, I will be found protecting and cultivating my own garden."

Pontiac gave the slightest smile, then said, "So will we all, Donoway."

chapter **14**

NEGOTIATIONS

On July 23, 1766, Sir William Johnson formally opened the great council of Oswego to establish eternal peace between white and red in the northwest, and to announce the adoption of new trading regulations that would, he insisted, benefit Indians for all time.

In the center of an enormous mass of seated Indians, Johnson stood under a temporary canopy of leafy boughs. The mob that filled this depression between the two British fortifications resembled October leaves clogging a dry streambed. Resplendent in uniform and medals, Johnson was surrounded by the most important chiefs and white officials, and beyond them were lesser leaders, most covered from the hot sun by the canopy. It was some mark of importance if an Indian or white was permitted a place in the shade, though the canopy was large and could shelter several hundred.

At one end of the structure, seated close enough to hear, but far enough back to talk without disturbing the speaker, Sutherland and Peter Defries listened to Johnson's remarks. Long-winded, as was appropriate with Indians, and weighted down by several great beaded belts of wampum, Johnson welcomed the nations. Offering wampum with each declaration, the baronet wished recent Indian dead a peaceful rest, the living no more mourning, and the hearts and ears of all listeners to be open for his words.

The heavy, ponderous Johnson exuded self-importance. Large eyes, dark and alert, his mouth, wide, he was overly pompous in bearing, further impressing the Indians, who saw him as a man of great power. They sat attentively as he told them to hold fast to the bright chain of friendship with the British, and to uphold past oaths of allegiance to the king.

"Children, you begin already to see the fruits of peace, from the number of traders and plenty of goods at all the garrisoned posts." A buzz of interpreters followed his words, which were

220

spoken in English. He talked of men of honor sent to reside at the posts and to address the needs of the Indians—the commissaries. He said gunsmiths would be assigned in considerable numbers to repair Indian firearms so they could hunt without difficulties. There would be no more abuses of the trade, Johnson promised, and he personally would answer any questions or problems that his commissaries at each post could not resolve.

Sutherland said to Defries, who was a longtime acquaintance of the Indian superintendent, "So Johnson's plans for a civilian commissary have been approved. Well, it all sounds nice, but I think your friend there cares more for his own profit than he does for Indian well-being. He wants power and influence in the northwest, and he'll do anything to get it."

Defries answered, "That's usual, ain't it? The only official I ever saw who wasn't after power for its own sake was Governor Murray, and he didn't watch out for himself! Look what happened once Cullen an' his cronies got their teeth into him."

Sutherland said Bradford Cullen and his family had visited Johnson that morning, and it was understood the merchant was gaining in Sir William's esteem.

Defries was surprised at that, and as he turned to Sutherland, the Indians gave a loud, guttural sound of approval at something Johnson had said. When the noise died down, Defries spoke. "I'm having dinner with Sir William tonight on some business of his, though I don't know what. I'll ask him directly what he thinks of Cullen. Nobody could esteem Cullen, Owen!"

Sutherland looked at Johnson, fat and honey-tongued, hypnotizing most of the Indians as a storyteller charms children. Sutherland said, "Cullen is a force to be reckoned with in the northwest, and Johnson will have to reckon with him if he wants to be the dominant ruler."

Defries considered that before saying, "Cullen's got all Montreal in his pocket, that's for sure. Our company's milkin' all we can for trade goods, but Cullen owns the cow."

Sutherland agreed, and added, "How about you and Mary going down to Albany and making a fresh start there?"

Defries was excited. He and Mary had once considered moving to Albany, where the Defries family lived, but had decided to stay on in the more important trading center of Montreal. Now that the city seemed to be firmly in the grip of Cullen, a move to Albany might be just the thing to revitalize the business. With a loud clap that annoyed the listeners nearby, Defries said, "That's a notion after my heart, man! When do we do it?"

"Can you get the support of Yorker merchants to supply you? Will Mary put up with Albany after French Montreal? I understand she likes it up there."

Defries said enthusiastically, "We'll get enough connections in Albany to supply two trade companies! An' Mary'll get over Montreal. Albany's a good place—not so many mangy New England Yankees like Cullen." He slammed his big paws together, again disturbing a few solemn listeners to Sir William Johnson, who was called Warraghiyagey—meaning "the man who does great things."

Sutherland said, "Mary does love Montreal, doesn't she? The French culture, everything from Britain right off the ship, the garrison, the pomp, the balls now and then—"

"Aw, don't go bringin' all that up, Owen! It don't do me nothin' to dance with perfumed Frenchmen! Nor Mary neither. I'm goin' to be happy in Albany, Jeanette'll be happy, an' so will Mary, if she knows it or not yet!"

Ignoring the black looks of men who wanted him quiet, Defries went into a colorful description of his home city, nestled at the confluence of the Hudson and Mohawk rivers, where "kids can grow up eatin' American, speakin' American, an' thinkin' like Dutchmen!"

The council adjourned after Pontiac made a brief acceptance of Johnson's interminable speech. The chief would address them the following day, as was correct protocol. That evening, Peter and Mary went to Johnson's apartment in the post commander's quarters, a stone building with simple but comfortable furnishings. Peter had already told Mary about Sutherland's suggestion they move to Albany and begin work for the company there, and her mind was full of thoughts related to such a drastic step. Also busy with worry for Emmy, the servant of the Cullens whom she had seen from a distance earlier that day, Mary was not in the best of spirits when they were shown into a dining room to be greeted by Sir William himself.

Dressed in the richest of garments, frilled with silk and glittering with silver, Johnson was the perfect image of a wealthy potentate. Peter had lost some of his past warmth for this man, but he was pleased with Johnson's courtesy to Mary, who had not met him before. The dining room had apparently been reappointed for the superintendent's stay, with new velvet drapes on the large windows, the woodwork polished to a soft luster, and new chairs placed around the long table.

Candles burned in silver sticks upon this table, which was set for seven. Peter wondered who else was invited for dinner, but he did not ask, knowing Johnson's taste for surprises and the dramatic. Peter could wait, particularly because he shared the Irishman's appetite for strong rum, which was served in a small sitting room adjoining the main chamber. Mary sipped a brandy liqueur and listened to the two old acquaintances talk of family and friends from Albany and Schenectady.

Peter had once been in partnership with Johnson and had supplied one of his military campaigns against hostiles. They had much to reminisce about.

By seven o'clock, both Peter and Johnson were adequately stiffened by drink, and the superintendent got to the bottom of things. Sitting in a luxurious armchair that reminded Peter and Mary of a throne—they were less elevated, in simpler seats—Sir William declared with some pride:

"Peter, my lad, I presume you are aware of the change in trade regulations, and of my plans to appoint commissaries to the various western posts? There are a hundred important men petitioning me for the position of commissary and assistant commissary in one or another trading post, but I want officials I can trust, men I can rely upon. You've served me well in the past, and I have no doubts you'll serve me even better in the future. Peter, it gives me great pleasure to say that I have chosen you as assistant commissary at the most important trading post of all!"

Johnson had expected Peter to be joyous and Mary to be excited. He hardly noticed their reaction, however, because he was chuckling contentedly to himself and downing another swig of rum. Peter was staring in amazement, and Mary was troubled. Johnson licked his chops and went on, looking directly at Peter:

"Can you clear up your personal affairs within the year? Do that, and I'll arrange to have you, your family, and your personal belongings transported to Detroit before winter sets in!"

"Detroit!" Peter and Mary exclaimed at once.

"Detroit! And as assistant to the new commissary, whom I'll appoint within a few hours! Quite a step up in your career, eh, Peter?" Johnson casually mentioned a substantial annual salary, housing, servants, and expense allowance. Peter was being offered an opportunity of a lifetime. Mary, too, knew it.

It meant breaking with the Frontier Company and allying himself with Johnson, who was indeed increasingly becoming a major lord in America. Peter had such little schooling that he realized any writing or record-keeping would be beyond him. He knew Johnson was aware of this, and asked precisely what he could do for the Indian Department. The baronet replied:

"Peter, this is not a post for a scholar or a weakling. Rather, the assistant commissary must be a man of particular influence among the traders, especially among the rougher kind. As you well know, America is changing rapidly, with a growing number of people becoming disaffected, almost treasonous to the crown; these rebellious elements defy law and order, come and go through Indian country as they please, insult the army, and so on."

Johnson took a drink and stifled a burp. "Now, I anticipate considerable hostility from this element when our commissaries take charge of the western trade; at the same time, I have no intention of scurrying to the military post commander to beg assistance to enforce my regulations."

He peered at Peter, who was beginning to understand what was meant for him. Johnson said the assistant commissary must be a strong man, able to defend the interests of the commissary, and capable of "knocking heads together when necessary."

He said, "After some years, when the system's working properly, there won't be any need for rough stuff, but in the time it takes to establish my organization, we'll need men on the spot who can support us, and win the immediate respect of traders."

Peter sat back, staring at the floor. "You want a fighting man as assistant commissary."

Johnson chuckled a long and rolling laugh that would have been appealing in other circumstances. He said, "Let's say a sergeant at arms, Peter. You're the one for me, and I know there's hardly a man in the colonies who would dare stand up to you, and fewer who'd dare a second time." He saw Peter's uneasiness and said, "I understand your loyalty to your company and to Mr. Sutherland, and I respect that, for I'll expect the same loyalty to me. But realize what's in the cards for the Frontier Company, my boy."

The young couple looked at him as he spoke. "The company is doomed to fail; the main adversary is Bradford Cullen and his fortune, and you can't overcome him. Have no shame at breaking with Sutherland, for if you stay with him, then your own self-interest and the welfare of your pretty wife will be at stake."

Peter wanted no part of this offer, as rosy as it might seem. One glance at Mary told him she felt the same. She was staring at her hands, not the slightest enthusiasm apparent. Naturally, Johnson had no doubt Peter would accept. To encourage Peter further, he added:

"I know you have hard feelings for Cullen, and at the same time you favor Sutherland's firm. Well, listen, you can do Sutherland a good turn and keep an eye on Cullen by accepting this post. How? As it turns out, I have some, ah, dealings with Cullen—land speculations and such—and I owe the man a favor or two. To satisfy my debt to him, I've agreed to name as the Detroit commissary his present factor at Detroit: one Farley Jones. Do you know him?"

Peter and Mary were benumbed, and hardly responded to this dismaying news. With Jones in such a position of authority at Detroit, Cullen would have tremendous leverage to harass the Frontier Company. Indeed, if Peter accepted this job as lackey and strong-arm man for Jones, it was possible that some of the trouble the commissary attempted might be hindered or tempered. Yet Peter despised the very thought of being subordinate to Jones—despised the whole idea of being a ramrod for Johnson. He was about to refuse flatly when there came a knock at the door.

Into the room strode a giant, dark fellow, powerfully built and haughty. Peter jumped up and embraced him, crying, "Brant! Why you look like a schoolteacher in those fancy clothes! Mary, this is Joseph Brant, a chief of the Mohawk, the man who saved my life in the winter expedition two years ago."

As Brant bowed graciously to Mary, the troubling affair of the assistant-commissary position was momentarily forgotten. Brant was Johnson's right hand and his most important confidant in all Indian matters. As a leader of the influential Mohawk, and as one educated in a Connecticut seminary, this warrior in his late twenties was on the rise in the northwest and in New York Province.

Tall and handsome, carrying himself like a prince, Brant

spoke to Mary in a deep voice, saying Peter had told him all
about her during that harsh winter campaign against hostile
Delaware in 1764.

Mary blushed a little, saying, "I believe it was you, sir,
who wrote Peter's letters for him, and also read mine to him."

Brant smiled and nodded: "There were times when I pretended they were letters to me from my own sweetheart, and
that did me good, too."

Johnson laughed loudly and called for rum to be brought to
Joseph, but Brant declined, saying, "Your other guests have
arrived, Sir William, and they'll be shown in if you're ready
for them."

With a twinkle of mischief in his eye, Johnson said, "There's
an ancient Chinese saying that the more two people fight, the
more alike they become. Well, then, we'll see whether our
guests in the next room and you, Peter, have anything at all
in common. Prepare, my boy, to dine in the company of Bradford Cullen and family."

Johnson laughed as Peter and Mary flushed and tried to
control their surprise. Brant, too, found it humorous and said,
"At least you know they're here; they have no idea you'll be
across the table from them."

Johnson declared, "Not across . . . next to them, Joseph! I
want our friends to get used to one another from the very start.
I'm sure Cullen won't like to hear that you're Jones's assistant,
Peter, but it suits me to have a little hostility; you'll both do
better jobs."

Peter composed himself and said, "Sir William, I ain't accepted your offer yet."

Johnson was taken aback and looked sideways at the young
man. "Not enough money?"

Defries was about to get up and end the whole matter right
there, when Mary touched his arm and said, "Sir William, this
is all such a shock to us. You must understand, we have several
things to discuss in private, if you would be so kind."

Peter was confused, but Mary smiled at Johnson in such a
sweet way that the superintendent was effusively cooperative
about leaving them alone for a while. As he and Brant prepared
to go out to the Cullens, Mary added, with a touch of pique:

"And it would please me, Sir William, if you would be a
gentleman and inform the Cullens thoroughly about us and of
your offer to Peter before we meet them at table."

Johnson was a bit disappointed that his sport would be less

entertaining, but he acquiesced and bowed to kiss Mary's hand. "Anything you desire, my pretty one. Do understand that my intrigues were intended as innocent jest—a way of breaking the ice between your warring families. Be assured, they'll know everything when you come in. But don't be overlong, my friends, lest dinner be spoiled."

When they were alone in the room and the door closed, Peter nearly exploded with anger. Storming back and forth, he said he would have broken the bones of any other man who behaved as presumptuously as Johnson. It was only his close family connections to the baronet that had governed his temper. Mary cooled him down, saying:

"Husband, listen to me. I know you'll never accept Johnson's offer, but let's not waste this opportunity to do some good with it. Here's my plan . . ."

Half an hour later, the guests sat in candlelight around a sumptuously laden table, a violinist standing nearby, his music softening a somewhat tense atmosphere. It was not Sir William and Joseph Brant who were on edge, for they drank and ate with gusto, joking and talking all the while. Neither was it Mary—who cheerfully sat at Sir William's right and made a point to laugh at the baronet's crude mirth—nor Peter, who was uncharacteristically polite. Seated between Mary and Cullen, he was as talkative and friendly to the merchant as only new business relations can be.

It was Bradford Cullen, Helen, and Linda Cullen whose simmering resentment tainted the dinner atmosphere. The happier Peter and Mary became, the more somber and reserved were the puritan Cullens. Helen, a wrinkled, graying woman in her mid-fifties, hardly said a word all through the first courses. The homely, dark-haired Linda, who seemed to be following her father's path to obesity, soothed any inner agitation with platefuls of French cheese, stuffed oysters, and pickled herring. Cullen was in good command of his outward emotions, and he talked civilly with Johnson and Brant, but he would not address Peter and Mary unless spoken to first.

It was clear that Cullen despised the whole idea of Defries being the assistant to Farley Jones. As commissary at the most important trading post in the northwest, Jones could serve Johnson and Cullen at the same time, with his prime allegiance secretly being to the merchant. Defries would know too much and be a constant annoyance to Jones. Cullen could try to pressure Johnson to have Defries posted somewhere else, but he was crafty enough to realize Johnson wanted his own man as second in command at Detroit. In appointing Jones, Johnson reciprocated for Cullen's alliance in some secret land speculation, but the superintendent would not permit an ally of Cullen's to run Detroit's Indian affairs without close watching by someone who was impossible to corrupt: Peter Defries. Throughout the meal, Cullen suffered, and Mary watched him closely, ever ready to twist the knife.

Talkative and high-spirited, Mary and Peter played on the nerves of the Cullens. Johnson and Brant were both drunk, and they joined in the giddy laughter and boisterous chatter.

"Detroit!" Peter exclaimed and slammed the table hard, causing Linda to spill cider down her chin. "Ah, Detroit! What a place, eh, Cullen? And you, Sir William, know it well. I've heard you made your mark there years ago, dancin' and romancin' the women until dawn."

Johnson modestly shrugged that off, but said there was indeed a certain French lady who still corresponded with him.

Mary sighed, "Detroit! How I love that place! The rough walls, the river, the friends we have, and the lowly soldiers, the greasy, smelly Indians—"

Peter, seated at her right, kicked her sharply on the shins and said, "From Detroit I'll carry out your commands to every dependency post in the northwest, Sir William!" He eyed Cullen. "That rascal Jones an' I'll make a hell of a combination, eh? Too bad Jones is such a bug-tit—sorry, ladies—and couldn't fight his way out of a feather duster if he had a club. But I'll take care of the scoundrel, don't you worry, Cullen. If things get rough, I won't let anybody hurt him too bad afore I step in—"

Cullen shoved back his chair. To Johnson he said, "Let's drop all pretense of amity, Sir William. I know why you've appointed this . . . this . . ."

"Careful," Brant warned, knowing Peter's fury when unleashed.

Cullen swallowed and told his women to get up. Johnson said, "There, there, let's not spoil a good start with such bickering. Please be seated, Mr. Cullen, and ladies. Dessert has not yet come round. No one thought this would be an easy alliance, but I'm sure it will be profitable"—he stared directly at Cullen—"for all of us. Now, let's overcome our petty quarrels and behave as associates, if not as friends."

Sir William's persuasive power came more from his high rank than from Cullen's willingness to be soothed. The merchant was just beginning this liaison with Johnson, and he did not want to damage it with a show of stubborn opposition to Defries. He sat down, fuming, but once more in control.

It was Peter who spoke next. "Maybe, Sir William, if Mr. Cullen here and I have a private chat, we can overcome some of our differences." He looked at Cullen, and grinned in a friendly way. "What do you say, old boy? Give me a few minutes in the other room, and I think you'll find me a very agreeable chap."

Cullen was suspicious, but with the encouragement of Sir William and Brant, he agreed. Peter winked at Mary as he and the merchant went from the table to the sitting room, saying they would be back in time for dessert.

Defries closed the door, and Cullen sat down heavily in the chair Johnson had occupied earlier. Wasting no time, Cullen said, "Get on with it, then. What do you want from me?"

Defries was in no rush. He sat down squarely opposite Cullen, who was brooding and angry, and got comfortable. Before Defries could say anything, Cullen spoke up:

"You must want something." He tented his pudgy fingers and leaned back, eyes glittering, half-shut. "You ought to know right now that I'd never trust you for one moment, Defries! I know what you'll do at Detroit: You'll be a spy for Sutherland, an accomplice with his company. Well, that won't be so easy. Farley Jones will watch your every move; you'll know nothing that will help Sutherland, and within a year's time, I'll grind your puny company to dust." He laughed in a short burst, more like a snarl. "Your turn to speak, fellow. Shall we be friends, then?" He snorted and looked away.

Defries was cold but exhibited no hostility. "If I'm assistant commissary under Jones, you'll feel my presence at every slimy turn you make, Cullen."

A question in his eyes, Cullen asked, *"If* you're assistant commissary? *If?* So, it is a bargain you want, then! You're not so noble and righteous as you and the rest of your associates make yourselves out to be." He gave that derisive snort once more, looked up at the ceiling, then back at Defries and said, "All right, my man, what is it you want?"

"Emmy."

Cullen could not believe it. His face fell, eyes searching Defries for some deception. "The nigger girl?"

"Give Emmy to me, and I'll turn down Johnson's appointment as assistant commissary."

Cullen actually seemed troubled. He had never heard such a preposterous thing in all his life. He tried to laugh, but what came out was weak and shallow.

He asked, "Do you expect me to believe . . . to believe that you would give up a post like this for a nigger servant girl?" A sneer came across his face. "Do we tell your wife about her, or would you prefer to keep her somewhere in secret for your pleasure?"

Defries clutched the arms of his chair, knuckles white, the veins of his thick neck bulging. He whispered, "Don't say anythin' like that again if you want to walk out of here."

Cullen swallowed involuntarily. He began breathing heavily, his lower lip working. "You'll strike that bargain in writing this very night? Sir William will witness it and even that savage Brant if I have to have two witnesses. Do I understand you correctly, fellow?"

"You do," Defries replied, regaining composure. "You'll turn Emmy over to me, no strings attached, and I'll never accept a position with Johnson."

Cullen had a light of triumph in his eyes. He slapped the arms of his chair, bounded out of the seat, and said, "Done! The hell with dinner! We'll fetch an attorney—there's enough of them doing business around here—and I'll have the document made official before morning."

About to depart to ask Sir William for paper, pen, and ink, Cullen stopped at the door, his hand on the knob, and stared at Defries. He might have said a number of things about foolish idealists and romantic dreamers, but he did not. Instead, he shook his head and muttered, "I don't understand you at all."

They returned to the dinner party to announce the news to Sir William, who was disappointed but in no way angry with Defries; Johnson was too big a man for that. Brant laughed uproariously at the news, and the Cullen women were speechless. Mary sat in silence, trying not to weep for joy.

At dawn the next morning, Mary rode a horse to the Cullen residence, a small farmhouse rented for the duration of the council. She found Emmy in an outbuilding, boiling clothes in a cauldron, turning them with a long pole. Emmy was surprised when Mary cantered up, and fear came into the servant's eyes.

"Missy Mary!" she exclaimed. "Please don't let them see you talking to me. Please, they'll beat me!"

Mary leaped from the horse and hugged Emmy, who broke down and embraced her.

Weakly, Emmy mumbled, "Please go now, Missy, please."

Mary's eyes were filled with tears, but she was laughing when she said, "Emmy, Emmy, you're free! They don't own you anymore! We bought you, and right now Peter's signing papers to free you officially! You're free, Emmy."

Emmy staggered a little, and Mary caught her. Eyes searching Mary, the black woman put a hand to her own head, as though to make sure she was not dreaming. Both of the women were shaking, one with excitement, the other with shock.

At last Emmy found the strength to say, "Missy . . . you mean it, don't you? Lord in heaven! Lord in . . . Free? What am I to do, Missy Mary? I never been free before." Bewildered, she rubbed her face. Mary's arm was around her waist. "Free. Where am I to go?"

Gently, Mary shook Emmy and said, "If you don't mind coming to Albany, you can be Jeanette's nanny."

Disbelief changed to a flood of dizzying passions that caused Emmy to laugh and cry at the same time, just like Mary. They held one another, wiping their eyes with Emmy's apron, and all the while the pot of clothes was boiling much too hard over a hot fire.

Emmy settled herself. A life of struggle and hardship had given her the inner self-possession to master even immense joy. She took a deep breath, and said, "Missy Mary, I'd be proud to help make my darling Jeanette the most beautiful, best-mannered lady the town of Albany ever did see!" Then, as Mary kissed her cheek, she added, "But I'm old-fashioned and strict and I won't let her get spoiled, or—"

Realizing what she was saying, Emmy stopped, then muttered, "Lord in heaven."

Standing at a window of the house, Helen Cullen watched everything. Perhaps her husband did not comprehend why the Defrieses had done all this for Emmy, but his wife did. Somewhere inside this tough old woman was the memory of more tender days, of love and self-sacrifice. As she observed the two friends so happily together, Helen felt a sharp twinge of regret, or envy, or perhaps even sentiment—she could not tell. Yet whatever it was that touched her heart, Helen Cullen knew she had neglected something important, something that gave life more meaning and worth than ambition, money, and power ever could.

A few days later, as the final act of the long and solemn performance at the Oswego peace council, Chief Pontiac made a closing speech to Sir William. Standing under the canopy of boughs, facing the multitude of Indians and several hundred whites, Pontiac was a noble though tragic figure whose days of leadership in the northwest were coming to a close. It was said that no other war chief would ever again organize or inspire an uprising such as that of 1763, when the Indians of the northwest very nearly shattered British power completely in a simultaneous assault on thirteen forts.

During the conference, in a number of smaller councils, specific terms of the end to hostilities as well as fine points concerning trade regulations had been worked out. Pontiac's final statement as supreme representative of the northwestern nations was expected to be simply ceremonial. He delivered the white wampum belt of peace to Johnson, saying all war belts sent out to the nations in the past few years would be recalled, and they would number more than one man could carry. Then he went on:

"Father, when you address me, you address all the nations of the west. Father, this belt is to cover and strengthen our chain of friendship, and to show you that if any nation lifts the tomahawk against our English brethren, we will be the first to feel and resent it."

Sutherland found himself struck by those words. In light of Pontiac's earlier warning to him that civil strife in America might force the Indians to choose sides, this statement promising loyalty to the king sent disturbing thoughts tumbling through the Scotsman's mind. The French had little hope or desire to reconquer Canada, and the Spanish on the Mississippi did not have the strength to challenge British America. Who, then, would ever lift the tomahawk against the British king in North America?

chapter **15**

BAD NEWS

The fall and winter of 1766 passed rapidly for the Sutherlands, caught up with the endless affairs of the Frontier Company. Peter Defries and Jacques Levesque—Levesque would stay one more winter in Montreal—labored heroically to find trade goods, but there were not enough to assure a season even as good as the last, when they had barely turned a profit. Furthermore, with the arrival of spring, Parliament placed import tariffs on such essential trade items as glass, iron goods, paper, and lead. The currency of the Indian trade, these products became so expensive in the American colonies that only well-financed firms such as Cullen and Company could purchase enough to make the most of the western fur trade.

In this time, Cullen grew steadily stronger, winning over many trappers and small traders who normally would have thrown in with Sutherland. Since the Frontier Company could not supply the wares essential to these men, they had no choice but to join Cullen. Otherwise they would starve.

Farley Jones had become Sir William Johnson's commissary at Detroit, replacing Lieutenant Parker as overseer of the fur trade. Parker continued as liaison between the military and Jones, but he was essentially subordinate in power to the new commissary. The replacement for Jones as factor at the Cullen warehouse was Caleb Soames, the former Cullen employee. This stocky, aging Hampshireman, who had been twelve years in the frontier trade, was glad to have his old job back, and was a good agent for his employer.

In this anxious, grueling time for the Frontier Company, Cullen did a booming business. Sutherland's firm was eroded away until by summer only a skeleton—including the original partners, Jeb Grey, Mel, and Nate—was left. Owen Sutherland felt the pressure mounting on his company, like some great, destructive avalanche beginning to slide down upon what he had created.

Briefly, Owen thought about Jubal Swain, who, it was said, lived in New Orleans with a stipend from Bradford Cullen. He had heard rumors that Swain and Jean Dusten were secretly shipping illegal French goods up the Mississippi to supply Cullen's traders. Thus, Cullen was tightening his hold on the northwest, gradually gaining control of the vast Mississippi Valley trade, which tapped the greatest waterways on the continent.

To Sutherland's mind came a vision of Niko-lota, whom he had not seen since Oswego a year and a half earlier. Perhaps the Delaware—who was likely still searching for the two Swain boys in Indian villages—would come up to Detroit this spring. That would be a good time, for the Frontier Company members would meet then to discuss their next step in the combat for survival.

He and his people held on tenaciously, their close friendships keystones to the existence of the firm. Mel and Nate overcame the rift that had resulted from the Matilda Merriwether debacle, and by now were both deep in the study of Indian lore, natural science, and northwestern geography in the attempt to locate the fabled burial mounds that Mel believed held treasure. Like Mel, Nate was becoming convinced these mounds must be somewhere near the confluence of the Mississippi and Illinois rivers; but neither had the funds to organize an expedition there, in the heart of Indian country.

When Mel was employed in some work for the company, tutoring or giving violin lessons to Sally Cooper and others, Nate often took up where his cousin had left off, working out, in his own crude way, theories and deductions about the location of the mounds.

Their quest was still secret, and no one else knew about the treasure map, for they had various explanations for their studies, including the search for a Northwest Passage or a theory about Indians being one of the ten lost tribes of Israel. Naturally, Jeremy Bently was very interested, but for the moment, Mel put him off by saying the work was too complex to explain, and too far along for anyone new to help with it.

Matilda Merriwether and Reverend Angus Lee had married

last July. Ella and Sally continued as Matilda's close friends and sometimes confidantes, though Ella preferred to avoid the young woman's tedious gossip and frequent complaints about other women in her husband's congregation. Ella thought Matilda was overprotective of Reverend Lee, for more than once the minister's new wife suggested that a certain coquette had winked at her husband during a service, or said some hussy lingered overlong at the chapel door, sweet-talking the minister at the end of the service.

Matilda's jealousy was perhaps understandable in a newlywed, but Ella hoped she would get over it soon. There were some indications that the woman's unfounded suspicions were beginning to be felt by Lee himself. Ella had noticed that Lee was not as buoyant these days, nor was he as relaxed and enthusiastic during sermons. It appeared he was being careful not to seem overly friendly to anyone Matilda might suspect as a rival.

But of greater concern to the Sutherlands than the family affairs of friends was the struggle against overwhelming odds to avoid the company being swept away by Cullen. By early summer, however, one reliable source of trade items was firmly established: In the Wees-konsan, Tamano and Little Hawk had reopened commerce with Plains Indian tribes who produced pemmican. The exchange rate of pemmican for what wares the Frontier Company could supply was advantageous, and Sutherland's firm remained solvent throughout that late summer and autumn.

The particulars of this trade were a closely guarded secret to prevent Farley Jones or Caleb Soames from cutting into the pemmican commerce. Sutherland and Tamano orchestrated the exchange of barrels of pemmican for manufactured goods from other free traders doing business at forts Pitt and Vincennes. This way, they acquired additional goods to trade for Indian peltry, which was then shipped eastward to Defries or Levesque.

At the end of fall 1767, the Montreal branch of the Frontier Company was pruned with the return to Detroit of Jacques and Angélique, who intended to go to Michilimackinac in a few months' time and establish a larger, more permanent company presence there. The only remaining French partners in Montreal were Dr. and Mrs. Devalier, whose responsibilities now included the obtaining of trading permits and the registering of *voyageurs,* though, in truth, there was very little of either going on.

The year ended with no promise of improvement in the company's fortunes. With the arrival of December came both the last mail from the east and the first major snowfall. Ella tramped through the whirling white clouds to fetch their mail from the military clerk's office, and was delighted to find a letter from her brother, Lieutenant Colonel Henry Gladwin. Now living in the family estate at Derbyshire, England, Gladwin took great interest in the relationship between the colonies and the mother country. Much of the letter dealt with politics and economics, and too little told of Ella's friends and relations at home.

Sitting before the fire in their living room, with the two youngest children dozing on the rug, Ella and Owen contemplated the letter, which she had just read. Neither of them was cheered by the news that the British had no workable policy for the American colonies. Gladwin wrote that any hope of fair and intelligent government was futile. Changing ministers, conflicts between Whig and Tory, and power struggles between rich and rising classes had left British government in disarray. The angry colonies were paying a bitter price for such unstable rule.

Sniffer nestled closer to the sleeping Benjamin, who took the otter's tail in one hand and sucked his thumb, letting the sleek tail fall across his cheek. As Sutherland watched the animal turn on his back and fall asleep, the memory of Henry Gladwin's closing words echoed in the silent room. It was as though the man were repeating Pontiac's own dark prophecy:

Where all this will lead us, I dare not guess, for the thought of civil war in America pains me most unbearably. Have you considered what you would do if this unhappy possibility comes to pass, my dear ones? Are you aware that the time might come when Parliament demands America obey? What if Britain uses force to put down continued defiance? You and your young trading company should (if you will forgive my boldness in suggesting so) prudently consider your response in the event of this unhappy outcome, and be prepared.

• • •

Outside, the wind dropped, and the storm abated. As they sat quietly, pondering the weight of Henry's words, the Sutherlands assessed their lives. Neither spoke, but their thoughts were similar, for throughout the past months conversation had dwelt on the same subject again and again. It was the recurring problem of how to go on from season to season, and they felt as though their movement was in a downward spiral.

Briefly, Sutherland thought about the debtor's prison that very well might be his fate should they fail to keep the company alive. That cruel reality cut into him with such force that he stood up. Without realizing it, he began to pace the room.

Ella saw his anxiety and ached for him. Sniffer opened one eye and gave a sneeze, which jarred Benjamin awake. The boy began to cry, jerked the otter's tail too hard, and sent the animal scampering across the floor, yammering in pain. Sutherland forgot his reverie and looked down at the otter, who lay down at his feet and rolled over to have his tummy rubbed. The Scotsman knelt to the creature and thoughtfully stroked him as a shaft of sunlight broke through the clouds and fell bright and warm on the floor.

By now, both children were wide awake and fussy. Ella picked up Susannah, took Benjamin on her knee, then looked at Owen. Both smiled at the same time, and he said, "Let's stop thinking and take a drive in the sled!"

Benjamin cried out in pleasure, and Ella agreed it was the best idea she had heard in far too long. She had intended to pen a reply to Henry, even though the letter would not go out to England that winter; she would put off writing it until they returned from the drive. Then her head would be clear, her heart not so leaden.

Soon they all were bundled in furs and woolens, Susannah swathed to her eyes. While Ella filled a wooden bottle with hot cocoa, Owen brought round a red sleigh pulled by a sturdy brown pony, and as they clambered in, they heard a shout. Jeremy and Sally came running through the knee-high snow, eager to come along, but Owen refused gently, saying they should stay at home with Sniffer and shovel the paths around the house. Moping and grumbling, the older ones turned away, Jeremy picking up Sniffer, who had come out of the house and obviously wanted to jump aboard as well.

Ella called out, "There's cocoa and raisins in the cupboard! But don't let Sniffer get into trouble." Owen cracked the small whip, and the pony sprang away—but not before Sniffer scrambled up on Jeremy's shoulder and hurled himself through the air, just managing to clutch the back of the sleigh. Jeremy and Sally shouted, but no one in the sleigh realized what had happened until the terrified otter scratched and clawed his way over the top of the sleigh and leaped into Ella's lap. Snorting and blowing in distress, Sniffer burrowed under the bearskin and blankets, much to the delight of little Benjamin, who soon had hold of the otter's tail. Contentedly the boy took his thumb and fell fast asleep once more.

It was a glorious day, with the clouds now far away to the east, the sun low and orange in the sky. Warmed by the hot cocoa they had brought, and snug in their coverings, the Sutherlands enjoyed the jingle of sleighbells and the swish of runners as they flew over the snowy track. So far, no one else had ventured out on the road, and they had the pure, hushed world of early winter all to themselves. The sleigh followed the unmarked road on the bank of the river, and before long they passed places where the French were clearing snow from frozen ponds. Here children and old folk gamboled, some playing *la crosse* on the ice, others skating.

The smell of woodsmoke from *habitant* cabins was comforting and homey, and seldom did they pass anyone without stopping for a brief chat and being asked inside for refreshment. They refused invitations, however, for they needed time alone, away from the fort. They went as far as the bridge over Parent's Creek, the one called "Bloody Creek" ever since so many British soldiers were killed fighting Pontiac there.

Slowing at the bridge to avoid a mishap while crossing, they heard loud, rough laughter and whooping from downstream, where the creek emptied into the Detroit River. One look told Sutherland there were scores of Indians down there, drinking and carousing. Sutherland knew better than to venture among drunken Indians, for they claimed no responsibility for crimes committed while intoxicated. These redskins must have procured rum illegally, because it was strictly forbidden to sell it to them. Ella was uneasy as Owen stopped the sleigh to watch the host of staggering, rowdy Indians and half-breeds milling around an enormous bonfire.

"Owen." Ella touched his arm, for he was engrossed. "The children are here."

He nodded and slapped the reins to drive the pony a little

farther, where there was a turnaround. On the way back, they again slowed to cross the bridge, and saw that many lanterns had been lit for the gathering, anticipating a prolonged debauch. Now it could be seen that trade tables had been set up, though it was against the law to trade on Sundays. Ella again urged Owen to get them home before there was any trouble. But just before he started the horse again, there was a crashing from nearby bushes, and a shadowy figure staggered out onto the road, then collapsed.

Owen handed Ella the reins of the frightened horse, then leaped down to the snow and hurried to the man, who had fallen on his face. Blood on the back of his frock coat indicated that he had been stabbed; when Sutherland turned him over, he was dismayed to see it was Caleb Soames. Cullen and Company's factor opened his eyes, blinking when he recognized Sutherland. He groaned, cursed, and got to his knees, pushing Sutherland away.

"How bad is it?" Sutherland asked.

Soames shook his head and managed to stand. "Get away from here," he told the Scotsman, who held him from falling. "I'll be all right. The son of a bitch that did this is dead, and when my men get hold of his pals, they'll all be rubbed out." He gave a savage look that Sutherland had never seen before on this hardy, once-decent man. "Go on, before you get dragged into this!"

Realizing that Soames had been in some kind of brawl with his customers, Sutherland let him go, then asked, "Why do you work for Cullen?"

Soames grunted in pain and said, "I owed him too much . . . I won't go under in debtor's jail. That's all I'm sayin'."

The factor glanced anxiously toward the raucous gathering, where his men and the trappers were arguing, drinking, and trying to cheat one another. Drunken Indians, however, were no match for Cullen's wily traders. His chest heaving, Soames strode away. He was tough, and it was tragic to see him follow this crooked path.

Apparently Cullen and Company made such great profits in illegitimate trading that it was worth risking the necks of employees to do it.

Sutherland got back into the sleigh, covered his legs with the bearskin, and took the reins from Ella. It was a relief to leave the buzz of many angry voices far behind, and before long they were passing down the quiet road, with night rising over the river at their left.

"Soames is lucky he came out of that scrap alive," Sutherland said, and Ella felt a chill in her bones to think how perilous even legal trading could be. "He was a good man, but he's going downhill fast because Farley Jones looks the other way when Cullen and Company do this kind of dirty work."

"You never want to talk about it," Ella said, "but just what is Farley Jones to Cullen these days? If you'd rather not spoil our afternoon . . ."

Sutherland looked at his pretty wife, who was flanked by Benjamin and Susannah, both asleep. With Sniffer's nose poking out between them.

He replied, "It's true, I'd rather not think about that, and there's no way to prove beyond doubt that Jones is secretly supporting Cullen, but he never misses a chance to get in a dig at us."

Johnson's first appointment as assistant commissary had mysteriously fallen ill and returned home that autumn; until the man was replaced, Jones operated with a free hand, regulating commerce and producing rule after rule to limit the movement of traders.

While traders were obliged to submit all goods to the commissary for inspection and tariff duty, Cullen's shipments were never delayed very long. The few wares of Sutherland's that were coming through, whether trade goods or peltries, were inevitably held up for days, sometimes weeks at a time until Jones got around to inspecting them. When he did, the ultimate in duty was wrung from them. Though in Sutherland's case Jones went strictly by the book and could not be accused of grossly overcharging, the amount of duty Jones charged on Cullen's goods was unknown.

Precisely what Jones's books said about which traders paid how much was also a question that no one but Jones—and no doubt Cullen—could answer. Jones had no secretary to keep his books, preferring to manage them himself. This way he made sure no potentially damning records slipped past to reveal conspiracy and favoritism on his part.

There was considerable discontent among free traders who were sure Soames was receiving illegal goods such as rifled guns and ammunition of a heavy caliber, as well as rum and other illegal drink. Yet this, too, was hard to prove, for after

Cullen's shipments were inspected by Jones, they were divided and delivered to Cullen and Company agents, who quickly sent them out of the Detroit area for trading to distant tribes.

Ella asked, "What about the trading going on back there? Shouldn't we report it to the post commander and have it broken up?"

Sutherland slapped the reins as his pony came out of a curve, and away they went at a fast clip. "No, lass, we can't turn that mob in, for it would earn us hard feelings with those Indians for a long time to come; anyway, by the time soldiers got themselves organized to get there, the party would be over and done with, and there'd be no one to arrest."

They drove home toward the lamplights on the ramparts of the fort. The snowy ground was turning bluish gray as night came on, the air sharply colder. As soon as they drove up to their house and stopped, the door of their cabin opened and Jean Martine hurried out. Excited, and obviously waiting for them, he helped Ella and the children down, and spoke quickly to Sutherland, who had climbed off to see to the pony.

"Strange things are passing at Michilimackinac, *mon ami!*" Martine declared, taking the sleeping Benjamin from Ella as he spoke. "Lieutenant Governor Rogers has been charged with treason and is under arrest."

Sutherland and Ella could not believe it. A man with the most promising career of any official in all the frontier being under arrest for treason was simply impossible. Jeremy ran out, his young face strained by concern, for already he had heard the tale from Jean. Since Oswego, he had admired Rogers, and the news that the Michilimackinac post commissary had clapped the major in irons was horrifying to the boy.

Sutherland understood immediately that Rogers had proven too great a threat to William Johnson's ambition for absolute rule in frontier America. Hurriedly, Jean explained his own theory that General Thomas Gage—commander of the army in North America—and Johnson had colluded to break Rogers, to destroy his reputation, and to prevent his inevitable rise in colonial government.

Martine said, "The charges are absurd—they say he is scheming against the crown for personal gain, that he is illegally making treaties with the Indians and spending money on gifts for them without the authority to do so! Madness, lies—I am certain of it." Martine handed Benjamin over to Jeremy, whose eyes were empty as he turned away to enter the house.

Sutherland spoke so only Martine could hear. "Lies they may be, but if Rogers is to languish up there in irons all winter, he'll surely die before he's brought down to Montreal for trial . . ."

Martine whispered, "The Ojibwa sent a runner down from Michilimackinac, and this was how I heard of the arrest; listen, those Indians love Rogers, and they want to attack the fort up there and get him free."

Sutherland thought about that and slowly shook his head. "Those days are gone, my friend; the Indians cannot take a British post in winter—"

"Then this spring or early summer!" Martine hissed. "The army had better get him out of there, or there'll be a massacre, just like in the old days."

Hearing all this, Ella, too, turned away. She moved mechanically, without thought, as she put her small children to bed. A little later, Owen came in, gloomy and silent. It was time to prepare dinner, but Ella was in no mood to do anything just then. Circumstances were so overwhelming that she needed a release. She had to take some decisive action toward overcoming it all.

Soon she was sitting at her writing desk, completing a letter to her brother in England. There was something in particular she had wanted to write to him long ago, but always had put it off, hoping for better times, for the company's success without looking to outside assistance. She wrote:

> I cannot express it more bluntly, Henry. We can perhaps survive one more poor season, but no more. We are in dire need of a commercial link to goods and credit. There is no other way to establish a system of trade, outfitting of traders, credit for Indian trappers, and shipment of peltry. America is strong despite economic hardship, but there is a critical shortage of hard currency. Our company's market is in Britain, and it is from Britain that financial support must come if we are to survive.

Ella was relieved when she finished the letter and sanded it, for this was a step she had long resisted taking. Owen's pride had held her back, but now there was no other recourse open to them. Henry was acquainted with many wealthy Britons; perhaps one would be interested in a partnership with the Frontier Company. Then Bradford Cullen would not wield such irresistible power as he did now. Whatever could be done for the firm, it had to be done soon, or all would be lost.

chapter 16

THE VICTIM

On a hot, muggy day in late June, 1768, the schooner *Gladwyn* appeared at Detroit, coming down from Michilimackinac. Sutherland stood on the landing, gazing at the black-and-white vessel, which was anchored some distance from shore rather than being drawn alongside the dock. He knew the reason for this was that Robert Rogers was imprisoned on board. The plans of the Ojibwa to raid the Michilimackinac prison had been foiled by the removal of the prisoner, who was now being shipped to Montreal for trial.

To Sutherland's side came Jeremy and Sally. They had also heard that Rogers was aboard, accused of crimes against the king. Recalling the resplendent image of the man at Oswego two years previous, the children found it hard to believe Rogers was shackled on board the ship named in honor of Jeremy's uncle, Major Henry Gladwin.

"If he's a royal governor," Sally said, with Sniffer in her arms, "why do they keep him in chains? Why don't they treat him with respect instead of being so cruel?"

Sutherland replied, "It seems to me they want to break him, destroy his spirit." Almost to himself, he said, "Perhaps even kill him so he can't testify in his own defense."

Sally was aghast. Jeremy flared angrily, "They're heartless scoundrels, no better than murderers! Somebody should help Major Rogers!"

Sutherland led them away from the ship, which bobbed in the current, riding high at anchor as though not loaded with much more than its human cargo. Few ships had ever made the journey to Montreal without being heavily laden.

"So it is with grasping men like Johnson," Sutherland said to them. "They start their tricks, then have to go farther and farther; sometimes—" he turned to peer at the ship "—sometimes as far as murder."

Jeremy bitterly comprehended that even if Rogers was not

guilty, his confinement would punish him harshly. Unless the charges were proven to be without the least foundation, the former Ranger would have no recourse at all against his ruthless enemies.

Jeremy said, "Then all they need to do is arrest someone they don't like, keep him imprisoned over a winter to break his health, and his death won't even be called murder?"

Sutherland looked at the boy. Jeremy was as tall as his stepfather's shoulder. He was shooting up rapidly, and was broad and lithe. At thirteen Jeremy had big hands and gangly legs that foretold height and strength. Now his young, impressionable mind was being molded by this raw view of government corruption; Sutherland saw the intense pain and disillusion in the boy's expression, and felt it himself.

Sally, too, was troubled, her face buried in Sniffer's furry back, a tear glinting on her cheek.

Jeremy asked Owen, "Is there nothing we can do to help Major Rogers? Nothing at all?"

Sutherland pursed his lips, walked with them from the landing, and said only, "We'll see."

The Scotsman left them at the fort's gate, hurrying away alone without explanation, as though something had come to mind. Jeremy and Sally turned to walk home, neither talking, their heads bowed. Close to the house, Sniffer sensed feeding time, fidgeted in Sally's arms, and sprang down, bouncing hard against Jeremy and throwing him off balance. The boy's pent-up fury burst loose, and he aimed an angry kick at the other, barely missing. Sally pushed him back with a cry of dismay. Fists clenched, mouth working, Jeremy was mad at the world, and he wrenched himself away from the girl, who looked from her friend to the startled otter and back.

"Jeremy," she said. "Jeremy Bently . . . what's got into you?"

He was red in the face, staring hard at the ground, shoulders hunched, and he would not face her. Gently, Sally picked up Sniffer and came to Jeremy, who grudgingly looked around, then slowly regained composure. Touching the otter, who sniffed at his hand, Jeremy apologized, and Sally tried to smile. The boy's shaking hand brushed against hers, and she held it briefly.

"Sally," he began with a sigh, "I'm a fool, I guess, but it all seems so wrong, so terrible, and I can't do a thing about it."

Looking over his shoulder at the ship framed in the water

gate, tears came into Jeremy's eyes, and Sniffer nudged at him.

A little while later, Jeremy and Sally sat with the otter in the southwestern blockhouse, which offered a good view of the backcountry and *habitant* strip farms. Sally was listening to the pretty *voyageur* song from her little music box, and Jeremy was reading part of the play Rogers had given him— a permanent loan, the major had said generously back at Oswego. He was reading the scene in which two white hunters murder Indian trappers and steal their valuable peltry. By the time Jeremy finished, he was depressed, for the murderous whites showed no remorse, scalping the dead Indians, regarding them as no better than animals. He put the book down and stared straight ahead; Sally gently closed the lid of the music box.

There was one scene in particular from Roger's play about Chief Pontiac that haunted Jeremy. It had a closing couplet that he repeated several times until the words hung like an echo in the sheltered blockhouse. In this episode, two traders intoxicate Indian trappers with drugged alcohol and cheat them heartlessly. In the end, one white, an inexperienced trader, asks whether these Indians will be bent on revenge when they recover and learn what happened to them. The old hand laughs this off, saying they'll take revenge, but upon other whites, for he and his friend will be long gone with their booty.

> The guilt is theirs, while we secure the gain,
> Nor shall we feel the bleeding victim's pain.

Whispering those last two lines to himself, Jeremy got up and went to the palisade. He gazed along the wall of the fort to where the ship lay, drifting in the current, anchor hawser tight against the stream. For Jeremy, the guilt belonged to Johnson and Gage, who had made Rogers their victim. The boy smashed his fist against the palisades, and said aloud, "And they'll never feel their victim's pain!"

Sally was by his side, looking at the prison ship. "Poor Major Rogers," she murmured. "Jer . . . we have to do something."

"We do." His eyes half closed as he thought of a plan. "We will!" Then his resolve faded as he watched a sentry pacing back and forth on the *Gladwyn*'s deck. The boy had no idea what he could do to make the suffering of Robert Rogers less painful, but he had to try.

• • •

Near midnight, under cover of darkness, a small canoe slid out from overhanging branches at the bank of the Detroit River. Owen Sutherland in the bow and Tamano at the stern paddled silently for the schooner. Lanterns were hung aboard ship, fore and aft, but there was no other light. The guards and crew were asleep, save for a watchman who could be seen leaning on his musket near the bow light.

In Sutherland's canoe were food and warm clothing and a couple of bottles of strong drink for Rogers. After asking a few questions earlier in the day, Sutherland had learned the prisoner was being kept in the ship's chilly, miserable hold belowdecks. He and Tamano worked their way around the schooner, keeping well out of the pool of yellow lantern light. They swung out into the river, to approach from that side, where no sentries at the fort would notice them.

It was a dangerous venture, for if caught, they risked being charged with attempting to free the prisoner. They intended only to supply Rogers with items necessary to sustain life, but a nervous guard and a bullet knew no excuses at critical moments.

The soldier on deck seemed to be asleep on his feet. He made no move as Sutherland's canoe eased under the high stern, and Tamano grabbed hold of the dangling rope ladder normally used to suspend crewmen for painting and chipping the ship's hull. The only sounds were the rushing water and the creak of masts and rigging.

Sutherland put his weight on the ladder and began to pull himself up, feet pinching the lower part of the rope for support. Then, instinctively, he sensed that Tamano had become alert. Hanging from the ladder, not daring to go up or down, Sutherland stayed where he was. Something was moving a little ways off in the river, a craft of some kind, coming directly at them. Sutherland eased himself back into the canoe, and Tamano prepared to paddle downstream if this was trouble. They were in reasonably dark shadow and presumed they could not be seen, but if they were spotted, speed and skill would get them clear before anyone knew who they were. They hoped to avoid a fight.

Holding his breath, Sutherland saw the other boat close in. It was a canoe with four persons aboard. Moving without a sound, it shot toward them, at the last minute almost ramming them. There was a muffled cry of surprise from the figure in the bow. By now, Sutherland knew who it was.

"Jeremy Bently," he hissed. "I needn't ask what you're doing, or you, Sally, or you others."

Struggling with an urge to lambaste all of them, including Tom Morely and Little Hawk, Sutherland dared not make any further disturbance.

"Get home," he whispered, and noticed Tamano was trying not to laugh. "You hear me? This is not your affair!"

Jeremy whispered, "It is! And if you don't believe me, look at the top of that rope ladder." Sutherland peered through the dimness and saw the upper length of the rope ladder had been disconnected from the railing and hung back down the ship's side. The ladder was secured on running gear fixed only partway up the hull, so Sutherland could not get aboard that way.

He stared at Jeremy as Sally whispered, "We saw that this afternoon, when we scouted the ship."

Tom said softly, "There's only one way in to the major, and that's through the porthole up there."

Jeremy added, "But it's too small for you, Pa. I'm going in alone."

Sutherland saw a picnic basket full of food in the center of the children's canoe. Moved, but worried for them, he insisted they leave off and go back to the fort. Then, after looking up at the small porthole Jeremy had referred to, he realized the youngsters were right. Only a boy could get through.

Tamano sighed and shook his head, saying, "They're growing up too fast, Donoway."

A few moments later, with Little Hawk boosting Jeremy up and the men helping to hold the children's canoe against the ship, Jeremy struggled into the porthole, which had been left open for air. Inside, it was dark and very close. In his pocket was a tinderbox and candle. Finding the stagnant air hard to inhale, he fumbled with his tinderbox, unsuccessfully striking the flint and steel again and again.

To his shock, a deep voice said quietly, "This ain't the powder magazine; explosives are forward, but you won't get my door unlatched, so you best go back out the way you came."

There was a hoarse chuckle and a clank of chains, then a cough from deep inside Rogers's chest, a cough that sounded painful. Jeremy recovered from his surprise and told Rogers who he was.

"Well, well," Rogers mumbled. "So you liked my Pontiac

play that much, eh? Come in to talk about it some?" He chuckled dryly and coughed. "Guess I could write a couple more by now..."

"Shh!" Jeremy ordered, surprised by the forcefulness of his command. Finally, he struck the light and touched the candle, which cast a soft glow in the cramped room. He looked about, but found no one. Rogers could not be seen. Then Jeremy held the candle over his head so he could see where it illuminated the floor. The boy gasped in horror. Rogers, a wraith of a man, a skeleton, with sunken, feeble eyes and big teeth, laying in his own filth, his clothes rotten and stinking. Great manacles gripped his legs, and Jeremy saw they were agonizingly tight.

He felt dizzy, and swayed.

"Easy, lad," Rogers said. "It ain't so bad, young fellow; you get used to the smell after a while." He moved and the massive chains on his legs clinked eerily.

Jeremy leaned against the wall, nausea and faintness and anguish causing him to reel, his knees to buckle.

"Steady," Rogers said in a powerful voice summoned from the very depths of his indomitable soul. "Steady now, and speak up. Why are you here?"

In the light of the candle, Jeremy saw Rogers had changed, his eyes now aflame, his face taking on a quality that told the boy this man was unconquerable.

Rogers said, "You've done well enough to get this far, now complete your mission and get on with a good withdrawal."

Jeremy took a deep breath at the porthole, glanced briefly at Rogers, then leaned out over the canoes. They were waiting below with the sacks of food and essentials. From his waist, Jeremy quickly unwound a rope with a sling on one end, then played it out. One by one he dragged up the supplies. When Rogers saw what was happening, he chortled weakly, and could not keep from coughing.

Jeremy got everything into the cell and brought them nervously to the side of the prisoner. Rogers said, "That's somethin', lad! But you know, what I'd like most right now is a swig of fresh water."

Jeremy found a bucket in one corner near the small door, but the water in it stank. He went to the window to toss out the water, but Rogers sat up and warned, "Don't do that!"

Taken aback, Jeremy realized what a foolish thing he had nearly done. The sentry above would surely have heard the splash. But there was no water at all in the supplies. He poked his head out the porthole and whispered, "He wants water. What'll I do?"

From up above came the ominous click, click of the sentry pacing across the deck, no doubt making his regular rounds. He would be at the stern in a few minutes. Jeremy was determined to get some water, even though Owen said they had no way to send up any.

Crouching at the supply sacks, Jeremy pulled out a small bottle of whiskey. Rogers saw it, and made a sound of approval. When Jeremy took it to the porthole, Rogers winced and asked what he was doing.

"I'll have them below empty it and refill it with water—"

Rogers almost cried out, but restrained himself, saying, "For water? Waste good whiskey for—for—" Then he sighed and licked his dry lips. "Waste it, lad." He breathed heavily. "I surely can use some clean water."

Jeremy fixed the bottle of whiskey to the rope, whispered down what he wanted to do, and began to lower it. The sound of the pacing sentry was very close now, almost overhead. If the man happened to look over the side, he would see the two canoes pressed against his ship, and the rope hanging from the porthole of his prisoner's cabin. It was certain Jeremy would not get out without some struggle ensuing.

The bottle went down quickly, but just a few feet from Sutherland, it slipped from the rope and fell through his fingers. Sally caught it, hardly knowing what she was doing. Trembling, she offered the bottle to Sutherland, both with blank expressions on their faces.

The sentry walked slowly across the deck. Sutherland uncorked the bottle. It was fine Scotch; he took a deep swig. The watchman's footsteps came along the railing, and stopped. They heard him yawn and begin to sing to himself. He was just above them, humming and rocking on his heels. They froze, listening.

Suddenly a voice came from somewhere, gruff and angry. "Be quiet there, will you, Russell?" It was Rogers, who startled all of them by shouting up through a hatch that vented from his cabin onto the deck. "Come over here, Private, and tell me what time it is, what day it is, and what you're doin' awake at such a disreputable hour anyway! Come here!"

The soldier grumbled and went across the deck, away from the railing. As the man talked to Rogers, showing a certain respect for his prisoner, Sutherland and the others acted swiftly. The precious whiskey was poured with distressingly loud glugs into Sutherland's felt hat. Then the bottle was filled with river water and hoisted back up to Jeremy at the porthole.

A few moments later, Rogers asked the soldier to go forward and find out whether the vessel's name, *Gladwyn*, was spelled with an *i* or a *y*, because the correct spelling was with an *i*. The soldier said the major was dead wrong in that, and they bet a piece of eight on whether the spelling was Gladwyn or Gladwin.

"Who the hell was Gladwin, anyway?" the private asked with a yawn as he tramped off toward the bow to check the ship's name.

Inside the cabin, Jeremy prepared to leave. With one leg out the porthole, he looked back at Rogers, and saw the facade of cheerfulness was gone. Sadness and suffering were in the Ranger's eyes. Jeremy gazed at them, knowing he would never forget this moment as long as he lived.

With a trembling voice, he said, "I wish...I wish you victory, Major Rogers."

The great soldier received that as though it had been thrown to him, something to be caught. He closed his eyes briefly, then looked back at Jeremy. He was aflame once more.

With a voice that croaked, he said, "It's Bently, isn't it? Jeremy?" He smiled and held up the bottle of water. "I'll remember you. Regards to Sutherland and the rest. I'm not done for yet. Tell them all that."

Jeremy nodded. Then, just before going out the porthole, he felt an awful wrenching pain in his heart, and with a quavering voice, whispered, "God bless you, sir."

He pushed out into the fresh night air. At the last minute he thought Robert Rogers had said, "God bless," but it might have been no more than a sigh.

Jeremy was changed. Everyone noticed he was less lighthearted, more introspective. He was carrying something he could not understand, something that troubled and consumed his thoughts. At first, Ella thought he would quickly get over the shock of having seen Robert Rogers in chains, but as weeks and months passed, the boy went through his days as though detached from reality.

Ella and Owen talked about Jeremy, wondering what they could do to brighten his attitude, to reawaken his boyish sense of wonder. Nothing they tried worked. Even Sniffer paid a price for Jeremy's absorption with the darker side of life. The otter was not cared for as before; his master seldom played with him, and it was up to Sally to take Jeremy's place in the creature's world. Tom and Little Hawk tried to shake Jeremy out of his shell of meditation, but they got back little for their efforts, often only a sharp word or silence. Eventually the boys resorted to good-natured teasing, which all too easily became barbs that stung. One day in September Jeremy fought both of them at the same time—a fight he lost, though he acquitted himself surprisingly well.

Owen told his wife one afternoon, "He's outstripping both the others in speed and—I hate to say it—in sheer savagery."

Ella sat down on a kitchen chair. Owen was near a window, watching the boy, who was out in the grass, reading Swift's satirical *Gulliver's Travels* for the fourth time.

Ella said, "I know he has a temper when stirred up, but I never thought of him as savage or cruel."

"Not cruel, but he won't give up, and even against his friends he was willing to hurt them to win the fight."

They had talked to the boy about the canker of bitterness, but Jeremy's growing cynicism and disillusionment with life had put down roots.

"We have to do something," Ella said.

Sutherland thought a moment as he looked through the window at Jeremy. The boy's book portrayed a fantasy world that was all too much like reality. In Gulliver's adventures, nations went to war over the proper way to crack an egg; the absurd lands of Swift's acid satire were easily recognized as the lands of Jeremy's real earth. The boy must have realized that, and it undoubtedly intensified his gloom.

Sutherland went to the living room, took a book from its shelf, and went outside to sit down next to Jeremy. The boy looked up and said hello, then returned to Gulliver.

After a few moments, Sutherland said, "Jonathan Swift is funny, isn't he?" Jeremy answered that it would be funny if it were not so true to life. Sutherland said those were almost his own sentiments.

"But at least Swift is not so grim and downhearted about life, eh? I mean he's a brilliant man of letters who knows more about world politics and social relationships than the likes of you or I will ever know, yet he still has the remarkable inner strength to tell us about all of it in a humorous manner, and with some sympathy for the Lilliputians and the people of Brobdingnag."

Jeremy was distracted, thinking about that.

Owen said, "Now, that takes real genius, real force of character, as I'm sure a fellow like you who's read so much will agree."

Sutherland became eloquent about the need for a man to take a realistic stand in life, yet not to see the world as either too bright or too bleak. Balance, he said, is the sign of intelligence, courage, and strength. Jeremy was listening when his stepfather said:

"There are lots of intelligent folk, lots of courageous ones, and even more who are just plain strong. But a man who combines those essential elements with a deep understanding of reality—as Jonathan Swift does—he's different, greater than all the rest."

The words sank in. As they sat in silence for a while, the boy turned them over. Ella was at the window, unable to hear what was said, but watching anxiously.

Sutherland went on, "If we let the sorrows of the world, or even the joys, rule us, then we'll be buffeted about like rudderless ships in a storm, without control, without... listen, without hope. And without hope we can't go on. With hope we can accept things as they are and try to change what we can without ourselves breaking."

Jeremy snorted. "Who can change things? Could you change things when Pontiac started his uprising? Could you see everything so clearly? Did you stop the killing?"

Sutherland was pained by these pointed queries. It was true; he had been unable to prevent a bloody uprising, even though the Indians trusted him. All he could do was to aid the army at the decisive Battle of Bushy Run, which destroyed the eastern uprising and resulted in hundreds of dead whites and Indians.

Sutherland said, "You have to make your stand somewhere, lad, and it's seldom a clear or easy choice."

Jeremy softened. "How does anyone know where to make a stand? Everybody has his own ideas these days. Liberty Boys blame the British for colonial troubles, and other people say that's not true, that we make our own problems and should try to solve them peacefully. Who can you believe? Maybe if I hadn't ever met Major Rogers I would've just thought he was a criminal like the government says, but when I saw him again... when I saw him like that..."

Jeremy's voice cracked, and he fought back a sob by taking deep breaths. Owen put a hand on his heaving shoulders, and Jeremy began to cry, leaning over, his face close to the book.

Sutherland said gently, "You listen to your own heart. Perhaps that's no comfort, for everybody says the same thing. But it's true. You have to decide for yourself what's right, and you have to be able to change, to take a chance when your intellect's not sure. But above all, you have to keep the bad part of the world from breaking your spirit, the way it's breaking yours right now."

Jeremy sighed and roughly wiped his face.

Sutherland said, "You've got a long way to go yet, and a lot more to go through." He gave the boy Voltaire's *Candide*. "There's an answer in here about confronting life's difficulties. If you recognize it, and you're strong enough, then you'll have a good basis with which to go on."

He stood up as Jeremy fumbled through *Candide*. The boy said a hoarse thanks, then rose, and walked away, carrying both Swift and Voltaire. At the garden gate he heard his mother call that dinner would be soon. Carefully she asked where he was going.

Looking back, Jeremy said, "I have to find Tom and Little Hawk, Ma. I'll be here for dinner; I just . . . have to tell them something."

Jeremy was better after that. Voltaire's message of cultivating one's own garden rather than seeking a perfect world was a way of looking at life that had touched him. Though still more serious and sensitive than he had been before, the boy showed an inner resilience that revealed itself in everything he did.

It was in late October that news came of Robert Rogers. Peter and Mary Defries brought it from the east when they came out for the company meeting. Rogers had been found not guilty of any of the charges. At first Jeremy was deliriously happy, but his relief was cut short when Peter said Rogers would be kept in prison all that winter and spring until a formal approval of the verdict came back across the sea from England.

"Innocent!" Jeremy loudly declared to a room full of adults. "He's innocent, but they keep him prisoner for months! What kind of government do we have? And why do we support it if it's so cruel?"

Jebediah Grey, who had joined the Frontier Company soon after his army discharge, said in a deep, slow voice, "That's what a lot of Americans are askin', son. That's what I'm askin', too."

"Careful," Lettie told him. As yet, they had not married, but they were close to it. "Don't say such things aloud, Jeb, lest thee be accused o' treason!"

Jeb grumbled, but others said Lettie was right, warning their friend not to speak his mind so freely, in case someone overheard who would have him arrested for his opinions.

"Don't forget what happened to Rogers," Defries said. "An' he was a lieutenant governor."

chapter **17**

ILLINOIS INDIANS

The approach of the main trading season, which would begin in late November, found the friends together at Detroit under a black cloud of uncertainty. There was much of interest to be discussed: Trade matters and the political situation were dissected and evaluated from morning to night throughout that entire first week of the Defries visit. Peter and Mary—accompanied by Emmy and Jeanette—had brought with them the latest issues of newspapers from New York, Philadelphia, Boston, Albany, and Montreal. Every article, every published opinion—two were essays by Sutherland on the emergence of the new American—was brought up in conversation, meetings, planning sessions, and table talk.

At this time there was relative peace in the northwest save for occasional raids and killings or robberies along the Indian borders with white settlements. Each attack and counterattack kept hatred between red and white at a high pitch in western Pennsylvania, the eastern Ohio Valley, and in the backcountry of the southern colonies. Peter Defries, who still had close contact with Johnson and the Mohawk Joseph Brant, knew much concerning the Indian situation. Recently he had attended a major council at the western New York post of Fort Stanwix, where a treaty was signed ceding Indian territory to the king.

"I guess Sir William an' his cronies feel proud about that treaty," Peter said, while sitting in a circle of chairs occupied by the Sutherlands, Levesques, Martine, Jeb Grey, Lettie Morely, Tamano, and Lela. "They claim to have defined once and for all the boundary line between Injun territory and settled land." He made a sound of disgust.

"I ain't no Injun lover, but if I was a Shawnee or Delaware, I'd be mighty hot over the Stanwix treaty! Why, they pushed the damned Injun border from New York to western Virginia back miles an' miles, an' them lands mostly will be sold by the king to speculators—pals of Johnson's near every one of them!"

Defries said the Six Nations—the tribes of Iroquois who had been rulers of the country that was sliced up—were the main signers of the treaty; but the lands given to the government actually belonged to the Delaware, Shawnee, and Mingo. Those tribes once had been in subjection to the warlike Iroquois, but all that had changed in the past decade with the Iroquois strength diminishing.

Defries shook his head, saying, "Everybody knows I admire a nifty trade when I see one, but I don't like cheatin'! Why, there weren't a Delaware or Shawnee within a hundred miles of Stanwix! Anyway, they couldn't have got close enough to Johnson to object for all the merchants, Injun superintendent deputies, commissaries, syndicates, an' agents, an' politicians all coddlin' up to Johnson like hens to a rooster! About made me want to puke. 'Scuse me, ladies. An' wouldn't you know that a lot of the land Johnson bought for the government with a jug of high wine an' a handful of trinkets is claimed by Johnson himself! That's right! He says Iroquois granted it to him long afore the law forbade private land dealin's with redskins."

Defries was boiling, and ended his speech with: "They named one of the rivers borderin' one tract as Cheat River! Good, eh? At least they got a sense of humor."

There was a land hunger among whites, growing more and more ravenous. Colonies were demanding that Parliament give them ownership of western lands; associations of speculators were claiming tracts of "wasteland" on the Mississippi, the Illinois, and all along the valleys of the Ohio and Kanawha rivers. One powerful syndicate, calling themselves the "suffering traders," demanded Indian land as restitution for losses incurred during Pontiac's uprising in 1763. This was only one of several groups petitioning Parliament and the king for grants in Indian country, some of whom said colonial charters gave them the right to take up land as far west as the Pacific Ocean.

The pressure such groups put on Parliament was tremendous; it was even common to form secret partnerships with members of Parliament and thereby secure their votes. The Indians knew all this, for there were many among them who were educated or who had friends in high places informing them of various intrigues to take their country. Leaders of the tribes knew what was coming and saw that full-scale fighting could again break out. Yet they tried to delay warfare either until they were protected better by the government or until they could recover from the 1763–64 hardships and arm themselves.

Sutherland said, "If general fighting starts, colonies like Virginia and Pennsylvania are sure to send their militia to attack the villages, hoping for one final war to destroy Indian power in the east once and for all."

Jeb Grey said, "Times are changin'. Folks want land, an' Injuns got land. Settlers won't be stopped by the government, nor by what little the redskins can send against 'em." He looked at Tamano and said, "Sorry, friend, but you know I'm right."

Tamano let his gaze fall to the floor. "It will not end without bloodshed. We will fight."

At that, the meeting lost its vigor. Affairs of business and politics seemed too abstract and petty when the specter of another Indian war arose. Such a war would stop all trade for a long time to come.

Peter and Mary Defries returned to Albany in late October as the weather turned sharply colder and the northwest settled into seasonal routines. This was the time for prime beaver trapping to begin, when animals had acquired thick winter coats. Beaver, otter, and mink pelts taken through December would be sleek and glossy because those fur-bearers lived off accumulated body fat. Fox were best taken in mid-November, for a few weeks later, the effects of winter and malnourishment would begin to tell on the animals. Their color would become less rich, the fur deteriorating in quality as winter dragged on. Detroit was growing busy in those weeks of the season. Trappers were supplied, given credit, and departed for upper lakes or the western country.

By late November, when Cullen and Company were resupplying scores of Indian and *métis* trappers who had already brought in one peltry harvest, Sutherland's firm was out of goods, having traded the few wares Peter and Mary had brought out on their sloop. There were no goods left to give to additional incoming trappers who needed gear, blankets, tools, pemmican, winter clothes, presents for their families, tobacco, and essentials such as cloth, needles, thread, and ammunition. It was turning out to be a tremendous year of harvest, and it pained Frontier Company members to close their doors by the last week of November.

Refusing to let this latest setback depress them, Frontier Company partners made the best of a difficult situation. Jacques and Angélique remained at Detroit, for there were no wares with which to establish themselves at Michilimackinac. Like the other partners, they were cheerful and optimistic, living frugally for the time being on their share of the meager reserve funds of the company.

Happily, Angélique Levesque gave birth in December to a tiny daughter named Sylvie Annette, who looked just like her mother. This babe became the personal ward of Sally Cooper, who was losing her responsibilities with Benjamin Sutherland, for he was more independent these days.

The older children were developing into young adulthood, and were forever a source of excitement and interest. Sally had plenty of girlfriends, and she also developed a particular liking for training sled dogs. Ella taught her what she knew about driving a team, which was considerable, and Mawak took the lessons further until Sally was a master with the sled.

The three boys, Jeremy, Tom, and Little Hawk—with James Morely now and again joining in—developed physical and woodsman's skills, learning *la crosse,* hunting, and canoeing under the eye of Tamano and Jacques. Sutherland taught shooting, swordplay, and languages. Mel and Reverend Lee also gave them a wealth of knowledge, while Jeb Grey's stories about modern warfare lent them a grasp of military maneuvers and life as soldiers. They came to understand the fur trade from daily experience, much of it drudgery, and James was best here.

Around Christmas came news that lifted everyone's spirits: It was the announcement by Lettie Morely and Jeb that they were to be wed. By now young Tom had accepted the former soldier, who treated him well and filled the place left by his late father. It had not been easy for Tom to change his attitude, but the encouragement of Jeremy and Sally had cracked through his reluctance.

Tom's opposition had been broken down in part by a conversation on a day of Indian summer in early November. He, Jeremy, and Sally were at the fishing pond south of the fort. There was an old, rickety windmill here, where they often had played when younger; but now, with Jeremy almost fourteen, a year older than Tom and Sally, their interests had drifted from climbing inside the abandoned mill to having long conversations about life while sitting around the pond.

The sun was pale but warm as Jeremy and Tom idled that Saturday afternoon, their fishing poles dangling in the water, brown leaves drifting steadily down to cover everything. Sally was off by herself, strolling near the river, dressed in a pretty white skirt and blouse she had made with the assistance of Matilda Merriwether Lee. Sniffer was diving for sport, but the boys did not care that the otter was scaring off their fish. The boys were talking about Jeremy's adventures at Oswego two years earlier.

Tom tossed a pebble into the water, and it plunked near Sniffer, who spun around to see what it might be. "You get all the luck, Jeremy, goin' to Oswego an' all while I sat home clerkin' at Ma's storehouse." He often complained like this, though his envy of Jeremy's Oswego trip had not been brought up before. Tom tossed another pebble, and Sniffer whipped after it, diving with a smooth movement that caused only the slight parting of water. "If my pa was still alive, he'd have gone, and he'd have took me along."

"What do you want, Tom?" Jeremy asked. "You want to go out with traders and see the wilderness?"

"Anythin' at all except lurkin' behind a counter like brother James, countin' skins, weighin' 'em, tryin' to keep trappers from cheatin' us. I want to see things, go places. I'd like Philadelphia, I'll warrant, or even Fort Pitt! Anywhere but this place, where nothin' happens to nobody no more."

Jeremy had wanted to ask something for some time, because he knew how Lettie and Jeb felt about each other, and how Tom was toward Jeb. He said, "Wouldn't it make things easier if you sort of made friends with Jeb Grey, and let your ma... make better friends... you know?"

Tom stiffened and tossed all his handful of pebbles into the pond. "Aw, Jeremy, I like Jeb well enough. Jeb's all right. I just can't reckon him as my pa. Nobody can be my pa, not like..." He did not want to say how close he had been to his father.

Sally appeared, fresh and crisp and clean; she dusted off a log, brushing away dead leaves, before sitting down like an aspiring lady. She had heard most of what Tom said, and it was not new to her, for she had talked before with him about Jeb and Lettie. Tom had always changed the subject, or showed so intensely the hurt of his father's death that Sally had not continued the discussion.

The boys hardly acknowledged Sally's arrival. Jeremy said,

"If Jeb married your ma, like they want, you'd have a whole different life, and you could go places."

Tom got hot. "Different life is right! Somebody to tar me if I ain't behavin' just so; somebody to tell me what to do even if I don't want to do it. He's used to bossin' privates around, and I'd be lower than the lowest lobsterback with him in charge."

Without thinking, Sally spoke up. "Wish I had a real pa like Mr. Grey."

She said the Sutherlands were almost like parents to her, but not quite. The boys thought of Sally's own loss, how she had witnessed the murder of her entire family, and they knew she had seen more hardship than both of them put together.

Tom said, "This is different, Sal."

"How?" she asked.

"Aw, I can't say; it's just different, is all."

Sally had no desire to bandy words. "Now you listen to me, Tommy Morely! You're being downright selfish about your ma and Mr. Grey. Downright selfish, and you know it! You want things all your way, but then you get sour because you have to work at the trading house; you want to be the man of the house, but you don't want the responsibilities. And more than that, you don't care about your ma. She loves Mr. Grey, and he loves her. If you weren't so much of a fool, boy, you'd see that! But they haven't tied the knot yet because they hope you'll come around and—"

"Go on," Tom said, embarrassed, and unwilling to yield his point. "They don't care about what I want."

"By Jove!" Jeremy exclaimed. "Listen, mate, I know what it's like to lose a pa, and Sally's got it straight about you. Stop wallowing about in your own pity and stop keeping your ma from her heart's desire. I couldn't be happier with Owen as my pa, but that doesn't mean I forgot my real father. But I don't want my mother to go alone all her life."

Tom tried to force his attention to Sniffer, who was ambling toward them out of the pond, wet and muddy, but Sally took up where Jeremy left off, her weeks and months of restraint falling away.

She ended with, "One day you'll be up and out, doing all that roving you want to do. Who'll be with your ma then?"

"James," Tom said and tossed a piece of fish bait to Sniffer, who caught it cleverly and went to Sally with it in his mouth. Sally hardly noticed the animal climb onto her lap as she scolded her friend.

"James! Why, you're more selfish than I thought, Thomas Morely! And you don't do the memory of your father any credit at all. I mean it! *James* should take on the responsibility, you say! Why I'm . . . I'm absolutely . . ."

Sally could not think of an adequate word, but she got no further as Tom said dryly, "Dirty. You're absolutely dirty, Sal."

She looked from Tom to Jeremy and then to the drenched Sniffer, who was munching in the lap of her new white dress. She shrieked and jumped up, throwing the poor otter to the ground with a thud. Her dress was covered with mud, lake-weed, and the juice of the otter's foul meal. Sally howled again, and Sniffer bounded into the pond, dropping his food as he fled. The girl swung away and ran home as her friends looked helplessly at one another.

After a moment, Jeremy said, "It's not easy being a female, is it?"

"They got it tough," Tom agreed.

"Sal should've been a boy."

Tom thought about that, then said, "I don't know, I kind of like her the way she is. I guess she grows on a body after a while."

A grin came over Jeremy's face. "You're sweet on her, you are!"

Tom blushed and threw an armful of leaves at his friend. "Mind your own business, Bently. She's just a girl like any other, and I ain't sweet on nobody, you bug-tit!"

Jeremy went on teasing, and Tom laughed at him, but he did not try very hard to prove Jeremy wrong. After a while, Jeremy told him to think about what Sally had said concerning Jeb and Lettie.

Looking serious, Tom answered, "I guess I have been thinkin' about it lately. I guess I've been thinkin' too much about it."

"You so set against it then?"

"I don't know anymore. You done all right with your step-father, I guess."

They left it at that for a few weeks, until Tom finally made his change of heart public at the Christmas Eve party in his family warehouse. When Lettie made the marriage announce-ment, big Jeb beaming at her side, Tom volunteered to toast their health. That made it a happy Christmas, whatever else was not so good. Then, at New Year's, the company was blessed with other news.

Tamano, Lela, and Little Hawk arrived on New Year's Day,

having spent two months in the Wees-konsan and in the Illinois country. To everyone's delight, the Delaware Niko-lota was with him, and they brought a load of peltry so great that it required three big dogsleds to haul it to Detroit.

Little Hawk was Tamano's exultant herald to Detroit. Commandeering a draft horse that Jeb Grey kept stabled near the western gate, he stripped down to the waist, heedless of the cold. Painted head to breechcloth in purple and yellow streaks of triumph, Little Hawk dashed bareback through the fort, whooping and screeching until everyone came out into the snowy streets. The big white horse thundered ahead, Little Hawk standing on its back, a makeshift rope rein attached to the halter. Even Soames and Jones left their offices to see what the noise was all about. When Little Hawk charged past them, he shouted down, "Long live Pontiac! Long live Frontier Company! Long live Pontiac!"

It was a magnificent spectacle as the young Sioux rode in savage glory, hanging from the horse's neck or riding backwards, laughing and howling in his excitement. The streets were filled with folk when Tamano, Lela, Mawak, and Niko-lota came in with their great burden of peltry. Detroit residents were used to an occasional free trader returning with a sled loaded down, but these were three, creaking under the weight of prime peltry. As the Indians pulled up, a crowd gathered outside the Morely warehouse, and Lettie, Jeb, and the Sutherlands came out to greet them.

Sutherland saw the bundled pelts, felt something leap within himself, and turned to Tamano, who was beaming. They greeted one another by gripping forearms, and Sutherland exclaimed, "If I'm dreaming, Chippewa, then you are a heartless manitou to play such a trick."

Tamano laughed. "We are all dreaming, and Chief Pontiac is our manitou, for he has called upon his trappers to aid us once again." He turned to indicate the sleds, where Little Hawk leaped down from his horse and joined the others. "These furs come from Pontiac's followers, and they need not be paid for until next season! The chief has blessed us with the bounty of a hundred trappers because he wants us to defeat the merchant named Cullen!"

Ella hugged Tamano, feeling immense joy. These furs were worth thousands of pounds sterling. The company had been given an unexpected chance. Once before Pontiac had aided the company by bestowing a gift of peltry on Sutherland, but no one had thought the chief would support the company like this. In the flurry of welcoming Niko-lota, and the reunion of friends, Sutherland noted bitterness in the eyes of one onlooker: Farley Jones.

The commissary snapped that Sutherland best get these furs inside where their duty could be estimated. "It'll cost a pretty penny before I'm done," Jones said.

Niko-lota replied, "Sharpen quill, little man. Pontiac send more, much more. You be plenty busy."

Scowling, Jones turned away, sputtering at Caleb Soames, who stood nearby, arms folded. Sutherland looked at Soames, who nodded in acknowledgment of his competitor's triumph.

To Soames, the Scotsman said, "Better than a knife in your back, Caleb."

The Hampshireman made no reply. Then he followed Jones to the commissary's office. They had much to discuss, as did Sutherland and his partners. This windfall boon from Pontiac changed everything. Where there had been resignation there was now hope; where there had been decline there was soaring prosperity. Tamano and Niko-lota said Pontiac wanted to prevent the ultimate triumph of Cullen's firm, which had caused such hard times for Indians in the past. Too many trappers had been robbed, cheated, and even murdered by agents of Cullen, especially by Jubal Swain and his band.

"It was easy for Pontiac to call upon his people to support the Frontier Company this winter, Donoway, for they know us and love us," Tamano told him as the partners gathered in the Morely house for a celebration, food, and drink. "Another shipment such as this will be here when the ice leaves the waters."

Niko-lota, who had unsuccessfully sought Willie and Joey Swain in the Ohio Valley for many months, lately had been in the Illinois with Pontiac. He laughed loudly and said in Algonquian, "Never would anyone expect the Indian trapper to give credit to the white trader! The manitous must be astonished at how the Indian's world has changed!"

Sutherland translated for the others, then Mawak grunted in pidgin English that he would not tell this story to his children's children.

"Nobody never believe grandfather's words if I speak about it, you betcha! Better say fur-critters jump in grandfather's sack an' ask to be nice English lady hat someday."

• • •

The April breeze blowing down the Mississippi caused Lucy Swain to shiver, and she drew the woolen cape about her neck, covering the red silk kerchief. Jubal had given it to her a few years ago, just before they married. Sitting in the middle of a whaleboat under sail, Lucy wished this exhausting journey north from New Orleans would be over soon. Saint Louis was still a hundred miles upstream, however, so it would take at least three days to get there unless the wind changed and came from the south.

"Drop sail an' start pullin', you water rats!"

Jubal was in the bow of the thirty-foot craft, which was pointed at both ends and carried a lateen sail. "Dusten, take the tiller an' send Spider to me; I want him to tell me about them villages on the right."

Jean Dusten, the renegade French *voyageur,* had been dozing near the stern, where the skinny Illinois warrior named Spide-toah was steering by means of a long rudder. Awakening with a snort, Dusten obeyed. The Indian made his way past Lucy, who was in company with two other women and six men. As the men ran out oars or lowered canvas, Lucy listened to Spider tell her husband about the cluster of brown lodges at the base of a ridgeline a mile away on the right shore.

This was the village of Kaskaskia, Spider said in his soft, nasal voice. His English had improved in the three years he had been based at New Orleans with Dusten and Swain. Though despised by many, Spider was loyal to Jubal, like a dog with a master he feared. Along with Lucy and Jubal, Spider and Dusten had done well enough at New Orleans. Managing the shipment of Cullen and Company wares and furs going to and from the north, they all lived on a stipend provided by Bradford Cullen.

Now, at last, they were moving back to the northwest. Smelling the fragrance of purple wildflowers carpeting the prairie, and observing a buffalo herd watering on the western bank, Lucy thought back to New Orleans and wondered whether all that had been real. Never before had she known such financial comfort, and if it had not been for her obsession with her lost boys and her loneliness in a foreign city, she might have been content to stay in New Orleans.

Her placid existence there had changed recently when Dusten and Spider had returned from a trip north, bringing word of a very special "task" required by Bradford Cullen. Lucy knew nothing about it, except that Jubal was wanted in the vicinity of Saint Louis, a primitive French Creole settlement founded a few years earlier. She did not care all that much about Jubal's business, although she wondered whether they would have stayed in New Orleans had her latest pregnancy not ended in a stillborn birth. Would Jubal have been less restless with a child to rear?

What mattered most, however, was that Lucy was resuming the quest for the boys. She had made Jubal swear to her that within a year they would head eastward, back to Pennsylvania and then to Fort Pitt, where they would search for the boys among the Ohio Valley Indians. Though this broad giant of a river was a beautiful sight, Lucy was tired of it after two long weeks of sailing. By now she regretted having freed the Delaware, Niko-lota, who had caused the destruction of their settlement. She was sure his promise to look for Willie and Joey had been false. He had fooled an anxious, vulnerable mother in order to escape. He had been clever, that Indian, and Lucy was sure she had made a mistake to trust him.

Jubal too had changed somewhat in their years at New Orleans. At first, he was in a rage over the destruction of his empire in the northwest, brought about by the men responsible for his defeats of the past and for the loss of his hand. But a new, lucrative association with Cullen had mellowed him, and he grew used to the good life, putting on weight. Though none of the men who associated with him dared stand up to him, he was less belligerent and not so often spoiling for a fight as a kind of diversion. Lucy liked to think that living with her had cooled Jubal's volcanic temper. Though he was hard and sometimes violent, no one had ever treated Lucy better, more tenderly, or shown such insatiable passion for her. She was sure he seldom, if ever, chased other women, and never once had he struck her without good cause.

As Lucy gazed at the point of land poking out from the right shore, she heard Spider say, "There lives the old bad dog, but he got too many warriors around, and the fort's too close with all them Redcoats."

Swain rubbed his thick beard as they approached the bend in the river where the muddy Kaskaskia flowed down from the northeast. This was a great village of Ottawa and Illinois, where Pontiac lived—"the old bad dog" as Spider called him, using the lowest of Indian epithets.

The whaleboat plodded ahead against wind and current, and Lucy got a close look at the sprawling village, surrounded by

scrubby trees and grassland. As they rounded the point and
turned northward once more, the small, white Catholic church
of Sainte Genevieve came into view on the left. Here, the river
was busy with canoes and pirogues, and even a British whaleboat with traders or soldiers appeared now and again. The right
bank was covered with lodges, and on the road running up and
down that side stood the imposing, whitewashed masonry Fort
Chartres, which had a British garrison.

Swain directed the whaleboat to take the western channel,
putting a large island between him and the fort, just in case
some curious officer decided to come out and look him over.
Though Swain was no longer actively hunted in the northwest,
there was no point taking any chances of being challenged and
recognized. He had a task to complete, and it would be easier
if the authorities knew nothing of his presence.

For an hour, Spider whined about Pontiac. He said, "That
old bad dog lives off the Illinois like a leech; he sucks their
blood and gives nothing in return but high words."

From the back of the whaleboat, Dusten called, "He's got
'em tradin' with that damn Sutherland, though. They don't
mind none about doin' that, Spider, or why would they give
him all their furs on credit?"

Spider whipped out his scalping knife and tomahawk, crossing them, saying, "Not much longer, *mon ami*. That bad dog
Pontiac will no more rule the Illinois after Spide-toah is finished."

Swain snickered and said Spider would earn two kegs of
rum when he was through. "And a brand new tomahawk! Then
we'll see about gettin' Sutherland, once and for all."

chapter **18**

A SACRED PLACE

By the end of April, the Frontier Company had much to celebrate. Thanks to Pontiac's furs, which had been sent down to Albany to Peter Defries, the season had been a triumph beyond Owen Sutherland's highest expectations. Even with the difficulty in getting trade goods, this incredible bounty of furs— combined with Peter's cunning—would help to purchase enough to fill the Frontier Company warehouses. Everyone connected with the firm was happy that spring, and the joy was compounded with the wedding of Lettie Morely and Jeb Grey.

Following the wedding came a general festival to mark the traditional May Day holiday, and Fort Detroit filled up with revelers who camped all around the stockade. It seemed the only unhappy folk at Detroit were Farley Jones and Caleb Soames. The factor had taken to drinking and was seldom sober these days, but even he turned out for the festival, which included picnics on the fort's hundred-acre common grounds, a great ox-roast paid for by Sutherland's company, and all sorts of sports, music, and dancing.

The first of May was perfect, sunny and warm. A large puncheon platform had been set up, eighty feet on a side, where folk dancing, fiddling contests, and early-morning church services were to be held. Reverend Lee gave the Protestant sermon to more than eight hundred Anglos, and Sutherland was amazed at the horde of new faces in the congregation. Lee spoke to them of loyalty to the crown and of the righteousness of peacemakers. In these troubled days, the sermon touched many who were wavering, confused about the future and their place in it.

After the service, Owen and Ella strolled with Reverend Lee to where Matilda awaited her husband at the finish line of the *calèche* race already underway. These furious contests among French owners of the two-wheeled pony carts were always as dangerous as they were exciting. Driving at breakneck speed, scornful of peril, the *habitants* were like Roman chariot drivers who risked their very lives for triumph. A thousand spectators lined the road, which cut through the grassy common ground.

Ella carried three-year-old Susannah, with whom she had developed a special relationship. Perhaps it was the result of the dangerous birth, but whatever it was that formed it, mother and daughter had a closeness that even Lee noticed. Susannah was a delightfully cheerful child, always laughing and imitating Benjamin, who scampered about with Heera. The other children were off on their own adventure. Ella set Susannah on her feet, and the child ran away, blond curls flying as she tried to catch her brother. As they walked, Lee observed that Ella and Susannah seemed to communicate without speaking.

Ella laughed and said, "I can't explain it, Reverend Lee, but from the start we've seemed to know one another's minds—though we don't always agree! I imagine that when she grows up, we'll talk more, but understand less."

"Yes," Lee said wistfully, "sometimes people talk but don't understand. Now Matilda and I . . ." He took a deep breath and asked, "Ella, would you mind it if Owen no longer wrote poetry?"

Owen chuckled, and Ella said, "Why he hasn't written anything but essays for the past year! I don't mind, so long as his essays don't get him in trouble with the authorities."

Sutherland said, "Poets don't worry governments, but nettlesome essayists do."

Sutherland's often harsh criticism of the British colonial system had been published widely in American newspapers, drawing irate dissent from those—both Whig and Tory—who favored free rein to buy and settle Indian lands in the northwest. So far, there had been no direct threats to Sutherland, but perhaps if he lived in the East, where punitive garrisons were stationed in discontented New York and Boston, he might have come under sharper personal attack.

Lee knew all this, but his troubles were less abstract than political theories. He said, "You both know how, ah, demanding my dearest Matilda can be once she sets her mind on something. Well, it seems she has her mind set on my writing poetry."

Ella was enthusiastic. "Won't you include some in your sermons?"

Lee looked unsure of himself, and even somewhat pained. "Ella, that's just it. I have enough trouble writing sermons, let alone poetry! I'm no poet. I wouldn't know where to begin."

Ella said, "Tell her that, then."

"I have told her, again and again, but she refuses to believe me. She says I'll never know until I try—and heaven knows I try again and again." He looked with plaintive eyes at Sutherland, who was thinking of an appropriate reply.

Lee was truly distressed, and that was understandable, if one knew Matilda. She was now in sight, sitting in a carriage under her parasol, watching them approach.

"What am I to do?" Lee asked. "As it is there's hardly time to compose a weekly sermon, let alone verse. My Matilda grows daily more disappointed, I'm afraid. It is a confounding pickle I'm in!"

Poor Reverend Lee, Ella thought, as they greeted Matilda and exchanged pleasantries. Matilda was always especially charming to Owen, for she thought his poetry enthralling and often told him so. Lee sat down next to her, and received scarcely a nod as Matilda gave all her attention to Sutherland, who stood with Ella nearby. The crowd was beginning to cheer, indicating the end of the *calèche* race, and Owen called the children to stand near him.

The *calèches* came on in a cloud of dust, the first carts dead even. Sutherland and Ella held Benjamin and Susannah tightly as the carts whirled along the track toward them. The din of the crowd drowned out the sound of horses' hooves, and the first animals seemed to float upon the billowing dust that rose behind them. In a wild rush, the foremost pony and cart sped by and crossed the finish line just inches ahead of the next one.

People were complaining or laughing, some shouting for the judges to nullify the victory, because it was Little Hawk who had won, and he had done it riding on the pony's back instead of in the cart. As it turned out, the boy was declared champion, and Jean Martine, whose pony and cart he had used, was commanded by the judges to pay tribute for the unorthodox drive by supplying a keg of hard cider to the other drivers.

This was typical of the festival's cheerful, generous spirit, and the day passed with increasing vitality and boisterous fun. The newly wed Lettie and Jeb Grey were the toast of Detroit, and everywhere they went they were honored. Everywhere, that is, until they encountered a tall, lean fellow with a game arm. He was drunk, and made a rude remark about Grey's well-known anti-Parliament politics, calling them treasonous. If not for the arrival of Sutherland and Niko-lota, and for

Lettie's begging her husband not to fight, blood would have been spilled.

Sutherland and Niko-lota persuaded Jeb to leave the man to his bile, for this was a day to celebrate, not fight. Then Niko-lota hesitated, looking at the lanky, dark fellow, who was staggering away, swigging homemade whiskey from a jug.

The Delaware said to Sutherland, "That is the one called Thrower, one of Swain's men from the Wees-konsan." As Lettie and Jeb went off, Niko-lota told the whole story about Thrower: how he had knifed Niko-lota's cousin and how Swain had broken Thrower's right arm, which obviously was lame now. Somehow, Thrower had escaped after the battle that devastated the renegade settlement. Sutherland had seen this man before, and knew him as a mean layabout who took an odd job now and again, often picking fights. Thrower Simpson must know a great deal about Swain, and the only reason Niko-lota refrained from killing the man who had fatally wounded his cousin was because he might be very valuable to them alive.

In the middle of his thoughts, Sutherland was dragged by Ella to the puncheon floor, where people were forming up to dance a reel. Sutherland put Simpson out of his mind for the moment, and joined in the dance, glad to see Ella so full of joy.

Throughout the fun, Ella tried her best to think of a way of changing Matilda's mind about Lee's not being poetic. She was distracted from these thoughts by the highlight of the day's celebration: the grand fiddling contest that pitted ten of the best fiddlers in the northwest against one another.

Playing on the platform before hundreds of people, the fiddlers were judged until there were five finalists—one each: American, English, Scottish, French, and a *habitant* who had some Spanish blood. The American was Mel, who was in stiff competition with excellent musicians.

Ella found it impossible to tell which of the other four was best after each had played for the last time. Then Mel stood up to play, first addressing the judges and hushed audience:

"According to the rules of this competition, I'm to play a song from my own country as my final offering." He shuffled a bit and flexed his shoulders to relieve the tension, then prepared to bring the fiddle to his chin.

"Since my mother was half Spanish and half French, and my father was half English and half Scottish, and since all of me is a Jerseyman, or I should say, American . . ." That got a tremendous cheer from the crowd, where there were plenty so drunk that they cheered whether they understood him or not.

"Since that's so," Mel said, placing the bow near the strings, "I'll play like this . . ."

With a flourish, he played the very same tune the Frenchman before had played, and though it sounded different, it was just as brilliant. He went right into the tunes of his English, Scottish, and *habitant* competitors, and the crowd gave rousing cheers as they realized Mel was making a point about the diverse nature of Americans.

He had them in the palm of his hand when he paused, saying, "This next melody needs new words, but it's as American as can be." As he spoke, he was slowly playing "Yankee Doodle." Picking up speed, he broke into a bright rendition that was so delightful that the insulting meaning of the song's words were unimportant. People hummed the tune, holding up drinking mugs or clapping in time. They loved it.

At the end, Mel was the winner, champion fiddler of the northwest, and there was no one, British or provincial, who had imagined "Yankee Doodle" could be so wonderful to hear.

Except for her wedding to Owen, this was the happiest day of Ella's six years at Detroit. Sitting around a bonfire at twilight, she even found a solution to Lee's difficulties with Matilda. Ella drew Owen into a conversation about poetry with the minister and his wife. Though Owen had been reluctant and self-conscious at first, he had followed Ella's lead, praising Lee's sermons for their "inner rhythm" and "subtle cadence" that had all the elements of modern verse. Matilda was impressed and pleased.

Ella piped up, "Why Shakespeare himself could not have expressed better what you said to your flock today, Reverend Lee."

Matilda, leaning forward, asked, "Shakespeare?"

Sutherland caught on. "The bard tries to say the same thing in *Macbeth*, when the assassin contemplates betrayal and murder of his king. But you, Reverend Lee, spoke just as forcefully of the meaning of loyalty in the face of the storm as ever Shakespeare did. Don't you think so, Mistress Lee?"

Surprised by such flattery, Matilda stammered but agreed wholeheartedly.

Ella said, "Poetry comes in many forms, and not all poets can master the distinctive poetry of the devout minister, who makes manifest the will of the Lord with every sermon."

Matilda let it all sink in. It took little more to persuade her that she was wedded to a master of the purest, most eloquent poetry of the age.

The Sutherland family departed just after sundown, walking slowly back to their cabin at the fort. They went hand in hand, Owen carrying Susannah asleep on his shoulder, and Benjamin shuffling along at his mother's side. The river was black, reflecting stars. Down by the water were small campfires, where people were singing and enjoying themselves. Canoes were pushing off for home with weary Indian and *habitant* families. The evening gun sounded as the Union Jack was lowered—a little later than it should have been, for Lieutenant Parker, the officer of the day, had himself celebrated overlong. Parker, who had been such a good friend of the Sutherlands for so long, was soon going to be leaving Detroit to take command of the lonely, isolated outpost of Fort Chartres.

Ella said, "Wouldn't it be nice to begin building at Valenya soon? Perhaps this summer, if we can afford it?"

Owen liked that idea. "With Pontiac's support in the future, we'll have the house built by next spring."

Ella leaned her head on his shoulder, then they heard a cry from someone running up the path behind them. They turned to see Niko-lota hurrying through the gathering dark, and when he came close, his face showed anger and sorrow.

He panted, "Donoway, Pontiac has been murdered!"

"Murdered?" Sutherland could hardly believe what he was hearing. Startled, Susannah awoke and began to wail. Her father did not notice, for his mind was whirling. "How? Who did it?"

"The Illinois coward, Spide-toah, tomahawked him from behind! It happened ten days ago; I just got word from an Ottawa chieftain who came in looking for warriors to go down to Kaskaskia and take revenge. Donoway, it is said that Jubal Swain is behind this killing, and that he is at Saint Louis!"

With Susannah howling, Ella standing in shock at his side, Sutherland knew why this had happened. Swain had been directly involved in the murder, but the force behind Swain was Bradford Cullen. There was no doubt that Pontiac's support of the Frontier Company was more than Cullen could take. The chief had been killed to cut off this bounty of furs for Sutherland's firm. A white-hot rage settled in the Scotsman, and it was felt more than seen by Ella and Niko-lota. Susannah was disturbed by the immense tension that enveloped her father, and she kicked until he absently handed her over to Ella. This news had struck Sutherland with the force of a cannon shot, but the disaster was compounded by what Niko-Iota said next.

"There will be much killing, Donoway; the Ottawa are taking the warpath against all Illinois tribes to make them pay for what their brother has done. No one will be spared. The Illinois are doomed."

It was the Illinois Indian trappers, in the main, who had supported Pontiac's call for furs to be sent to Sutherland's company. If those tribes fled or were destroyed, the source of peltry would vanish with them. Swain and Cullen had wreaked terrible havoc once again, for no one could stay the hand of the vengeful Ottawa.

Though Sutherland said nothing at first, Ella knew what he was thinking, and she was not surprised by what he told Niko-Iota, then translated for her:

"I'm going down there! We can catch Swain if we move fast. I'll ask for volunteers, ten men in all, and we'll lay a trap."

Ella, fighting down fear, asked, "What about Farley Jones? He can stop unauthorized armed parties from going into Indian country, and you know he'll try to stop you."

Sutherland seemed not to hear her, his mind already on plans that would snare Swain near Saint Louis. Absently, he said, "Jones doesn't matter."

But Ella remembered the fate of Robert Rogers, who was viciously imprisoned by a post commissary. She knew Farley Jones mattered very much.

Things happened swiftly. By noon of the following day, word had raced through Detroit that Sutherland was going south after Swain, the murderer of Chief Pontiac. Owen's cabin swarmed with volunteers, red and white alike, offering to settle matters with the renegade. Sutherland could not take a large force with him, for supplying and equipping them would be impossible, and he had no formal permission from the army to go. He turned all but a handful away: Tamano, Levesque, Jeb Grey, Niko-Iota, Little Hawk, Mawak, and two others—Colin O'Donnell, a young Irishman and a former soldier employed by the company, and Alain Moreau, a *voyageur* who had many acquaintances in the Illinois, where he was born.

These were few, but enough for what Sutherland intended. He would use guile and stealth to isolate Swain, then kill him. Although Spanish authorities would throw them in jail if they were caught west of the Mississippi without a pass, Sutherland was willing to take that chance. He and his men could slip across the river, perhaps disguise themselves to move among Indians and *habitants*, then dig Swain out of his hole near Saint Louis.

By now, Sutherland had learned much from Niko-lota, who had queried the Ottawa recently arrived from Saint Louis. There was no doubt that Spider had done the killing, with Swain as instigator. Before long, Ottawa would swoop out of the north and take revenge on Illinois people whether they were guilty or not. In that attack, Swain might be frightened off and flee south to Spanish New Orleans, and there be safe from Sutherland.

As the Scotsman turned away the last volunteer with thanks for his offer, Sniffer darted in fright under the settee. Ella looked up to see Farley Jones at the door, his face ugly and threatening. Dropping the leather shirt she was mending for Owen, Ella stood up.

Owen put down his claymore, which he had been oiling. "What do you want, Jones? Speak up and get out."

"Don't be so impudent with me," Jones said, waving a letter with a wax seal, which he tossed on the table. "That's what I want, and you'll heed it or what was done to Rogers will be nothing compared to what happens to you."

Sutherland nearly pounced, but Jones scurried away and shambled out the garden gate.

"What is it?" Ella asked, coming quickly to her husband, who had picked up the letter and was breaking the wax.

Reading quickly, he said, "It's an official order from Commissary Farley Jones forbidding any armed party to go into Indian country . . . on pain of immediate arrest upon the charge of inciting the Indians and disobedience to the duly authorized commissary of the Indian Department."

"Oh, Lord." Ella put a hand to her forehead and leaned against the table.

"This won't stop me," he said. "I've been authorized to get Swain before, and Jones won't keep me from fulfilling a charge already given by Governor Murray."

Ella knew her husband was thinking with his heart, not his

head. "Owen, whether he can ultimately prove you guilty of a crime or not doesn't matter! He can arrest you, as they did to Rogers, and then—"

He took Ella in his arms and held her. She was trying not to cry. There was no question about it: He was going, and that was that. He kissed her. After a moment, Ella drew away from him and returned to the leather shirt.

"I'll have this mended in a few minutes."

There was a knock at the door, and they saw Mel and Nate standing there, hats in hand. The men were invited in, and when they offered to volunteer for the expedition, Owen apologized, saying there were enough already.

They had been prepared for this.

"Mr. Sutherland," Mel said carefully, "there's something my cousin and I have been meaning to tell you for some time now. It's about something that a man of your education might know... You see, sir, we have this treasure map..."

In the next ten minutes, Mel and Nate talked as quickly as they could about their map, Mel's theory, and the virtual certainty of the ancient burial site being at Cahokia, right across the river from Saint Louis. Sutherland's mind was moving fast, another plan developing that might draw Swain out of his refuge. The Scotsman believed nothing about Mel's buried treasure or the history involved, nor did he care just then. But he saw a glimmer of light: He might have before him the elements for a ruse with which to bag Swain.

"Do you know the man known as Thrower Simpson?" Sutherland asked Mel. "Well, find him and tell him I want to make a deal with him. This is what I have in mind..."

Shortly, Thrower, more or less sober, was sitting in Sutherland's cabin. Dressed in soiled linsey and doeskin, he chewed tobacco and let his long legs sprawl in front of him. At first he maintained a look of disdain on his darkly handsome though grimy face, but Sutherland ignored the man's attitude; he would put up with it if the result was the capture of Swain.

"Thrower," Sutherland said, "I guess you know more about Jubal Swain than any man at Detroit."

"You guess right." He worked his right shoulder as though the very mention of Swain brought back pain. His arm had never healed from Swain's cruel break, and it bothered him, though he was still deadly with a throwing knife in his left hand. "But ain't nobody kin prove nothin' about me an' him."

"You want to pay him back for ruining your arm?"

Thrower looked around for a place to spit but saw none. Sutherland let him be uneasy, and said, "You work with us, and I'll let you be the one who finishes him off."

Thrower had difficulty talking because his mouth was full. He did not have the nerve to spit in a flower vase on the table, as he would have done in a lesser man's home. Awkwardly, he stood up and got rid of the juice out the window. Coming back to his chair, he asked Sutherland just what he wanted.

"Go to Swain, and tell him I'm at Cahokia looking for Indian burial grounds."

Thrower leered and shook his head. "What 'n hell you be doin' that for, by gad? Injun burial grounds? You some goddamn scientist or somethin'?"

"There's a reason, and you'll learn it if you bring Swain in. Tell him I'll be digging there in three weeks; if he's got the guts, he'll come over to kill me . . . maybe even get rich while he's at it."

Thrower was confused. His cheek stuck far out with the wad of tobacco, which did not move as he thought hard about this.

"You want Swain to come kill you?" He guffawed again, but really was not sure whether he should laugh or not. "I don't git it."

Sutherland said, "You convince Swain to come after me, and I'll do the rest. He won't know I'm ready for him, because he'll think you're just an old pal of his trying to get back on his good side, right? Say we hired you as a laborer for the digging, and we had no idea you were a friend of Swain's. He'll think we're easy pickings, and he'll come over. We'll know he's coming, because you'll lead him in by the way I tell you to. Then we get him, and you get him."

Thrower's eyes glittered with a kind of hunger. Perhaps it came as he thought of killing Jubal Swain. Perhaps there was another reason. After some thought, he started chewing again, and said:

"That hoss ain't no child, son; you're jokin' with some crafty son of a bitch." He eyed Sutherland, who made no reply. "Your plan better be foolproof, or this nigger ain't interested."

Sutherland told Thrower about Mel's search for an old Indian culture at Cahokia, saying it would be simple to set up Swain. "You have to convince him you want to get back on his good side by crossing me and leading him to us."

Thrower thought it through, saying finally, "What makes you think that boy'll believe me? He knows I got a grudge against him."

Sutherland sat back in his chair and considered that. After a moment, he said with disappointment, "Maybe you're right. It'd take clever talk and a deal of stomach for a man to take the chance I'm asking you to take."

Thrower chewed faster.

Sutherland said, "I judged you wrong; I need someone who's smarter than Swain and has nothing but ice in his veins. You know anybody I can count on who's man enough?"

Thrower got up, went to the window, and spat. His face was drawn when he turned around, eyes hard.

"You got yourself a spy, Sutherland, but I'll be paid good for it, by gad, or I don't leave Detroit."

They made a bargain, and when Thrower left, Ella came downstairs, having heard everything.

"You can't trust him," she said immediately.

"I know," he replied, buckling on his claymore. "He'll join Swain, and that's what I want. Thrower will try to set us up instead of Swain. Swain will think we don't expect Thrower to double-cross us."

"It's so dangerous," Ella said and hugged him.

"It is, but I want to finish Swain this time . . . I want him to come to me for sure. If he knows we're there, he'll come. I'll be ready. It's something that has to be done, Ella."

Ella did not like the risk. She did not want her husband's life to hinge on the erratic behavior of a man like Thrower Simpson. Yet she had no better plan; no one did. And when Sutherland explained things to the others, they, too, were willing to gamble that Thrower would lead Swain to them. They only hoped Swain would come for them on their terms, not his own.

The night before the men left, the families of the partners in the company shared a good dinner. The evening was not a festive one, but everybody accepted what had to be done. Jeremy, eating in silence next to Sally and Tommy Morely, had resigned himself to the fact that he could not go out with his father. Though nearly sixteen now—big and well made—Jeremy did not have the experience of the other men, or even Little Hawk. Sutherland was proud that Jeremy was willing to accept his limitations.

Jean Martine lifted his glass of wine to toast the men who

would be going out, and the others raised their glasses and drank. Angélique, whose baby slept in a crib nearby, gazed at Jacques, and their eyes caught and held. Jeb put his arm around Lettie's shoulders, and Tamano and Lela remained sitting quietly, though there was no question what each was feeling. Ella took Owen's hand under the table and squeezed it tightly; tonight, when they were alone, she would hold him as though he were never going away.

Three weeks later, Sutherland's party paddled down the east bank of the Mississippi, which was overgrown with trees right to the water's edge. Here and there was a cluster of Indian lodges near the water, and across the river, though not to be seen from here, was the village of Saint Louis. If Sutherland's plan went as it should, Thrower would cross the river in the next few days and find Swain.

Each time Sutherland urged Mel—who was in his canoe with Tamano and Little Hawk—to put in to shore, the fellow insisted they go farther. They turned up a small stream through some forested flats, and behind came a canoe with Levesque, Thrower, Nate, and Mawak. A third canoe bore Jeb Grey and Niko-lota. With them were Alain Moreau—the stocky, cheerful young *voyageur,* clean-shaven and proud—and Colin O'Donnell, a big redhead of thirty, with blue eyes and a bushy mustache.

The journey from Detroit down the Illinois River had been long and hard, the weather hot, and game scarce. There was little time to hunt, for they had moved fast, and day after day their diet had been mostly pemmican and peas, enough by now to disgust even the voracious Mawak.

Mel followed his map, and seemed to know exactly where he was going. Though Sutherland was more concerned with finding a place to ambush Swain, Mel's excitement and rising hopes convinced him to press on up a small stream until they arrived at a village of Cahokia Indians. This place was a dismal clutter of shabby lodges, badly kept vegetable plots, and was overrun by a horde of snapping dogs. The inhabitants were hardly to be seen, for they were petrified that Sutherland's party had come to wipe them out in revenge for Pontiac's death. These poor people, a tribe of the once-strong Illinois Confederacy, had generations past faded and grown weak. After some time, the Cahokians were persuaded to come out, but when they recognized Mawak as an Ottawa, they quailed, begging his forgiveness. Mawak was appropriately stern with them, but he longed to shed no blood. Yet his very presence made the tribe cooperative, and they answered, through Alain Moreau, all Mel's questions about the area.

They said there was, indeed, a great flattopped hill nearby to which they did not dare go, for it was a "place of spirits." Mel was trembling with excitement, knowing he was finally closing in on his objective. After a few more questions, and a polite sharing of tobacco and bread with these sad Indians, Sutherland led his men away through the trees to find a good campsite. Once again Mel took the lead and insisted they follow him.

"Look, Owen," he said as they tramped along a hunting trail through swamps, "you want to defend high ground, right?"

Sutherland replied that such was often military principle, but he cared only for the right spot to overpower Swain, wherever it was.

"If this place is what I think, you'll have an ideal ambush! There will be very few trails there, and—" He stopped short, gaping ahead. Pointing, he gasped, "There it is!"

All Sutherland saw was a gentle rise above the trees, a small wooded ridge, and nothing more. Mel burst away up the trail, and the others followed wearily. They had no idea what this nervous fellow was after—except for Nate, who caught the excitement and dashed up the slope behind his cousin.

Sutherland followed through the woods, picking his way up soft ground that seemed to have been tilled once, though it was a rather steep slope. Near the top, the trail turned downward again and did not go all the way to the crest. Here Sutherland saw where Nate and Mel had barged through the thick undergrowth and forged ahead, breaking through saplings and fallen deadwood.

From above came a cry of joy, and when Sutherland found his two forerunners, they were clapping one another on the shoulders and jumping up and down. He reached the top of the ridge, which was bare of all trees for a circle of forty feet in diameter. With others behind grumbling at this increasingly steep climb after so many days of canoeing, Sutherland asked what the yelling was all about.

Then he thought he knew why Mel and Nate were excited: This place had a remarkable command of the flats on all sides; and even though it was only a hundred feet or so above river level, it offered a glorious view of the Mississippi Valley. With his spyglass from here he could see distant Saint Louis, and they could easily spot canoes crossing the river.

He commented on this to Mel as the others collapsed all around and caught their breath, complaining that this was no place to camp, for there was no water here. Mel replied, "That's fine for you, Owen, but look, and you'll see that I've got other things in mind."

Mel began to point out small rises here and there that dotted the swamps and flats. Sutherland was not impressed, thinking them only hillocks, though they did occur in an unpredictable and illogical manner, as though nature had placed them whimsically. There was no other high ground of any size within five miles, but these small circles, or mounds—as Mel named them—stood scattered around this main rise all the way west to an inlet of the river, five miles off.

Mel said, "If my theory's right, those are burial mounds, and each of them contains secrets! Count them . . ." There were many, and as Sutherland looked down, he found it easy to pick them out of the overgrown flatlands.

"There's quite a large one," he said, pointing to a rise directly across a fairly open area below. Then he noted that there was a linear formation of several rises—mounds—on the right and left of this open ground. They seemed to form a sort of inner courtyard. "Quite interesting."

Mel told Sutherland that the mound they stood on was man-made.

"So enormous? By Indians? Are you daft, laddie?"

"Look," Mel said, taking Sutherland around the perimeter. "Can't you see it's square? And below us, there's another tier, also flat and rectangular! Owen, this is something to stun modern natural science."

A gravelly voice said sharply, "We go now! No should be here!" It was Mawak, who looked grim and troubled. "This is no place for Injun! No place for white man! We go now!"

Niko-lota agreed, saying to Sutherland, "My people have the ancient Walum Olum—the Red Record—and it tells us about such sacred places as this." He looked at Mawak, who was nervously fidgeting nearby. "The old medicine man feels something, and I believe we should not be here. This is a magic place."

Sutherland translated for the others, and Mel said science and reason were real, but magic was not. Then Jeb Grey grumbled, "Magic or not, it ain't got water, an' I want to soak my feet an' my arse afore I bed down tonight; let's get down, make camp, and talk later."

The rest agreed. Mawak and Niko-lota were the first to leave the flattopped mound, and as the men filed back down to the trail, Tamano stopped near Sutherland and said:

"I, too, have heard legends of such places, Donoway." He was uneasy. "It is not good to be on this mound. Great things have come to pass here, and it is not for us to stand upon it."

By now, Sutherland did not know what to think. Sure enough, Mel's deep research and scientific methods had brought him accurately to this mound. That told Sutherland that some truth might lie behind the fellow's deductions that this must be some relic of a past civilization. Sutherland conceded that much, but the superstitions of the Indians about alleged spirits and forces manifested here failed to move the Scotsman. Linking up Mel's science and Indian beliefs would take considerable reflection on his part before he made any final judgment. For the moment, at least, his immediate worries were neither theories nor pagan superstition. He had to be ready for Jubal Swain.

chapter 19

DEFEAT

The next morning, Sutherland stood on the stream bank as Thrower Simpson pushed off a canoe and climbed in. The man had his instructions: Make Swain think he had double-crossed Sutherland, and guide Swain into a trap on the western trail leading to the flattopped mound. Swain and Thrower would be expected at dawn after five days.

Sutherland told Thrower, who backed his canoe into the sluggish creek, "Tell Swain we'll be gone on the sixth day, so he has to come for us or lose his chance at me. And don't forget, take the west trail—we'll have a guard there all the time, so we'll spot your approach before you get within a mile of us."

Levesque was at Sutherland's side, and he called to Thrower, "Keep your arse down when the lead begins to fly."

Jeb Grey yelled, "Wear a flower in your hair so I don't plug you first."

Thrower sneered, and said he was not concerned about the marksmanship of a former soldier. "Don't worry about Jim Simpson! Just leave a piece of Swain for me when it's done."

He turned the canoe and paddled away, the others watching him until the ripple of his craft in the water was all that was left of him. Dragonflies flitted through the muggy air, and clouds of mosquitoes plagued the men as they talked among themselves about what Thrower would really do.

Levesque said, "If all goes as we think and Thrower really does join with Swain, they'll come after us before the five days is up."

Sutherland said, "That's what I expect. Even if Swain wonders whether Thrower is a Judas or an ally, by the time he gets done puzzling through which it is, he won't know what to believe. But he'll know where I am, and he'll come for me with all his men, one way or the other."

Levesque loosened his red waist-sash and retied it. "I hope, *mon ami,* we are ready when he comes."

The rest of the plan—which Thrower did not know—was to establish a false camp at the foot of the great mound, and there keep a fire lit through each night. Around the fire would be dummy figures lying as though asleep. When Swain approached, he would be seen by one of the guards placed at the entrance of both trails leading past the mound. Sutherland's men were divided into two hidden camps, without making fires at night; each camp was positioned near a trail to move on Swain's force when the warning was given by either of the guards.

The plan hinged on the two guards staying alert for Swain's arrival. Then, when Swain attacked the dummy camp, the trap would be sprung. It was a complicated plan, and Sutherland was uneasy about it, yet he had no better way to draw Swain out of Saint Louis.

Sutherland worked tirelessly, taking extra shifts of guard duty, patrolling endlessly for sign of Swain, and going among the Cahokia Indians to learn what they knew about the renegade. The other men on the force were also always on the lookout, taking only brief rests, but no one worked as hard as Sutherland.

While the other men patrolled or rested, Mel and Nate dug a pit in the east side of the great mound. The other whites were uninterested in Mel's progress, but the Indians, even Little Hawk, seemed troubled. Several times each hour, Mawak drifted close to the digging to watch Mel and Nate labor furiously with pick and shovel. The old Ottawa never came too close but observed from a distance, saying nothing.

When not on guard duty, Mawak and Niko-lota sat together, talking quietly about what they considered a sacrilege. They were not yet so upset that they demanded the digging to stop, but they muttered about dire consequences and curses. Ignoring them, Mel and Nate dug on, almost obsessed in their frenzy to find treasure. When Mel discovered a copper amulet the size of his thumb, it caused considerable excitement in the party. The amulet bore the image of a bird-man, Mel said, indicating that this civilization had contact with South and Central American cultures currently being unearthed by Spanish explorers.

That first day ended with even Jeb Grey and Colin O'Donnell digging when they were not on guard duty. In the evening the men split into two groups, with the Indians and Sutherland joining Mel and Nate at one of the concealed camps. Those who were off duty—including Sutherland, who was taking a much-needed rest—talked in darkness, slapping at mosquitoes and gnats, the chirping of crickets creating a din in the forest around them. Mel and Nate were excited, but the Indians were morose.

Mel exclaimed, "Why, there's scores of mounds around here! We could dig for a hundred years and still not uncover all they hide."

Mawak muttered, "Ancient ones not give up old secrets so easy."

Nate smacked a mosquito on his neck and declared, "I ain't after secrets; I'm after gold, old fella! If there's more jewelry down there, ye'll get yer share, too, an' ye'll be the richest medicine man in creation! Don't that cheer ye up?"

Mawak said, "Maybe it go bad for you. Mawak heart troubled . . ." He got up and moved away into deeper darkness near the trees, where he could not be seen. From there he said, "Take care, friend. Whites not understand . . ."

Mel, exhausted from his hard work, called out, "If Indians don't come into the modern age, the age of pure reason, not superstition, then they'll be crushed by progress!" His voice cracked: "Mawak, I'm not transgressing against Indians! I want to know who they were, and thereby who they are today! Science can tell us much, and I believe if we find treasure buried with the dead here, then others will seek to dig and to learn about your past! Mawak, Indians will be respected as never before; don't you want that?" No reply. "Please believe me, I want no part of defiling what is holy to you, but in the name of science, we must go forward! We must cast aside fear and superstition once and for all! Really, Owen, I'm not one who would ruthlessly dig up graves . . . I have a calling, a—a—"

Mel sighed. In the dimness, Sutherland saw him lie back and pull a blanket over his shoulders. The Scotsman knew Mawak was rich in lore, and knowledgeable in what his people called medicine. There were times when he thought Mawak a kindly but senile fellow, harmless and amusing, but tonight Mawak had sounded strangely dynamic. There was an air about the old man that told of something deeper than one who was no more than a tale-spinner who liked rum. There was something, but Sutherland could not tell what, that tugged at his mind. He wondered whether Mawak actually knew old secrets that no white man ever would know.

Further, it was unusual for Mawak to abstain completely from drink, and he had been sober from the very moment they arrived at the mounds.

Sutherland got up and strolled to his old friend at the edge of the clearing. The Ottawa acknowledged Sutherland with a faint grunt. The Scotsman looked up at the velvet sky sparkling with stars. Through the trees he saw the top of the largest mound, and presumed Mawak was contemplating it.

"What is it about this place that makes Mawak so cheerless?" Sutherland asked in Ottawa.

Mawak thought a while, then replied, "Were it not for the need to avenge Pontiac, Mawak would not remain here; there are ghosts, there are memories, and there are forces beyond my understanding—and I understand much of my people's medicine. This is a sacred place, Donoway, and we should depart soon."

Sutherland was impatient. "We have come far, Mawak. We have come for Swain, and soon he will be in our grasp. Would not the ancient spirits want us to avenge Pontiac?"

"Avenge him, yes. But while we are here, we should not dig into the center of . . . into the . . ." For just a moment, Sutherland had the eerie feeling that Mawak was drifting off, then the Indian's voice came forth clear and strong. "This was once the center, the source of a great fire, a great power that has never been equaled since. To be party to its defilement haunts my Indian blood, and tortures my soul. Ah, Donoway, my heart is in great pain . . ."

Mawak slumped against a tree, and Sutherland grabbed him to prevent a fall. He helped the old man back to his bed near the others and eased him down. Breathing heavily, Mawak said he must sleep, must dream, and remember. Niko-lota joined Sutherland, the young warrior a darker silhouette against the night all around.

The Delaware said, "Old Mawak feels more things than I do, yet what I feel I dread."

With that, Niko-lota went out to relieve Levesque, who was the guard on the trail nearest to their campsite. On his way to the sentry post, the Indian stopped at the false camp, pausing at the edge of the trees to make sure no one was lurking nearby. Then he went to the fire and piled it with wood, stacking enough to burn all night. Before leaving the campsite, he glanced up through the trees at the top of the mound. He could not look at it for long, and turned away to take Levesque's place.

The following day, the digging went on, with the four men finding more bits and pieces of a forgotten people—shards of pottery, flint arrowheads, and some beads made of seashells. The heat of the sun was overpowering, and at midday all but Mel stopped working. When he returned from his patrol, Sutherland had to persuade Mel to rest before he took sick and collapsed, but he did not pause for very long.

"This is it," he exclaimed, eyes glazed. "We'll find the barrow of a king, and with the body will be treasure!"

Deeper and deeper went the hole, which was six feet square and twenty feet down on a steep angle into the side of the mound. Near suppertime, Sutherland heard a cry of astonishment from the site. He was coming back from a scouting trip toward the river when Mel's voice rose in an almost hysterical wail of joy. Sutherland trotted forward. Though the heat was oppressive, Mel was leaping and skipping about, holding something over his head. The others in the hole, dirty and running with sweat that blackened their clothes, were leaning on tools, watching with a mixture of excitement and concern as Mel cavorted happily. The Indians appeared just before Sutherland came close enough to see what Mel was holding. As Sutherland ran into the clearing, Mawak howled with anguish and charged Mel, knocking him down and snatching away what had been found.

Sutherland and Niko-lota caught Mawak, holding him back from attacking Mel, who lay stunned on the ground, foam flecking his lips.

Mawak was shouting in English, "No more! No more!"

Niko-lota and Sutherland had Mawak by the shoulders, trying to calm him, for he was shaking, head to foot. In Mawak's hands was the skull of a child.

Near nightfall, in their lonely campsite, Sutherland's group sat in silence. Mel had recovered, though he was light-headed and nauseated from exertion. With Mawak's assault, the digging had stopped, and now Sutherland was trying to mend things between the Indians and Mel. Nate sat nearby, also spent from so much work. He was talking to Sutherland, saying there was surely treasure down below, and old Mawak must realize that only ignorant superstition was causing all this trouble.

After a while, Sutherland was only half-listening. He had been moved by Mawak's anguish, and still saw the image of the old man with much ceremony replacing the skull in the hole. No one had opposed him, though Nate had been uneasy, knowing that something important was so close at hand.

Niko-lota sat with his head hanging, and Mel was huddled in a blanket, not a word coming from him since regaining consciousness. In the gathering twilight, Sutherland watched them all, and now and then looked through the treetops at the mound. He did not believe any ancient power spoken of by Mawak could affect him, yet it was repellent to desecrate whatever graves lay under the mound.

Nate was saying, "This is only some old burial ground what don't belong to nobody! Why, it ain't even their tribe, not Ottawa, not Delaware, so what's eatin' 'em?"

Mel sighed, a sound that was loud in the heavy, muggy silence. He looked over at the Ottawa and said, "I have thought much about all this, Mawak; my heart has been hard and closed. I don't know what to say to you, but I'm sorry if I have done wrong here."

Mawak said nothing, but Nate exclaimed, "Now what in blazes makes ye so down in the mouth, cousin? For God's sake, Mel, after all these years o' searchin' an' scrabblin' an'— I mean after all this ye be on the brink o' success, an' ye be apologizin' over Injun superstitions? Listen, I respect Mawak here, an' I like him, too, but that don't mean I have to believe what he believes, nor fear what he fears neither! Why, I ain't no heathen! I'm a . . . a . . ."

Mel said emptily, "Grave robber."

Nate slapped his forehead and howled in a prolonged moan of exasperation. "I ain't! I ain't! This ain't no churchyard, by gad!"

Mel said, "All my research, all my studies never prepared me for what I'm thinking now, cousin, though it was always plain for any fool to see." The others listened as Mel explained how his pure reason now had nowhere else to go, unless it was incorporated "with what we call faith; or is it called piety, or reverence? Whatever you call it, I encountered it the hard way the moment Mawak struck me.

"I might never have grasped it if the shock of that blow had not brought me back to reality, forced me to think about what I was doing, and about this place and its true meaning. This mound was built by a great people for lofty scientific and religious purpose...and here I am, with pick and shovel and arrogant icy reason guiding every stroke, gouging away at something that my own reason tells me was created by a power higher and purer than even my own reason itself." He looked at Sutherland and said, "Does that make sense to you?"

Nate groaned and appealed to Sutherland, "Tell the boy what's what, will ye, Owen? Appeal to that natural law an' reason both o' ye worship so much!"

Sutherland looked at Mel and then at Mawak. Without meaning to, his eyes drifted again toward the crest of the mound. He made no reply as Nate went on with urgency:

"There be treasure here, Owen!"

"Perhaps."

"The boy's figurin' has paid off, an' ye can't deny it! Whatever else ye believe about this place, ye got to admit Mel's been right up to now, an' we got to believe he's right about the treasure! Don't ye believe that, Owen?"

Sutherland was still looking up at the mound. "Aye. This is a special place, and likely even there's treasure...of some sort here." He gazed at Mel, who looked away. "But a man has to make decisions about things, and how far he wants to go to get at them, to possess them."

Mel looked around, eyes big and sad in the dusk. He said, "I...I suppose I might have been wrong...about the treasure part, I mean."

"Wrong?" Nate exploded and leaped to his feet. "How kin ye say ye been wrong, when ye ain't been nothin' but right? What'n tarnation? Cousin, ye be a doodle-brain! Ye be a doodle-brained, addlepated...*scholar!* That's what! An' if it wasn't my sentry-go right now, I'd give ye a piece o' my mind that would make me sorry in the mornin'!"

Nate picked up his rifle and bag of ammunition, grabbing a handful of parched corn. When no one was looking, he also put in his shirt a flask of rum, for he felt like drinking to forget his disappointment with Mel. He stomped off into the woods to relieve Jacques Levesque, who would sleep at the other camp tonight, then with a few of those men go on a scout at dawn. They would scour the countryside and visit with the Cahokia Indians to ask again whether they had any worthwhile information about Swain.

Soon after Nate left, Mawak, Tamano, and Little Hawk went out on their own nightly patrol toward the creek. They would swing around the dummy campsite, follow the water-course toward the Mississippi, and later scout behind the great mound before returning once again by way of the false camp. By five in the morning, they would come back to Sutherland's position, their duty then taken over by Levesque's patrol. In this way, the area would be well searched for Swain's band, and with the two sentries posted on the only trails, it would be difficult for Swain to surprise them.

After the Indians departed, Mel let his head fall on his forearms, which rested on his knees. He sighed, and Sutherland said, "I'll take your watch later tonight, laddie. Get some sleep, and think about all this. I have to do the same."

Sutherland lay down and drew up his blanket as night settled over Cahokia. He found it hard to still his mind, which was in turmoil with conflicting ideas. He wanted to sleep, for in two hours he would be awakened by Nate, and then he would take a four-hour shift, his and Mel's. He was tired and anxious, yet sleep came only slowly. After a long time, he checked his pocket watch. It was nearly ten, and Nate would be back in an hour.

If Mel was correct about these mounds, then the heritage of North American Indians was far more spectacular than pop-ularly believed. Indians were not a primitive race that never had risen higher than its present development. Rather, they had been powerful once, highly developed, and linked to kindred civilizations thousands of miles away. Could Mel uncover truths that would astound the scientific world? Did the legends of Christian, Jew, and Indian have a common source? If under-stood, could the meaning of Cahokia alter the entire under-standing of human history? And what should Sutherland do about it? Help Mel dig, or support Mawak's beliefs that this was a holy place to be left undisturbed.

What would he do if this were a churchyard in Aberdeen-shire, Scotland, and the graves were his own forebears, and Christian? The answer was clear. Its relationship to this Cahokia burial ground could not be denied. He accepted the answer, and with it came welcome sleep.

Sutherland awoke to hear wind rustling through the trees. It was dark, though the sky was starry and gave some light to the clearing. He tried to see the time on his watch, but the hands were difficult to see. Then he realized something was wrong. It was an hour past midnight. Nate should have awak-

ened him long ago. At that same moment he knew there was
no breeze at all.

Hardly moving, he felt for his claymore, sliding it slowly
from its scabbard. Only he and Mel, sleeping twenty feet away,
should have been in the clearing. But men were at the edge of
the trees. How many he could not tell, yet they could not be
friends or they would have shown themselves.

His rifle, leaning against a boulder nearby, was loaded, but
too far to reach without starting trouble before he was ready.
He wanted whoever was out there to show themselves first.
Where was Nate? Then, there was no more time for questions;
someone was creeping out of the woods, crawling on all fours
toward Mel. Sutherland gripped the sword. The shadow slipped
to within a few feet of Mel, and Sutherland saw the dull glint
of steel. Another figure came out of the woods, crouching low,
and then another.

Without making a sound, Sutherland leaped to his feet and
sprang over Mel, his sword slashing and stabbing with silent
ferocity. It was Spider he cut down, and the Indian gave out
a curdling shriek of agony. Near the bushes, a rifle pan flashed,
igniting a torch that flared brightly, illuminating the clearing.
Sutherland sprang past the writhing Indian, answered the death
rattle with a war cry, and rushed Jean Dusten, who brought
his rifle up to fire. But the claymore struck first. The gunbarrel
was knocked aside as the hammer came down, and the shot
missed. Dusten whipped out his tomahawk and tried to defend
himself. Sutherland's blade whisked over the Frenchman's head,
causing him to reel in terror.

Then Mel was at Sutherland's side, swinging a shovel like
a wild man, charging the figure holding the torch. This was
Thrower Simpson, who had led these killers through the woods
to find Sutherland. Simpson tried to switch the pine torch to
his game right hand and pull out a throwing knife at the same
time, but as he did so, Dusten took the point of Sutherland's
sword and staggered back, ramming against him. The torch
fell. Sutherland whipped it up, throwing it into the forest at
the same instant as a rifle went off.

Sutherland was jerked around, a bullet crashing into his hip.
He spun, falling, but held on to his claymore. The shock of
his wound dizzied him, but he managed to roll away immediately from where he had fallen. In the next instant, a shadow
leaped to that very spot and, letting out a fierce scream, struck
the ground with a tomahawk that threw off sparks as it hit

rocks. Then the clearing was black and silent.

Sutherland lay still, listening. Two men were moving in the darkness. Was Mel one? At that moment, he found himself close to his rifle. Edging toward it, making not a sound, he took the rifle by the butt and lifted it to himself. The throbbing pain in his hip was hideous, and he could barely move without gasping in agony.

He tried to make out who was with him. In a few moments, his men might arrive, having heard the musket report, but that was no sure thing, for the patrol could be a mile off. Was Nate alive? Was the other camp already overwhelmed? Did Swain have more men with him?

Bringing the rifle to bear on a moving shadow, Sutherland used all his willpower to keep from groaning in pain and re- vealing himself. He feared the shadow might be Mel. He dared not fire until he knew. His eyes made out the other man, and he was certain there were only two. If they both were enemies, he could bring down one, but the other would know where he lay, and he would not move fast enough to escape. In the darkness, Sutherland heard whispering, and the clatter of a ramrod driving home a bullet. They were together. Neither of the men was Mel.

Then the shadows were backed by trees, and Sutherland could not see them. He had to wait, listening as they scoured the ground. One of them kicked at a body. Sutherland's rifle was awkward and cumbersome. The pain caused his eyes to go suddenly out of focus, sweat drenching him. All he could hear now were mosquitoes buzzing. The others had stopped moving.

There was a rattle in the bushes at Sutherland's left, and he swung instinctively, realizing too late that the sound was a thrown rock meant to startle him. He had made a mistake, and the first shadow loomed, quickly charging in. Sutherland's rifle went off with a flash and a loud bang, lighting for an instant Thrower's face, revealing utter disbelief. He collapsed onto Sutherland's feet, wrenching the injured hip, and it took all the Scotsman's strength to heave the body off and slide away.

Leaving his useless rifle near Thrower, Sutherland dragged himself across the ground until his back was against a tree. Swain might hear Sutherland move, but the renegade could not be sure there was not another bullet for him. Sutherland listened for anything that would tell him where Swain was. He thought he heard the cry of friends coming to the rescue, but was not sure. They had better come soon. The pain was a torment, and it was difficult to pay attention to the darkness. His leggins were wet with blood. Sutherland gritted his teeth and held his breath to stay conscious.

The claymore felt immensely heavy, hard to hold. His ears rang, and images darkened and faded before him. Through the trees he could make out the skyline of the great mound. Gazing at that bulk against the stars, he felt himself fading away, almost forgetful of peril, when a shout came from the distance, and another. His party was definitely on its way, making plenty of noise, pretending to be more numerous than they were, because they feared the worst and hoped to scare off Swain.

Sutherland's eyes were open, but nausea, pain, and dizziness obscured his vision. He fought against losing consciousness. Was that movement over on the right? He thought he was still conscious, but could not be sure. Holding the claymore as though it were a spear, he drew his dirk from his leggin. A shadow flitted back and forth, hard to follow, silently closing in, not offering a clear target. It might be just ten feet away now, or perhaps it was not there at all. His eyes went out of focus. The pain bore him away, away to merciful unconsciousness . . .

"Sutherland!"

The rasping voice came from straight ahead. Sutherland, in his dream, sensed the body had moved to the left in the same instant. It was as though he could actually see Swain dart aside, could see him through the blindness of night and delirium. He let fly with the claymore, roaring with the force of his throw, then rolled away, over and over, hearing Swain snarl—the retort of a wounded beast.

The trees came alight with torches flashing here and there. This was a desperate method of counterattack, but Sutherland's men had no time to lose, and risked their lives to save him.

With only the dirk in hand, Sutherland lay on his right side, battling against passing out. He heard movement to his left. He tried to turn that way, knife ready.

Then, "Die, Sutherland!" echoed inside his murky consciousness. A gun went off, blazing like a sun in darkness. Pain smote his right side, and he began to slip from reality, refusing to cry out, refusing to surrender to the awful, throbbing agony overwhelming him.

Footsteps. Distant shouting. Someone running in. Did he
see torchlight or was it another shot that a dying man could
not hear? Sutherland groaned, giving himself away.

At first light, Tamano and Little Hawk ran back up the trail
from the Cahokia village. Niko-lota, Levesque, and Moreau
were following Swain, who had stolen a canoe at the village
and had made off across the river in darkness. Worried, the
two Indians burst into the clearing, where Mawak was working
his medicine on the unconscious Donoway. Tamano and the
others had pursued Swain through the forest soon after they
had found Donoway lying badly wounded in his camp, Mel
Webster unconscious beside him. Webster would be fine, but
Sutherland was gravely hurt, bleeding badly, and only half-
alive. Not half-dead, Tamano told himself. Half-alive! Alive!
    He ran to Mawak and fell to his knees at Sutherland's side.
The Scotsman was ghastly pale, his bandaged body covered
with a blood-soaked blanket. The bullet that had struck his
ribcage had not penetrated, but the other had lodged against
the pelvis. In the five hours since the fight, he had not regained
consciousness, raving in delirium, and calling out for Ella and
his children.
    Swain had escaped alone, leaving Thrower, Spider, and
Dusten lying dead. Nate Breed had been found dead at his post,
knifed, an empty rum flask at his side. The killers had crept
through the woods, avoiding trails, and come in behind Nate.
From the tracks, it was clear they had been watching, waiting
many hours. The fact that Nate had drunk too much rum in his
anger explained how Swain had managed to kill him, and thus
eliminate one of two key guards. A good man was lost, but at
least, for the moment, Sutherland lived.

Sutherland's vision was of hell, hot, painful, hard. He heard
familiar voices. There were moments when he saw familiar
faces, but always the faces vanished before he could speak,
and the voices made no sense, talking from across a lake, far
away. He wanted to drink that lake water, all of it, drink it
down, cool his burning body, slake a thirst that only hell could
scourge him with. Tamano, Mawak, Little Hawk all were there
in hell with him, standing on the mound, and so was he. They
were telling him something he could not understand, though
he wanted to.
    Mawak loomed above him, and behind the old medicine

man was a blue sky with soothing clouds. There were birds chattering, there was shade. Sutherland was neither in hell nor dreaming. Mawak was working on his hip, which seemed to belong to someone else. The old chief labored away, his tongue sticking out in concentration. Sutherland seemed to drift into his own body, and with this sensation came horrible pain that caused him to moan.

His friends were at his side then, looking down at him, and he began to piece together what had happened. Tamano gave him water, and he asked questions.

Mel appeared, his first answer. Looking haggard and weary, a huge welt on the side of his head where Thrower had struck him and knocked him out, Mel knelt down and answered Sutherland's next question.

"They killed Nate before they attacked us," he said, his voice breaking. Mel tried unsuccessfully to clear his throat, looked down, and shook his head. "I wish I could say something . . . or do something to change it all, Owen, but I—"

Sutherland could not sit up, but he laid a hand on Mel's shoulder. There was nothing he could say, either. For the rest, Sutherland learned the bitter news that Swain had got away, and that some of them were following him across the river.

Jeb Grey knelt at Sutherland's side and said, "Thrower betrayed us, as you thought he would, but that devil Swain was too sly."

"That was my mistake; I'm sorry . . ."

Swain and the other three men had been the only attackers, figuring on surprising Sutherland by slipping through with a small force rather than the large one that had been expected. Tamano said Swain was wounded, and had left a trail of blood down to the Cahokia village.

Sutherland asked, "My claymore?"

No one had seen it, only the empty scabbard. Swain must have the sword, a token, a reminder of the vendetta not yet carried to its end. Weak, and still in danger, Sutherland must be brought to nearby Fort Chartres, to be treated for his wounds. He lay back, trying not to think about the pain and the frustration. Thinking of his family and of the future, he looked up to see Mel, a shovel on his shoulder, leaving the campsite.

He called to Mel and asked, "You intend to stay on here, and dig?"

Mel looked down and shook his head. "Only as long as it takes to bury Nate . . . and fill in the excavation on the mound.

I don't belong here ... though it's too late to find that out; too late to learn ..." He choked up, then went off, with Jeb and Colin following to lend a hand.

Too late, thought Sutherland. Yes, too late to bring back Nate, too late to wish he had never led these men on such a dangerous mission. His distress over his failure caused as much pain as that in his body.

This thought and its convoluted wanderings troubled Sutherland as he was carried on a litter to their canoes, then to Fort Chartres. Glum and angry, he spoke little during that time, even when reunited with his old friend, Lieutenant Parker. Recently made commandant at this lonely outpost, Parker had just sold his commission in the Royal Americans and bought one in the 18th Royal Irish Regiment. The 18th would be garrisoned in the eastern colonies one day, while the Royal Americans were a wilderness regiment, whose junior officers had little prospect of promotion when stationed far from the halls of power.

Parker saw to it that Sutherland received the very best care available, though old Mawak seldom left his patient's side throughout the first week in the post infirmary. Doctored, plastered, and well fed, Sutherland mended quickly. His spirits sank even lower, however, when Tamano came in with word that once again Swain and his wife were in full flight from Saint Louis.

A large force of Ottawa warriors had descended on the Illinois villages, slaughtering hundreds of innocent folk. Then they had surrounded Saint Louis, demanding that Swain be given up to them. Before then, however, Swain had escaped, sailing downriver to New Orleans. Yet he would find only brief refuge in that city, Tamano said, for the Chickasaw and Creek were also furious over Pontiac's murder. As they had done before, when angry with the French, these strong tribes would march on New Orleans and threaten the city until Swain was produced. Sutherland had no doubt Swain would escape New Orleans before any Indians caught up with him. Bradford Cullen had considerable trading interests down there, and any one of several coastal vessels he used for smuggling could spirit Swain back north to a British colony.

Lying dour and beaten in his bed, Sutherland gazed up at the white ceiling, wishing he were home again, vowing to start all over. Like Mel, Sutherland had to sort out an answer to a nagging question: Was his quest for Swain to continue year after year? He thought not. He would rather build the house at Valenya, surround himself with loved ones, and guide the Frontier Company through these turbulent times. Other, younger men could deal with the likes of Jubal Swain, until the day that law took root in the northwest.

Sutherland was convinced he would become strong enough to fight Swain again, but in his heart he knew he was not a young man any longer—that he had his limits. Unless there was no other way, he would have no part of another hunt for Jubal Swain, a man like the very devil himself.

One rainy afternoon, Mel Webster sat next to Sutherland's bed and listened as the Scotsman told of a young colonial botanist and scientist named John Blair, who lived in Philadelphia. Blair was acquainted with Dr. Franklin and corresponded with scientists in several colonies. He had come to Detroit a few years ago, and there befriended Sutherland and other members of the Frontier Company before returning east to teach at the Philadelphia Academy.

Sutherland spoke highly of Blair and of prospects at Philadelphia, where Mel had recently decided to go. The two friends were as somber as the cloudy, damp weather. They were parting, both bearing a burden of guilt from the latest conflict with Swain. Mel felt miserable about having led Nate on a fortune hunt, only to result in his cousin's death. Sutherland was still filled with self-recriminations and doubts over Swain's taking him and his men by surprise, even if it was because Nate got drunk and let the enemy pass. Sutherland should have put more men on the watch; he should have been there himself!

As Sutherland handed over a letter of introduction to John Blair, he tried to cheer Mel up, saying they would certainly become great friends.

"You want secrets from ancient civilizations, and John wants to find the Northwest Passage; I'm sure you'll have much to tell one another, and perhaps he can find work for you at the Philadelphia Academy."

Mel thanked Sutherland, saying he intended first to go with Niko-lota through Shawnee and Delaware country. They would travel up the Ohio River toward Fort Pitt, and on the way he would visit Indian towns no British whites had ever seen. At the same time, Niko-lota would continue to search for the sons of Lucy Swain in that region, intending to honor his word to her. Also, the Delaware still hoped the boys would attract Lucy, who would bring Swain along. Then, one way or another, Niko-lota and Swain would come to a final reckoning. Sutherland made no comment when Mel told him this. He was sick of vengeance, sick of the name Jubal Swain.

Yet for all that, Sutherland knew the time would come when once again he and Swain would come face to face. Like the empty scabbard that once had held the claymore, the warlike side of Sutherland's soul had lost something in the conflict with Swain. Until the day Swain's evil was driven completely from the northwest, however, Owen Sutherland would not truly rest, could never find peace. As he half-listened to Mel talk about the coming journey eastward, Sutherland fought to shake off the taunting image of his old enemy. It was with great difficulty that he turned his thoughts to Mel.

The young man was saying, "And on the way I'll take a look at some remarkable mounds Niko-lota knows about— Only looking this time, of course." Mel smiled wistfully. "No digging."

These two hoped to meet again the following summer, 1770, when Jeremy and Sutherland came to Philadelphia to enroll the boy in the Academy.

"Perhaps he'll be a pupil of yours," Sutherland said, shaking hands as Mel stood up. "You and John Blair have turned his mind to important things, and I thank you for that, my friend. Godspeed."

Mel departed, and Sutherland closed his eyes. He tried to sleep, but his leg was terribly sore. It was almost time for the attending army surgeon to administer laudanum to ease the pain. Then another kind of pain rose in Sutherland to think that so much misery could be caused by Bradford Cullen. A man respected by his peers, a leader of a British colony, Cullen had not been held accountable for what he had done. That made Sutherland all the more sullen and ill-disposed toward the system of government that corrupt men like Cullen could use to protect themselves from justice. Cullen was at this very moment smugly prosperous in Montreal while hundreds of Illinois Indians lay slaughtered in ruined villages because of the evil done by the merchant's hirelings.

A dry, spiteful anger festered inside Sutherland as he pondered how to bring Cullen to justice once and for all. It would not be easy, for Cullen had such great influence in the government of Lower Canada that it was unlikely he would ever be tried there. Taking the law into his own hands and dealing with Cullen directly was wrong, Sutherland knew, because he would be throwing away his life.

A trial would be best, because even if Cullen were not convicted, his reputation would be damaged beyond repair. Anyone of common decency would be repelled by what Cullen had done in secret with Jubal Swain. But who was there who could prove he was allied with Swain? Who would testify that he had financed so much killing?

Farley Jones could, but only an extreme change in his circumstances would give him the reason to be a witness. Jubal Swain would die before he talked. Then Sutherland thought about Lucy Swain, who had been with her husband throughout, and who must know who paid him for all he had done. She was a possibility, but to find Lucy and bring her forth as a witness against Cullen was as unlikely as persuading Jones to tell the truth about his employer. She might be anywhere in the colonies, perhaps never again to cross Sutherland's path.

These vexing thoughts filled Sutherland's mind as the surgeon came in to give him a dose of laudanum. Just before Sutherland took the cup, Lieutenant Parker appeared. Realizing Parker wanted to talk, Sutherland asked the doctor to wait with the laudanum.

The lieutenant had the look of a man with some deep inner hurt. Sutherland hoped there would be no more bad news, but he became tense immediately when Parker asked the surgeon to leave them alone for a while.

Sutherland tried to sit up in bed, but the agony of his cracked pelvis was too much, making him break out in a heavy sweat. He took a drink of water as Parker sat down. Turning his tricorn over and over in his hands, the young officer at first said nothing more than asking for Sutherland's health.

"It would hurt less if Swain were done for," the Scotsman said. "Don't waste any time, James. What's on your mind?"

Parker took a deep breath, stood up, then violently threw his hat against the closed door. He stared at Sutherland and declared, "I have orders to arrest you!"

A bolt of pain shot through Sutherland's body, but he did not show it. Holding his breath until the ache subsided, he watched Parker pacing back and forth.

Sutherland asked, "Is it Jones?"

"It is, that rat! He won't win anything in a court of law, he knows that—"

"What charges?" Sutherland could have guessed, but he had

not the strength to conjecture, and wanted the answer put simply and clearly. Parker said Jones had accused Sutherland of illegally entering Indian territory without a pass; of leading an armed party out with the intention of stirring up Illinois Indians; and of inciting the Ottawa against Saint Louis. Parker went on with some additional absurdities, which would not stand up when the evidence was presented to judges.

Yet the question was not whether Sutherland ultimately would be proven innocent, but whether he would survive imprisonment under the heel of the vengeful Farley Jones. Parker said Sutherland was to be sent under guard to Detroit, later to be shipped east for trial. Since it was only September, Sutherland could be taken east before winter, and he mentioned that to Parker.

The officer picked up his dented hat and shook his head. "I'm not supposed to bring you to Detroit until the end of October, according to my orders . . . because the jail at Detroit is full of prisoners—"

"What prisoners? My people?"

"No, thank the Lord. But it seems there's a growing group calling themselves Liberty Boys who are behaving insolently to the authorities—meaning Jones and the commander. They're rabble-rousing, threatening to tar and feather anyone who doesn't agree with their opposition to Parliament's laws for northwest."

This was part of the conflict Sutherland had seen brewing for so long, in which people were increasingly taking sides in the many disputes between Parliament and colonial government. Newcomers from the East in particular were coming out to Detroit with an inborn hatred of all British authority. There were growing numbers of arguments, brawls, and even blood-feuds between both sides. Parker said some Liberty Boys had taken up lands they bought illegally from Indians, then built cabins. The army, as required, was throwing them out and burning their homes.

Parker said, "It's getting ugly, Owen. We're still isolated here at Chartres, and it's still quiet up at Michilimackinac, but Detroit's boiling over with people; I'm afraid something's soon to break apart if Parliament doesn't find a way to soothe colonial defiance. Why, there are troops quartered in Albany, troops in Boston, in New York, and they're forcibly billeted upon people who don't want them there . . ." He continued pacing, saying that before long he might be posted to some eastern hotbed of dissension, where his uniform would make him despised by many people.

As Parker spoke about these things the immediate burden of arresting Sutherland was momentarily forgotten. The lieutenant understood why Americans were so hostile to Parliament, but said, "The unfair part is that the army pays the price! We're between colonial rabble-rousers who are after power, and Parliamentary mercantilists who are getting rich from colonial markets. Soldiers represent Parliament, so Americans abuse us. The result is that we retaliate and abuse colonials, and there we have the cycle of eye-for-an-eye that results in even more chaos, and in full jails in Detroit . . . where . . ."

He stopped talking and pacing. The weight of what was before him was felt once again. Looking at Sutherland, Parker said, "Tell me what you want to do, Owen, and I'll help; no swine of a commissary will make me arrest you, to be kept imprisoned all winter the way they did Robert Rogers."

Parker was standing at the foot of the bed. Sutherland knew leaving would be hard, but if he stayed at liberty in Chartres, he would compromise Parker, who could be ruined, perhaps even arrested for insubordination. There was only one thing to do.

"I have to send word through Peter Defries to William Johnson; he won't let Jones get away with this. I can't stay here, but you'll be blamed if I escape, James."

Parker shook his head and smiled wistfully. "The soldier who brought the express was with us on the expedition against Swain, and he's a friend of Jeb Grey; he came in before dawn, and only the officer of the day knows he's here. The fort commissary doesn't even know about the messenger or the order to arrest you. As far as anyone's concerned, that order hasn't come in yet."

"I'll go . . ." Sutherland tried to get out of bed, but the cruel pain from his hip swept through his body, nearly causing him to faint. He sat on the edge of the bed, Parker holding him from falling. The lieutenant said he would arrange private lodging in the nearby French community until Sutherland had healed well enough to travel.

"What about the others—Grey, Webster, Levesque . . . ?"

"They're all mentioned in the express; I should arrest every one of you, but I won't know your whereabouts if you have already taken to the woods."

Thus it was arranged to move Sutherland to the farmhouse belonging to an acquaintance of Alain Moreau. Parker sent a return express to Jones saying Sutherland and his men were no longer in the fort, and nowhere to be found. At the same time, the messenger took a letter secretly to Ella and the other women. It told them to depart quietly in early November for Fort Michilimackinac, where the Frontier Company had a small warehouse and lodgings. They would be joined by their men before winter, and, with the country snowbound, Jones would be powerless to harass them until spring. At the same time, Sutherland sent word to Defries of all that had happened, requesting that he go to Sir William Johnson and have Jones's order countermanded. Johnson's reply would not likely reach Detroit before ice closed the lakes, however. That meant Sutherland and his friends would be isolated at lonely Michilimackinac over the winter.

Parker said the commander at Michilimackinac would aid Sutherland; further, the post commissary there was loyal to Johnson, and unlike Jones had no dealings with Bradford Cullen. It was obvious that Cullen had put Jones up to arresting Sutherland to break the Frontier Company, and in this way had once again inflicted a telling blow.

There would be little trading done by company members from Michilimackinac this season unless the trade goods from Detroit could be moved up there clandestinely. To try that, however, would risk Jones's getting wind of Sutherland and his friends escaping to Michilimackinac.

At Detroit, Ella was dismayed to learn the men of the company could not return home. Only Jean Martine was not charged with a crime, yet as a partner in the company, he temporarily lost his trading license at the orders of Jones. So did Sutherland and the others with him, and thus Jones effectively closed down the Frontier Company for the season. Though its Detroit warehouses were filled with trade goods—those Peter had purchased with the money earned from Pontiac's furs—the firm was forbidden to do any business until the case was decided in the courts. Jones even padlocked the Morely and Martine warehouses, so the goods could neither be used nor transferred north.

In early November, under cover of night, the women and children stealthily slipped away from their homes at Detroit. Ella, Lettie, Angélique, Lela, and their children were taken off in the sloop *Trader*. Word was planted that the sloop was heading east, as usual, so by the time the ship reached Michilimackinac, it would be too late in the year for word to go back to Jones and give them away. The last army dispatch boat from that fort left for Detroit just at this time, following the western shoreline all the way, thus not on the route of the *Trader*.

As they sailed up the Saint Clair River, Ella stood alone at the ship's bow. Jeremy, Sally, and the little ones were asleep below in the hold; the other women were in the cabin, preparing for bed. A bitter wind came sweeping out of the north, cutting through Ella's cloak, and she was grateful for the cold. Let the snows, the ice, the cruelty of a harsh winter take the northwest tightly in its grip this year, and protect Owen. Let them all be safely isolated at distant Fort Michilimackinac until spring, when Johnson's aid would surely prevent Jones from imprisoning their men. The wind bit through her, and Ella invoked it to blow even colder. Soon she would be with Owen, where the hand of Bradford Cullen could not harm them. Closing her eyes as gusts whipped icy spray from the rising and falling of the prow, Ella prepared for the worst. Settling into the steady rhythm of the *Trader*, listening to the sounds of ship, river, and wind, Ella resolved at this moment never to allow hardship to overwhelm her.

PART THREE

White Foaming Waters

Military Canoe Expedition

chapter **20**

RESPONSIBILITY

The winter of 1769–70 was indeed hard in the upper reaches of the Great Lakes. By mid-November the waterside palisades of Fort Michilimackinac were bordered by ice and drifting snow, and the lakes froze solid soon after that. Never in anyone's memory had there been a more bitter, prolonged cold snap so soon, but Ella was relieved. For now, they were safe.

At Michilimackinac, all was as Parker and Sutherland had hoped. The commander was a dedicated professional not given to appeasing civilian commissaries of the Indian Department. After the notorious treatment of Robert Rogers, soldiers at Michilimackinac resented all Indian Department officials. The middle-aged commissary who had replaced the persecutor of Rogers was careful not to antagonize anyone needlessly. A quiet man who favored dallying with a Chippewa squaw more than he liked to work, he was no threat to Sutherland or the others that winter, and knew nothing of the orders to arrest them.

After years of hard work, the time at solitary Michilimackinac was at first restful for the Sutherlands, though they regretted the cost of missing the trading season. They made the most of the peace and tranquillity in a silent world blanketed with snow.

Michilimackinac was a tenth the size of Detroit, but built generally the same. Its score of dwellings were sturdy log or squared-timber affairs with steep roofs covered by cedar-bark shingles. Private homes were in several row houses with five-foot picket fences enclosing small gardens. The residents' houses were invariably also trading shops, except for a few belonging to prosperous merchants who had separate storehouses rented from the king. The largest structure in the fort was the graceful Church of Sainte Anne, patron saint of *voyageurs* from Louisburg to Lake of the Woods. Next to the small graveyard of the church stood a one-story log barracks recently built by men of the Royals. The barracks was massive, with a pair of fine brick chimneys and a shingled roof.

Sutherland's firm had a small storehouse of French-style vertical logs, and they divided it into apartments by putting up temporary walls for Grey's family, and for Tamano and Lela. The Levesques, who had not expected they would be coming up to Michilimackinac under these circumstances, had their own residence, and the Sutherlands shared three rooms in an adjacent building. Finding lodgings for so many might have been impossible, but when word passed among traders that Jones had forced Frontier Company partners to winter here, places were immediately offered, and Colin O'Donnell and Alain Moreau found lodgings with *habitants* outside the fort.

Cullen and Company had no permanent factor here, preferring to ship goods from Montreal out to traders each spring. A few men at Michilimackinac were regularly employed by Cullen when his company's canoe brigades descended on the trading post, but these fellows were not concerned about their employer's hostility to Sutherland. Thus, there was no way Jones could learn of his prey's location that winter, and for now they were safe.

This new home was exciting for the youngsters. Jeremy, Tom, James, and Sally were all content at the change in surroundings. Little Hawk was the only one who felt restless. At eighteen, too old to live in Tamano's small house, he went with Mawak to the nearby Chippewa village. At first he was looked upon with suspicion because he was Sioux, the enemy in this country, which was dominated by Chippewa. Since many of them were relations or friends of Tamano, however, the warrior's recommendation of Little Hawk defused any possible trouble. The young man was taken into the lodge of Tamano's aged uncle, Calla, whose home would do for the winter; but Little Hawk felt a powerful inner urge compelling him to move on, back to his own people, far to the southwest.

When he met a niece of Tamano's, one called White Dove, Little Hawk was distracted from the longing to return to his people. White Dove was a fine-looking cheerful girl, robust and very self-confident. There were few men who could outrun her, though many had tried to catch her in the race as well as in love. Though at fifteen she was eligible for marriage, she had never committed herself to anyone. Being without a father—

hers had been killed in the English wars—White Dove depended on her great-uncle Calla to decide whom she married. Skilled at womanly tasks, she bore promise of being an excellent squaw. Little Hawk knew this but hardly noticed White Dove's domestic ways, caring more for the challenge she posed to him: Like most of the Chippewa, he could not outrun her, and that galled him.

Perhaps there was something deeper between Little Hawk and White Dove, but neither expressed any particular infatuation during those first weeks at Michilimackinac. From the start they were fierce competitors—he showed off as a masterful rider, even in snow, and she raced alongside his horse just to tease him. They were not lovers, though those who observed them knew such things could change.

The other children had lots to do with winter games, chores, and studies. Though Mel and Reverend Lee were no longer at hand for book learning—which the children pursued independently—others were there to instruct them how to survive and succeed in the wilderness. Old Mawak in particular was a demanding teacher, whose knowledge of the forest and the creatures living there was unmatched by anyone. He was a thorough, careful guide, gentle when the young ones were troubled or impatient, strict when they were lazy or overconfident.

Ella and Owen watched with admiration as the older children began to take their places in the world of adults. They even marked the change in Benjamin and Susannah. The boy grew out of sucking his thumb, though he still had a soft spot for Sniffer's tail when he slept. Too often, though, he teased the aging otter, irritating and confusing Sniffer with his tricks, and the animal was no longer playfully young to accept such sport.

One day, when Ella was home alone with the two youngest children, Benjamin tied a beaver pelt to the sleeping otter's tail, causing an uproar in the apartment as Sniffer went wild at the scent of his mortal enemy. Biting and snorting, whirling around the room in fear and anger, Sniffer banged against walls, beds, and tables, knocking over candlesticks and chairs. Ella was frantic, and Benjamin's laughter soon changed to dismay as he realized Sniffer might really hurt himself if not stopped. No one could catch or calm the otter until brave little Susannah, who was in bed with a cold, sprang out and grabbed Sniffer, heedless of his nipping and panicky scratching.

"Good Sniffy, sweet Sniffy," she cooed through her cold,

petting the trembling otter, distracting him from the beaver fur. Susannah sat down on the floor, fair curls spilling over her nightgown, and Ella commanded Benjamin to untie the fur from Sniffer's tail.

Sheepishly, the boy did so, Susannah all the while soothing the otter. At the very moment Benjamin was done, Susannah set Sniffer free, then leaped up with a shriek to clutch at her brother's hair. Fighting and screaming, Susannah and Benjamin went at it like wildcats, and before Ella could pull them apart, Jeremy returned, running into the house, and caught them up, one in each hand. Squirming with anger, the children wept and howled until their older brother gently placed them in their respective beds. Leaving them there to cry themselves out, he then went to his distraught mother and calmed her down, suggesting she sit before the fire and have a cup of tea.

As Jeremy poured for Ella and himself, she regained her composure and looked at her son from a new perspective. How he was changing, and what a fine young man he was! It did her heart good that amidst all the turmoil and uncertainty of these days at Michilimackinac, there was much to be thankful for, and her children were foremost of all.

Before long, Owen and Ella found themselves too often distant from one another, though neither intended it. Owen was constantly deep in thought or fighting back both the mental and physical pain that would not relent. The commander of the fort had a respectable library, which Sutherland often visited, and he spent his time reading and writing, and he was ever ready to debate politics and world affairs. This increasingly acid, argumentative manner was unlike him, but Ella understood what he was going through. She tried to ease his troubled heart by small kindnesses that usually were not noticed or appreciated until too late.

Snug and clean, their lodgings were similar to those of their friends. The residence could better have been larger to accommodate the four children, but with Jeremy and little Benjamin on bunk beds in one room, and the girls berthed in another, they managed. Owen and Ella converted a storage closet into their own sleeping chamber, and closed it by a curtain. That small room was Owen's world week after week as he recuperated from his hurt.

He was not eating well, nor exercising enough, and because of his dejection a kind of bitterness pervaded the entire house. Ella found it hard to talk with Owen. Whenever she brought up his health, or said he should rest more and write less, he grumbled that he would be fine as soon as he could move about again. He never wanted to discuss trade business, because that subject made him all the more angry with life in general. Any talk about the future left him black and gloomy.

Owen's prolonged confinement and dismal pessimism worried Ella, and more than once she urged him to look on the brighter side. But his thoughts went ever deeper in the political and social turbulence of America. He believed there had to be a general solution, a way to create a better and just society that was designed precisely for American conditions, not British. Often he stayed up late at night to read or write, getting up early in the morning to continue.

He devoured tracts by Rousseau, Locke, Voltaire, Swift, Bacon, Diderot, Franklin, Sewall, Smith, Defoe, Tully, Virgil, Homer, and on and on—every philosopher and thinker he could find who might shed light on the nature of man and the application of natural law to modern America. He analyzed, synthesized, and dismembered promising ideas, theoretically applied them, then sought others to dispute and test the merits of his reasoning. Often Ella was his first audience, but she wearied of incessant philosophizing and experimentation, telling Owen bluntly that she would like to drive him ten miles from the fort and let him walk home—or crawl, if it would help clear his mind of thoughts that it ground up like so much grain.

"You need to purge yourself, Owen Sutherland," she told him as he sat in bed, buried in an essay by the famous Massachusetts Bay politician James Otis. He did not look up, scribbling notes to himself, legs covered by a blanket against drafts. "Do you hear me, Owen?"

He absently peered over the book, his brain still working. "I hear you, lass. You want to take me for a drive, but I can't go until I read this..." He glanced at the window, where a light snow was falling. For just a moment, he gazed at the tranquil, gray peace of winter enclosing his house.

Ella said, "Beautiful, isn't it?"

"Aye," he replied, as though seeing it for the first time. Stiffly, carrying the blanket, he hobbled to the window, his legs sore from poor circulation. Ella saw him, in that fleeting moment of her thoughts, as an old man, withered and tired, forgotten by the world. "Beautiful, indeed. Too bad I have this essay to write and Mr. Otis to digest. What a mind that man has, Ella." He looked at her, surprised to see a tear in her eye.

"What is it, lass? Are you ill?"

He came to her, taking her in his arms, which were strong, the way she knew them. She shook her head and took a deep breath, shuddering just a bit.

"I just don't want you to change so . . . I mean I don't want you permanently suffering from either your injury or . . . or your bitterness!"

She drew away from him, going to the fire, where a teapot stood, keeping warm. Owen was back at the window, sorry for how she felt. He understood why Ella was so concerned for him, and he admitted that the past weeks had been more difficult than any others in his entire life.

As though from a distance, he said, "Lass, this time won't last forever; it's just that I have something to say, though I don't know just how to say it yet . . . or how to say it in a way that's both clear and engaging." He watched her pouring two cups of steaming tea near the fire. Susannah was asleep in a chair. Benjamin was out playing with Jeremy and Sally, who had taken Sniffer with them. The only sound was the flames crackling.

He asked, "Can you just stand it for a little longer?"

She collected herself and said, "I can stand it if you don't poison yourself with ideas! You can't change the world!"

"Someone has to!"

"You?"

"Us! All of us! Perhaps a whole nation, a new people in a new country with a new start that no other people have been afforded since the Etruscans founded Rome! There's a mood in America, a tidal wave of thought that is a vanguard of a new age! Thought that merges with action, and has the power to put all that—" he gestured to the books piled around his bed in the small alcove "—all that into reality, step by step, the way the colonies emerged from the forest. I can help change the world, and so can you and our children, Ella."

She sat down, staring at her cup. Then, as he sat on the edge of a chair opposite, she handed him his tea and said, "What about simply cultivating our own garden?"

He sipped the tea, gathering the blanket around his legs like a man whose strength is sapped before his time. Ella could not look at him, and she turned to the fire.

He said, "The northwest is only part of our garden; we can help cultivate all British America, and from it will grow a new world to vie with Rome for power and with Greece for genius!"

Ella heard him, but she did not care. She was not so interested in changing America. Owen's ideals were fine things,
but if they transformed him for the worse, envenomed him
because they were fragile ideals while reality was cunning and
cruel, then she wanted no part of them. She made no reply.
With his cup of tea, Owen limped back to bed and began to
read again, as though Ella were not even in the house.

Ella's man was changing from the carefree rover of the
wilderness to the abstract thinker whose ideas were as profound
as those of the most important minds of his country. Soon she
was tired of Michilimackinac, worried about the spring, about
Jones, and about a possible trial. She could not lose herself in
his theories because she was not made that way, and when
little Susannah caught a cold that lingered and lingered day
after day, Ella's nerves frayed.

The strain of it all bore down hard on her, but she was
strong. With the support of her friends—Lela, Angélique, Lettie, and even Sally—Ella would get through it all, difficult as
it was. Regardless of her distress, she still had faith that her
Owen was producing a body of work that one day would mean
much to the northwest, and to America. Without complaint,
she did her utmost to help his writing continue uninterrupted.

Though Owen got around better with every passing day, he
was pale, almost thin, from lack of fresh air and vigorous
exercise. It took considerable prodding from Ella to get him
up and out for walks around the fort; and when the wind was
not too strong they went beyond the walls to watch the children
play the popular Indian game, snow snake. This involved hurl-
ing a long staff of burnished wood along a channel of ice, with
the winner being the one whose staff traveled farthest.

Ella enjoyed these diversions, but it was seldom that Owen
gave them his full attention. At such times he did not talk
much, his thoughts cluttered with ideas and problems. When
he did converse, it was invariably about his work. Ella prayed
that the weather would break with a January thaw, for she
would see to it that he laid aside his words and took up snowshoes and went hiking with her. If there was going to be a
January thaw, it was still several weeks off, however, and Ella
knew she would have to be patient with her man and his com-
pulsive writing until then. How she longed for something to
slow his fevered, racing mind, anything to loosen the cynical
bindings that seemed to be tightening relentlessly around him.

The day came, two weeks before Christmas, when Owen

presented Ella with a leather folder filled with essays on the need for a total American political change. He had gone to great lengths to recopy each essay so that they were neatly written, and as polished as he could make them. It was with a good deal of uneasiness that Ella took the work, knowing how much her opinion meant to Owen. She longed to be genuinely helpful and constructive in her critique, and hoped she was up to it.

That afternoon a raging blizzard pounded Michilimackinac, so Owen and the children were confined to the same small dwelling throughout the three hours Ella needed to finish reading. He hardly spoke the entire time, though he played chess with Jeremy; meanwhile, Sally looked after Susannah and Benjamin so Ella could have time to herself. The house was quiet, for both Sally and Jeremy knew how important the essays were to their elders. Near dinner hour, Jeremy and Owen talked in hushed voices about the coming summer and plans for the boy's enrollment at the Philadelphia Academy.

Jeremy had been bottling up a serious question for some time now, and after every aspect of his education had been discussed, he finally asked, "Pa, can we really afford to send me there?"

Sutherland looked at the boy, the chessboard between them; he nodded once. "We can, son. Don't worry about that."

Jeremy was not convinced. "I am worried. I know how much we've lost, and I know the goods in Detroit won't bring us anything until a year or more . . . I don't want to be a burden—"

"Let it lie," Sutherland said, more sharply than he meant. "We'll get you to Philadelphia one way or the other. Your education is essential, no matter what it costs."

"Don't you see, Pa? I don't want to do it this way if it means others have to go without!"

Just then, Sutherland saw Ella rising from the rocking chair near the fire, and he sat up, anxious for her comments. He waved Jeremy off, saying not to bother about such problems just then. Jeremy was not content with Owen's offhand manner, and wanted to talk this through. His mother was approaching, however, her face showing weariness from prolonged reading and apparent distress. Jeremy got up and went to his room, troubled and annoyed that his own worries were so unimportant to his parents. Sally began to prepare the meal, for the little ones were hungry.

Ella sat where Jeremy had been and brushed back a wisp of hair. She laid the essays down on the table, not meeting Owen's penetrating eyes. There had been much to digest, too many ideas and opinions to sort out easily, and she needed time to think before voicing her opinion. Giving her no time at all, Owen asked, "You don't agree? You don't like it, I can see that."

"No, no, Owen, it's not that I don't agree, for I do. But there's so much here, that I can't so easily pick out point by point and discuss—"

"What then?"

"Wait! Don't rush me, Owen. You took weeks to write this, so at least give me the simple courtesy..." She covered her eyes and tried to think clearly.

He apologized, but his impatience was not tempered. "I had hoped you would think it strong, to the point."

"It is. It is that, yet... yet I think it's also harsh and abrasive."

"So are the times we live in, and the people who lead us, the ones I've written about." His fingers thrummed on the arm of his chair, his legs moving nervously.

Ella took a deep breath before continuing. "It's gloomy, Owen. It's right, and it's unmasking, and it's a deep, sharp analysis of our country's situation, but it's so very dark, so lacking in any kind of uplifting humor save for cynical sarcasm."

Ella's emotions, after living with this day after day, escaped unbidden. Perhaps she was more blunt than she should have been, and as she talked Owen stopped tapping his fingers. His legs became still, and he listened to his work being taken apart page by page, idea by idea. The tension and enthusiasm drained from him. He had not expected such a shattering response.

He had thought his essays fairly scathing, but true enough to awaken Americans and British alike to undertake a whole new beginning. Ella thought them overcritical. He had intended his warnings of brutal frontier warfare to be clear and well framed. She thought them cold and holier-than-thou. He wrote about the need for Indian self-determination and sought to evoke sympathy from whites who had humanitarian motives. She said this section was too abstract, without life, compassion, or substance. "It fails," she said, "to portray the real character of the Indian to eastern colonials."

Before Ella was finished, the children had gone to bed. Sniffer and Heera were asleep by the dwindling fire—these two had come to be companions by now—and the north wind howled down the chimney.

Ella said, "You fail to see the positive, the good that is in our people, Owen. You don't consider all those on both sides who are sincerely working for justice and liberty, and if you can't acknowledge them, you can never consider yourself one of them. This essayist sounds like a bitter old hermit stuck in the frozen north, alone and sour, flailing at the world with grand ideas that have no heart, no soul, no real meaning for anyone trying to live in the middle of all the turmoil!"

He understood. He could not deny anything Ella said. His hip gnawed at him. He moved in the chair to relieve the discomfort, then tried putting the leg up on a stool. Nothing worked. Ella was quiet now, feeling the chilly draft as the fire died down.

"Owen," she said, and reached over to take his hand. "You know how hard it is for me to say this, and I know how difficult for you it is, but you have to see no one can change the world overnight . . . perhaps our world not at all."

He looked sharply at her, firelight flickering in his dark eyes, which were sunken and shadowed by seven days of non-stop writing. Ella reached to touch his other hand. He held hers but looked at the floor.

She said, "We'll come through this, just as we've come through everything else!"

"That took all I had to give, but you're right, it goes nowhere."

"Owen—"

"Nowhere, just like me."

"Owen, we'll come through this, and so will the colonies. I have faith that even the Indians will make their way. It will all work out because others feel the same way you do."

"There's no easy answer!" He stood up, pain shooting through his leg, and he let it get to him, sitting down heavily. The bone was healed, but the muscles, the ligaments, and tendons were atrophying and needed exercise—which he knew, but had put off until the series of essays was done. "For a month I've been writing with gall and not intellect."

"Don't write from intellect alone, Owen, but from your heart!"

That touched him deeper than he would have expected. After a moment he picked up the sheaf of papers and began to thumb through them, seeing how Ella's critique had been so perfectly to the point. Phrase after phrase, page after page, was a slashing attack on a system of government that was vulnerable and perhaps even deserving of it. But, as Ella said, his writings had nothing constructive, nothing uplifting, and hardly the smallest gleam of faith in the triumph of human goodness.

Putting the essays on the table, he sat back and said, "How can I tell anyone what's the right political direction, when my own life is so riddled with failure and—"

"Owen, Owen. Now you're being unfair with yourself, and that's why your essays, for all their brilliance, are not good enough!"

"No. They're not good enough at all. But I'm not sure I can do any better. . . ."

He sighed and took her hand again, grateful for what she gave him, feeling as though he had nothing to give back to her or to anyone.

Ella said, "In the springtime we'll make a new start—"

"I can hardly walk! Hardly get from my chair to my bed, woman! I'm not sure I'll be able to travel any distance again—"

"Owen! Have hope!"

"Hope?" He moved to relieve the discomfort, but was unsuccessful. "If it was only myself . . . if it was only me that I had to think about, then I wouldn't be so low. But I'm responsible for all of you, and for the others who followed me to Cahokia. They're all suffering because of me."

"They wanted to go."

"They didn't have to go, and if I hadn't been such a stubborn—"

"No one regrets it, Owen."

"I do."

"Owen, it hurts me to hear you talk so. They all chose to go, just as you did, and they knew Jones might cause trouble. They're here because they did the right thing."

"That's just it, Ella! We did the right thing, but I failed them, as I did at Swain's settlement! Ella, so many have died because of—"

"Because of Swain! Because of Cullen!"

He shook his head, and Ella saw grief he had never before allowed anyone to witness. He rubbed his eyes with one hand and gripped hers with the other. Ella felt shaky but held back, staring at the fire, wishing she knew what to say.

She whispered, "All I care about, Owen, is us, and our own

garden . . . All we can do is cultivate it."

He turned to her, and a warm smile crept across his face. She wanted to see that, and smiled back.

"I've been cultivating my garden, lass, but it's got ground-hogs in it. . . ."

Lying in bed, listening, Jeremy wished there were some way he could help his family come through this difficult time. Almost sixteen, he was on the threshold of going out into the world. He was eager to travel to Philadelphia this summer and enroll in the Academy, where he had been accepted thanks to the influence of Benjamin Franklin and the botanist John Blair. Jeremy had decided he would one day study medicine.

There was a shortage of funds to pay for his schooling, however, and that troubled Jeremy. What little of his own he had saved had gone into trade goods now locked up in a Detroit storehouse. Next winter those goods would earn enough money for the Academy, but there would be nothing for 1770, meaning he really should wait until 1771 before attending. That would take some strain from his family, but it was a long wait, too long. He was anxious to get on with his studies, for others at the Academy had begun their education much younger than he. If he waited another year, he would be studying while other young men were striking out for themselves.

Jeremy was too long for his bed, feet sticking up, arms hanging over the sides. Weighing close to a hundred and sixty pounds, he was remarkably strong, and did a man's work when it came to physical labor. Whenever he could, he escaped the confining walls of the fort, often going hunting with Mawak, Little Hawk, or Tom Morely. He had learned much about the wild, and was the best shot of the three boys. Like them, he was bursting with youthful energy. He missed Detroit, which from here seemed a bustling metropolis, with its two thousand whites and as many Indians. Out here were only a couple of hundred Indians in a small gathering of lodges near the fort, and nearly all the hundred or so whites were native French. British traders or more worldly Frenchmen from Lower Canada generally went east when winter settled in, so Jeremy had only his family, close friends, lonely soldiers, and backward *habitants* for company.

Jeremy longed to prove himself to his stepfather. Lately chess had been the only way he could compete, and by now they were an even match. For more reasons than one, Jeremy wanted Owen to get well quickly, because then he could test his strength against him.

Already he held his own in wrestling with Tamano and Levesque, and in all of Detroit, only Tom Morely was better, though not by much. If Sally was watching them wrestle, Tom was impossible to beat. It seemed the girl was a jinx for Jeremy, because he had trouble concentrating when she was watching him wrestle with Tom. Morely was so strong that concentration and quickness were the keys to beating him; but Sally had an unexplained way about her that never failed to disrupt Jeremy's concentration.

Yet it was not the thought of wrestling or the boredom of Fort Michilimackinac in winter that kept Jeremy awake that night. It was the lack of funds to pay for his first year at the Academy. He knew a way to raise the money, but at this time of year it was dangerous for any but the most experienced woodsman. That, he knew, was precisely what Owen would tell him if he asked his stepfather's permission to go. So he would not ask.

Ella was half-asleep next to Owen when she thought she heard Jeremy up and about the house. It was before dawn on a bitter-cold morning, and she wondered drowsily why he was stirring so soon. She thought no more of it and fell asleep again against her husband. When she awoke, there was a note on the table saying Jeremy had gone trapping, alone, and that frightened her. She told Owen, and he got out of bed quickly, for the moment ignoring his aching hip.

Ella read Jeremy's note aloud, ending with, "... it's my responsibility to earn my own keep, so I'll return in two weeks with enough fur to pay my way at Philadelphia and perhaps a little over for some presents when I come home."

Jeremy did not say where he had gone to trap, and that angered Sutherland as much as it troubled him. The boy was a good trapper by now, but he should not disregard the great danger of going out alone.

"I admire him for his pluck," Sutherland said, stiffly donning winter clothes as Ella watched. "But he shouldn't take such risks by himself. Someone has to go out with him..." Indecision showed on the Scotsman's face, because he would have gone along himself were he completely fit.

Ella said, "Perhaps Levesque or Alain Moreau can find him; I could take a sled out with someone, too."

Sutherland was absently flexing his leg, working blood into the muscles. "You have the other children. It's my responsibility to bring him back and let him find a partner."

"But your leg. Is it healed?"

Sutherland said, "It'll never be healed unless I go out. It's well enough to catch up to the boy before nightfall. Don't worry, lass, I'll have him back for breakfast, perhaps even tonight for dinner."

chapter **21**

CHALLENGE

Dressed warmly in a blanket coat, leggins stuffed with straw, a beaver hat, and with a scarf over his face to protect his lungs from the cold, Sutherland tramped on snowshoes along the trail of his stepson. Jeremy moved much faster than Owen had anticipated. Also hiking on snowshoes through this stony country that required considerable climbing up slopes and across ridges, Jeremy had set a grueling pace. This was no ground for sled dogs, and that was why Sutherland had taken only Heera, who loped ahead, free and excited to be out.

In contrast with the capering dog, who sniffed at Jeremy's tracks, Sutherland lumbered awkwardly as he made his way along the side of a hill. He had not expected his hip to be so very tender, and his disturbing lack of wind complicated matters. He was not making as much time as he had intended, and by the look of Jeremy's tracks, was not gaining on him. The boy would have to rest before long, however, and no doubt Sutherland would come up on him then.

Jeremy was less than an hour ahead, he estimated, and had been trotting much of the way. It was normal that a man would run on downhills, making good time when he could, but Jeremy was moving at top speed for long stretches, and still had not taken a rest.

Owen, too, could have run this distance without pause half a year ago. Indeed, Ella was right to say he had let his body go during this past time of recuperation and writing. By midday, the injured leg was less sore, though it was not as flexible or resilient as it might have been. Every time he made a misstep, or the snowshoe came down on a hole, awkward movement jarred his leg so that he felt it right up to his shoulder. He had to concentrate to run, had to watch the trail, keep balance, and think about his body.

This was the first time in Sutherland's life that his body had not responded naturally, easily, to his will. Movement was no longer second nature. Hurrying took concentrated effort, and by early afternoon he was soaked through with sweat. Being wet out here, where the wind was sharp and strong, was dangerous if he was not careful. He dared not pause very long, for if he cooled off too quickly, he could catch a chill from which he would never recover. He was tired but would not make camp until he caught up with Jeremy, which he was sure would happen before evening.

He was amazed when, by the end of the afternoon, Jeremy was still far ahead. Perhaps the youth was even widening the distance between them. Sutherland attributed it to his own weariness and lack of exercise, and yes, even to his age, for he was well past forty now. Then he realized that Jeremy was carrying considerable gear, including several traps, food, weapons, and tools. Sutherland had only his rifle slung across his shoulders, an extra blanket with some essentials and a day's provisions rolled up over his back, and a tomahawk at his hip.

Jeremy had come out for two weeks, and was probably lugging a hundred pounds. Sutherland thought about that and realized it was quite a run he was making, by any standards. He laughed to himself, aware of his own advancing age and of the boy's surging manliness—a son to be proud of—and forgot the discomfort of his hip. He picked up his pace, glanced at the lowering sun behind, and whistled up Heera from a rabbit hole. Jeremy was posing a worthwhile challenge. Sutherland would give it all he had. In the back of his mind he knew that even were he fully well, the boy would require some determined running to catch.

On he went, with Heera stopping frequently to lick ice from his paws. The dog was tireless, making five miles for every one of Sutherland's. The countryside became rougher, cut by steep gullies and lorded over by sheer gray cliffs that shadowed the trail. Before setting out, Sutherland had persuaded Tom Morely to tell him where Jeremy was headed, though Jeremy had told Tom not to reveal where he was going. It was obvious that Jeremy was taking a considerable risk, so when Sutherland pressed for the answer, Tom told him about a small lake that Sutherland knew. It was a few days' march from Michilimackinac, a spot too difficult to reach for trappers with sleds and lots of gear. High among the ridges, it was a frozen swampland of black spruce, where Mawak sometimes took the boys while hunting elk. Beaver were there, at least three big lodges. Only the most enterprising trapper would have endured the hard climb to clean them out. Enterprising or desperate. Sutherland admired Jeremy's motives in going after this fur, and again his esteem for the boy rose.

By dark, Sutherland knew he would not catch Jeremy in time to camp together. He found a sheltered cove beneath outcropping rocks, where a cluster of balsam pines offered shelter and bedding. There, exhausted, he made hurried camp, summoned the strength to build a fire, and huddled close to it, boiling snow for tea. He was sick to his stomach, having pushed himself too hard this first day out after so long a confinement. As he sat before the roaring blaze, he felt his back and leg muscles stiffen. By exercising them vigorously, he barely kept them from cramping.

Then he took a small bottle of camphor and witch hazel and rubbed the liquid into his body—every part was sore. His feet had blistered, and now he felt their discomfort more than he had when running. He should have known better than to push so hard on snowshoes before getting used to them again.

Where was Jeremy, he wondered? Probably just over the next ridge. Of course he had been saying that to himself all day, but that next ridge was never crossed. Heera had caught a snowshoe hare and brought it back, but Sutherland was too tired to eat anything. He left the game to his dog, lay back in the heat of the fire, and fell soundly asleep.

Morning found him aching worse than he had in his small lodging at Michilimackinac. Sitting up in the faint light of dawn, he moved only with pain. Slowly he plied the embers of his fire with wood, and soon had a strong blaze going. More camphor massaged into his limbs, a pot of tea, and boiled pemmican made with berries gave him back some vigor. He was impossibly stiff, but by the time the sun was up, he had finished breakfast and was back on the trail, tramping along sluggishly.

He knew it would take at least a week of hard running before he would be strong and supple again. He did not like to think it, but he suspected Jeremy had been on the trail since before sunrise. If that was so, Sutherland soon would have that week of running. And from now on he had better keep an eye out for some game, for he had brought little food to sustain him if the boy kept up his remarkable pace.

• • •

Three days later, on a bright, crisp afternoon, Ella carried Susannah to the fort's water gate. She stood just outside the palisade, bathed by sunshine, gazing across the vast white blanket that stretched to the horizon from points of land to her left and right. It would be Christmas soon, and she hoped her husband and son would return before then. She set down Susannah, who scampered toward a young soldier on sentry duty. Stamping his feet against the cold, the friendly private chatted with the child about Father Christmas and her New Year's resolutions.

Susannah then asked, "Do you know where Daddy and Jeremy went?"

The sentry knew the story, for little occurred at Fort Michilimackinac without everyone hearing about it. He looked at Ella, wondering whether she was as anxious as he thought she might be. Ella smiled and said, "Daddy and Jeremy will be home soon, Susannah, you know that."

The soldier touched his hat to Ella, then spoke to the child. "Susannah, I saw your daddy go across the straits, and he told me that if you asked, I should say he'll be back as soon as Jeremy is ready. And he also said to ask you for a nice kiss." He bent over, and Susannah kissed his cheek. To Ella the sentry said, "I've got a sister about her age back in Ireland, and I hope she's still askin' about me."

Later, Ella and Susannah went home, where Sally was looking after Benjamin. Unlike Detroit, Michilimackinac had no spinet to while away Ella's time and distract her mind. She missed much about the larger fort. Though there were so many good people living at this lonely fort, she longed to go home to Detroit, where they would make a fresh start this spring. Yet they would lose Jeremy, who would go east to begin his own life anew. How quickly the years passed! Strange that they flew so swiftly away, even though the recent days of not knowing where Owen and Jeremy were had dragged out so slowly.

There was a knock at the door, and as always in the last few days, Ella jumped up, hoping for good news. It was Levesque, with Tamano and Little Hawk. They said perhaps they should go out for Owen and Jeremy, just in case something had gone wrong. Ella wanted to agree, but then she thought about Jeremy's desire to prove himself, and Owen's need to pit himself against nature once again.

Ella went to the window and looked out at the sun and shining snow. "If you think they're in danger, then I'd be grateful that you go." She turned to face them. "But Owen's been in danger before, and somehow I think wherever he is now, he has to do this alone, as does Jeremy."

Though he was troubled, Tamano said Ella was right. "Donoway is like a young warrior; he must find himself, and he must do it alone, even if it means looking death in the eyes."

Ella's heart skipped.

Levesque said, "And your son must also find himself." He spoke to the others, "We will give them ten more days, as is fitting. If they have not returned, then we will go out."

As they left, Tamano lingered a moment; and before Ella closed the door, he said, "Come and visit Lela. Share her joy, for she is with child."

Through a howling wind that whipped up snow and ice into swirling clouds that covered the sun, Sutherland and Heera struggled along Jeremy's vanishing trail. Sutherland had barely been able to keep close enough to the youth to find the track, which was almost obliterated by drifting snow. Often it seemed to have disappeared altogether, but Heera had found it each time. Five days had passed since Sutherland set out from the fort, and his food was gone. Heera had caught another rabbit, which sustained them, and once Sutherland had fired at an elk, but had missed. Heera's eyes glittered from hunger, and if he had been a different dog, Sutherland would have worried that he might turn on his master. Yet Heera was faithful.

Light began to fade from the sky, and the wind dropped. Darkness, blue and sparkling, began to overtake them, but Sutherland did not stop to make camp. Now he knew for sure the lake Jeremy wanted was just over the near ridge, beyond shadowy pine trees that carpeted the high ground. Sutherland would be there in half an hour if he kept moving. He was weak in body, but his spirit was steadily rising. Fired with determination, a new will drove him on despite physical pain and weariness. His sore hip actually hurt less, or perhaps he had forgotten it. His legs were still not as strong as once they were, but they did not fail him, and they had regained some suppleness and conditioning. On he pressed, tramping up a steep slope, following tracks almost a day old. Before long, he would see Jeremy's campfire.

Sutherland's mind, long since abandoning political theory

and flighty abstractions, dwelt now on what he would say to the young man he would soon encounter—a young man who had left boyhood behind forever. With the likes of Jeremy in this younger generation, there was no reason to fear for America's future.

As for himself, Sutherland comprehended but did not try to analyze the change coming over him. For the first time since spring he was glad to be precisely where he was: toiling desperately with every ounce of strength through a bitter, beauteous, cold wilderness that could kill him. Winter felt no compassion for idealists, held no reverence for noble theories. Yet for all its primitive majesty, the northwest winter was not to be feared. It was not hostile to Owen Sutherland, for it was part of him, and he of it. He belonged out here, evolving and creating a whole new relationship with his world, a relationship that was intangible, yet very real.

This winter ordeal caused Sutherland to rediscover the balance he needed to harmonize with natural law and order. Simple, though profound, realities must be accepted and used to survive in the wilderness, and those same realities could guide a nation if its political leaders understood them. Sutherland had refound his desired place in the natural order of things.

He ran on and on through twilight, not with the strength of a young man, but with the power of an experienced one who knew his limits and wasted nothing. After all that had happened in the past year, Owen Sutherland had hope, and he was content with his life—except for the blisters.

Jeremy had been in camp for half a day when night came on, crisp and bitter cold. He had lost no time setting up traps as he came down into the frozen marshland of black spruce. He was after martens, and his road of traps had been half set out before he returned to camp for the night to eat and sleep. He was tired from the merciless pace he had set for himself since leaving Michilimackinac, but his emotions ran high. Stronger than even he had expected, he had tramped on, stimulated further by a rush of exhilaration at being able to travel so far, so fast.

He boiled some pemmican in a pan of snowmelt over his blazing fire, relishing the heat, body soaking in warmth. There had been times during the journey when he had felt detached from his body, watching it, feeling it move, as though it were new to him. The gangly arms and legs of a year ago were now long and lithe. His hands seemed not so big now that his forearms had thickened, and he could almost feel the muscles of his chest and back rippling with even the simplest motion.

Only one thing bothered Jeremy as he smelled the steam from the boiling food, and that was the set of wolverine tracks he had seen that afternoon. The wolverine, or Indian devil, as whites named him, was the most vicious and feared beast in the northwest, more savage than a wounded bear, more cruel than a drunken Indian. To be roving about before dark was unusual for the wolverine—*carcajou,* the Indians called him, meaning "bad dog," that lowest of names. Normally it hunted at night, but this one was likely very hungry, perhaps having trouble finding food, and that made him doubly dangerous. Jeremy had laid his trap road knowing he risked trouble with the *carcajou,* who could destroy every bait and pelt if it got on the trail of traps. Jeremy took this chance, for he had little time left to snare martens if he wanted them at their peak. In December their pelts were deepest brown, glossy, and thick. A couple of dozen of them and some beaver would bring enough money to pay for a year of schooling. When Jeremy's personal trade goods at Detroit were exchanged next year, more funds would be available to continue his education.

Even now he was tempted to check his sets, but it was too dark, and since he was out alone, he must take no unnecessary chances of a mishap. The food was cooked, and he hungrily tore apart the boiled pemmican, drinking snowmelt from another pan, later munching on some of his mother's raisin bread saved until now. After a good meal, he yawned and lay back on a blanket spread over balsam branches. He had not taken the time to build a proper lean-to, but for one night in the shelter of evergreens, he was out of the wind and warm enough.

The fire was well built, smoke rising into a sky sparkling with stars. In a few days, Jeremy would go home, burdened with pelts. Feeling sure of himself in a way he had never known, he dreamed about those furs. He could see them, feel them, those worth the most having silver gray or golden brown tips on their rump hairs . . .

A terrifying shriek rang out, and he sat up, hand on his rifle. Another screech of fury set his hair on end, and he knelt in his blankets, trying to tell where it came from. Vicious snarling, lasting a couple of minutes before it stopped, told that the wolverine had found a trap. The set was seventy yards off through the trees, on packed-down snow near the edge of a thicket. Something had been caught there, and the Indian devil had torn it apart.

Jeremy gripped his rifle. His marten road could be pillaged. He understood why Indians feared and hated the wolverine, calling it an omen of bad luck for the hunter it chose to harry. The *carcajou*'s terrible scream had caused fear in the young man as nothing ever had. This beast could be following the trapline right toward him, for there was another set baited no more than twenty yards from camp. If the wolverine was coming, it might attack, and would never retreat.

As Jeremy checked his priming and readied himself, he thought of what old Mawak had told him about Indian devils. The wolverine was believed by Indians to be a condemned hunter who in life had slaughtered game wantonly, and upon death was punished by being incarnated in the body of the nastiest, most murderous creature on earth. It was said that once a *carcajou* found a trapper's line, he had best abandon all hope of working in that region. Killing the wolverine was almost impossible, but if one succeeded in that, then extreme bad luck was sure to result. Jeremy did not believe a wolverine had the soul of an Indian, as Mawak had said, so he was willing to kill it, no matter what he had been told. This wolverine could stop him from doing what he had come here for, and no threat of bad luck, nor even the terror the animal called up, would make Jeremy flee this place.

Once while out hunting he had seen a wolverine kill a large buck, had watched as the bulky *carcajou* leaped down from an overhanging branch to dig teeth and claws into his doomed victim. The wolverine was incredibly strong, though it weighed only thirty pounds and had short, stout legs. Its claws were big and powerful, its courage even more immense. Jeremy had stared in amazement and revulsion as a brutal whirlwind of long black fur ripped the buck apart. Indeed, the wolverine was a devil, a perfectly created killer. He had hurried away as the wolverine brought the screaming buck to its knees, not staying for the horrible end.

Listening for even the slightest sound, Jeremy sensed more than heard the wolverine approach. He got up, rifle ready. Moving out of the firelight, drifting to the edge of the evergreen stand that surrounded him, he peered into the darkness in the direction of the baited trap, and waited. He neither heard nor saw anything, but felt a presence, eyes watching him. He was nervous, mouth dry, heart thumping.

He stepped forward quietly, snow crunching underfoot, a sound that was loud in the hushed woods. Even his own breathing gave him away. It was good the breeze was in his face, putting him downwind from the wolverine, which he knew was close. He hardly moved, listening, nostrils flaring like a wild animal on the hunt.

Then he knew he was the hunted. There was a scrape on a branch to his right, and he swung the rifle up, saw the shadow against the stars, and fired. As the priming flashed, the flare of powder lit the animal's eyes, and it sprang.

It had taken Sutherland longer than expected to cross the wooded ridge. Now he moved through darkness, following Heera, who was scenting Jeremy's trail. From the slope, he saw the inky, vast swamp below the vault of blue-black crystal sky and stars. Then, just as he discovered the distant glow of the campfire, the sound of a rifle and the wolverine's shriek stopped him. He had heard its cry a little earlier, but now it was quite close at hand. Heera whimpered to run, Sutherland gave him his head, and the big dog bounded away. Sutherland hurried behind, struggling through drifted snow, face stung by branches. He moved by instinct more than sight, making for the campfire and the frenzied snarls of the wolverine attacking something.

Then there was silence, save for the clatter of branches and the sound of himself running. Close to the campfire, and to where the wolverine had struck, he was anxious, about to cry out Jeremy's name, when Heera howled, long and loud. A moment later Sutherland entered the clearing where the fire burned brightly, but his stepson was not there, nor was the dog.

"Jeremy!" His voice evaporated into the night. "Jeremy! Where are you? Heera?"

Sutherland turned quickly at movement in the bushes. Heera bounded toward him, tongue hanging, eyes red in the campfire. The dog led him into the trees, where Jeremy's tracks could be seen. Calling his name, Sutherland crashed through the thicket, then called again, but there was no reply.

In the dimness, he sensed Heera close at hand, then heard the dog savage something. A few steps closer, and he found the carcass of a big wolverine, a bullet in its side, its throat stuck with a hunting knife. Heera had made sure it was dead. Sutherland searched about for some sign of Jeremy, then heard a soft moan to his left. The campfire gave enough light for him to find the young man, who was lying against a birch tree, blood on his forehead, arms, and chest. At his stepfather's approach, Jeremy cried out and tried to fight, but Sutherland grabbed him, and with difficulty held him down. In a moment, Jeremy came to, but lay shaken and faint from the wolverine's fierce attack.

Owen examined his body, which had been bitten and scratched in many places, then hefted him back to the fire and laid him on a blanket. Tossing dried comfrey root into boiling water for a poultice, Sutherland began to search out the wounds, which included claw-marks across Jeremy's chest.

After a moment, he said, "Your clothing was thick enough that none of these is too deep." Sutherland noticed a welt on his stepson's forehead. "Seems like the critter clubbed you with a log."

Jeremy gave a weak smile, and Heera came to him, licking his hand and nuzzling close. "I guess I ran into a tree limb; after I shot the devil, he still came on, and took my knife in its gizzard. He backed off, and I wanted to put some room between us so I could reload the rifle; that's when I ran into the limb." He patted Heera, saying, "Good thing you came along to finish him, friend, or I'd be finished instead."

Sutherland dipped a handkerchief into the comfrey brew and wiped the youth's head. The poultice would do well enough to treat him, and they could start back in a few days. He told this to Jeremy, adding, "But first you can teach me a few things about laying a marten road; and with us and Heera to lug the pelts, we ought to clean out those beaver lodges, too."

Jeremy grinned, though his body hurt. Philadelphia seemed possible, not a dream at all.

Christmas Eve was lovely, a soft snowfall laying its hush over Fort Michilimackinac. Window after window glowed with light, and the Church of Sainte Anne shone within from the yellow light of whale oil lamps and candles in preparation for midnight mass. A Protestant service would be held at the same time by the British chaplain in the fort's council house, and everywhere folk were in a festive spirit. Some officers and their women went caroling through the fort and, after singing, were invited in for a dram at *habitant* and British homes alike. Ella sat by her frosted window, knowing they soon would come to her house.

Ella's children were dressed neatly for the approaching service. They sat on the rug near the fire, with Sally teaching them checkers, and Sniffer curled up close by. Sally glanced at Ella, and they smiled at one another, each aware of the other's thoughts. For all the joy of the season, they were almost melancholy, but held up the best they could. Owen and Jeremy had been gone two weeks, and tomorrow their friends would go out to find them. Tom had revealed where Jeremy was going, and after breakfast, he, Levesque, Mawak, Tamano, and Little Hawk would depart on the hunt.

Sally heard the carolers singing for the Levesques next door, striking up the cheerful hymn, "God Rest You Merry Gentlemen." When the song was done, the singers went inside, laughing and talking, to partake of hot cider or eggnog. Ella's own house had been gaily decorated by her and the children in spite of their uneasiness at the men being gone. Mistletoe hung in the main room, and Ella had adopted the German settlers' custom of setting up a small fir tree in a keg near the window. The tree held a few small tallow candles made just for the occasion, and was garlanded with a bit of red trade ribbon and a white handmade rose of Sally's.

On the table were mugs, plates, sweets, and pastry, all carefully prepared by Ella and Sally days in advance. Ella had baked a dozen gingerbread Yule men—figures eight inches high, decorated with raisins—as her family had made them for generations. Already the children had picked out the ones they wanted.

Over the fire steamed a pot of spiced cider, and nearby stood a cool pitcher of eggnog. After church services, friends would come back to the Sutherland house, to celebrate the start of Christmas festivities. Other than Owen and Jeremy, all that was lacking was the traditional Yule log, which the Sutherlands had always kept at Detroit. As was customary, it was a great bole of an oak tree, partially burned up on Christmas Eve; what remained was saved all year long until next Yuletide. This being her only Christmas at Michilimackinac, Ella had no log without her men to bring home a new one, as ceremony required.

She could do without it, of course, one other thing missing from this Christmas so far from home. She heard the carolers come out of the Levesque house and gather to sing at her window. The younger children gleefully jumped up to peer out at them.

Ella sat by the fire, listening as they sang her favorite, "The First Noel"—and it was so beautiful, she had never heard it sung better. In a moment, they would come in. She hummed along and prepared to take the cider from the fire. Even before the song was done, there came a rattle at the door. They must be especially thirsty, Ella thought. Then the door was thrown open, and, as she turned in surprise, the children squealed with delight, and Sally cried out. The cold night blew into the room, and with it strode Owen and Jeremy, a great gnarled Yule log on their shoulders. Heera scampered back and forth, Sniffer pawing at him, and Ella flew past the animals and into Owen's arms. The singing went on, louder now. Sally threw herself at Jeremy as the little ones capered up and down, shouting and calling to be picked up by somebody. The men were almost bowled over, the weight of the log, their gear, and a bundle of pelts causing them to stagger and laugh as their family embraced them.

With a joyous shout, Owen and Jeremy tore away, dropped all but the Yule log, then laid it carefully in the roaring hearth. Then Sutherland and his wife were in one another's arms again, Susannah and Benjamin climbing up and tugging at them. Sally dragged the startled Jeremy off to one side, where the mistletoe hung from a rafter, and before he could protest, kissed him fiercely. Ella and Owen gazed at them, seeing Jeremy's arms out wide, Sally holding him close. Even Benjamin and Susannah were staring, for they had never before seen the older ones act quite like this.

Hours after the caroling, the church services, and the jubilant invasion of friends, Ella and Owen lay abed, listening to the fire, watching the red glow flicker over the ceiling. Owen had told how Jeremy shot the wolverine, stabbing the wounded, attacking animal, which bit and scratched him in many places. The subsequent harvest of marten and beaver pelts had been excellent, completed in only two more days. The wolverine pelt was not taken, for Sutherland had enough of the Indian about him to prefer burying it and not keeping any reminder whatever.

Ella pressed against him, closed her eyes, and drowsiness overtook her. Just as she fell asleep, she thought she heard

Owen say he had come upon a way of revising his essays to give them more life and feeling. Ella made no reply. She was so happy then, and tomorrow would be a most wonderful Christmas Day.

Much changed for the Sutherlands. Though there was yet the impending confrontation with Farley Jones, their lives had been rejuvenated by the almost complete recovery of Owen and the rapid maturation of Jeremy and Sally. Their son was close to manhood, and shone with a confidence that spoke of intelligence and burgeoning physical strength. They did not know quite what to do with Sally, who could not have been more like a daughter to them. The notion of adopting her, however, had been put aside, virtually permanently by now. Perhaps it was for the better in more ways than one that Jeremy was going to Philadelphia for four years. In that time, Sally would grow to womanhood, and would have to accept it that her childhood infatuation with Jeremy stood in the way of a full life and a real love.

So far, Jeremy had not returned the same feeling Sally displayed for him, and that, thought Ella and Owen, was no doubt why she loved him all the more. Tom Morely was coming to visit almost every day, spending lots of time with Sally, and it was obvious he was infatuated with her. It was also apparent that she did not share his affections. This was all new for Ella and Owen, and they realized it might intensify before long. Spring had a way of bringing such things to fruition, though in the spring, Jeremy would depart.

For the sake of Sally, they hoped the lad would be gone before matters between them became any deeper. It worried the Sutherlands that Jeremy's education might be stopped too soon, or that Sally's early womanhood would be cut short by children and a home to keep.

A cloud over all these things were the charges against Sutherland and the others. As winter relented, and ice began to recede, Sutherland completed his essays. While he worked, Ella saw in him a new vigor, restored vitality that expressed itself in many different ways. He exercised every day and worked astonishingly hard. His former despair and despondency was gone. Owen was his hearty self again, and somehow even stronger. He had come through an ordeal that had scarred him, but the scars had healed, and he was, like Jeremy, more sure of himself. Now the question was whether these latest essays were better than those written earlier during so much pain, frustration, and heartache.

The day came as late-March winds were whipping a sheen of water on the ice into sparkling ripples. Ella was outside in the warmth of the afternoon, reading a volume of poems by John Donne, when Owen came to her. The leather folder was again full of essays, and he handed them over. She took them, looking closely at him as she did so. He seemed tired but happy. Asking for the volume of Donne's, he said he needed to clear his mind. Leaving her there, he went for a walk down to the water, Heera padding along beside him.

Ella watched them go, then went inside, sat down at the table, and began to read. From the very first she was absorbed, and for two hours her attention did not wane. In that time she read the narration of a fictional character Sutherland had created: the venerable Indian sage named Quill. Living somewhere in the distant northwest, Quill observed the civilized world from the perspective of a wise but unpretentious man. He might have been an educated Mawak or a primitive Voltaire with a dry sense of humor. Sutherland wrote as the unbiased translator for Quill, presenting his subject's words in correct English rather than the common pidgin language of most red men:

> . . . for among his folk Quill is a great orator, whose eloquence rises far above the plodding language we know as modern English. Quill's images of nature spirits, visions of wise animals who reason and speak, and legends of ancient worlds unknown even to the Greeks, are beyond the power of this pen fully to apprehend; but if the reader be generous, Quill's words may be meaningful and perhaps enlightening to those who value candor.

In the course of these essays, Quill commmented upon British America as an Indian might see it. He was balanced in his judgment of Whig and Tory, who were at opposite poles of the American political conflict now developing into open hostility.

Quill understood the terms Whig and Tory as his native ear heard them: "whick" and "towhee." The whick, he knew, was an unbeautiful bird that existed only at Sault Sainte Marie, and was notorious as a quarrelsome noncomformist who pecked at anything, whether hungry or not. The towhee, a gaudy finch known for raucously scratching the ground for food, was always ravenous, with an insatiable appetite. Neither group of birds, whick nor towhee, appealed to him because they cared nothing for the welfare of Indians. He said both groups were poised to tear Indian country asunder for personal gain.

Their names, said Quill, were appropriate choices, but he suggested there were better terms, even more in keeping with the characteristics of these parties. Whicks ought better to take the old Gaelic word an Irish trader once had used—"whig," which meant horsethief. Towhees, he said, would be aptly called by the Irish name for outlaws—"tories."

In these essays, Quill expressed hope that Indians would take their rightful place in the system of government supported by both parties. Quill spoke of the great Indian leagues and confederacies, such as that of the Iroquois, which were founded on the equality of man, of tribe, and of nation. He described leagues brought into being many generations past, and maintained throughout war and the coming of European culture. The Iroquois League, he said, was a remarkable example of six nations cooperating for the good of all. The unity of the American colonies into one such league could also be achieved if whites had the respect for one another that Iroquois regarded as a natural law of life.

Then Quill referred to the famous Massachusetts political essayist and thinker, James Otis, who had led opposition to Parliamentary oppression and unjust taxation of the colonies.

> Mr. Otis has raised his voice bravely and nobly in the cause of freeborn British subjects in America, white and black, but there is no mention in his writings of the red face. If untold thousands of Indians are not to be considered freeborn subjects of the same king as the eloquent Mr. Otis, then how is it that every treaty we have signed with our sacred mark refers to us as subjects? Do these documents lie?

> Or is the term "freeborn" inappropriate when the subject is of Indian blood? Yet that cannot be so, for Indians are as free as the wind, as jealous of their liberty as even Mr. Otis, and just as willing to fight for it.

Quill was not always so grim. When lighthearted, he poked fun at whites with the affection of the humanitarian whose troubled mind is full of love for his fellow man. Often he employed Indian metaphors, legends, anecdotes to make his

points, and Ella thoroughly enjoyed each essay as she read it
swiftly, without pause. Owen had clearly laid out the Indian's
case, and likewise the case of the northwest territory. He said
the destiny of Indian country was vitally linked with that of
British colonies, which were turning westward. The rights of
Indians who dwelt in that territory were as essential to American
liberty as were the rights of whites and blacks:

> The Indian has been a wandering hunter, a man of
> the forest, but his days as such are numbered. Just as
> his forefathers, with the coming of guns, neglected the
> bow and spear, so will his sons forget the primitive life
> of the woods, and will take up the ways of whites. For
> better or for worse, this will happen, and those Indians
> who have seen the power of white civilization will not
> flee it.
>
> Just as some Iroquois have houses that are finer than
> many white neighbors, just as Cherokee keep estates
> resembling those of the gentlemen of Charles Town, and
> just as the Indians of eastern Pennsylvania are becoming
> craftsmen and husbandmen as clever as their white in-
> structors, so, too, will other Indians east of the Father
> of Waters make their way as equals. For too long whites
> have looked upon Indians as a race to be exterminated.
> In that fatal course lies warfare and a poisoning of the
> soul that will take generations to heal.
>
> Before us unfolds an age of hope, of faith, of reason
> and natural law. This Indian longs for the day our peoples
> will go forward in peace, cooperation, and mutual re-
> spect. May the Great Spirit will it so.
>
> Quill has spoken.

Ella dashed from the house, hurrying down to the river,
where Owen was repairing a canoe suspended upside down on
a rack. She leaped at him and whirled him around in her happiness.

In the summer, these essays would be taken to Philadelphia
to be published in Franklin's *Gazette*. They would be reprinted
in periodicals from Montreal to Saint Augustine, and perhaps

even in Great Britain. Quill would speak to thousands, saying all men are equal, and all governments accountable to those they govern.

chapter **22**

NEW BEGINNINGS

In the early weeks of April the melting time came to Michilimackinac. Frozen straits turned dark at the shoreline, a border of weakening ice that crept steadily outward, until the entire surface was no longer white. Winds buffeted and tortured the ice, breaking it up, pushing it in floes against the shore. The days warmed, and waterfowl returned in flights like arrowheads, settling on beaches and mossy banks. In the fort itself life changed, for no one could venture beyond the walls as mud and morass thickened everywhere.

In these long days of waiting, green shoots of fern squeezed through the ground and gray shadows of pussy willow appeared along creek-banks. Trickling, rushing, flowing water of snowmelt and thawing groundwater covered the land, sluiced over cliffs, and swelled streams. The ice highways on the rivers turned to slush; trails that had led across snow became impassable; and even the streets and gardens of the fort were formidable obstacles to normal movement.

It was a common complaint that summer was too short to be worth the hell of spring breakup. The strain of cabin fever was felt in the extreme during these warm, breezy days, when the outdoors was so marvelous and yet so abominably impossible to traverse because of the mud.

Late in the month, the booming, shuddering ice out on the straits quieted, disintegrated, then began to drift away, leaving open water. The Sutherlands knew that farther south the lakes had already become navigable, so if Defries had succeeded in persuading Sir William Johnson to override Farley Jones, word could have come already to Detroit. It was likely the next ship that arrived at Michilimackinac would bring news, and there was some concern that before Johnson's order reached Detroit, Jones might send a vessel of his own to Michilimackinac. If the commissary had learned Sutherland and the others were here, he would surely attempt to place them under arrest.

With every passing day, the Sutherlands and their friends at Michilimackinac grew increasingly anxious. As the ice left the lake, hurled in glistening piles along the shoreline, Ella and Owen knew a moment of decision had come. Unwilling to put off longer what they must face, they resolved at the end of April to go down to Detroit no matter what awaited them.

The day before they were to depart, a shout came from the sentry in the southeastern blockhouse that a sail was in sight. Ella and Owen were in their house packing goods into canvas bales when the yell rang through the fort. They hurried out into the bright sunlight and accompanied the crowd of residents and off-duty soldiers making for the landing. Partway there they were joined by the Levesques and the Greys.

None of the partners spoke, all aware that this vessel might carry orders for their confinement. Worse than that, Jones himself might be aboard to see to it that imprisonment was speedy and harsh. Despite what might happen, the friends had agreed not to resist with violence, for that would be just what Jones and Bradford Cullen would like.

Passing through the double set of gates opening to the landing, the friends did not share the excitement of most others, who looked forward to first word from the East. Royal artillerymen in blue coats scrambled around a fieldpiece in the center of the parade ground, their white breeches and gaiters spattered with mud. The loud report of the gun startled the crowd, causing babies to cry, and Ella's younger children huddled close to her legs. Like their mother and most other women at the fort, Susannah and Benjamin wore wooden sabots, which were perfect for the mud. The men, too, wore clogs or else boots, the better-dressed with spatterdashes to protect their breeches.

The salute from the ship clapped and rolled across the water, white smoke puffing from the side of the vessel, which was within half a mile by now. Its sails bright against dark blue water, the sloop heeled to port and scudded swiftly toward the fort, close enough now to be recognized.

Sutherland was the first to see this was his own sloop, *Trader,* which had come all the way from eastern Lake Erie. Jones could not be aboard, but word from Peter Defries surely would be. That lifted the spirits of all of them. When the ship drew close to the landing, dropping sail and throwing a bowline to the whaleboat rowing out from shore, Peter and Mary were unmistakable on deck, waving and calling to their friends.

Hearts pounding, Ella and Owen stood at the end of the landing, waving back, eager for the message from the beaming Defrieses, who were near Emmy and Jeanette. Ella was trembling, and she took Owen's arm, the children shouting with excitement, jumping up and down beside her.

The *Trader* was towed laboriously to the landing, where men waited to catch the cables and tie her up, but even before the ship came alongside, Peter Defries got the megaphone from the sloop's master and bellowed to Sutherland:

"Sir William sends his regards! All's well that ends well, an' Farley Jones can go to hell!" He roared with delight and clapped the railing with his meaty fist. "Hey, laddie, I'm a poet just like you!" He laughed again, and Mary gave him a poke to stop his clowning.

Sutherland was leaning nearly over the edge of the dock, grinning at the mischievous Defries. Even before the Dutchman shouted again, it was obvious things had gone their way.

"Jones is out as commissary!" Defries yelled, so close now that there was no need for the megaphone. "Charges are dropped, trading licenses are restored, an' you can all go home on the *Trader*!"

The partners cheered and hugged one another, and so did their many friends from Michilimackinac who knew of the conflict. As the ship was made fast, Peter clambered up on the railing and sprang onto the dock, his massive weight shuddering the planks as he landed. He embraced Sutherland, who, laughing, lifted him off the ground in triumph.

The others gathered around, clapping Defries on the back as he shouted down, "Sir William's broken with Cullen completely! Says Cullen's embarrassed him with all Jones's dirty tricks, an' too many folks are thinkin' the superintendent can't run his own Indian Department. Anyway, Cullen's a Whig these days, an' Johnson don't like Whigs!"

At that moment, Sutherland noticed a stranger aboard ship, who followed Mary, Emmy, and Jeanette down the gangplank. He was a short, bewigged gentleman of middle age and wearing immaculate clothes. Sutherland, still staggering under Defries, saw the fellow nod in greeting.

Chuckling, Defries said proudly, "Mr. Raymond Graves of London, sir, this here bully is the gent you're lookin' for. Owen Sutherland, meet a friend of Colonel Henry Gladwin, a merchant who come out to this godforsaken wilderness just to do business with us."

Ella broke off admiring Jeanette, and gaped in amazement. Could this plump man, grinning so politely, tipping his hat to her and Mary, be the answer to her troubled letter? Dignified and forthright, Raymond Graves smiled warmly at the Sutherlands.

"Honored, mistress," he said, bowing to Ella. Then he shook hands with Owen, who had set Defries back on his feet and seemed unable to grasp what he had heard. With a twinkle in his dark eyes, Graves was saying the wilderness was magnificent, not godforsaken at all, and to Ella added, "Mistress Sutherland, permit me to be so bold to reveal that last year Henry read your letter to me! After all you wrote of the Frontier Company, I thought it a splendid enterprise that would complement my shipping and mercantile house in England."

Ella gaped at her astonished husband, while Peter Defries chortled happily. Mary gave Ella a hug, and nearby the Greys and Levesques were listening with wonder. Sutherland looked from Ella to Graves and back, beginning to comprehend.

Owen said, "Permit *me* to be so bold, sir, but are you offering to supply us with trade goods on credit in return for our peltry?"

Graves said it was so, adding that he had always wanted to see the northwest. "I was a frigate captain during the great war, and I know every port and inlet of the American seaboard; when my ship gave passage to Henry Gladwin on his return to England I heard him describe the wilderness in such glowing terms that I resolved to visit it one day. Now I've done it!"

Upon Ella's urging, they all returned to the Sutherland home, talking as they walked about how Graves and Gladwin had schemed to establish a British source of supply for the Frontier Company. By the time they crowded into the little house, Graves had made it clear he knew everything about Bradford Cullen's intrigues in the Indian trade. Willing to invest in the Frontier Company, Graves offered thousands of pounds of credit, and would take charge of shipping and fur sales to Britain.

"It's like a dream come true," Ella murmured, standing after the others all sat down.

Graves smiled, and an elated Defries slapped the merchant's leg so hard it stung. Sutherland, full of ambitious plans, asked when they could receive the first goods.

The merchant motioned in the direction of the waterfront and said, "As soon as your men unload the *Trader*."

Defries cried out, "Owen, the ship's stuffed to the yardarms with the finest, most Injun-pleasin' doodads, geegaws, an' trinkets that ever made a redskin feel white! With this shipload, an' with the storehouse already full at Detroit, nobody, not even Cullen, can match us now!"

Angélique Levesque stood up and declared, "From here we can send canoe brigades out to Rainy Lake and beyond!" Then she held her abdomen and sat down, for she was well along in her second pregnancy. As an expert in the trade, Angélique quickly rattled off where goods ought to be sent, and which *voyageurs* would be best to hire for various routes.

As the Frenchwoman spoke with mounting excitement, Owen sat back contentedly, sensing that for the first time their combined skills, knowledge, and trade relations finally would be exploited to the utmost.

Jacques laughed to hear Angélique so excited, and said, "The upper lakes will be picked clean of prime peltry, and the Indians there will be the handsomest-dressed in all America!"

Defries told the rest of his tale, explaining that his meeting with Sir William Johnson had come at a time when the Indian superintendent was furious with Cullen's abuse of the western Indians. In collusion with Jones, Cullen had cheated and oppressed so many tribes that complaints had come thick and fast to Johnson's home on the Mohawk.

Defries held up a hand, saying, "There's more! If you know Sir William, you'll know he don't give somethin' for nothin'! So, in return for droppin' charges, he wants Owen to take his nephew, Guy Johnson, under his wing an' get him the trust o' the Injuns in the Illinois."

Guy Johnson was about to take control of the Illinois department to learn more about managing Indian affairs. Not only did Sir William desire to strengthen his own influence in the West, but he was grooming Guy to step into the post of Indian superintendent within a few years.

"Sir William's terrible sick," Defries said, adding that the man suffered from syphilis and fevers resulting from a fast and hedonistic life. "He might not last much longer, so he wants a man he can trust to prepare Guy well over the next year or two."

Sutherland gladly accepted Sir William's bargain, saying

he could renew trade with the Illinois country tribes at the same time as he counseled Guy Johnson.

"This is the opportunity we've always wanted!" He grinned at Ella, who was radiating with joy. "This year, we'll even begin to build our house at Valenya!"

So it was that Ella's half-forgotten letter to her brother in England brought the Frontier Company to the brink of triumph in the fur trade. From the outset Raymond Graves was taken to the hearts of all the partners. He was like a kindly, wealthy uncle to the young folk, and was a trove of knowledge about London, Edinburgh, Paris, Amsterdam, Philadelphia, and New York. As a former naval officer, Graves had seen much of the world, had fought against the French in several great sea battles, and was now a leading figure in London society.

Sally in particular was enthralled by him, and wanted to know everything of fashion, taste, and new styles. The men asked about politics, which were ever more sour between Britain and the colonies. In his turn Graves was fascinated by life in the northwest. During those days before the return to Detroit, he struck up a close friendship with Jacques Levesque and Jeremy Bently. These two showed him much of the country and the people, informing him of the subtle things a fur trader must know. Graves intended to return to England that autumn, so he had little time to waste, learning all he could and taking sincere interest in everything.

In return, Jeremy had much to ask concerning the study of medicine in Britain after finishing the Academy in Philadelphia. That appealed to Graves, who briefly had studied medicine, which was still his first love after the sea.

"But as the eldest son, I had to follow the family tradition and join the Royal Navy, though I might have been happier as a doctor of medicine."

Graves was walking along the beach near the fort as he said this, and listening were Jeremy and Tom. They carried fishing poles, and at their side was Sniffer, who was spoiled by the gentleman's ever-full pocket of sweets.

Graves gave his attention to the otter, and the lads climbed onto a rock to cast their lines. Sitting in the sunshine of a windy spring day, they saw Sally come down the beach to join Graves. She wore a white dress, her bonnet hanging at her neck, auburn hair full in the breeze. Graves said she reminded him of his own daughter, about her age. They walked along the beach, she barefoot, he with hands behind his back.

"He's so rich," Tom said, gazing thoughtfully at Graves. "An' look at Sally, she acts like the daughter of a duke, don't she?"

Jeremy saw her, carrying shoes, slowly moving along the beach at the merchant's side. "It's true," he said absently. "Sal's almost getting pretty."

"*Gettin'* pretty! Why you must be blind, Bently! She's been danged pretty for a long time!"

"You think so? I never thought much of it."

"Look closer, you bug-tit! She's the best-lookin' girl I ever seen; an' I mean ever, anywhere!"

"You haven't seen so many." Jeremy cast his line again; something surfaced not far away. "Why don't you marry her, then?"

"Me?" Tom colored and yanked his own line from the water to rebait the hook.

"You'd like to, wouldn't you?" Jeremy stared right at his friend. "If you ask me, you're ready to settle down and sink some roots."

"Mebbe. Yeah, why not? What do you want to do, be a schoolteacher or sawbones in Montreal or New York Town?"

"Or London or Edinburgh—"

"Or Chinee or Africay or the Spice Islands!"

Jeremy chuckled. "I do want to travel. Don't you?"

"What for?" He stuck himself with the hook and grimaced, then fixed the worm and cast again.

"What for? Why, to see things, of course. And if you're going to marry Sal, then you'll have to travel, because she tells me she wants to see things." He felt a tug on his line and was hardly listening as Tom muttered:

"Yes, I guess she does want to do that. I guess she'd like to travel with you, though, not me."

Jeremy lost his catch and gaped at Tom, who was rather downcast. "With me? What are you saying, boy?"

"By gad, you're a lout, Bently!" Tom stood up, drawing in his line. "How're you gonna teach anybody anythin' if you ain't got the wit to see when a pretty girl's got a soft spot for you?"

"You're mad!" Jeremy laughed more loudly than necessary, so that Sally turned to look at him and waved.

Tom saw no humor at all.

Jeremy declared, "Morely, you're the one's blind! She can't think the way you're saying she does, 'cause she knows I'm going away, maybe forever."

Tom paused. "Forever. That sounds grand, Bently, really grand for you."

"Don't you want to go somewhere special?"

Tom jumped down from the rock. "If things work out that way, I suppose I'd go."

"You mean if Sally wants it, eh?"

Jeremy attempted a good-natured laugh. Tom shook it off, then went to join Sally and Graves, who were walking back along the beach. Jeremy could not concentrate on fishing. Did Sally really feel that way about him? It was not possible! She was a friend, more like a sister than . . . than anything else. He watched Tom saunter up to Sally, snatch her bonnet, and dash away. Sally raced after him, leaped on his back, and down they tumbled laughing and shouting. They were a good combination, those two. Sally would be much better off with Tom, that was sure, because Jeremy had too much to do, too much to see.

As she jumped up and ran off, long legs flying, hair streaming behind, she looked more like an Indian girl than a white woman. He liked that about Sally. She was free and fun to be with; she would make Tom a good wife, and he was sure to keep her happy. Unless, that is, she really wanted to see the world.

For the Sutherlands and their friends, departing from Michilimackinac was more difficult than expected. Though the outpost had been so far from home, a certain attachment had been formed and new friends made here. The Levesques would stay behind as factors for the Frontier Company, and later Sutherland would inform Jacques of the results of the dispute with Jones.

The most difficult parting was Little Hawk's, for he had fallen in love with the Chippewa maiden, White Dove, and she with him. The young warrior was determined to return to his home country that summer, but first he must travel to Detroit to gather his belongings and his share of trade goods locked up by Farley Jones. One morning, he found White Dove walking near the lake, staring out at the massive island called Michilimackinac. It was a place of enchantment held sacred by Indians.

She turned when she heard Little Hawk ride up and, as he dismounted, ran to him, trying not to weep. As they embraced, he promised to come back and ask her uncle to have her as his wife.

"In Sioux country I will trade all I have for horses as the bridegroom's tribute, and then your uncle will be the richest man in your village; White Dove and Little Hawk will never part again."

She said, "My uncle is already a rich man, Little Hawk, and he needs no horses; he has told me already I can marry you . . . if you ask."

Little Hawk raised his arms and leaped in delight. With a yell of joy he mounted his horse, and lifted White Dove up beside him. Together they galloped back to the village for her uncle's formal permission. Then, halfway there, Little Hawk swung his mount toward the fort to find Tamano and Lela, who could not have been happier to hear the plans of this young couple. Tamano gave a load of trade goods to be used as gifts in exchange for White Dove.

Little Hawk said, "These will do for now, but when we return from Sioux country, I'll bring a herd of horses for your old uncle to admire all day long and be proud of!"

They rode off to the village, and Tamano and Lela felt the loss to think Little Hawk would leave them after they returned to Detroit. Yet all was well, for Lela was big with child, strong, and healthy. The infant would be large, Tamano thought, for never had he seen a pregnant squaw so enormous. In her sixth month, Lela was content. The child would be born at her home near Valenya, and she could hardly wait.

By June of 1770 it seemed there had never before been so many leave-takings in the lives of Ella and Owen Sutherland. They had bade farewell to friends at Michilimackinac, particularly the Levesques; then, upon returning to Detroit, Little Hawk and White Dove had departed for the Gathering of Waters. At Detroit, the Defries family and Raymond Graves had sailed east on the *Trader,* traveling to Albany, where Graves would embark for England. It had been a time of triumph and sudden success mingled with the melancholy of parting.

Among the triumphs was Sir William Johnson's removal of Farley Jones as commissary at Detroit. Jones left in a bitter, vicious mood, returning to Montreal and his patron, Bradford Cullen. His replacement was an honest man who neither bore ill will toward the Frontier Company nor favored Cullen and Company. It was apparent immediately that Cullen's firm could not repeat its success of past winters, when Sutherland had been hard-put to procure enough trade goods. The Frontier Company was ascending, and Cullen and Company was being sorely challenged. Even though Cullen had ample wares, few Indians would voluntarily trade with him unless deeply in his debt. Not only could the Frontier Company offer better goods at favorable exchange rates, but also the Indians naturally preferred to do business with Sutherland. Caleb Soames had Cullen warehouses stocked to overflowing with trade goods, but few trappers would buy.

The future of the peltry trade lay in the hands of Owen Sutherland and his partners. With all his money tied up in trade goods, Cullen would be hard-pressed to pay his creditors if he could not turn those wares into pelts for resale abroad. Sutherland had heard from Defries that Cullen was more and more engaged in land speculation, purchasing new tracts opened by Indian treaties. As part of a combine, he resold this land in parcels to associations of settlers. There was immense profit in this, but the drawback was that not enough land was to be had for these greedy speculators.

The most dependable way for speculators to acquire lands was to accuse Indians of hostilities, then to fight a punitive war that ended in territory being taken in payment for alleged depradations. Unfortunately for the likes of Bradford Cullen, there were no major Indians wars either underway or likely to begin soon. It was true that the frontier along the Ohio River and in the backcountry of Virginia was a dangerous no-man's-land where small groups clashed. Yet there was no real justification for whites to attack any tribes. None had taken the warpath, despite years of friction between them and squatters or white surveyors spying out Indian country.

For the Frontier Company, Detroit was a very happy place that summer, and adding to the delight of the partners was the birth to Lela of twins, a boy and a girl. Sutherland had never seen Tamano happier; Lela was lavished with attention and showered with gifts for her babes. This event brought joy to Valenya, where the couple lived in a bark lodge, and made the imminent departure of Little Hawk and his new wife less painful.

In those pleasurable weeks it seemed Detroit and the distant northwest were havens from the misery and conflict scourging

most of British America. During the winter, troops had fired
on a rowdy mob in Boston, killing several in what Yankees
declared was a massacre. American political leaders had called
for a congress of colonial delegates to discuss deteriorating
economic relations with Britain; but this meeting had been
forbidden by the government, which feared the potential hostility of a unified America. Soldiers were being billeted on
people who did not want them, and in New York Town an
ugly brawl had occurred between Sons of Liberty and the local
garrison. On the frontier, too, Indians were passing belts calling
for a general council to discuss an alliance against white incursions, but so far fighting had been only sporadic.

Among many encouraging events at the straits was the beginning of a new house at Valenya for the Sutherlands. Jeremy
refused to depart for Philadelphia until the house was at least
framed and the roof put on. He, Sutherland, and many friends
labored throughout the month of June. They transported timbers
and planks from a mill across the river near the fort, dug out
the foundation, gathered fieldstone, and laid up the fireplace
and stone walls. Construction of the main floor was completed
by the end of that month, and then a house-raising was held
in early July, with scores of people coming across the water.

Massive timbers had already been squared, and mortises
and tenons were cut into them by Jean Martine, a skilled car-
penter, who had come over for a full week, enjoying his work.
On the day of the raising, gangs of men stood up the two side
frames, pushing them into place with spearlike poles. Another
group lifted the timbers spanning the width of the house, and
inserted their tenons into the raised walls. Ella watched with
excitement as her new home took form, even grander than she
had imagined it would be. After the main structure went up,
the men swarmed over it, hammering in studs, beams, and
planking to complete the entire framework and roof just before
supper.

Exhausted, cheerful, and proud of their handiwork, men,
women, and children lit a huge bonfire that could be seen all
the way downriver to Detroit. They made music, danced and
feasted late into the night, then camped under the stars, to
dream of their own homes being built eventually in just this
way.

Inside the darkened house, which smelled of pine and of
pitch preservative, the Sutherlands all slept on the floor, bedding down on balsam as though they were on the trail. It was

a wonderful feeling to lie looking up at the rough beams of the roof, to imagine a ceiling and a second story with bedrooms. Ella and Owen, for all their weariness, could hardly sleep for talking about furniture, the kitchen, where the children would have their rooms, and so on.

Ella said, "Jeremy won't have a place here; it seems strange and unreal to think he's grown up."

Sutherland could see Jeremy in his mind, laboring under great timbers with the strongest of them, matching his raw power against even that of big Jeb Grey, and doing almost as well. Once Jeremy knew how to employ his fine body better, he would be as formidable as anyone Sutherland had ever seen—anyone, that is, but Jubal Swain.

In the Virginia port city of Alexandria, Lucy Swain also lay awake that night, Jubal snoring at her side. The heat was terrible, so oppressive that Lucy got up and went to a window for air. They lived in a fine, rented brick house, but how she longed to go back to the hills! She had been here half a year, and now she wanted to leave this strange place, where folk looked at her as though she were less than they. She and Jubal were well-off, thanks to Cullen's continuing stipend, but she felt inferior to these women of Virginia. Compared to Lucy— a simple backwoods woman—even the lowest of Tidewater females seemed dignified.

Jubal's nasty chest wound had healed since the fight near Saint Louis, but it had been a long time in closing. The claymore that speared him had penetrated deeply, and only her man's tremendous strength had kept him alive in those first weeks after he came back to her. They had fled to New Orleans, then took a Cullen ship to Alexandria. She turned to look at the claymore, where it hung like some trophy above the mantelpiece—or perhaps more than a trophy, it was a reminder.

Here at Alexandria they had recuperated, drawing a monthly wage from a local merchant house where Cullen had an account, yet they had done nothing at all to earn it. She knew well by now that Jubal was a hired tough, fighting for his living. There was no more pretense that Cullen employed him to manage some aspect of the peltry trade.

Lucy had also learned Jubal was involved in the murder of Chief Pontiac, but she preferred not to inquire deeply about it. She only hoped in the future he would pursue less dangerous missions for Cullen. Already he had told her Cullen wanted the country near the Little Kanawha River looked over for possible purchase once the government acquired it from the Indians. Jubal had said Virginia claimed that region and would inevitably settle it, one way or the other. A week ago an agent of Cullen's had come by—that sorry-looking creature named Farley Jones—and told them to be ready to leave next spring for Fort Pitt. From there Jubal would go on a scout into the Ohio Valley.

At last they would be doing what Jubal swore to her they would do, going to the country near Fort Pitt, where Lucy was certain her boys still lived as slaves of the Shawnee. Lucy had not lost hope, and even now she tried to imagine them with the flaming red hair of their dead father, Matt, as well as of Jubal, his brother. She wondered if they looked like her or Matt. Willie, the eldest, had been the image of his father when kidnapped six years ago. Joey had been more like Lucy. Willie would be almost sixteen, a man by frontier standards, and Joey a year younger. That relentless misery welled in Lucy, and she went back to bed. As she lay down, Jubal turned heavily toward her. Somehow, she would find them; Jubal would take her to them, right into Indian villages. If anyone was man enough to do that, he was. For that reason Lucy was willing to accept whatever he did for a living. One day his fierce power would bring them through the most dangerous country of all, and there Lucy would be reunited with her sons.

Lucy felt at her tummy. She was almost sure she was pregnant, and that thrilled her. At the same time, she worried that she would be unable to journey into the backcountry.

Jubal's arm went around her, and drew her close. She resisted, feeling too melancholy, but he pulled harder. Then she said, "Jube? Wake up, Jube."

He mumbled, half-asleep, and tried to kiss her, stirring with annoyance when she avoided him.

"Jube, I want to go find the boys soon. Hear me?"

One eye partly opened, he grunted assent, dragging her against him. But she struggled, for she wanted a more definite affirmation. She repeated the question, and he lay back with a great sighing groan.

"Lucy, girl . . ." He grumbled at how stubborn she could be when this torment haunted her. "I know, girl, I know. C'mon, now." He tried again.

She pushed him back. "I want to go afore the child's too big to carry, or too young to travel with."

Frustrated, Swain made a sound of exasperation deep in his throat and lay on his back, legs up. "Girl, we move from here when Cullen says we move." He rolled on his other side, his back to Lucy. "He'll send us there, equipment, supplies an' all, an' we kin find the kids then; but yuh gotta be patient, don't yuh know?"

"It's been so long." Lucy gave a shaking sigh. "Six years."

He was already dozing.

She whispered, "Oh, God . . . six years."

Here in Virginia she was so close to the Shawnee towns! A few weeks' travel westward was the heart of Indian country. She would get there. Jubal would take her—she would make him, for she knew how to get what she wanted from him. She would find Willie and Joe, and no one would stand in her way, not even Jubal.

chapter 23

BLACK CLOUDS

The time came for more farewells, these the most poignant of all. In late July, Jeremy prepared to leave Detroit for Philadelphia. His family had returned to the fort from the house at Valenya, which would not be complete and furnished until Sutherland came back in October. For Ella, this parting with her son was like a deep wound that gave no pain, but sapped her strength. Yet she would have it no other way. It was for his own good that he go. She had accepted this, and that was why his departure caused no pain; but it was a profound loss.

Early on the morning of departure, the Sutherlands and friends gathered at the beach, where a half-canoe was drawn up, loaded and ready to go. Tamano would accompany Owen and Jeremy to Pitt, and on to Philadelphia. It was hoped that on the way they would find Niko-lota, who was said to be in the valley of the Ohio. Many people were on the shore in the gray light of dawn, but neither Jeremy nor Sally were to be seen.

These two were a little distance from the beach, at the abandoned windmill. Sally had taken him here because she had something to give as a keepsake. They were up on the second floor of the decrepit mill, watching the crowd on shore. Though coming here had been Sally's idea, she had not said a word in the fifteen minutes they had been alone, nor had Jeremy spoken. After all, it was she who wanted to talk. Anyway, he could think of nothing to say.

Jeremy sat with his legs dangling out the window, and for a moment remembered how often they had come here as children. The ground had seemed so far down back then, and his legs never reached like this to the door header below. It was funny to think how one grows, and he mentioned it to Sally. Wearing linsey and buckskin, holding his felt hat in his lap, he was the very image of a frontiersman. Sally was dressed in yellow, with a golden ribbon in her long hair. She leaned out another window that overlooked the water, and when he spoke, she agreed but said no more.

After some time, Jeremy realized the others were waiting for him. He had to go, he said, and Sally sprang from her window to grab him, and keep him a moment longer.

"Hey, careful, girl," he cried, nearly falling out. "Trying to break my neck?"

He was grinning, but she was serious. Almost inaudibly she said, "If it kept you here longer, I might."

He laughed and took her by the shoulders, his right leg still hanging out the window. To his surprise Sally pushed against him suddenly, her arms going around his waist, head pressed to his chest, eyes closed. It was awkward and precarious for Jeremy, for the window sill was rotten and began to give way.

"Sal," he said, off-balance, and trying to get back in.

"Jer!" She thought he was hugging her close, not realizing he was nearly out the window. "Oh, Jer, Jer!"

"Sal!" His voice cracked—to her it was with passion, but really it was fright. He tried to get into the room, but Sally was in his way, crushing against him, squeezing and breathing hard. The wall creaked and sagged outward. "Sal, let me just . . . I mean would you . . ."

"Anything, anything, my Jeremy!" Her eyes shut tight, and all that she knew was his body, his voice, and his hands clutching her shoulders.

She gasped, "Don't let go!"

"I won't, Sal, I can't . . . I have to . . ." He was sure they would tumble right through the disintegrating wall. "Sally, will you . . ." This happened in a twinkling, and Jeremy needed all his strength to heave inside, recover his balance. To accomplish this tricky maneuver, he picked up Sally, and she went limp. Arms about his neck, lips on his cheek, she seemed uninterested in putting down her feet. To his surprise, she was lighter than he thought, very firm and soft. He would miss her. She was hardly moving, and for a moment he thought her unconscious.

"Sal, you all right?"

She shook her head.

"You fainting?"

She nodded.

"You want salts or a doctor?"

She shook her head.

In the distance he heard the blast of a hunting horn—Tamano's signal that it was time. That opened Sally's eyes. There were tears in them.

He said softly, "I have to go."

Gazing at him, she sniffed, "Aren't you wondering why I asked you here?"

"Uh . . . sure. Why? To say good-bye?"

"To give you something. It's here, inside my blouse."

Jeremy's eyes widened when Sally told him to take it out, and he cleared his throat with a kind of squeak. She closed her eyes. When he did nothing, she opened them again and asked whether he did not want his going-away gift.

Trying to hold her up and find what it was that bulged near her tummy was not easy. Had the young man's mind been cooler he would have stood Sally on her feet, but she was quite helpless, and he thought she might collapse if he tried that. Using a bent leg and one arm to hold her, he slipped his hand inside her blouse and very, very carefully felt for the package there.

He succeeded in finding it the first time. Almost disappointed that it had been so easy, Sally dropped to her feet, watching as he unwrapped the paper. Her heart was thumping as she observed his surprise at finding the rosewood music box she treasured so.

"Sal, this is too much. I can't take it."

With shaking hands she reached to open it. The sound of the *voyageur* song tinkled around the mill, and in the background Tamano's beckoning horn rang out.

Sally whispered, "It's yours to remember me by. It's got a happy sound, so when you're lonely, play it and think of me." She was compelling herself to be cheerful, and he was grateful for that, because he felt empty and sad beyond words.

"I have nothing to give you in return. . . ."

"Just keep it, and care for it for both of us, and that will be enough." She spoke so quietly that he felt drawn to her, then was close, and kissed her. Their eyes closed, the music box between them, playing happily. Sally's tears ran down Jeremy's cheeks, and he put his arms around her, his young strength squeezing the breath from her so that she laughed and kissed him harder.

"It's time," he said and kissed her again, wondering what this new sensation was all about and whether it was anything like love. Stepping back, his hand in hers, he told her, "I'm glad we never adopted you, Sal."

"Oh, Jer!" She kissed him roughly and held him. The music box wound down slowly, and they listened to the few, final, hesitant notes. It stopped completely. In answer came the horn. Their time together was finished.

The journey to Fort Pitt was a welcome time of friendship between Owen and Jeremy. Tamano, too, would miss the boy, who had been an apt pupil in the ways of the forest. He hoped his own son would be as fine a man as Jeremy was becoming.

Their stay at Pitt was brief, though long enough to resupply and get into a brawl with some Virginia toughs who picked a fight with Tamano. There had been six of them, braggarts and eye-gougers, but they were no match for the newcomers. When it was done, the trio were the talk of Fort Pitt—a place bustling with frontiersmen anxious to take up lands to the west. Sutherland liked Pitt less now that it had turned from a military outpost into a sprawling frontier settlement with a village, professional whores, and gangs of layabouts as mean and shiftless as the crew they had whipped.

As they canoed away up the beautiful Youghiogheny River toward the Allegheny Mountains, Jeremy reflected with some satisfaction upon the brief but exciting visit to Pitt. Not only had the fight given him reason to remember it, but afterward they had met a tall Virginian who commended Jeremy for his prowess. He was a gentleman, as was immediately apparent by his fine clothes and dignified manner. Yet he took particular interest in Jeremy's wrestling skills, saying he had been a fair scrapper in his youth. He had invited the three of them to dinner, later, out on the lawn of his inn, taking a few lessons from Jeremy.

Now, paddling in the bow, Jeremy chuckled to think how he had thrown the man, though he was very big and tremendously strong. The fellow had come back hard, and had put Jeremy down a couple of times himself, though the youth was the better wrestler. The strangest part of it was that the Virginian had been so refined and handsome before they wrestled, but when he removed his false teeth, he looked unexpectedly fierce.

Unlike the many Virginians of lower classes who came to Fort Pitt to squat, this man was a speculator and surveyor. He claimed lands near the Kanawha River mouth, which had been granted to officers who had served in the French and Indian War. After they had wrestled, while they played billiards and drank brandy with the fellow, Jeremy learned he was a member of the Virginia House of Burgesses and a colonel in the colonial militia.

He could not remember the man's name, though he and the others had been invited to visit him sometime in Virginia. Turning to Owen, he asked who the gentleman was.

"That, laddie, was the very same one who started the whole French and Indian War that led to the Great War for Empire; in fifty-four he led militia against the French Fort Duquesne that used to be where Pitt is today, and he was beaten badly. That fighting caused Parliament to declare full-scale war against France.

"His name is Washington, and he may not be much of a soldier, but he's a bloody good billiards player."

"And a wrestler," Jeremy replied. "I liked him, and I hope I meet him again some time; too bad he's one of those damned land speculators stirring up the Indians."

They left their canoe at Fort Bedford, bought horses, and rode over the Alleghenies, through rocky, spectacular mountains that delighted Jeremy with their beauty. Even Tamano was a capable horseman by now, having been taught by Little Hawk, just as he had instructed the Sioux in handling a canoe.

The country changed, hills giving way to woods and tilled fields. Cabins yielded to clapboard houses; split-rail fences and thorns became whitewashed boards, and trails turned into wide turnpikes, deeply rutted and busy with travelers.

In the wilderness Jeremy had been completely at home, but as they drew near Philadelphia, passing neat, prosperous farms on busy roads filled with strange people he had never imagined existed, he became quiet. Absorbing everything, marking for future investigation all he saw, Jeremy stopped asking question after question as he had done all the way from the Alleghenies to the Schuylkill River.

Sutherland enjoyed the astonishment of his stepson that morning, as they moved along the Lancaster Road, mobbed by people and wagons heading for the city. There were too many different sorts of folk to inquire about, and Jeremy simply gaped, front and back, side to side. There were somber Quakers, pious Moravians, well-dressed Christian Indians, prosperous German farmers, and Calvinist Scotch-Irish backwoodsmen as poor and proud as Quakers were rich and modest. Great Lancaster wagons loaded with hay twenty feet high caused Jeremy to stare for a full minute before Owen called him to catch up with them. It struck him that he was indeed on the threshold of the second-grandest city in the British Empire. He was arriving as a student in the best academy in the colonies, and would for four years be a genuine Philadelphian.

He could hardly comprehend, believe, or stop thinking about it. When the city came in sight as an endless horizon of houses and steeples above a line of trees, Jeremy whooped like an Indian, setting his horse on its hind legs. Tamano—just as excited as Jeremy—challenged the youth to a race. Before Sutherland could restrain them, they bolted over a hedge and into a field of clover. Galloping for Philadelphia, they leaped fences, crashed through groves and orchards, and hurdled streams in their headlong dash. Not the rider they were, Sutherland raced behind, hoping the constables of Philadelphia would forgive their exuberance.

When Philadelphia heard that Owen Sutherland had returned, Jeremy and Tamano were further amazed by the magnificent reception he was given. Owen had intended to hire rooms in an inn, but Governor Penn himself gave an audience and offered Sutherland the same exquisite quarters he had shared with Ella in 1764. Back then Sutherland and Benjamin Franklin had narrowly prevented wholesale destruction of the city by rebellious frontiersmen who were incensed at the government failing to protect them during Pontiac's bloody uprising. To prove their strength, the Scotch-Irish borderers had determined to wipe out Christian Indians harbored in Philadelphia.

It was during this turmoil that Sutherland first made Swain his enemy by beating him in a fight. Swain had caused much of the trouble in Pennsylvania by murdering his own brother and blaming it on Christian Indians, many of whom were later massacred or died of disease. The dead Indians also included the sister of Niko-lota, who succumbed to smallpox. Now that Sutherland had come back a hero, Jeremy found himself living like a prince in the elegant house on the Delaware River, where his mother and Owen had honeymooned.

Sutherland, too, was surprised and gratified at his warm reception in Philadelphia. The only disappointments were that Franklin was abroad in England as a representative of the colony in government and economic matters, and that the aged black servant who had attended them in 1764 had departed. Sutherland was told the educated, wise Botany Lee recently had bought his and his daughter's freedom, and returned to Virginia.

For the rest, Philadelphia was as gracious, splendid, and hospitable as he remembered it. Grown much larger over the years, the city was swollen with every kind of American ever made. Tiny Detroit did not throb like this, for all the restless folk crammed into that fort. Along with Owen and Jeremy, Tamano was welcome in the house, provided he forsook donning bear grease or paint. These days, as it turned out, the Chippewa took an interest in civilized things, and even wore some of the clothes available to guests of the house.

At the Academy they learned that John Blair, the botanist, was also away; and Mel Webster was said to be somewhere in Indian country with Niko-lota. While at Fort Pitt, Sutherland had hired a young Mingo to carry a message to the Delaware, saying he would stop at that post on the way home. Perhaps he would meet Mel out there, also. For the moment, however, what mattered was getting Jeremy settled in before Sutherland departed at the beginning of September.

That chore was easier than Owen had expected, for Jeremy was an immediate center of attention. At the many social gatherings they passed through as in a whirlwind, the young women in particular took to Jeremy, and he had more invitations to tea and to tour the city than even his stepfather. For just the briefest moment, Sutherland sensed himself aging, and it was a mellow, contented feeling. When Jeremy was there, women hardly noticed Owen—Ella would be glad to hear that. The lad was smooth and confident through the inevitable avalanche of females that engulfed him wherever they went.

As they rode home in a carriage one evening, just before Sutherland was to return to Detroit, Jeremy was advised not to let studies suffer because of his social life. He laughed, and said he was so impressed by the Academy that women would have to tear him away. "And this, too, assures that I'll be studious," he said, opening his shirt to reveal white scars from the wolverine that had attacked him. "It costs too much to attend the Academy, so I won't let it go so easily."

Half-dozing nearby, Tamano muttered, "Indian devil bad luck, they say; maybe it better you forget school and marry young rich girl instead." He began to laugh. "Maybe it bad luck if you become good scholar instead of rich, lazy husband."

Jeremy smiled. Absently, he reached inside his frock coat and brought out Sally's rosewood music box. Opening it, he listened to the song. Sutherland looked at Tamano, who grinned and turned to the window. Softly, they all began to sing, remembering their faraway home, each wondering what lay ahead of Jeremy and whether he ever would come back to them.

The months that followed Sutherland's return to Detroit were happy and prosperous. Frontier Company operations multiplied and expanded to take in the entire northwest from Fort Pitt to Rainy Lake and beyond, from Montreal to Saint Louis. The great, fur-rich drainage basin of the northern Mississippi became the domain of the Frontier Company, and Bradford Cullen's firm—short of loyal trappers—virtually collapsed. Sutherland's house at Valenya was finished, painted white, and became an inspiration for the other ambitious settlers and traders living near Detroit.

Tamano and Lela were comfortable in a smaller house, feeling uneasy in the spacious Sutherland home. The Indians and their friends built a fine cabin in a peaceful cove secluded from the river and just out of sight of Sutherland's place. Unlike Tamano's house, the residence of Owen and Ella was full of light, with real glazed windows, polished hardwood floors, and a handsome staircase with a curved balustrade leading up to the bedrooms.

Like the Sutherlands, all the partners throve in this time. The Greys moved out of the fort and built down the shore from Valenya, on land Sutherland had been granted years ago by the Ottawa. Jean Martine was content to stay in the fort, purchasing a house he renovated, and taking to wife a middle-aged French widow. More and more folk were coming to Detroit, and the straits filled up with people who found it difficult to acquire lands from any but French *habitants*. Impatient, eager to buy from Indians, these newcomers were thwarted by strict government controls on such settlement. Detroit, though not as bad as Fort Pitt, was an increasingly lawless place. Rough, land-hungry men arrived on every boat from the east, or came in by bateau or canoe. For all the disruption they created at the fort, they were an important source of profit for the Frontier Company, which supplied them from Jean Martine's sutler shop.

To Frontier Company partners, Detroit was a haven in a stormy time. From every part of British America came news of unrest, riots, deepening hostility between supporters and opponents of government. Jeremy's letters from Philadelphia told of the changing climate in America, which was increasingly anti-Parliament. Most troubling of all his letters was one in which he told of ambitious land-speculation schemes that requested British government grants as far west as the Mississippi and the Illinois country.

Indians knew about these schemes, and they often stopped by at Sutherland's home to ask for clarification on just what he thought whites intended to do. Sutherland, however, really did not know, for he was satisfied to stay out of active involvement in Indian affairs as much as possible. Still, he was often asked for his opinion, and whites at the fort also respected him, no matter what side of the colonial conflict he supported.

At Detroit, or in the Illinois with Guy Johnson, he was contentedly remote from worldly turmoil. Raising his family, managing affairs of the company, and enjoying long journeys into the wilderness with Tamano, he had never been happier. Jeremy, too, for all the ominous news contained in his long letters, was progressing well at Philadelphia. As the years passed, the young man's intentions to become a physician were beginning to be realized. To do so meant going abroad, and already arrangements were being made with Henry Gladwin and Raymond Graves. Coinciding with Jeremy's anticipated departure in 1774 was the ambition of Peter and Mary Defries to sail to foreign ports. It was decided that when the time came, they would all leave from Philadelphia on a ship being built in that port for the Frontier Company.

Despite the troubles in America, the Sutherlands were able to remain neutral for the most part. Of course, there were some who were jealous of their company's success. More than once Owen was accused by Tories of being a Whig, and by Whigs of being a Tory, generally because of the provocative Quill essays. Published in Franklin's *Gazette* and reprinted in publications abroad, the observations of the mythical Indian sage were well known, and seldom failed to stir either heated animosity or fervent agreement. Even Dr. Franklin wrote from London to praise Sutherland's work, and a letter from George Washington in Virginia did the same. Both men, however, questioned whether Quill was realistic in his dream that Indian lands be protected from white encroachment until the nations learned to wield political and economic power. America's destiny, these two men wrote, depended on westward expansion, and all that could be hoped for was that white migration would be peaceful and controlled.

Sutherland knew Washington and Franklin spoke for most of America's leaders, and he also realized that to influence such men would require decisive action on the part of Indians themselves. Education, organization, and strong alliances to solidify their position were essential, and must be achieved soon. It was the only way of stopping the white tide westward until the tribes proved to the likes of Washington and Franklin that Indians could stand as equals in American society. If that time came, then whites would be forced to respect Indian lives and property.

As the years passed, animosity intensified between whites and Indians. There had been a severe uprising among the Cherokee in June of 1773, and several large Indian councils held at Fort Pitt had been charged with the threat of a wider war. One Delaware chief warned that black clouds were gathering fast in his country, and this statement was widely repeated in the colonial press. To Sutherland's mind, whites invited a war, knowing it could only result in serious defeat of any tribes who rebelled. Such defeat meant new treaties and additional land cessions to the colonies who were victorious. The cycle would begin again: opening more lands that bit into Indian country; settlers buying up everything available from speculators who enriched themselves; and whites once more looking greedily upon the next vulnerable Indian ground.

During that time, Sutherland's main efforts—after family, company, and essays—went into the education of Sir William Johnson's nephew in the Illinois. Guy Johnson was capable and tough, fair with the Indians, and highly respected by them. By late 1773 Sutherland's work was done with him; the Scotsman had made a powerful acquaintance who one day would succeed Sir William as superintendent of the northern Indian Department.

In attending to his busy life, even a day of reckoning with Jubal Swain faded from Sutherland's mind. Cullen had been defeated, and Swain's ruthlessness was no longer felt. Only the old scars and the empty scabbard for his missing claymore recalled those harsh moments of combat. Sutherland was willing to let the past go. Now was the time to build, not destroy.

Around Fort Pitt, October of 1773, the forest was a fire of orange and red, but Lucy Swain saw none of it. Her own small

world enfolded the daughter born two-and-a-half years ago, a
red-haired, robust baby named Eloise. These days Jubal spent
most of his time scouting western Pennsylvania and the Ohio
River lands for Cullen, estimating the extent of flats and woods,
locating rivers and lakes. He had not been especially excited
at Eloise's birth, for he wanted a boy; but Lucy's love made
up for what the child's father lacked.

Fort Pitt was now called Pittsburgh, and had a squalid village
laid out. The forks of the Ohio swarmed with people, most of
them Virginians—in particular militiamen here to replace the
garrison of regulars who had abandoned the post a year earlier.
The government had taken its soldiers from several frontier
forts, including Chartres, in order to send troops to the distressed eastern cities. The evacuation of Pitt had opened the
way for an invasion of Virginia Longknives, sent here by their
royal governor, Lord Dunmore. These Virginia militiamen ag-
gressively enforced their own government against rival claims
to this land by Pennsylvanians.

It was often violent here, but Lucy did not mind, though
her life was far different from what it had been in Alexandria
or New Orleans. Even with her beloved daughter, Lucy was
sworn to continue the search for her sons. Jubal had learned
that Willie was said to be living with the Mingo not far from
Shawnee towns on the Scioto River. More than two hundred
miles from Pitt, these clustered villages held thousands of
Shawnee, Delaware, and Mingo—this last a mixed people of
Seneca and Delaware blood—and it was the center of the
territory still remaining to them. Here were the sacred council
fires, the graves of ancestors, a place where few whites were
welcome. If Lucy could, she would have walked to that very
country alone, and for the sake of her sons dared penetrate the
dark forest between Pitt and the Scioto. No more than a handful
of whites could venture there and hope to survive. One of them,
Mel Webster—friend of Niko-lota, the Delaware—was a can-
didate for adoption by that tribe in the coming year.

Since 1770 Mel had become a sort of eccentric wanderer among
the Indians of the vast Ohio Valley. Known to the tribes as
Singing Bow because of the violin he often played for them,
he was esteemed as a harmless, though entertaining, medicine
man, kindly and wise. Mel had learned much Indian lore, and
spoke every language within five hundred miles, having even
conversed in Cherokee and Chickasaw. Protected because of

his fame, and beloved for his openhearted ways, Mel could go wherever he chose in this part of Indian country.

He spent half his time at Philadelphia, where he lectured and studied botany and natural sciences; the rest of his days were strewn from village to village, teaching English and practical, technical skills: the use of a magnifying glass to make fires; the building of wind and water mills, and the employment of saws and woodworking tools. At Philadelphia Mel became a close friend to Jeremy Bently, instilling in the young man a profound understanding of Indian culture, both contemporary and prehistoric. This same subject became Jeremy's second love after courses leading to his intended study of medicine.

During these years, Mel often traveled in company with Niko-lota, helping search for Willie and Joey Swain. In the spring of 1774, they learned that both Joey and Willie had been returned to the whites more than three years earlier. The younger son, Joey, had vanished, but Willie had come back to the northwest, preferring the wild life of an Indian to the toiling drudgery of the settler. He had married a Mingo woman, and now lived with the respected and peaceable chief named Logan. The first meeting of Niko-lota and Willie took place just after winter, with Mel on hand to witness it.

Niko-lota and Mel entered the hamlet of Logan, who lived, contrary to what Lucy believed, east of Pitt in a good cabin, and there they saw a fine-looking group of Indians. Most of these Mingo were children, though there were several warriors, their wives, and visiting relations. Logan's people had well-cultivated fields and gardens, with sheds and corrals that would have done a prosperous Pennsylvania settler proud.

Logan welcomed them, and Mel was impressed with the imposing figure of this chief, who had been named for a white friend of his father. A leader who had refused to join Pontiac's rebellion years earlier, Logan was generous and outgoing to all whites but Virginians, whom he hated for their cruelty and hostility to Indians. Tall and regal, wearing a heavy buffalo robe against the cold, he invited the visitors to join him, and sent for one he called Red Panther. This eighteen-year-old warrior, said Logan, was admired by older men, known for his great strength and fierce temper.

The chief and his two guests were seated on chairs at a pine table when the door opened, and in came a giant, red-haired young man with a full beard. Instinctively Niko-lota leaped up, hand on his knife. Mel jumped between them, and the startled redhead crouched to defend himself.

"This isn't Jubal Swain!" Mel cried out to the shocked Delaware.

Soon, Willie Swain—Red Panther—understood that these two had come looking for him. Mel told him that he was the image of his uncle, and the young man replied, in a voice deep and slow, "I'd rather think I'm like my pa."

He sat down, and they were brought tobacco. After the appropriate introductions and polite ceremony, Logan allowed the Delaware and Red Panther to converse. Niko-lota soon realized that Willie did not know Jubal had murdered his father in 1764. Not mentioning that at first, Niko-lota told all about Jubal's involvement in the white attacks on Christian Indians that year—attacks that ended with the Delaware's sister dying, and with the murder of many others.

"I have sworn to kill Jubal Swain," Niko-lota said, staring at the white man.

Red Panther showed no emotion, saying, "I care nothing for him, only for my mother; I haven't seen her for nine years. She deserves better than him, but she's chosen, and it's her life, wherever she is."

Niko-lota's hatred of Swain rising within, he spared Red Panther nothing. "Your mother's husband is the killer of your father."

Red Panther's face paled, his eyes bulging. Niko-lota related all he had seen that terrible day, when Jubal had murdered Matthew Swain in order to have his wife. As a result of that killing being blamed on Aleta's people, many innocents had died, their blood on Jubal's hands. After Niko-lota spoke, a profound silence came over the room. It was so heavy, the tale so sorrowful, that several squaws and children who had been idling nearby—including Red Panther's wife and their small son—departed in haste. Mel thought Willie Swain might have a fit, he was so agitated; but a few words from Logan steadied him. There were tears in the young man's eyes, but they did not fall as he stared at Niko-lota, who said:

"I have vowed my life to avenge my loss upon this evil one."

Hoarsely, Red Panther said, "And I give mine, brother. If I slay him first, it shall be for your sake, also, and the blood of my uncle shall wash away our tears."

"So it shall be," said Niko-lota, taking the other's arms. "I shall never rest until Jubal Swain is dead."

• • •

With the beginning of spring 1774, Sutherland received a letter from Jeremy saying there were plans to call the colonies to a great congress at Philadelphia that fall.

Americans are infuriated with new laws giving royal favorites a monopoly on tea, and surely you must have heard of the Tea Party in Boston last winter. Also, here at Philadelphia tons of tea lay rotting in warehouses, for no one would stoop to purchase anything that would benefit a despicable monopoly. It's the same in Charles Town, where opposition to Parliament's tyranny is widespread and increasingly well organized. Parliament is desperate, proven by its continued use of so many punitive measures against Massachusetts because of the Tea Party. Yet abusing that colony for its refusal to bow to despotic regulations has only served to alert other colonies that they might be next if they do not lick the boots of Parliament.

To many influential Americans one recent act of Parliament was the most intolerable of all: The Quebec Act reorganized the northwest territory, restoring to the Province of Quebec the old boundaries that had been ruled by France. These lands north and west of the Ohio River were no longer to be claimed by any other colonies. This act denied all assertions of royal charters, which more than a century earlier had doled out to colonies all the territory to the "western waters."

The provocative Quebec Act had been under consideration by Parliament for a full year, because the question of how to govern the northwest territory had remained unsolved ever since the victory in the French and Indian War a decade earlier. Unlike other of the so-called Intolerable Acts passed at this time, the Quebec Act was not intended to punish colonies for defiance of British commercial and tax laws, yet it struck America like a bolt of lightning.

Bursting to take possession of the northwest territory, scores of influential men refused to accept this act. To plan a united colonial response to the Quebec Act was one of the most important reasons for the coming congress in Philadelphia.

Jeremy wrote:

There are deep-seated fears that Parliament desires to impose a despotic French-style government upon all the colonies. This continental congress will undoubtedly unify Americans against such tyranny; Britain will be forced to reconsider its poorly thought-out and executed colonial policy, for if it does not, I dread to think of the consequences. I mean bloody civil war.

Sitting on the stoop of their house at Valenya, Owen read Jeremy's letter to Ella. The house was grand, two stories high and painted white, with a steep roof of cedar shingles, and two glazed windows flanking the front door. As they sat in the warm sunlight pouring down, the Sutherlands felt Philadelphia and Jeremy's life there was a world apart. Owen remarked that the lad was becoming quite versed in political affairs, and Ella said that Philadelphia must be an intimidating whirlpool compared with the tranquility of Detroit.

Sutherland was reading on and smiling to himself. "Not so intimidating. Listen."

Jeremy wrote:

It's a blessing to have found new lodgings at last in the Academy residence hall, for my old room near the Statehouse had been hellish on account of that damnably deafening big bell hanging in the belfry there. Hour after hour it tolls, loud enough to shatter glasses and make short work of anyone ill and on the verge of death. All the neighbors complain, but no one has been able to quiet that abominable thing since it was brought over from England in Fifty-two.

They say it cracked twice when first rung, but these thrifty Quakers recast it both times, and it's a testimony to their determination and their stoic natures that it rings so appallingly loud. Would that it cracked again, for even though I'm now across the city, its distant tolling still unnerves me and awakens me from sleep, though its din is scarce a fraction of its former ferocity.

As a gesture of affection for the monster, Mel Webster and I climbed in secret to the bell tower one night and muffled the clapper in rags. It took three days until anyone bothered to go up and remove our handiwork, which is evidence of the love others bore for the glorious silence we bestowed briefly upon our city.

By the way, the inscription on the Statehouse fiend is "Proclaim liberty through all the lands unto all the inhabitants thereof." Indeed the giant is capable of being heard anywhere in the colonies if the wind is right. No doubt when I return to Detroit, there will be nights that I awaken, sure I hear the thing toll the hour!

To Ella, her son sounded like another person, whose time in Philadelphia had changed him. On one hand she was happy for that, and on the other, she missed the child, who was gone forever. When Owen finished the letter, full of cheerful news and hearty optimism, she went inside to play her spinet, which had been purchased recently from the fort.

A new commander was over there now, and he hardly knew the Sutherlands at all. Owen seldom was asked by the army for advice on Indian affairs, and he liked it that way. The spinet, which Ella's brother had bought for the garrison just before the uprising of Pontiac, had fallen into disuse, lying virtually abandoned in the old council house. Buying it had been easy enough, and Owen had floated it on a bateau across the river a few days earlier.

The spinet sat in one corner of the main room, where a fire was lit against the chill of April. Ella sat down at the instrument, gazing into the flames of the hearth. Thinking of Jeremy, she remembered faraway days, when he was young. It would be wonderful to be with him when they traveled to Philadelphia later that summer. Then they would see him off for Britain.

Outside, Owen listened as Ella began to play. He lit his pipe and in the distance saw a couple of canoes shoot across the river toward Valenya. His attention was given over to the soft music, and he hardly noticed the canoes pull onto shore until the voice of Jeb Grey attracted him. Jeb and Jean Martine were at the head of a few other leading community members as they trudged up from the beach. Owen stood to welcome them; Ella heard them come, and stepped outside. Obviously this was no social visit, for their guests seemed grim and self-conscious, removing their hats in greeting.

"Owen," Jeb began, even before Ella could invite them inside for some refreshment, "we come to you as representatives of the whole caboodle 'round here, British and French and American.

"Owen, I guess you heard about the congress bein' held in Philadelphia for the continental colonies?"

Sutherland said he knew about it.

Jeb cleared his throat and said a large number of folk had voted to send an observer from Detroit to the congress this fall. They wanted someone they could trust, who was smart enough to understand "big words an' foolish blabber, an' didn't git edgy rubbin' elbows with squires an' delegates."

With that, Jeb shut his mouth and stared at Sutherland. The Scotsman, pipe in hand, stared back. Nothing was said for a moment, though there was plenty of shifting of feet and looking around until Sutherland asked:

"Can your observer have the company of his family?"

"He can!" Jeb replied and almost grinned.

"And does he have to present the position of Detroit in any particular light at Philadelphia?"

"Only the truth as he sees it."

"And will he be obliged to vote in any particular way if asked to voice an opinion by the colonial delegates?"

That got some hemming and hawing, and Martine said, "Well, Owen, it's like this—you...I mean our observer is not a politician, and he is being sent down there to listen and report, not vote. You see, this observer has been chosen by both Tories and Whigs."

Sutherland thought about that a moment, then asked, "Why don't the Tories send their man and the Whigs send theirs?"

Martine and the others chuckled as Jeb said, "Tories an' Whigs out here both voted to send the same man as their observer...you!"

Jubal Swain had been in camp with a gang of Virginians for a week now, and had stayed drunk most of that time. At first there had been much rivalry with these dozen toughs, for they scorned anyone not from their home province. Since Swain was from New York, then Pennsylvania, he had to prove himself, and did so brutally, taking on three of them at once.

Camped near a broad creek on the south side of the Ohio River, they had been delayed by rainstorms from crossing over to survey a few thousand acres for their employer, Bradford Cullen. It was early afternoon when the rain finally stopped, and by now their keg of rum was drained. Most of them were surly and eager to get back to Pitt, to carouse after drawing their wages from Farley Jones, who represented Cullen there. The forest was wet, the river rushing fast, and they could not get over until that night at the soonest. That made them all the more disgruntled, for they were soaked to the skin, their food was going bad, and all were too drunk to hunt. Swain dozed in the lean-to, a fire spitting away in front, mosquitoes plaguing him. He was startled when the shout of one of his men awoke him.

"Injuns! Goddamn Injuns! Lookee here!"

Swain leaped to his feet, rifle cocked, but began to laugh when he saw that the man who had called to him was dragging a couple of young squaws by the hair, a few children running alongside, yelling and crying. The men would have some fun.

Then there came a call at the far side of the campsite, where the trail entered the clearing near the river. Some young Mingo braves came rushing in, obviously intending to save the women who had been abducted. Carrying only tomahawks, they were afraid, however, to start anything serious. In the next moment, as the Virginians laughed in the faces of these young warriors, more Indian women and elderly men arrived, all members of the same traveling party.

The Indians were horrified to see the two squaws so rudely treated by these Shemanese, the Shawnee word for Longknives, used now to describe any Virginia frontiersmen. An old man approached Swain, babbling at him in a weak but courageous voice. Half-asleep, and drunk, Swain understood not a word the man said. Meanwhile, Swain's followers, grinning wickedly, surrounded the Indians, looking over all the other Indian women, whose children clutched at them in terror. The Virginians were silent, making them all the more threatening. By now there were five women, three warriors, a couple of aged men, and a dozen children in this part of the clearing.

When the old man ended his tirade, he turned to the warriors and told them to gather their families and depart. The warriors looked uncertainly at the fierce whites all around them, the stink of liquor heavy in the air. The two squaws were still being held by the hair. Quiet words were spoken to the other women, who collected their children and tried to get through the ring of frontiersmen.

The ring did not open. The warriors and old men whispered to one another. One Indian put a hand on his tomahawk, another stepped close to his squaw.

Swain began to laugh. The whites grinned and leveled rifles. The Indian women screamed. Children howled. The men tried to shield their families. The old man turned to shout at Swain, who raised his hook and struck savagely. The Shemanese rifles banged simultaneously, and in the next instant the Indian men were shot or tomahawked. The old man died last, flailing with his scalping knife until Swain's tomahawk finished him. Several children were shot, and the two captive squaws died in that first firing, but the Virginians captured the other shrieking women. The children were sent fleeing off in shock, and the surviving women were dragged screaming into the lean-to.

These were the people of Logan, and among the dead were Red Panther's wife and son.

chapter **24**

VALLEY
OF THE OHIO

Just before the Sutherlands departed for the East on the
sloop *Trader*, another letter came from Jeremy, saying he had
been accepted to study at Edinburgh University, thanks to the
influence of his uncle Henry Gladwin. The joy that news brought
to Valenya spread quickly, and on the last night at home, they
celebrated with a great party, filling the house with music,
song, and laughter.

Offshore the *Trader* was anchored, its lights bobbing yellow
against the black river. Sally Cooper and Tom Morely walked
along the beach, enjoying the night air and listening to the
happiness from the house. Sally was content, excited to be
going to Philadelphia. She hardly noticed how quiet Tom was,
and told him all about her plans, relating much that Jeremy
had written in his letters. Tom made no reply, and walked in
silence as Sally hummed to herself. She was slim and pretty;
he tall, strong, and quite handsome.

In the four years that had passed, Tom had never declared
his heart to Sally. Though he had tried more than once, he was
too shy, afraid she would refuse him. Whether it was that she
always had anticipated his words and cut them off by inten-
tionally changing the subject, he could not tell; but he knew
well enough that Sally did not feel the same about him as he
did about her. For the moment, Tom accepted that, but he had
some hope that she would change.

After strolling a while he asked, "You think you'd want to
live someplace like Philadelphia, Sal?"

"Oh, yes!" She skipped once as she said that. "Or if not
there, then perhaps London . . . or Edinburgh; I really don't
know. What about you?"

He shrugged and tossed a pebble into the water. "I guess
anywhere's all right, long as I'm with folk I like; I don't know
much about the folk in them places. Do you?"

"No, not yet, but I will once Jeremy gets there. He'll write me all about it!"

"He write you much? I mean write just you an' nobody else."

Jeremy did not write to her alone, so Sally sighed, trying not to show her feelings as she said, lightly, "Oh, he doesn't have to write just to me, 'cause I can . . . you know . . . read between the lines, and sort of tell when he means something special for me . . . you know."

Tom merely nodded and was silent for a while. Finally he said he would really miss Sally when she was away, and she said that was nonsense, for there were lots of other friends there, and all the girls fancied him. Then she could not avoid seeing the sadness in Tom. She stopped walking and put her hands on his shoulders. He felt a chill up his spine, and at his sides, his hands were clammy.

Sally said, "Why, this is the happiest place to be in all America, Tom, maybe all the world! You should be glad to be here instead of some riotous city where everybody's in arms and fighting one another."

That did not work, so she tried to say the time would pass quickly. That did not help, either. She promised to write, and he urgently insisted she keep that promise.

"Tell me about everything, about Jeremy, and the congress, and all about them folk in Philadelphia! Gee, that's a strange word . . ."

"It means 'city of brotherly love'; it's Greek, you know." She took her hands away and began to walk on, but he grabbed her arms and turned her toward him.

"Sal, I don't like that term, 'brotherly love,' because the way things've been, Jeremy's like your brother, an' if you ask me . . . it ain't right for you to *really* love him, don't you think?"

Sally laughed a littly shyly. "Brotherly love means just that, like brother and sister—nothing . . . more."

He asked whether she wished it were something more between her and Jeremy, and Sally became slightly annoyed.

"Look, Tommy Morely, he's just a friend, like you are—"

He tightened his grip, saying, "I don't want to be just a friend . . ."

Sally yanked away, pleading, "Don't, Tom, please don't."

"Sal, you know how I feel about you, an' you can't—"

She put her hand over his lips. "Don't say this now, not

when I'm going away. I can't think straight about anything now, Tom. If you...if you care for me, then don't make it so much more difficult. Please?"

He relaxed his grip and took a deep breath. Looking at the dark ground, he said, "Anything you say, Sal."

Then she kissed his cheek, meaning only to be kind, but his lips turned to hers, and they met, briefly, but with fire. She pulled away, almost breathless.

Even Jeremy's kiss had not felt like that.

The journey of the Sutherlands to Philadelphia was leisurely and idyllic. Taking ships and whaleboats as often as possible, they arrived at Albany in early July, weary but in good spirits. They had heard rumors of increased strife on the southerly borderlands, with some talk of an important Indian council being held on the Scioto River that spring. Yet Sutherland felt no driving compulsion to find out what it was all about. Others could take on responsibility for Indian matters; he had another life, a peaceful one. It was not until he met Peter Defries and joined him in a meeting with the sickly Sir William Johnson that the gravity of the danger came home to him.

While Sutherland's and Peter's families were sight-seeing at Albany, the two men sat with Sir William on the lawn of the great stone mansion, flanked by stalwart blockhouses that were as strong as any Indian defense in the colonies. Johnson sat in a litter, which had been carried out by servants; he looked very ill, consumed by a reckless life of indulgence and frequent hardship. While his guests drank brandy, Johnson took only tea, complaining considerably about it. He told Sutherland that the situation in the Ohio Valley could blow up and become a general war that would ravage the frontier from the Mississippi to Albany.

"There are war belts flying thick and fast as ever Pontiac sent them out, Owen; there might be serious trouble on the Virginia and Pennsylvania border this year, and if that happens, the doom of the Mingo, Delaware, and Shawnee will be sealed."

He sipped his tea, making a face as he did so, and lay back weakly. Sutherland was told about the massacre of Chief Logan's people that had prompted the gathering of tribes as well as touched off raids up and down the frontier. Johnson was weak in body, but his voice was decisive and strong.

"There are whites who want this war, Owen; the Indians know it, and have tried to avoid a major confrontation. Insult after insult, murder after murder was forgiven or ignored, but it's gone too far now, and the red tomahawk's been taken up again. And you know what that means for Governor Dunmore."

Defries said, "Injuns're playin' into that rascal's hands!"

Lord Dunmore, royal governor of Virginia, was contending with Pennsylvania for control of the Ohio Valley, claimed by both colonies. In past years Dunmore had sent his own colony's settlers and local officials into land ceded by the Indians at Fort Stanwix, but Pennsylvania settlers already living there had resisted. The result was open fighting, feuds that cost a number of lives, and a state of virtual open war between whites around the former Fort Pitt, now named Fort Dunmore. The Virginia governor had there hundreds of his militiamen—Longknives, as they were called—waiting for his arrival. Before long he was going to march against the villages of the Scioto, and take all the land for his colony.

Sutherland was dismayed. "It'll take thousands of militiamen to get in there and out again, as well as a few good companies of regulars—"

Johnson held up his hand, coughing and spitting phlegm into a handkerchief before going on. "Dunmore will have three thousand men in two main columns, but the troops will all be colonial militiamen; only half of the army, his personal force, will be commanded by regular officers."

Sutherland scoffed at that. "The all-militia column will cut and run if a combined war party of three tribes hits them; not even Bradstreet with a professional army could fight his way out of the woods after being ambushed! Militia have never won a major Indian battle alone."

Defries said, "That's just what them militiamen intend to do—win; all by themselves if need be, without Dunmore or regular officers."

Bewildered at first, Sutherland declared, "That's a sure way to lose: Divide your troops and attack without any coordination."

Defries looked to Johnson, whose eyes were half-closed. The Indian superintendent let a cynical, knowing smile pass his lips as he said, "Dunmore doesn't think that will happen at all, my friend; he knows the Longknives want to win as badly as his regulars. When they win, Virginia can take a chunk of Ohio Valley as punishment of the tribes. You see, Dunmore and quite a few other Virginians have claims to that very land."

"A royal governor?" Sutherland exclaimed. "He's starting

an Indian war because he'll profit on land speculation?" He stood up, fury mounting to think that the tribes of the Ohio Valley and the Scioto could be massacred for the benefit of a few wealthy men. On the other hand, if the Indians somehow won the first battles, hundreds, perhaps thousands of whites would be wiped out before it was all over. Yet no matter how these first engagements ended, Indians could not win, for ultimately the regular army would be assembled to destroy them.

Johnson said, "Lord Dunmore could have prevented all this, but when the Indians retaliated for the murders of Logan's people by rubbing out a couple of stray traders, Dunmore called out his militia, and they came running—"

Defries interrupted, "Because they'll all get military land grants, too, for having joined up! Neat, ain't it?"

Pacing back and forth, Sutherland asked whether the Iroquois and the western tribes would join the Ohio tribes. Johnson said he believed he could hold the Iroquois after addressing them at a council planned for a few days hence. If Sutherland had taught Guy Johnson well, his nephew would keep the western tribes quiet.

"At least until the progress of the war is apparent," Johnson told him. "But a major Indian triumph on the Ohio would put us back ten years in the northwest; all the nations will rise, and the slaughter will be fearful on both sides. There is no one, but Lord Dunmore himself, who can end this before it gets worse. Yet I fear he will press on to the bitter end, no matter what the cost in human life."

Sutherland asked whether it was generally known that Dunmore was involved in illegal land speculation in the very same country he was marching against. Johnson said he had just sent a letter to the government revealing all this, but by the time an answer came from England, the war would be in full prosecution, the Indians probably overwhelmed.

Sutherland was astounded. "But the Proclamation of Sixty-three, the treaties at Stanwix and Hard Labor! The king himself has said colonial governments must keep out of Indian land without Parliament's backing! Dunmore's ignoring all of that by taking his militia in; it'll get him recalled on the next packet to Bristol!"

Defries snorted. "He'll likely resign first if things get too hot for him, an' get fat sellin' off his new land."

Johnson leaned forward, taking a sip of Peter's brandy and savoring it. "You see, Dunmore knows the mood in America, and he realizes that a royal governor who supports a popular policy of taking Indian lands will be widely supported. Though he defies past government policy, Parliament will be going against popular opinion if it dares cross him or remove him; the Commonwealth of Virginia and all those influential to-bacco-planters-turned-land-speculators will back him up. After all, he can simply say he was protecting his frontier from Indian attack."

"But there's something else!" Sutherland had a gleam of hope. "What happens if the Virginia militia triumph without the aid of regular troops? Dunmore will be embarrassed, and so will the entire British military establishment."

"Quite, quite," Johnson mused, recognizing a chink in Dunmore's armor. "If Virginia militia alone can defend American frontiers, Americans don't need the army, don't need to be taxed to pay for the army, and don't need garrisons in our cities to keep them from rioting against those same taxes . . . Hmmm . . . quite right."

Dunmore was running great risk by permitting an independent force of militia to march without the control of regular officers. If they were victorious, or even fought well, Dunmore would be tumbling Parliament's house of cards with respect to the alleged need for a strong military presence in America.

"In addition," Sutherland went on, "if the Indians immediately sue for peace, then Dunmore will have no justification for wiping them out, will he? If he dares attack after the Indians formally call for peace, then the proof of his personal interest in causing a war will further condemn him as an adventurer bent on clearing that country by bloodshed!"

Defries grumbled, "What good will all that do the damn Injuns if they're already dead or their towns're burned down?"

Sutherland was pacing again, aware that somewhere in this reasoning was a way of heading off disaster for the Ohio tribes. There was only one course to follow: These arguments had to be brought home to Dunmore immediately. The governor might call off his army if he saw how this rash war would jeopardize his ambitions and career.

Voicing Sutherland's thoughts, Sir William said, "We need a man who can stand toe to toe with a royal governor." He finished Peter's brandy and poured another. "However, in time of war, a man who defies a governor in the field, but fails to make his point forcefully enough—"

Defries added, "—An' all the while accuses that royal governor o' corruption—that man would be crow bait in the mornin', an' no questions asked."

Defries looked away from Sutherland and at the wide expanse of Johnson's lush fields on both sides of the Mohawk River. Sutherland was staring at the same tranquil scene, but seeing none of it.

Defries then downed his brandy, toasting, "It might be worth a turf jacket for me to spit in a governor's eye once."

Sutherland looked round at him, then at Johnson, a profound calm in the Scotsman's expression. He said to Peter, "You'd get lost in a field of clover, never mind the Ohio Valley forest."

"True enough," Peter said, taking more brandy. "That's why you'll have to come with me."

Sutherland grinned, and so did the others. It was, for an instant, as though he were ten years younger.

In the next few days, the Sutherlands and Defrieses sailed down the Hudson, stopping only briefly at bustling New York Town to take on water and supplies. Then they set off down the Jersey coast for Philadelphia, and it was a thoroughly enjoyable journey save for those times when they could not ignore what Owen and Peter soon were to face. Yet when Sutherland had told Ella he would go to Lord Dunmore and attempt to stop the campaign against the Ohio Valley tribes, she was not startled nor even surprised. Already, Mary had told her much about the backcountry misery and the march of the Virginians, and she knew what her husband had to do.

It was mid-August when the vessel beat up the Delaware River, putting in at the port of Philadelphia. The youngsters were incredibly giddy, but poor Sniffer was terrified at the sights, sounds, and odors, and he refused to come out of the cabin. Peter and Mary stayed with the ship, and within half an hour, the Sutherlands had hired an open mulberry phaeton. Dressed in their best city clothes, they spun through the streets of Philadelphia, Owen driving toward the Academy, where Jeremy lived. They had written him of their coming, and expected he would be waiting for them.

They clattered along the cobbled streets, soon surrounded by many young gentlemen who were excited about the end of their school year. Sally was astounded, for never had she seen a city like Philadelphia, and the imposing red brick and white trim of the Academy were marvelous to behold. The horses were nervous, and pranced onto a narrow footpath bordered by grassy lawns. Sutherland laughed as he steered them toward the three-story residence hall where Jeremy lived. This building was set at right angles with the massive main hall, which had a delicate white steeple and a pair of grand pillars that flanked its center door.

Ella cautioned Owen to hold the horses, but it seemed the college men liked the fun, and they cheered as the Sutherlands rambled through them right up to the residence. Sutherland stopped at the corner of the building, guessing by past letters which room was Jeremy's. Standing up in the carriage, he blew three blasts on a hunting horn, further delighting the students— a few of them shouted greetings to Sally, who modestly ignored them.

Jeremy's window flew open, and there he was, waving with both arms, then clambering out and shinnying down the vines that covered the walls.

Owen and Ella leaped from the carriage to embrace him, and he whirled his mother around until she shrieked, laughing. As he turned to his stepfather, a momentary shadow passed over Jeremy's face, as though something was troubling him. Then they shouted and hugged one another, each trying to lift the other off the ground, neither succeeding because of their hilarity.

Ella dragged Jeremy clear for a quick inspection. Dressed in faded brown breeches and a cotton shirt that needed mending, her son looked very much the struggling student living on little money and working hard. Yet he was bigger and more handsome than ever, massive in the shoulders and as tall as Owen, who said he hoped college life had not softened him too much.

"Some," Jeremy said, "but Mel Webster and Niko-lota come now and again to drag me out to the woods . . ." That troubled look overtook him again, and he was about to speak, when Sally could stand it no longer. She swooped off the carriage and threw her arms around him. He whirled her, too, then they parted, and both looked painfully self-conscious.

Jeremy saw Sally as though she were a stranger—a beautiful stranger—and stood back to admire her. Sally thought him a dream. Compelled by her pounding heart, she touched her throat to slow her breathing. Then Benjamin and Susannah assaulted Jeremy, and he lifted them together, groaning that they were positively huge and surely had been eating whole bears at once. Then he was gazing at Sally, and his parents took note. The little ones made it difficult for Jeremy to look at her, so Owen dragged them off, intending to let the young folk talk without distraction.

Sally said, a little stiffly, "I hope the pleasures of the city have not changed you too much, Jer. My, you look wonderful!"

Sally was about to speak further, but Jeremy cut her off, turning to Owen, and saying seriously, "Mel Webster was here last night, and he'll be back as soon as he knows you're here. Pa, Jubal Swain is at Pitt."

Ella gasped, almost fainting. Sally put an arm around her, and the little ones became silent. While all around them cheerful, carefree students enjoyed the end of the academic year, the Sutherlands learned once more of Swain, the discovery of Willie, and of other equally harsh news:

"Niko-lota has taken the warpath," Jeremy said, almost whispering. "I don't know if he's begun raiding cabins..." His voice broke. "But he might..." He fought to master his turbulent emotions. "Mel came in from the backcountry a couple of days ago, and said the Virginians intend to wipe out every Indian they find. The Indians are mad, too. Chief Logan has already taken thirty scalps to avenge the loss of his family, and Pitt alone is filled with blood-thirsty militiamen, nearly two thousand. There's more, south on the Greenbrier..."

Standing in bright sunshine, with the gentry of the middle colonies coming and going, the Sutherlands spoke of war. Jeremy said the second force of eleven hundred militia under Colonel Andrew Lewis and Captain George Rogers Clark, both respected fighters, was massed at Camp Union in the Alleghenies. Lewis was to descend the Kanawha River to the Ohio, and there meet up with Dunmore and his regulars, who would come on bateaux and flatboats. They would unite before marching overland, burning villages all the way westward to the Scioto River.

There came a shout, and they turned to see a reedy, tall fellow in buckskins, with long blond hair and a scraggly beard, come hurrying along the cobblestones toward them. There was no mistaking Mel Webster, who hurled himself into Sutherland's arms, embracing the family, children and all. It would have been a joyous reunion had the gloom of war not overshadowed it. There was much to ask about Mel's adventures in the wild, so they took themselves off on the phaeton to the City Tavern for a meal. There they got all the news from a distraught Mel, and it was a sorrowful dinner, indeed. Afterwards, Ella and Sally took the children away, and as Sally departed, she exchanged a lingering glance with Jeremy, who clumsily asked, "How's Tom these days?"

Unexpectedly, the memory of that farewell kiss Tom had given her came into Sally's mind, and she replied awkwardly, "He's wonderful . . . I mean, he's well, and sends his warmest regards."

When the others left for the lodgings being rented during the stay in Philadelphia, Sutherland, Jeremy, and Mel discussed the Scotsman's plans to go with Peter Defries and intercept Dunmore near Pitt before his main army engaged the Indians. Explaining about Sir William Johnson's letter to the government revealing Dunmore's secret land transactions, Sutherland was interrupted when Mel said:

"Johnson's dead."

The Scotsman could hardly believe it.

Sutherland and Defries had left Albany just before word of Johnson's death came in, and once aboard ship they had heard nothing of it. Mel said his last act was to convince the angry Iroquois to stay out of this war, and thus had prevented a general uprising that would have devastated much of the northwest. The western tribes, too, has been persuaded to keep out of the war by Johnson's nephew, Guy. So it was that Niko-lota's Delaware, in alliance with the Shawnee and Mingo, stood alone against the might of Virginia. The Indians did not have a chance unless Sutherland headed off Dunmore and peace was made.

Mel insisted he go with Sutherland and Defries. "In case a war party catches you. They nearly all know me, and that will get us safe passage."

Sutherland agreed and thanked him. Then Jeremy spoke up, "I'm going, too."

They looked blankly at him, then at one another. Jeremy went on, "Don't expect me to stay behind here when you're both chasing royal governors and Virginians through the woods." He stared coolly at his stepfather, who, after a moment, put a hand on his shoulder. Sutherland wanted to refuse him, but could not.

"It'll make you appreciate Edinburgh all the more, lad; just don't leave me behind this time! Show some respect for age!" Jeremy was elated until Owen said, "Let me be the one to break it to your mother, son."

· · ·

Before dawn the next morning, the four of them were on the trail, galloping along the Lancaster Road, making for Harris's Ferry and the track to Pitt. It would take two weeks of hard moving to get out there, and they hoped Dunmore could be found before he was too far downriver. Strapped to Sutherland's side was the empty claymore scabbard. He wanted to have it with him, in case Jubal Swain had kept the sword.

Just then, at Fort Pitt, Swain stormed about the slovenly cabin where he and Lucy lived with Eloise. He was in a foul mood, grumbling about goddamned soldiers, goddamned officers, goddamned governors.

Lucy was sitting at the table, pouring milk for the pretty child, who looked around fearfully every time her father threw something down or kicked the crude furniture. Swain was half-drunk, as usual these days, and Lucy was careful not to touch off violence. She knew him well enough to let this storm pass. What did she care, as long as he did not beat her or the child? He was doing just what she wanted, and she believed she was very close to finding Willie and Joey now.

Jubal had resisted her demands when first she wanted him to join up as a scout for Lord Dunmore; but she had pressed and pressed, nagged and complained, wheedled and pouted for weeks on end until he gave in. She wanted him to seek out Willie down on the Scioto, and make sure her sons were safe during the fighting.

He was muttering, "Got to traipse all the way to Camp Union an' back with the goddamned governor's goddamned fly-blown dispatches! I never jined up to haul my arse through no woods for no governor's fancy!"

He glared at Lucy. She gave some bread to Eloise, saying nothing. He was about to leave on a dangerous hike of nearly two hundred miles through the woods and mountains with an express message from Dunmore for Colonel Andrew Lewis. It was written down, but also memorized in case he lost it. Lewis was to march or take bateaux to Point Pleasant, a small peninsula at the confluence of the Ohio and the Kanawha rivers. Then he was to cross over without delay and engage the Indians in nearby villages, but on no account was the Virginia militia to advance alone upon the larger dwelling areas at Chillicothe on the Scioto.

Known as a man who could accomplish this dangerous but

crucial task, Swain had been sought out by Dunmore soon after Lucy persuaded her husband to join the scouts. Swain did not fear the danger, but he despised the labor of this oppressively difficult journey.

He went to the mantelpiece and took down the Royal Highland Regiment claymore Sutherland had thrown at him, and shoved it in a scabbard that was a bit too small. Angry at having lost his precious freedom until his enlistment expired in three more months, he rammed the claymore home, swearing when it did not fit. Then he jerked it out again and threw it into the corner of the room.

Turning on Lucy, he said, "Girl, I ain't gonna let yuh forget this for as long as I live! I should've never listened to yuh, an' never got in with government sons of bitches! I ain't no goddamned soldier!"

Lucy stood up, eyes downcast, and came to him, putting her hands on his heaving chest. He made no response. Then she looked into his eyes and took off the red silk kerchief he had given her long ago. It was a bit tattered, but she prized it as a symbol of their life together. Tying it around his thick neck, she kissed him, quieting him.

Then she said, "You're doin' all this for me, Jube, an' I won't let you forget it neither." She kissed him again, remembering the bitter arguments between them when first she tried to persuade him to join the Virginians.

"Jube, when this is done, an' we have the boys back again, you'll be glad you did somethin' good, somethin' right, an' did it for me."

He, too, recalled how she had threatened to run out on him if he refused to press home and search for her lost sons. Then, as she kissed him passionately, pressing him back toward their rumpled bed, he forgot his anger, his hatred of commanders, and swept her into his arms. He would not see her for months, and no squaw could satisfy him like Lucy. No woman could.

Jubal had been gone two days when there came a sharp knock at Lucy's cabin door. She was washing clothes near the window, and poked her head out to see who it was. She saw the ghost of her dead husband, and screamed in terror, stepping back from the window, eyes wide. The door was thrown open, and in rushed Willie Swain, pistol and tomahawk at the ready. Eloise shrieked, huddling on the bed. Willie, dressed in white man's clothes, had come to Fort Pitt for one reason.

"Where is he, Ma?" He approached her, menacing, casting about the room for some sign of Jubal. "I come to kill 'im! Where is he?"

Lucy staggered back against the log wall, kept herself from falling, and closed her eyes. When she opened them again, with the screams of her daughter ringing in her ears, she knew it was all too real.

"Willie," she whined and ran to him, clutching him close. "Willie, Willie, Willie, Willie, Willie—"

He shoved her away, and she crumpled against the table, banging her head. It was as though he felt it, too, and as Lucy slumped to the floor, he threw his weapons aside and leaped to her. Lifting her in his arms, Willie felt a mighty surge of anguish, and his body shook.

He broke down, sobbing, and when he could speak, moaned, "Ah, Ma, what's been done?" He held her against his chest, his face buried in her hair. As Lucy came to, she put her arms around Willie and held him tightly, with all her might, so she would never lose him again.

Painted for war, Niko-lota stood in the huge Chillicothe town in the center of massed warriors from three peoples—Shawnee, Delaware, and Mingo. The mood was solemn, without the usual delirium of taking the warpath. Even though a large force of fighting men had been assembled—nearly one thousand—there had been little dancing and chanting, few boasts of certain triumph or promises to drink the blood of the advancing She-manese. Seated in a vast host that filled the council grounds and eddied around bark lodges, these Indians were well aware of the peril they faced.

At this very moment Andrew Lewis's men were preparing to cross the Ohio River and devastate the countryside. This mighty gathering, magnificent in its array of colors and fine-looking men, was not strong enough to stop all the advancing soldiers. Everywhere Indian faces were painted black and red for war, but there was no light in the eyes, and even now leading chiefs were undecided on what course to follow.

There had been many speeches this morning, for and against meeting force with force. Niko-lota had vowed never to sur-render, and there were hundreds who would go with him to attack the well-armed Longknives, even if it meant defeat. Yet the greatest war chief of the day, the one named Cornstalk, had not cast his vote in favor of battle. At this very moment, another respected elder, Pucksinwah, was calling for an attack, standing in the midst of the warriors, saying, "The great chief Pontiac united us against the Shemanese, but we were defeated; treaties were forced against our will, lands sacred to us were taken, driving us back, and they harried our borders. The Shemanese have treated us like dogs!"

The warriors growled and uttered angry agreement with Pucksinwah; he was a stocky man, fully painted and feathered, wearing silver armbands, and for clothing only the simple breechcloth that would serve him best in the fury of battle.

As the belligerence of the warriors grew, Pucksinwah declared, "Again the enemy have come, like locusts, like wolves; Pucksinwah will die where he stands, or he will triumph!"

Yelling and shaking weapons, the Indians leaped up, spirits lifting at the devotion of so outstanding a warrior. Pucksinwah sat down near Niko-lota, and the chief's six-year-old son, Tecumseh, ran to his father, proud and beaming. A full ten minutes passed until the tumult quieted; then Cornstalk rose. He was a fierce man, noble of bearing, though not yet painted or adorned for battle. At first, raising his powerful arms to the skies, he tried to reason with his people, warning them they were not numerous enough to win. Darkening the gloom of his fighters, he called on them to send emissaries to the Longknives and sue for peace.

"There is no man who can say Cornstalk fears death!" His voice rang out over the silent audience. "But before engaging in this coming war, brothers and cousins, we must first attempt to make peace. Always I have striven to serve my people. Now I offer myself as ambassador to the Longknives, if that is what you wish."

The silence deepened, warriors staring at the ground, sorry to hear such a revered fighter oppose their determination to do battle.

After a moment, Cornstalk lowered his arms, and said, "But if it is your choice to fight, Cornstalk, as always, offers himself as your leader in battle!"

A shock went through the multitude. Niko-lota leaped to his feet, waving his rifle. "Lead us, O Cornstalk! Lead us to victory or to death! Lead us!"

The thousand were all shouting and cheering, jumping up and down, united in this desperate gamble for one great triumph that might repulse the Shemanese onslaught. Cornstalk hesitated, then went to Pucksinwah's side and reached down for a jar of vermillion held by Tecumseh. The warriors roared as he streaked his face with the colors of war. They would fight. They would attack in the mightiest single war party ever assembled by the nations of the Ohio Valley. In his passion, Niko-lota lifted the laughing Tecumseh over his head. Pucksinwah looked on, his expression distant, as though he knew the battle's outcome, yet accepted it for the sake of honor.

Nor was Cornstalk exultant. He had seen much of war and knew what lay in waiting. The Indian could not win, he could only fight and fight again, until the young ones were all dead, the old ones left with memories and broken hearts.

On the west bank of the Ohio River, Red Panther sat on horseback, concealed by yellow and scarlet leaves, watching flatboats and canoes swarm downstream toward Shawnee country. In his week at Fort Pitt, he had learned much about the movement and size of Dunmore's main army, and knew there were too few warriors to resist once the southern division united with Dunmore. Floating downriver, like leaves after an autumn rain, soldiers, mounts, beeves, and supplies filled every craft—an army of plenty in contrast to the poorly equipped Indians.

Behind Red Panther, his packhorse whickered, and a third animal bearing Lucy Swain and her daughter pawed the ground. It was time to depart. Red Panther intended to join the Indians in the coming battle. He had taken his mother away from Pitt—both of them dressed in civilized clothes—and she hardly cared. Her mind was twisted, spent from the turmoil of what her son had revealed. To think that Jubal had murdered her husband, Matt, then won her, was the final cruelty. It had nearly shattered Lucy's will to live.

Lucy had not objected to following Willie, not asking why or where they were going. She lavished attention on little Eloise, but said nothing to her son. That he intended to use her to bait the trap for Jubal mattered not at all. To Lucy, save for her precious child, life was empty of purpose and held no solace, no sympathy. She watched her son remove his linsey shirt, dig powders and grease from his pack, then mix up war paint.

It had come to this, thought Lucy. It had come to an end that she could not have dreamed—and yet, it could not end until she faced Jubal one last time. That might be the end of her. . . . Eloise nuzzled against Lucy's breast, sucking her thumb and smiling so beautifully. As though stabbed with ice, Lucy knew it could not end so, not while Eloise still needed her. She wept, her brittle self-control crumbling, washed away in tears.

chapter **25**

SHEMANESE

A few days later, with October bright and glorious on the Ohio Valley, four riders trotted along the same trail used by Red Panther and Lucy. Owen, Jeremy, Peter, and Mel rode single-file, pursuing Dunmore. The track beside the river had been widened by soldiers and packtrains following up the main army, and some miles farther back Sutherland's party had passed an enormous herd of cattle being driven along—enough to feed soldiers for weeks in the wilderness. This campaign was in deadly earnest, well organized, and capable of pounding its way through Indian country right to the Mississippi if Dunmore chose to do so.

More deeply troubled than ever, Sutherland knew that if he failed to sway Lord Dunmore, the consequences for Indians would be brutal. The nations of the northwest would never recover from such a blow, and deep inroads of settlement would follow the army as irresistibly as the flood through a broken dam. As these thoughts haunted Sutherland, the image of Jubal Swain recurred to him time and again. No matter what the outcome of his confrontation with Lord Dunmore, he would ride on and find Swain. This was not a blood vendetta; this was not an obsessive quest; this was a mission to put a stop once and for all to the mayhem Jubal Swain caused again and again in the northwest.

A few days later, Sutherland caught up with Dunmore's army, camped at the marshy outlet of the Hockhocking River. The sight that met Sutherland's group as they rode out of the trees was impressive, the panorama opening into a broad swath of flat bottomland shorn of forest. A stout stockade was going up to pen in hundreds of cattle, and two thousand confident men in buckskin and linsey were pitching canvas tents or building lean-tos. The uproar mingled with the bellowing of cattle: shouting, laughing, and singing men; the steady batter of three hundred axes and the rasp of as many saws. Suddenly and irrevocably, the wilderness of the virgin Ohio Valley had been violated. Torn raw and muddy out of the forest, this temporary camp would be the staging area for Dunmore's massive advance into Shawnee country, where he would link with Lewis near the Kanawha River.

Drawing up their horses to watch the jockeying of flatboats and canoes out on the wide river, Sutherland felt almost puny just then. The invasion of an army so great, by frontier standards, was indeed like the descent of locusts, as Indians had described it.

Liquor flowed freely in the camp, and the score of sweating, redcoated regular officers were hard put to maintain discipline. The militiamen were cocky, always raring to fight, and had not the slightest doubt of eventual victory over the Indians. They bore no love for Redcoats or for authority of any kind, but obeyed Dunmore because they believed this war would destroy the warlike Ohio tribes once and for all.

Sutherland heeled his mount ahead, asked an agitated regular officer for the tent of the governor, then moved through crowds of milling Virginians busy with the modest, yet essential chores of an army. Latrines were dug and lime thrown in; stock driven and chased into pens; sentry duty divided among companies; and here and there a man slept in the warm autumn sun, rifle and gear at hand.

Just before they reached the tent beneath a flapping Union Jack marking it as the headquarters of Lord Dunmore, Peter Defries pointed to the beautiful river and its wooded banks as far as the eye could see.

"No wonder the Virginians want this country; why, it's almost as pretty as the Hudson Valley."

Defries spoke for them all as they admired the Ohio, which was flecked with whitecaps. "Ohio" came from the Indian word meaning "white foaming waters," and it was the prevailing southwesterly winds that caused this river to froth. On the far bank, flats were thickly forested, and beyond the trees was a continuous chain of modest bluffs reaching into the southwest. It did not take a farmer's eye to tell how fertile this land was, so overgrown with oak, walnut, and cherry trees. Near Dunmore's tent rose a massive sycamore, like a lord above the rest, and at least twenty feet in diameter. A line of militia officers and soldiers waiting to see the governor on army business wound right around the tree. As Sutherland took in the majesty of the valley, this rugged camp diminished in the perspective of forest, river, and mountain. The Ohio country would never be the same again, no matter what the immediate outcome of the war. Indian country had been breached; what lay beyond would be taken, too, by another generation of strong and fearless people like these.

A shout from within the tent distracted Sutherland, and he heard a distincly Scottish voice meting out a severe reprimand. A young militia officer came stumbling out and stalked off, muttering in anger. Sutherland dismounted, but the Redcoat sentry at the tent entrance prevented him going any further, demanding his business.

"Owen Sutherland presents his compliments to Governor Dunmore," he replied, removing his hat. "I have a personal message to deliver of the utmost urgency."

"They're all urgent, so get at the end of the line, sir, if you please." The soldier indicated the file of militia officers and couriers, all impatient and annoyed at Sutherland's moving ahead of them.

Sutherland said his business was not related to affairs of the army alone, but was more important. At that the first man in line, a squat, dark frontiersman who wore a feather and seemed more Indian than white piped up.

"Army business comes first 'round here, Mr. Sutherland, especially if ye've come to speak for Injuns." He spat tobacco juice, to the disgust of the sentry.

Sutherland recognized this grizzled fellow as Simon Girty, a well-known professional scout who had been raised by Indians after his parents were massacred during the French and Indian War. Girty had been through most major campaigns of the Pontiac uprising, serving the army but not particularly liked by soldiers because they considered him an Indian-lover. He told Sutherland his own interview with Dunmore was next, and he was carrying dispatches back and forth to Andrew Lewis down on the Kanawha.

Sutherland again tried to get past the sentry, but was firmly refused. The militiamen waiting in line complained loudly, causing Girty to sneer and snicker to himself. Then he asked Sutherland what he wanted Dunmore for.

"To stop the war before it starts, and save your friends on the Scioto, Simon."

Girty's face fell, though the other whites laughed with scorn. It was obvious this man would rather have the Indians left alone, even though he earned his living from the army. Whispering, he told Sutherland he had just come up from Lewis's force, which was determined to destroy the villages without the leadership of the governor and his regular officers.

"Ain't easy to stop them Longknives," Girty murmured. "Dunmore's the only man can do it, an' he's squattin' here too long." Looking about at other whites, sure they could not hear him, Girty went on. "Lewis an' George Clark are hot to bust up 'em villages; they'll cross the Ohio in two days, then Dunmore won't see 'em for dust an' smoke."

Sutherland told him he had a way to make it plain to Dunmore that Lewis must be stopped. Girty eyed him with interest; then Sutherland said, "Tell Dunmore who I am, and say I've got a copy of a letter from Sir William Johnson concerning him. It's addressed to the Board of Trade."

Girty was called in, and a moment later, came out to beckon for Sutherland. While the unruly Virginians yelled and complained, Sutherland went into the cool tent, leaving his other companions behind. There he confronted a lean Scotsman with curly brown hair and penetrating eyes. Wearing a splendid scarlet uniform with ample gold braid, Lord Dunmore exuded authority. He leaned back in his camp chair, hands on the desk before him.

"Simon here tells me you're the same Sutherland who fought with Bouquet, and with Henry Gladwin..." Dunmore had heard much about Sutherland, and in his refined burr, said he was grateful to receive a message from the late Sir William Johnson, "though it's a bit unusual to get a dispatch from a dead man."

Sutherland handed over the envelope with the Indian superintendent's red wax seal. Dunmore opened the letter and motioned for Girty to depart. Sutherland nodded to the scout, and when he turned back to Dunmore, the man's face was already livid, his hands shaking. Sutherland remained calm as Dunmore scanned Johnson's accusation declaring the governor to be marching against the Indians purely for personal gain.

"This... this is outrageous!" Dunmore slammed the letter to the desk and jumped up. Leaning toward Sutherland, he demanded, "What gives you the impudence to show this to my face, Sutherland? You may be something special at Detroit, but you're only another fur trader here, and the fur trade is forbidden until my war is carried to its end! You better have a good answer, or I'll call the guard and throw you in irons!"

"That won't change anything, Governor." Sutherland's face was close to Dunmore's. "The truth will be known in Parliament by now, and when it's coupled with the inevitable triumph of colonial militia operating without government regulars, you'll be yanked home before Christmas!"

"Watch your tongue, man! Are you sure you're a Scot? You're as insolent as any damned American." Dunmore's hand was on his sword; instinctively, Sutherland felt for his empty scabbard, but his claymore would have been no use just then; reason was wanted, not violence. "I've given specific orders to Colonel Lewis not to attack the main villages without me, and he won't defy me."

"He might if his Longknives can't be held back."

Sutherland had touched a nerve. Dunmore seemed to be listening to the raucous din of his sprawling camp of Virginians, rowdy and half-wild. It was apparent the governor had his hands full controlling even his own division of the army; there was no way he could guarantee the conduct of an independent force seventy miles away.

As Dunmore pondered what Sutherland had said, a loud yelling began among the militia officers in the file outside. Both Scotsmen listened as Virginia militiamen poured abuse on the very notion of regular officers. Apparently someone had touched them off at just that moment, and one and all, they declared regulars were worthless in an Indian fight.

"Good to have 'em along, though," someone cried out, "'cause their lobster arses make easy targets, an' the Injuns don't worry us woodsmen none!"

The Virginians laughed at that, several adding brief tales they had heard about Redcoats, such as having shot their own men in terror during an Indian ambush. Sutherland recognized a few of the voices chiming in. The lustiest was Peter Defries, obviously having fun; but Jeremy, too, was adding to the banter, saying Redcoat officers were not so bad.

"Why, the other week in Philadelphia a whole flock of them put on a burlesque for the city, and it was quite entertaining; they looked good in skirts."

Peter laughed overly loud at this, saying the only time a Redcoat officer could smell blood without fainting was when a private was flogged. Insults became harsher, for unknown to Dunmore, Peter and Jeremy had passed bottles of rum among the backwoodsmen. Dunmore was about to leave the tent in a cold rage, when one mild-mannered voice rose in defense of

British officers. Mel Webster declared that at least they had good music. He whipped out his wooden flute and piped away at "Yankee Doodle," so infuriating the Virginians that by the time Dunmore stormed out, they were pushing and shoving past Defries and Jeremy to get at Mel, even a few punches being thrown.

After considerable shouting, threats, and calling upon the regular officer of the day, Dunmore restored some order to the furious Virginians. By now, Jeremy, Peter, and Mel had vanished, and only Sutherland remained. The militia were so peeved at Dunmore for berating them that they stamped away. Where there had been thirty impatient backwoods officers waiting for an interview, there were none by the time the disturbance was over.

If matters had not been so desperate, Sutherland would have enjoyed the spontaneous ploy conjured up by his friends. Instead, he remained serious, and said, "Furthermore, if I can bring the Indians to a peace council, Governor, you'll have to hold back Lewis or be accused of perpetrating a brutal slaughter solely for your own profit."

Dunmore was grave, rubbing his forehead, and looking over the teeming camp of rough-and-ready militiamen. There were plenty of British members of Parliament who rated Indians higher than provincials, and Dunmore knew where they would stand if Virginians ran amuck.

"Can you bring me their chiefs? If they won't attack, I'll hold back my armies. But there's little time; these woodsmen want blood or a rock-hard guarantee their homes will be safe from attack."

That same afternoon, Mel and Sutherland galloped off toward hostile country to keep the Indians from starting the bloodshed. While Peter remained with Dunmore's army to keep in touch with its progress, Jeremy crossed the Ohio and rode with Simon Girty for Andrew Lewis's army, which was making camp at the mouth of the Kanawha. Girty had a dispatch from Dunmore forbidding Lewis from attacking.

Both pairs of men journeyed on opposite sides of the river through the nights of October 8 and 9. They moved fast, with Jeremy and Girty making the best time, for their side of the Ohio had few war parties because of the strong force of Virginians there. Sutherland and Mel avoided being seen by passing groups of warriors, keeping to the trees as much as possible in order to get close to the Indian towns before being discovered. They did not want to risk being captured by warriors who might not know them. If that occurred, there was no guarantee of safety. Twice they had to elude Indians on foot who spotted them and gave chase; both times they escaped, heading steadily westward for Chillicothe and the main Shawnee towns.

Like Mel and Sutherland, Jeremy and Girty walked their horses at night. They were picking their way along the riverbank trail before morning of October 10, when Jeremy saw movement out on the water. He and Girty left the horses tied, and crept to the water's edge. In the half-light the surface of the river was alive with canoes, dozens of them. Indians were crossing, keeping complete silence, then sending the boats back for more men.

Lewis was camped just a mile downstream.

Girty whispered, "The attack is on," and they scurried back to their horses. "We got to warn Lewis, afore it's too late!"

Jeremy said, "You go for Dunmore and tell him! I'll get to Lewis!"

Girty stared out at the shadowy canoes drifting over the Ohio, landing downstream, and blocking the trail along the river. He nodded. "Yer right. Dunmore's got to come now." He grabbed Jeremy by the shoulder. "Listen: Them woods'll soon be full of Injuns, so go the long way 'round to the east of this peninsula. Leave yer horse behind; he won't get through the swamps. Go now! Watch yer arse!"

They split up, and Jeremy got his rifle and gear from the nervous animal. Girty had earlier told him where Lewis was making camp, and he had studied a map of the area before leaving Dunmore's army. He would have to move carefully, by instinct, but he knew his business in the woods. As he trotted along in the dark, down hunting paths or through thickets and cane, he could visualize the host of Indians coming stealthily ashore. If the Virginians were ready, the Indians might withdraw before a general battle commenced. But on the other hand Lewis could be wiped out if taken by surprise.

At that very hour, Sutherland and Mel were dragged into the Chillicothe village and thrown to the ground. A group of young braves had surprised them on the trail and spared them only because they knew Mel. To them Sutherland was a stranger, and they would have slain him had Mel not interceded. Mel asked for Cornstalk or Niko-lota to meet them, but the aged men who were left to manage the hushed village said their war chiefs had alredy gone to wipe out the Shemanese on the river, and would not be back until they were done.

Only women, children, and old men were here, so the grown boys who had captured Owen and Mel stayed behind as guards. There was no way to prevent a battle now; stopping the Virginians seemed beyond hope.

Sutherland and Mel were led away, the weight of defeat heavy on them. As the whites walked through gray morning light to a lodge, hundreds of silent women and children stood staring at them. Sutherland had failed these people, whose destruction was at hand. If Cornstalk defeated Andrew Lewis, it would be full-scale war to the death when Dunmore arrived. More armies would come if Dunmore failed, but surely he could not fail. He had two thousand men and provisions for months. Winter would find these squaws and their brood wandering in the northwest in need of pity. Shawnee, Delaware, and Mingo would cease to exist.

Mel bent down to enter the lodge, and Sutherland took one last look at the people watching him. Their only real chance lay in their men being beaten back, driven home to sue for peace. Yet if that happened, the death wail would haunt this and fifty other villages.

Sutherland wrenched himself from their curious eyes, but turned back quickly when he saw a familiar face: Lucy Swain, her child in arms, stood with the Indian women, gazing at him.

As a young warrior tried to push Sutherland into the lodge, the Scotsman called to her, "Where's your man?"

Emptily, Lucy said, "He ain't my man no more."

Until now, Jeremy had moved silently through shadowy woods tinged with the hint of reds, yellows, and oranges of an approaching autumn morning. He had worked well inland from the river, curving southeast toward the place whites called Point Pleasant: a heavily forested spit where Lewis had camped, the river protecting three sides. So far Jeremy had been cautious, but now something urged him to hurry. Not only could the Indians strike at any moment, but he was being followed.

The hairs on the back of his neck prickled, his whole body soaked with sweat. Having traveled hard for two days and nights without a rest, he now needed all his strength to keep ahead of whoever was after him. Splashing through streams, pushing into canebrakes that lashed and slowed him, he kept running, running. Whenever he looked behind he saw nothing. The woods were utterly silent, but Indians were trying to catch him. He changed directions three times, twisting off to the right or left in case they anticipated his route and took a shortcut to lie in wait. The Indians dared not fire at him, lest they alert the camp, which must be near by now.

His rifle loaded and ready, Jeremy would fire a warning shot if he had to, and take his chances getting away. He only hoped the shot would be heard, for he was not sure how close the camp might be. Each time he tried to cut to his right, there seemed to be someone coming up fast in that direction. It was apparent his pursuers wanted to keep him from going that way, where Lewis's force lay. He ran and ran, beginning to feel more than see that his pursuers were closing in. He had to do something quickly, before he was too late—

Someone was above him. Jeremy sprang forward just as a body dropped silently, steel cracking the back of his head. It was a glancing blow that staggered but did not stun him. Reeling forward, Jeremy dived into a mass of laurel, rolling when he hit the ground, and spinning quickly as his attacker followed. The Indian jumped blindly after him, leaped into a rifle butt that smashed him squarely in the face, and went down with a vicious thud.

On every side men were crashing through the bushes. Surrounded, Jeremy squirmed under the laurel and brambles, hoping the Indians would pass him by. Naked legs moved close and slowed. Jeremy felt eyes as though they were spears, probing, searching. He dared not move, hardly breathing, but the man he had knocked down stirred, his leg sliding through dry leaves. Did the Indians hear the man move? The stunned Indian lay concealed from other warriors, whose legs were passing everywhere, though there was not a footfall to be heard. A voice called softly, apparently seeking the injured warrior, who was breathing heavily, his foot moving again. Legs, moccasins, were inches away, at least six Indians searching, aware Jeremy was hiding close by. They called for their companion. Jeremy, lying curled up on his side, could have cut the legs out from under the nearest Indian, who was on tiptoes peering over the laurel thicket for his friend.

The man lying near Jeremy turned over and groaned. Legs flitted around the laurel, then the warriors came through, cautious of making noise. Jeremy took his chance, quietly sliding out the other side into the clearing, and springing to his feet.

He stopped suddenly. The bushes were full of warriors, all drifting ahead, wraiths in the gray dawn. Standing still, like a deer sensing the hunter, Jeremy had not been seen, though the nearest Indian was twenty feet away. Behind the laurel, the other warriors were helping their groaning friend. They would come out soon, and would see Jeremy if he did not get away.

Through the trees to his right he noticed the light of cook fires. This was Lewis's camp, and the Indians were on the perimeter. Militia were notorious for not posting sentries, relying on their hunting parties to detect enemy movement. These warriors had crept close enough to overrun the Virginians, who were stirring now, talking and laughing, their woodsmoke drifting through the trees.

Jeremy had no choice. He brought up his rifle and fired. The shot was deafening, and at once a dozen black eyes turned toward him. He sprang for cover as the entire forest rang with fierce war whoops and a wild explosion of gunfire. He crashed through bushes, bullets zinging close by his head and thunking into trees. Someone stepped in his path, rifle aimed point-blank. Jeremy dived at the Indian's feet, crashing him to the ground in the very instant the rifle fired. Then he tried to escape, but the warrior grabbed his leg and tripped him. Down he went, the din of war whoops and gunfire obliterating all clear thought. In the next moment, a greasy, painted Shawnee was grappling for Jeremy's throat. A tomahawk glittered in the pale light.

Instinctively, Jeremy moved his head. The blade bit the ground close to his ear, bit once more, and he snarled, throwing the Indian off. Up he leaped, making for the camp, intending to burst through the Indians and flee for his life.

Then the Shawnee again was on his back, dragging him down. He yanked the man over his head and clubbed him with the butt of the rifle, but did not hit him hard enough, having not yet comprehended that he must fight mercilessly or die. The warrior was bloodied, but he struck back, trying to get up, flailing viciously with the tomahawk. With his rifle, Jeremy knocked the tomahawk away, but the warrior pulled a knife. This time Jeremy swung the butt with full force, and the Indian slumped to the ground, his head split open.

Jeremy hesitated. This was not why he had come. He did not want to fight, but to stop the battle. It was then he realized blood was running from a tomahawk wound on his forehead and a bullet had burned his shoulder. He came to his senses. All around, the forest was alive with men fireing and whooping.

To these Indians he was just another white man—indeed, an enemy—for he had warned the Longknives. He took cover behind a tree and quickly reloaded.

From here Jeremy could see the Virginians through the thickets, pouring lead into the forest in deadly volleys that sent clouds of leaves fluttering down. Their drums beat to arms, fifes whistled, and officers shouted commands. Though he was only thirty yards from the perimeter of the camp, Jeremy dared not run that way, lest he be shot by Virginians. He had to take cover until it was safe to join the whites.

Just as he ducked back into thickets, bushes nearby rustled, and through them pushed five Shawnee. They saw him and yelled. He had no choice but to turn and fire. The first Indian, a slender young man his own age, grabbed his bloodied face and fell backward. Jeremy crawled away, trying to put more bushes between himself and the other warriors, knowing their rifles were coming up to shoot.

Immediately, there was a sudden roar of gunfire, but it did not come from the Indians. A gang of Virginians charged out of the trees, overwhelming these Indians in a furious counterattack. Someone shouted that he had warned them just in time, and helped him out of the undergrowth. As Jeremy heaved clear of the bushes, his companion gave a mighty pull and lifted him to his feet. Jeremy saw the iron hook.

He was no more than three feet from Jubal Swain, whose face was alight with battle-madness. Grinning, Swain nodded once. "Do I know you, boy?"

Almost ten years ago, Swain had kept Jeremy prisoner, but did not recognize the young man now. Unable to speak, Jeremy thought how easily he could break the man's skull with his tomahawk. He lifted it a little, but hesitated, aware Swain had just saved his life.

"That ain't no use." Swain indicated the tomahawk, which had splintered at the handle. Jeremy stared stupidly at his weapon, and in the next moment, Swain said, "Use this for now, but I want it back, hear?"

He shoved something into Jeremy's arms, then dashed away, following the rest of his men, who were meeting stiff resistance a little way off. Jeremy stood there, by the Indian he had killed, and in his hands was Owen Sutherland's claymore.

Before Jeremy had even a moment to contemplate the ugly irony of his situation, a sudden fierce shouting rose from Swain's party and their opponents. Jeremy looked up and saw Swain leap over fallen trees to fight hand to hand with a big Shawnee warrior. At that time, dozens of Indians began to swarm from the trees, outnumbering the Virginians. Jeremy moved without thinking, instinctively, like an animal of prey, and took on the first enemy at hand. He was a middle-aged, experienced Delaware, whose tomahawk chopped and slashed in a confusing blur as he silently tried to kill Jeremy. The claymore parried as though it had a life of its own. Jeremy's skill as a swordsman had never before been tested by a real foe, but he was very good. The blade flicked defensively, without the slightest effort. The Delaware tried his utmost, grunting and panting, feinting with his feet, circling; and through it all, Jeremy was as much spectator as combatant. He could have run the man through with ease, but he did not want to kill again.

He tried to speak, but the Indian was wise, saw his chance, and struck. Jeremy's claymore met the handle of the tomahawk, just inches from his ear. He twirled the Indian's weapon into the air, and the Delaware was left helpless, eyes betraying his horror as he stopped, standing motionless.

Jeremy hesitated once more as a rough battering of humanity rushed by him. He heard Jubal Swain's roar: "Git back! They's too many, kid! Run!"

Swain dashed past, in full retreat, a wounded Virginian over his shoulder, the man's blood running down Swain's back. The Indians were almost upon Jeremy. They came on in a crowd, their yelling, echoing voices and a loud crackling of gunfire mingling with the smells of war. Jeremy spun to get away but, from the corner of his eye, saw his beaten opponent move. A blade glinted, and turning back, Jeremy barely avoided the knife. In the next motion, he drove his claymore into the Indian, up to the hilt, the force of the thrust knocking his own breath away.

Before the Delaware hit the ground, Jeremy was flying for his life, bullets zipping past, taking down two of Swain's group. Jeremy yanked one man off the ground and dragged him and his rifle away on the run. Other Virginians appeared from the trees, opened a furious fire upon the pursuing Indians, and, for the moment, saved Jeremy and his companions.

Yet even this second force, commanded by a burly red-headed young man named George Rogers Clark, was driven back by the relentless Indians. As he withdrew, Jeremy had hardly time to load and fire. All the while he bore the injured Virginian along from tree to tree, not knowing if the man was alive or dead. He cried out for someone with a doctor's skills, but there was no one. Jeremy was responsible for the fellow, whose rifle he fired, whose ammunition he used, yet he could not have described what the casualty looked like. Because of the tumult, the fury, and the danger on every side, Jeremy could only fire and move, load, and fire again, then move once more. The Virginian line, formed up loosely through the forest, fell back slowly. The Indians came on, attacked weak places, overwhelmed outnumbered parties, and drove through the white defenses, threatening to burst past this line and into the camp itself.

There were times when Jeremy knew cold fear, others when he felt nothing, understood nothing other than killing, taking cover, fighting body to body, eye to eye, with whoever attacked him. The whites were desperate, the Indians fanatical, though disciplined. The defenders reeled, regrouped, and fought back, their line yielding to the breaking point.

Finally Jeremy left his wounded companion with another man whose leg was shattered and who could not move. With Clark and Swain in the lead, he counterattacked recklessly, charging into a thicket full of gunsmoke and flashing rifle muzzles.

He leaped into the bushes, heedless of danger, and there met a Shawnee his own age, whose rifle, like Jeremy's, was empty. They caught one another by the throat, went down heavily, and rolled over and over in the underbrush. Swearing and punching, kicking, biting, and scratching, they might have been alone in the world, mortal enemies, whose survival depended on the other's instant death. Jeremy avoided looking the other in the eyes, and actually had no chance to do so because of the quick, painful pounding of the Indian's fists and feet. Jeremy's sword was no use at such close quarters, but they both tried to pull knives.

The Indian raked at Jeremy's eyes as Jeremy rolled over on top of him. When the Indian tried to keep Jeremy's roll going and get on top himself, Jeremy got control, flipped up the youth head over heels, and yanked out his knife. As he hit the ground hard, the Shawnee went for his own knife, but the jarring fall threw off his hand's movement, and in the next instant, Jeremy caught him, drove him back down, and killed him. Then Jeremy collapsed in a heap, the madness draining from him in a rush, as though it were his very blood.

All around, the forest was a harsh crescendo of shrieks and

roaring gunfire, shouts of conquest and howls of agony. Jeremy could not look at the youth he had just killed, could not take back the bloody knife, did not want to move for the horror of it all. He could not tell how long he lay there, but it was no more than a few minutes, though it seemed an eternity. The fighting surged and flowed all around him; he knew he must get up and go on. He had to go on, keep killing, or he would die himself. Slowly, with great inner pain, he rose, recovered his rifle, and calmly reloaded it. Though he was concealed in a thicket, lead flew dangerously all around. He did not care. He had no fear of death just then. His eyes, mind, soul, focused only on reloading that rifle. Methodically he rammed home the ball, and an Indian bullet thunked into a tree trunk near his head. He did not flinch. He replaced the rammer alongside the barrel, hefted the weapon, and looked out at the world through a haze of icy determination.

He took a deep breath and, with narrowed eyes, marked where he was, where the Indians were, and what he had to do next. Not far away, Jubal Swain called out, and Jeremy knew it was there he had to go. Stepping over the dead Shawnee, he carefully pushed through thickets, moved like a shadow between trees, and rejoined his men. He would fight because he had no other choice. He would not throw his life away, and no one would take it from him without a battle. For Jeremy Bently, nothing ever would be the same again.

The Indian assault was well led and daringly executed. The hasty defense of the Virginians bent under the determined attack, but did not break. Swain and the others were driven back to the main defensive line of fallen trees cut down to protect the camp, and Jeremy went with them, his stepfather's sword stuck in his belt. Swain was too absorbed in the battle to ask for the claymore back, but when that moment came, Jeremy would have to do something, though he knew not what.

For hours, frontiersmen and Indian fought in orderly battle lines, but from cover, in the way of wilderness wars. Lying behind a newly felled tree, Jeremy became a soldier, like any other, in the desperate attempt to keep the Indians from breaking into the camp. The forest was a steady din of shrieks, groans, angry oaths, and gunfire like an endless storm. Officers bravely directed their men, moving along the firing line, skillfully coordinating concealed fighters against a hidden enemy. It was a marvel to Jeremy how leaders such as George Rogers Clark maintained command over scattered forces without relying on headquarters to send frequent instructions.

Hour after hour the fight raged, with whites pushing Indians away from the main camp, then Indians sending flanking parties, who maneuvered as well as any regulars, to force their enemy back. Give and take, attack and counterattack, the battle of Point Pleasant swept along a width of one mile, and the most intense fighting took place within a depth of only two hundred yards.

As the morning wore on, warm and windless, the air became so thick with acrid gunsmoke that it was difficult to breathe, and every man's eyes ran with tears. Faces smeared with powder burns, blood, and sweaty dirt, the combatants fought from tree to tree, bush to bush. Singly, and in small groups, they pounced upon one another, grappling hand to hand, looking into the eyes of those they slew, or who slew them.

Despite the Indians' initial advantage of surprise, the Virginians were heroic and stood their ground under the sort of massed enemy gunfire that had thrown trained regulars into disorder during the French and Indian War. Indians, too, fought courageously. Had Jeremy not given the alarm, their attack would have overrun the camp, and by now the Virginians would be in flight, trying to swim the rivers under deadly fire.

Battling alongside Clark, Jeremy knew he was in company with the best of fighting men. The tall, bronzed Virginian had a calm way about him that instilled confidence. Like other provincial officers—so many of whom had been shot down by now—Clark was methodical, decisive, and heedless of danger. He cared about his men, talking quietly to those close at hand, calling out encouragement to subordinates who kept in touch with the rest. He took an interest in Jeremy, knowing the young man had saved them from destruction. Clark taught him a few things, such as to move after he fired so the Indians could not locate him and set him up to be picked off.

Often, a man might know an opponent was directly ahead and, in a personal duel, would try to outsmart him. A favorite Indian tactic was for one warrior to distract a concealed white man by taunting him, while another silently moved to get a better angle. Then, when the Shemanese showed himself to fire at the first warrior, he was shot. It was an effective tactic, and many a Longknife died that way before the troops became alert to it.

By now, Jeremy had given up the notion of finding Colonel Andrew Lewis and delivering Dunmore's command not to en-

gage the enemy. Not only was the message absurd now, but
Lewis was impossible to find in the carnage.

The struggle thundered on, an equal contest unprecedented
in frontier warfare, both sides treacherous and crafty, cautious,
but recklessly brave. Back and forth the fight surged and ebbed,
as one side took ground, and the other slipped behind the salient
to cut off or attack from another angle. Streams ran red in that
beautiful forest. The sun climbed over a hell of acrid smoke,
and the place stank of sweat and blood. As the day ground by,
men suffered from thirst and hunger as much as from wounds,
but no one willingly left the lines. Rifles were little use in hand-
to-hand fighting, and the tomahawk or knife often became the
bloody weapon of the moment. For Jeremy, the weapon was
Owen's claymore, wielded in desperation.

About midday, the Indians' assault subsided, and firing
slowed up and down the line. Jeremy took this grateful moment
to rest, kneeling behind a rock, forehead on his musket butt.
Nearby, Clark was talking to another man, telling him to keep
an eye out for any sign of renewed attack. Then the Virginia
captain slumped down behind the same rock protecting Jeremy,
who did not look up.

Mouth dry, eyes sunken and bleary, Clark breathed deeply,
composing himself. After a moment, he asked Jeremy who he
was. When he heard of Jeremy's original mission to Lewis,
and of Dunmore's desire for a treaty, Clark gave a derisive
snort and looked away.

"If you lived where I do, friend, you'd talk differently."
His voice crackled from thirst; though he was only a few years
older than Jeremy, this big redhead seemed ageless, vastly
experienced, and wise. "With God's help, we'll win today,
and then we'll go on to rub these vermin out completely; that's
the only way my people can live in peace!"

Clark closed his eyes and leaned his head back, half-dozing
in the bright sun, yet obviously alert at the same time. Jeremy
began to clean his rifle, poking burned powder from the vent
with a wire pick. He wondered just what had brought him to
all this. How had he ridden so hard to stop a battle and then
become the first one to kill in it? In the heat of combat, it was
so easy to kill; even easier to die. Now, more than anything,
he wanted a cool drink of water. The gathering stillness in the
woods around them was good, but he would have traded some
of the peace for a drink, would risk his life for it. His nose

was choked with dust, his throat parched so he could hardly swallow, and his whole body ached.

In the distance, off on the far left of the Virginian line, gunfire increased again, as though there was a new attack over there. Clark immediately became conscious, listening. Other militiamen looked to him, some commenting that the heavy firing might mean the whites had broken through.

Clark said, "Or the redskins are trying to get into the camp."

Jeremy quickly reloaded, even though the gunfire was a long way off. The shooting was very fierce, obviously an intense conflict.

There came a shout from behind, and Jubal Swain burst out of the trees, running in a crouch toward Clark. Jeremy had not seen much of Swain that day, and now put his hand on the claymore. He would not give it back, no matter what happened next, but Swain hardly noticed him—perhaps did not recognize him, filthy and bloody as Jeremy was. Swain brought a message from Colonel Lewis.

"Red niggers's tryin' to bust through on the left flank, Cap'n! The colonel wants yuh to do the same to them, right now! Shelby an' Isaacs already be movin' on your left, an' your own boys should hustle along the Kanawha shoreline afore swingin' in to give the varmints hell!"

Swiftly, Clark called up his fighters, who magically appeared from concealment, ready to move. Swain ran off with Clark's reply that he would strike immediately. Though all tired and thirsty, the Virginians and Jeremy set off at a dogtrot through the trees, collecting their men as they went. They rushed down to low ground not far from the broad Kanawha, slipping fast along the banks. Their scouts went out first, and before they had been away ten minutes, one came back with word that the Indian lines were just ahead. Jeremy and others looked longingly at the cool water, so close at hand, then forgot about it for now.

Hardly saying a word to his men, Clark arranged their battle order, dividing them into fighting bands that knew their roles and worked as a team. The frontiersmen drifted forward and came up to their waiting advance scouts. Lurking behind trees, they saw single Indians here and there, clearly scouts of their own, while their main body struck the Longknife left flank. The distant firing was even more furious now. The battle might hinge on the next few minutes. Clark moved, his men encircling the pickets and killing them without a sound, one by one.

The Longknives moved deliberately, but fast, covering three hundred yards before they were discovered by a larger group of warriors prepared to fight back. Then the shooting started, lead flying thickly, buzzing all around, and dropping men on every side. Jeremy fired and reloaded as quickly as he could until he remembered the Virginians took careful aim, not wasting a shot. He did the same and here the better marksmanship of the whites told devastatingly against less skillful Indian riflemen. Though Indians were better at concealment and ambush, the Longknives picked them apart, relentlessly driving them back toward the heavy fighting on the left. The battle became widespread again, and the Indians stiffened their resistance. Word came to Clark that the enemy had left off assaulting the camp; finding themselves outflanked, they were retreating, leaving dead and wounded on the field.

Clark's men exulted and pressed onward, eager for a rout. Jeremy, too, felt his heart leap, thinking the horror was almost over. At last he could get a drink! They rushed ahead, Indians vanishing before them, hardly firing a shot in reply. Then, after a hundred yards of headlong pursuit, the whites ran into a tremendous blast of gunfire and smoke. Men scattered, and Jeremy dragged a wounded Virginian to shelter. The Indians had rallied, and this well-timed, withering volley stopped the Longknives completely.

Finding cover to shelter the wounded militiaman and from which to fire, Jeremy peered through the smoke at howling Indians whooping in defiance. As soon as the Virginians were positioned to shoot back, however, the warriors melted into cover. The shooting became controlled. Now and again Jeremy heard the mighty voice of some chief exhorting his fighters to stand fast and shoot well:

"Oui-shi-cat-to-oui! Be strong! *Oui-shi-cat-to-oui!* Be strong!"

It was Cornstalk, and near him were Pucksinwah, Red Panther, and Niko-lota, rallying their men to hold back this dangerous maneuver by Clark. The Indians had stopped giving ground, and now were entrenched in a solid defensive formation on higher terrain that was heavily wooded. They would be hard to drive out. Clark and his men had paid heavily for their bold attack; they were content to rest now and let night come on. Tomorrow they would fight again—this time to the death.

Soon, firing and war cries faded away, the only sounds

being wounded men groaning, or an occasional taunt hurled by one side or the other. The whites withdrew a little distance from their enemy, and Clark counted his company's survivors: fifty left of the eighty who had begun the battle. For the remainder of that dismal afternoon, no more than desultory shooting broke out here and there. Clark told his men to give their rifles a good cleaning before they reloaded, and to hold their weapons ready. Jeremy, his rifle gone over, sat backed against a tree watching others near at hand lie down, bind wounds, or have a smoke.

Someone passed a skin bag of tepid water, and Jeremy took his share—little enough, but precious. Only Clark had the stomach to eat the beef jerky that he himself offered around, but the water went quickly. Jeremy felt a kinship with these men, though they opposed much that he and Owen Sutherland believed in. Constant warfare with Indians was the Longknife inheritance, a way of life, and Jeremy respected their bravery and unselfish sacrifice.

When someone grumbled that the water bag was empty, another man said there was a pool down through the bushes not far from them. After a moment, Jeremy offered to get a refill. Clark grinned and said he would go along. The men covered them as they got up stiffly and went into the thicket, the Virginian in the lead. Darkness was coming on.

Moving swiftly, silently, into no-man's-land between the two forces, Jeremy nearly tripped over a dead Shawnee. Clark saw the body, and came back to cut away the scalp. Jeremy sickened, and retched, but Clark chuckled softly. "I was going to give this one to you . . . Guess not."

He stuck the bloody hair into his shirt, and they slipped along a narrow game path. Above, where it showed in patches between the treetops, the blue sky paled. The land fell away here, and it was quiet, with only an occasional pop, pop of rifle fire some distance off. Neither man talked.

They saw the glint of light on a swampy pool and went toward it with great care. Near its edge, Clark stood guard while Jeremy drank his fill and soaked his head and chest. The splash of water sounded loud in the stillness. Jeremy filled the bag, then watched while Clark drank. Dragonflies darted through rays of light that slanted long and low through the trees. It was a pretty spot.

The men rose to go, Clark first, Jeremy covering their back. Then, as Clark passed into a canebrake, Jeremy spotted movement behind. He dropped and hissed to the Virginian, but apparently was not heard. Tense, Jeremy began backing along the trail, following Clark. He saw someone among cattails, took cover, and brought up his rifle. Aiming at a shadow among dense growth across the mirror of the pond, he waited.

"Hey, Longknife! What do ye see?"

He was not sure where that cry came from. More to his left. Where was Clark? Had he heard it, too?

"Shoot!" The voice cackled, then hooted in mockery. Jeremy stayed behind the tree, drawing a bead on the silhouette. "Don't miss, Longknife!" Startled, Jeremy realized the voice was even further to his left now. He eased to his right around the tree, inching slowly, trying to make certain of a target.

"Here!" Jeremy knew where the man was, and fired. Missed! An Indian's howl of derision infuriated him, and he reloaded quickly. "Don't be nervous, Longknife!"

Jeremy saw another outline behind some brambles. Sighting perfectly, he made certain this time, squeezing the trigger. The rifle jumped, the ball hitting the man for sure. He edged forward a little to see better. On his right came sudden movement. They had him. There was no time to duck. The bullet hit his side, and he did not hear the shot that got him.

chapter 26

TO THE DEATH

As they had come, the Indians withdrew by birch boat under cover of darkness. The Longknives had held the field, though the Indians had wrought terrible destruction upon them. Two hundred and fifty whites had fallen, nearly one hundred of them dead by nightfall. The Indians had not suffered so heavily, but their only chance for victory had melted away. They departed in silence, ashamed at being compelled to abandon most of their thirty dead, who lay where they had fallen.

Still strong, determined to avenge their losses, Lewis's army soon would cross the Ohio either to attack or to join with Dunmore's two thousand. Niko-lota, in the last canoe to cross from the east bank, hung his head in exhaustion and defeat. Pucksinwah had died in the fight, as had many other important chiefs. The warning of Cornstalk proved correct. Indians could not withstand the power of the white man, and now there was nowhere to turn.

Red Panther lay beside him, badly wounded in the stomach. He had fought bravely, and had been hit in a swamp near nightfall, while attracting the fire of a young Longknife who was himself shot down by Niko-lota. That had been the last real fighting of the day, and then the Indians had passed the word to withdraw.

Already, some warriors were vanishing into the forest in fear of the Shemanese. Tomorrow there would be even fewer fighting men left to stand up against the Longknives. All was lost.

At dawn, back at his village, Niko-lota found Sutherland, and fell into his friend's arms, weak and melancholy.

"I have done all I can, Donoway; it is finished with my people." Sutherland and Mel helped him sit down, and teary-eyed squaws, their hair cut short in mourning, brought bowls of boiled squash and venison. Too dejected to eat, Niko-lota told everything about the battle, and Sutherland asked anxiously whether Jeremy was there.

Surprised to learn that Jeremy had gone to stop Lewis's army, and might have been caught up in the battle, Niko-lota recalled the last Longknife he had shot. The same one who had wounded Red Panther, this young Shemanese had looked so much like Jeremy that the Delaware had almost not fired. Sick at heart, he told this to Sutherland, who paled and turned away.

Niko-lota gasped, "I did not . . . take his scalp, Donoway, so I cannot be sure; more Longknives came up fast and drove us back. That was just before the end, and we withdrew."

At dawn the next day, so troubled that it was difficult to speak, Sutherland stood in the circle of chiefs and warriors and told them he would confront Dunmore on their behalf. Word had come in that Lewis's army was assembling bateaux to cross the river. Dunmore's army too, was on the move, marching across country, straight for the main Chillicothe villages, burning and destroying lodges, fields, and orchards as it came. Near Niko-lota was Tecumseh, son of the dead Pucksinwah. Serene and self-controlled despite his father's death, the child heard every word Sutherland said. The rest of the Indians, too, listened intently, but none replied for some time. When no one else spoke, Cornstalk rose, his body bruised and cut, eyes gleaming with an inner fire.

In a shaking, though forceful voice, Cornstalk said, "You told me you would fight and triumph, but I counseled peace; we have fought well, brothers and cousins, but my soul cries out to the heavens for the loss of so many beloved young men, who have fallen, and yet we have not triumphed."

He looked around at stony, sullen faces. "Now the Shemanese come for us, and we cannot win." The hush was painful until Cornstalk shouted, "If we fight on—" He yanked out his tomahawk and grabbed his little son, holding him under the weapon, about to strike. A shudder ran through the Indians. "—Then we fight to the death! First we must kill our squaws and children!"

Women averted their faces, and men gaped in dismay. Cornstalk's son did not cry out as his father shouted at the people, "Tell me it must be so, and I begin here!" There came no answer. Even the wind fell silent.

Cornstalk let the tomahawk down slowly, and released the

boy. "I cannot stir your hearts to one last battle. Very well."
He flung the tomahawk down, its head burying in the soil. "I
shall go to Dunmore and ask for terms of peace. Donoway
shall be my interpreter, and I shall give myself as hostage to
guarantee the good faith of my people. Let us pray the war is
finished. Cornstalk has spoken."

Torn apart by an intense longing to cross the Ohio and search
for Jeremy, Sutherland compelled himself to crush that yearning in order to stop another battle. He rode with Cornstalk
toward Dunmore's approaching army, cold reason directing
him in this last effort to save the Indians. Earlier, Mel had
departed from the village with Red Panther and Lucy. Her life
was in danger because the Indians had lost the battle, so he
left her to look after her daughter and her wounded son in a
secluded camp on a hill overlooking the Scioto River. Then
Mel had crossed over to Lewis's army with the message that
the tribes desired peace negotiations, and while there, he would
seek out Jeremy.

It took Sutherland a full day of riding to come up with
Dunmore's vanguard, then he and Cornstalk were taken to the
governor. To Sutherland's relief, Dunmore already had resolved to prevent the militia from torching the Shawnee and
Delaware settlements. Defries, who met Sutherland and Cornstalk after the Scotsman's council with Dunmore, said the Virginians in this force were like mad dogs, killing every Indian
they ran across, scalping man, woman, and child.

"It'll go bad if Dunmore can't stop Lewis," Defries said as
guards took charge of the somber Cornstalk. "An' the way
Dunmore drags his arse like a snail through the woods, he'll
never come up with Lewis in time."

There was nothing else to be done except to remain with
Lord Dunmore, to see the man did not change his mind. The
governor was courageous, a dependable leader, but he moved
slowly, bringing up supplies, and making elaborate camps before pushing on the next day. Though couriers galloped back
and forth between the two armies, it was clear Lewis's force
had not stopped its advance. The governor grew steadily more
enraged as he received ambiguous replies from Lewis to his
commands to stand fast. Ten days after the Point Pleasant
battle, Lewis had crossed over the Ohio and was massing for
the final assault. Virtually unopposed, he faced confused and

defenseless Indians, who believed Cornstalk was arranging a peace.

Because of Dunmore's decision not to attack, disgust and frustration unsettled the ranks of his own army, except for the professional officers. Rumors flew that Dunmore wanted the full credit of destroying the villages, preventing Lewis from winning glory for colonial troops. At the mercy of the Longknives was the very heart of a people who had battled with them for generations. The villages of the Scioto and Ohio valleys were thick with scalp poles, and cruel war parties had been sent out from here year after year. This was the sanctuary for fleeing raiders, a dark and dangerous ground where Virginians had dared not venture until now. At last they had broken through, and the end was in sight. Dunmore must unleash the militia, the troops asserted, and let them fight their own way. If he did so, there would never again be a burned cabin, slaughtered family, or stolen child in the backcountry settlements of western Virginia.

Dunmore ignored these pleas and plodded on, making an unprotected camp at the eastern edge of an oval grassland seven miles long by four wide. He was in sight of Cornstalk's town to the west, and near several other large villages along the Scioto River. But Lewis was closer to the Indians. Dunmore said Simon Girty had been sent to the Scioto towns to make sure Cornstalk's request for peace terms was supported by other chiefs; until Girty returned with confirmation, Dunmore lingered. Sutherland was troubled, for they must move faster to intercept Lewis and, face to face, give the ultimate command to stand fast.

When Girty came in, he brought ominous news: Lewis intended to march soon on the villages. Just as Dunmore ordered the scout to ride the few miles to the Virginian's camp with another blunt order to halt the advance, a horseman came galloping over the plains, long arms flapping, blond hair shining in the sunlight.

"Mel Webster!" shouted Defries, attracting the attention of the governor himself. "He comes from Lewis's camp, Your Excellency!"

Sutherland and Dunmore called to Mel, who saw them and galloped toward the grove of trees where they stood. Shouting "Lewis is marching! He's on the attack!" Mel bounded from the horse, and Sutherland caught him.

Dunmore cried for his staff to mount up, and in the next moment, twenty horsemen in scarlet or homespun whirled across the plain. Defries brought their own horses, but before Sutherland mounted, he asked Mel about Jeremy.

Gasping for breath, Mel said, "He's hurt badly, but alive!"

"Thank God!"

"Somehow he got hold of your sword!"

"Swain!"

Sutherland leaped onto his horse, and Mel shouted that Jeremy was with other wounded in Lewis's packtrain. Riding like a demon, Defries at his side, the Scotsman raced after Dunmore's party. As he passed near the Indian village, he could make out crowds of women and children collected in the center of the lodges. The men were together in small knots, and seemed to be without weapons, completely helpless. Sutherland and Defries pounded through long grass, making for Congo Creek, where Lewis had made camp the previous night. Soon they reached high ground above the creek, and saw the arrayed militia army formed into marching columns, flags waving, drums and fifes sounding.

Sutherland and Defries crossed the creek to where Dunmore and his officers had dismounted and were in a confrontation with Lewis. As Sutherland leaped from his horse, he saw Colonel Andrew Lewis, a lithe, dashing figure, dressed elegantly in the fine plum-colored frock coat of a country squire. A cool veteran of the French wars, Lewis stood squarely before Dunmore. They were like stags about to charge. All around, disgruntled Virginians leaned on rifles, listening. Among them was Captain George Clark, who had come out of the battle unscathed and was as eager as any to mount an attack.

Lewis shouted: "I prefer, sir, to have this out before my whole army and not privately in a tent as you request!" His voice lifted over the force, and the militia began to drift from their ranks to close around the cluster of officers. "As you can see, Lord Dunmore, I've already struck my tents, for this army is at war, not dallying like—"

"That will do, Colonel Lewis!" Dunmore was fuming and touched his sword. He might draw if Lewis insulted him further. The Virginians were surly, muttering among themselves, someone even bold enough to shout for an immediate assault. As the troops began to clamor, Dunmore did not hesitate, shouting, "Silence in the ranks there!"

The militia sniggered, Lewis doing nothing to still them. His blood up, Dunmore and his handful of officers were like scarlet rocks in a sea of brown and linsey. Sutherland and Defries dismounted, making for the packtrain that they saw at the far side of the army.

Lewis shouted that his men had paid in blood for the ground upon which Dunmore's army now camped so complacently. Dunmore sputtered, having no answer to give.

Lewis removed his tricorn and pointed toward the Indian villages. "That's where I'll pitch my tent, sir, and there we can talk further, when you're ready!"

Dunmore took on an expression like a beast about to spring. His Redcoat officers closed behind him, and Lewis's men joined their commander.

By now, Sutherland gave not a damn about them, and pushed through angry militiamen to find Jeremy. Defries with the horses fell behind.

Another outcry went up from the militia, for they wanted to get on with the fighting. Sutherland could still see Lewis and Dunmore, the provincial colonel throwing his hat to the ground, spinning to face his men.

Offering his back to the royal governor, Lewis blared, "Gentlemen, prepare—"

His order was drowned out by a bellow from Dunmore, whose sword glittered in the sunlight as it sprang from the scabbard. Lewis wheeled, hand on his own sword hilt, but he did not draw. The troops became quiet, waiting, shifting uneasily. The Virginians were full of malice, but so was Dunmore, and to defy him was treason, to fight him mutiny, for which they could be executed.

Eye to eye, Dunmore and Lewis were fused by tremendous force of will. If Lewis defied the governor, his men would surely back him, and rebellion of bloody consequence—the nightmare of governors and colonials from Maine to Florida—would begin.

Unrelenting, Dunmore spoke loudly, in a measured voice heard by all. "Colonel Lewis, command your men at once to fall out and pitch their tents. Obey, or draw your sword and defend yourself!"

Just then, Sutherland saw Jeremy lying on a blanket thirty yards from him, and his heart leaped. A woman was bent over his stepson. Lucy Swain!

In the next second, Colonel Lewis picked up his hat and again slammed it to the ground and stamped on it, then glared at Dunmore. The point of the governor's sword was inches from his face.

Sutherland could not move, transfixed by the crisis, by Jeremy, and the sight of Lucy. Suddenly the woman turned and ran, leaping on her Indian horse and galloping off. Only Sutherland and Jeremy seemed to notice. The rest focused on Dunmore's sword. Lewis was shaking, every wrathful inch of him, and his fists, which were slowly rising at either side of his body, were trembling.

"So be it!" Lewis abruptly cried out. "The blood those red dogs spill in the future will be on your head, Dunmore! But there will come a day of reckoning between you and me! Upon my solemn word, there will be a reckoning for this!"

Storming away, Lewis ignored the governor's order to have the men fall out. Just as furious as his subordinate, Dunmore roared, "Captains, dismiss your troops until further notice! Officers assemble here in ten minutes! Any man disobeying will be shot!"

At the very moment the infuriated Virginians turned away without their captains giving the order, Sutherland saw Jubal Swain galloping after his fleeing wife, who was riding into the trees of a bluff above the Scioto River.

Shoving through swearing, milling Virginians, Sutherland broke clear to Jeremy, who gasped his stepfather's name as they embraced. The lad was wounded in the side, but the ball had passed through, cracking ribs, and taking much blood from him. Though weak, he was overjoyed to see Owen.

"You did it, Pa! It's over!"

Seeing that Jeremy would be all right, Sutherland watched Swain riding into the trees a hundred yards away. In a voice hardly audible over the tumult of complaining backwoodsmen, Sutherland said, "It's not over yet."

He stood up as Jeremy said, "Lucy Swain was here begging for a doctor, but she ran off when she saw Jubal; her son's in a lean-to up on that ridge." Jeremy, too, had seen Jubal pursue Lucy. Aware of what would happen next, he held up the claymore that had been concealed under his bloodstained blanket, and handed it over. Sutherland rammed the sword into its scabbard, and picked up Jeremy's rifle and ammunition. Quickly loading the gun, he tried to catch sight of Defries, who had the horses. Nowhere in view, Peter was likely still surrounded by the great crowd of militia on the parade ground. Looking at the trail Swain had taken, he knew there was no more time to waste.

After grasping Jeremy's hand, he sprinted away to confront Jubal Swain for the last time.

Lucy's horse picked its way up the slope, through a dappled forest thick with fallen leaves. Birds and squirrels darted out of her way as she urged her mount on, taking backward glances, finally seeing what she feared: Jubal was following, shouting her name. Just ahead was Willie's lean-to, overlooking the river. Her daughter, Eloise, slept inside, and Willie lay outside on a blanket, near a cooking fire. From here was a fine view of the valley, with a sheer drop straight down to the Scioto. Red Panther was still smeared with black and red war paint, his stomach swathed in blood-encrusted bandages. When he heard Lucy ride in, he lifted his head, eyes blurring.

"Ma," he called as she ran to his side and cradled his head. "Give me water, Ma."

Hands shaking, Lucy brought a bowl of water, then heard the clop of Jubal's horse as it came up the trail. Afraid to turn around, afraid of looking at him ever again, she did not know what to do. Red Panther drank thirstily, then fell back, chest heaving, fresh blood staining his bindings. Then he, too, heard the hooves, and gave his attention to the trail. Lucy moved to block his view, but he eased her away. When he saw who was coming, Red Panther's body became taut, his expression fierce.

"Lucy!" Jubal shouted, and jumped down from the horse, uncertain whether to berate or embrace her. She could see by his watery eyes he had been drinking.

Her son made to rise. "Willie, Willie," Lucy pleaded, holding him down. "Think of yourself. Don't reopen that wound. Please . . ." She glanced over her shoulder and gave an involuntary whimper. Jubal was walking toward her, rifle in hand. "Willie, don't do anything . . . Please!" She tried to push him back down, but Red Panther's breath was coming in quick, short gasps, a sound in his throat like a saw rasping through wood.

"Who the hell's that, girl?" Jubal demanded, coming close. Then he muttered, "Well, so yuh found him after all—"

Lucy whirled, gesturing for him to stay back. Annoyed,

Swain came on. Lucy jumped up to stop him, but he shoved her lightly aside. That was enough to take his attention from Red Panther.

Back on the narrow trail, racing as fast as he could, Sutherland scrambled up a steep slope, rocks and dirt sliding free as he hurried to reach Swain. He heard someone screech in murderous fury, and tried to quicken his pace, but the trail was long and difficult.

At that moment, Red Panther screeched again and sprang for Jubal's throat, driving him backwards and knocking away the rifle. Swain bellowed and threw Red Panther savagely to the ground. Lucy screamed and leaped between them, but her son got to his feet and attacked again. Hampered by his own frenzy, the young man was easy to avoid, and Swain stepped aside, more surprised than angry.

"What in hell—" Jubal shouted. "Damn, Willie, you're like a slimy redskin!"

Red Panther hit the ground, grunting in pain. Blood running from his stomach wound, he scrambled on all fours at Jubal, who put a hand up to calm him. Jubal was about to speak when Red Panther hit him full in the chest, taking him down heavily. Lucy whined, grabbing the fallen rifle, and trying to club them apart.

"Stop! Stop! No, Willie, don't! Jubal, please! No! Not any more! Not any more!" She swung the rifle uselessly, for she did not have the heart to strike either of them with all her might.

But as the struggle intensified, and her son's blood splashed over her husband and the ground, Lucy screamed in terror, raised the rifle over her head, and this time brought it down as hard as she could. Jubal took the blow and looked at his wife, pain and puzzlement in his eyes, but he shook it off. The impact shuddered through Lucy's body, yet it did nothing to stop them. Inside the lean-to, her daughter cried, but Lucy did not hear. She fell to her knees, sobbing and quivering, praying for this fight to be stopped before Willie was killed.

Sutherland heard Lucy scream at the top of her lungs. He was close to the end of the path, and could see gray wisps of the cookfire.

Spitting blood and swearing, Jubal fought the big young man onto his back, pinning him and shouting at him to keep his head. But Red Panther wrestled free, gouging and scratching, and Jubal yanked out his own tomahawk. Lucy screamed again and struck Jubal with the rifle butt. He was about to turn to her but was punched in the face by Red Panther. Stung, Swain surged almost out of control.

"Enough!" he roared and brandished the tomahawk at his opponent, fighting him down with his hook. "Enough! I've killed men for less—"

Red Panther somehow got the advantage and knocked Jubal back. They brawled on the ground, rolling over and over in a tangle of bloody bandages, fists thudding. Then the youth's hands were again at his uncle's throat. Howling in fury, Jubal threw the tomahawk aside to have his good hand free. Half-drunk, he turned mad, for his nephew, refusing to give up, actually hurt him with savage punches. As they fought, Jubal started hitting back harder, kneeing, and using his elbow.

Held together by locked arms, the two men battled to their feet, then Red Panther howled and slammed Jubal down, and with a wicked kick broke Jubal's nose. Dazed and bloody, Swain lost all control. Through pain and rage he began to see the face of his dead brother, Matt. In a blur of movement he tripped Red Panther, clamped a hold on his head, and battered it against the ground, shouting, "Damn, Matt! Damn, Matt! Damn!"

Lucy jumped on Jubal, scratching his face and biting until he threw her off, knocking the wind out of her. Then he pounded his victim, fists punishing, though the youth was helpless by now.

Sutherland took the last yards with all his strength, brushing aside branches that overhung the path, leaping ahead. He cocked his rifle as he bounded clear of the trail, saw the lean-to, then heard Lucy scream.

Jubal was lost in the delirium of nightmare. Staggering wildly to his feet, he whipped the unconscious Red Panther over his head. At the brink of the cliff high above the river, he reached back to hurl the body over. In an almost inhuman voice, Swain shrilled:

"Die, then! Die, if that's what you want!"

In the next instant, with Lucy's shriek echoing in his mind, Swain hesitated, recovering himself, as though suddenly aware of what he was doing. He had no chance to change his mind. A rifle shot rang out, and he staggered as the ball slammed into his back. Swain crumpled to his knees, Red Panther held over his head. He swayed, and turned, amazed to see Lucy holding the gun, her expression horrified. As though in a trance,

Jubal laid his nephew's body down, then said, "Lucy, girl..."
He shook his head once, not understanding. He closed his eyes,
then opened them, seeing Owen Sutherland approach, claymore
drawn.

Blood trickled from Jubal's mouth as he tried to speak.
"Lucy? I can't see yuh. Where be yuh, Lucy?"

Sutherland sheathed his claymore. There was no use for it
now. After all that had driven him, there was nothing more to
do.

Staring at the dying Swain, Sutherland absently took the
rifle from Lucy. Her hands reached out for Jubal, but she could
not move. The only sound was the child crying. Swain tried
again to speak, his voice faint:

"Lucy, you hear? The...kid's..." His eyes closed, and
he collapsed forward, dead.

Lucy let out a long, low moan that rose, helpless and sorrowful, from deep within. Sutherland felt it. Lucy ran to the
body and dropped to her knees, laying her head on Jubal's.
The Scotsman's hatred of Swain was gone, replaced by pity
for Lucy, and by wonder that such a man could be loved.

Red Panther stirred, and Sutherland knelt down beside him.
Conscious, though badly beaten, Red Panther gazed at Sutherland, who wrapped the bandages about his bloody torso. He
needed a doctor, but with care he might live. Seeing his mother
huddled over the body, Red Panther called to her.

Slowly, Lucy Swain sat up, in her hand the tattered red silk
kerchief Jubal had given her so very long ago. She touched
the kerchief to her lips and gave a shuddering sigh. Sutherland
came to her side and, taking Lucy by the shoulders, eased her
to her feet. Eloise was wailing louder now.

He said, "Go to the child; I'll take care of your son."

Looking down at Jubal, Lucy had to lean on Sutherland.
After a moment she began to turn away, then hesitated. She
let the red silk fall, fluttering, onto her man's body.

The war was over.

Lord Dunmore made peace, without further killing. On their
march home, aware that Parliament trembled at the gathering
of such a strong body of warlike colonists, the captains of the
Virginia militia held a meeting. On behalf of the entire army,
they declared unfailing allegiance to King George III, saying,
"...we will, at the expense of life and everything dear and
valuable, exert ourselves in support of his crown..." But the

resolution ominously went on to say that Virginians would "exert every power within us for the defense of American liberty . . . when regularly called forth by the unanimous voice of our countrymen." This was a clear defiant warning to the government, especially in light of the successful war waged against a strong body of Indians.

The resolution also thanked Governor Dunmore, expressing the militia's respect for him, and asserting that he underwent the "fatigue of this singular campaign for no other motive than the true interests of the country."

The Delaware River frothed with a northern wind, the black water and stormy gray sky deepening the November chill that brought the memory of winter to Philadelphia. The city had bade farewell to the delegates of the First Continental Congress, and Parliament was already angry at the congress's firm declaration of American rights and opposition to taxation without representation. The maintenance of the British Army in America without colonial consent was also denounced by the congress, which, as its last act, set a date for a second congress in May.

Owen Sutherland, who stood on a dock with his back to the cold wind, had missed the congress because of the conflict by now known as Lord Dunmore's War. He would return in the spring as an observer from the northwest territory, but just now, politics were far from his mind. He looked up at the trim ship moored to the landing, a vessel just built for the Frontier Company. With Owen on the dock were Ella, the children, and Sally, all muffled, huddling together. It was difficult to get warm when one's heart was heavy. This was the parting with Jeremy, who at that moment was limping up the plank gangway to the deck of the new schooner, christened *Yankee*.

Though pale, still weak from his wound, Jeremy was determined to go to Great Britain before winter. As Peter and Mary Defries helped him onto the deck, he turned and waved to his family. All the lingering farewells had been said, and he looked down at his loved ones for the last time. Mel, too, was on shore, holding Sniffer, who cocked his head, his black eyes sad.

Much had happened in the past weeks to change the situation of the Frontier Company: Lucy Swain, conscience-stricken, was willing to testify against Bradford Cullen, bearing witness that the merchant had paid Jubal to wreak havoc in the northwest territory. Her son still lived, recovering from his wounds at Chillicothe, where Niko-lota was caring for him. Though Red Panther refused to return to civilization, Lucy and her daughter dwelt with friends of her first husband in the back-country near Carlisle, where Sutherland would call upon her next spring. Then formal charges would be brought against Cullen in Montreal.

Jeremy wondered how all this turmoil, as well as the deepening conflict between Parliament and colonies, would end. Soon he would see things from the British perspective, and he looked forward to that. He did not, however, like leaving his family and friends behind, especially Sally, who had been with him constantly in the past weeks of recuperation.

Calling out, "See you in two years!" Jeremy put on a brave show, but could not help sniffing. It must have been the chilly wind. On the dock they all waved, Ella and Sally wiping away tears.

A sailor heaved on a line, and Jeremy stared, sad, but also excited to be going to Scotland to further his studies. As the gangway was raised from the dock he took a last glance at Philadelphia, the great city under a haze of woodsmoke darker than the storm clouds. The ship swayed as the bowlines were cast off, and on the quarterdeck the vessel's master spoke to the mate, who shouted through the wind to men aloft. Sail was unfurled, the helm was brought about, and a longboat towed the ship's bow away from land.

Jeremy and the Defrieses, with Emmy and Jeanette, made their way along the railing, waving and calling out good-byes, the others on shore steadily waving back, some with both arms. To keep as close as possible to them all, Jeremy moved to the stern of the ship. Sails began to fill, snapping like gunshots as the wind caught them. How beautiful Sally looked! He had not asked her to wait for him, but he thought she would. He knew now how very much she meant to him. He would come back to her.

Taking the music box from his coat, he held it up, opened, for her to see. As he listened to its song, she stood with hands to her lips, watching, no longer waving.

The ship was forty yards from shore when Jeremy noticed a quick movement and saw Mel lurching toward the end of the dock. There was a shout as Sniffer skidded off the edge, leaping far into the icy stream. The otter surfaced, swimming with amazing speed right at the schooner, which was coming about, anchor dragging to head the bow downriver.

The otter reached the *Yankee*, Sutherland and the others watching in fascination as it swam back and forth below the ship's stern, sniffing and blowing in distress at losing Jeremy. Sally leaned against Ella, the otter's frantic helplessness mirroring their own emotions.

Then Owen gave a shout of delight. "Now the lad'll have someone to look after him in Britain!"

Jeremy, in spite of his sore body, had swung down a ratline that dangled over the ship's side, and with his feet against the hull, leaned over with one arm and caught up Sniffer. Everyone on the landing cheered as Peter Defries hauled Jeremy aboard. Mel whipped out his wooden flute and began to play "Yankee Doodle."

"Godspeed!" Ella cried.

"Come back soon," Sally whispered.

The wind gusted, swelling the sail, white against the storm clouds. The longboat cast off and rowed clear. The *Yankee* heeled graciously to port, then skimmed downriver on a westerly wind blowing hard across the sea, to England.

A Special Preview of the
Opening Chapter of
Book 4 in the
Northwest Territory Series

REBELLION

by
Oliver Payne

On sale October *1983*
wherever Berkley books
are sold

chapter 1

Hugh Meeks snorted and laughed to himself as he said, "Ain't it a fine day for a brawl, Farley?"

Farley Jones, the slender, aging companion of Hugh Meeks, coughed nervously as he peered landward and shuffled his feet on the deck of the sloop tied up at the landing of Fort Detroit. Clerk and lackey for Bradford Cullen, the powerful merchant, Jones was watching a large crowd gather on the expanse of open ground just outside the fort's western gate. If Hugh Meeks, that treacherous pirate with the guile of a serpent, did what he intended this bright December morning, there would be cracked bones and caved-in heads among the folk of Detroit, white and red alike.

Taking a sidelong glance at Meeks, master of this vessel, Jones wondered where Bradford Cullen had found the hulking roughneck. Surely the wharves of Boston and New York could not have produced the likes of Meeks, whose savage temper tyrannized tough sailors, and whose wit and seamanship won their admiration and respect. More likely it was the West Indies, the old Spanish Main, or the buccaneer haunts of Barbados that had nurtured Hugh Meeks. Cullen must have discovered him in the sugar trade somewhere between New England and the Caribbean.

Unlike the people on land, Meeks and Jones were not soldiers or frontiersmen, but like these people of the northwest territory, the two men in charge of the sloop *Helen* made their living from the lucrative fur trade that harvested peltry from Rainy Lake in the west to eastern Iroquois lands on the frontiers of New York Colony. Only recently hired by Bradford Cullen, and having docked the *Helen* at Detroit but two days ago, Meeks was new to the northwest. It was his duty as shipmaster to run Cullen and Company's vessel across Lake Erie, through these broad straits at Detroit, and up to distant Fort Michilimackinac, carrying fur and trade goods. His employer also had another use for Meeks: to take on Cullen and Company's foremost competitor, Owen Sutherland, hand-to-hand. After years of bitter rivalry, Cullen had resolved to put an end to Sutherland.

Jones wondered whether Meeks underestimated these frontier folk, thinking them less hardy than seamen. If he did, he was wrong, and even the thick wooden belaying pin the man was taking from its place on the gunwale would not intimidate the likes of Owen Sutherland. In the past, Jones had spent years here at the center of the northwestern fur trade, working as a clerk. Detroit was the hub, the emporium for half the continent, where thousands of Indians brought in their peltry, and hundreds of whites made a living buying the furs with manufactured goods and rum. These folk were tough and resilient, and the clerk knew Meeks would have his meaty hands full if he fought Sutherland.

A former officer in the famous Black Watch Highland Regiment, Owen Sutherland had recently come back from Philadelphia. Sent there as a delegate by frontier folk of every political shade, Sutherland had been trusted to listen closely to representatives from the colonies, to ask questions related to the trade and the northwest, and to inform the people of Detroit about the current hostility between Parliament and America. A platform of planks, white in the sunshine, had been built on a rise overlooking the blue, rushing water of the river. Sutherland would soon mount it to speak, and the crowd was eager to hear him.

Just how Meeks would carry out Cullen's orders and attack Sutherland, Farley Jones could not tell. There was not a man in this country fearless enough to challenge the Scotsman face to face; but then, Meeks was no duelist, he was a brawler, shrewd and cruel. Furthermore, the excited, anxious crowd was smitten with a dangerous anger—anger that split them into two camps.

For months, perhaps years, lines had been drawn between those who favored Parliament—the Tories—and those who demanded more American rights and liberties—the Whigs. As Jones observed the growing crowd, he recognized familiar faces from the past, and already knew who was on which side. There was ready hatred there in the mob, with each party blaming the other for whatever unfavorable contributions beset their country. Raw nerves might be touched and the crowd goaded to sudden violence if Meeks did his work well.

Jones watched the dozen sailors of the *Helen*, all handpicked by Meeks, assemble near the gangplank and take belaying pins from their master. Meeks was even more imposing in the big greatcoat and tricorn he wore, but his face was alight with good humor as he spoke a word to the men and clapped their shoulders before sending them down to mingle in the crowd. With clubs secreted in coats or breeches, these rogues knew their orders.

Meeks noted a flurry of movement a hundred yards off near the fort's gate that meant Owen Sutherland was coming. Then he turned, with his left eye half-closed, to look at Jones.

That cunning, squinting stare caught Jones off guard, and the skinny clerk could not look away. Like a serpent, the pirate was, Jones thought, a deceiver whose very eye made a man shiver.

"Will ye not come along and have a lick at them lubberly rebels, matey?" Meeks cackled and came alongside Jones, who had to wrench his face away from the penetrating gaze and look again toward the land. He saw the tall form of Sutherland dressed in buckskins moving through the parting crowd.

Meeks jabbed an elbow into Jones's ribs and offered a belaying pin, as thick as the clerk's arm. Jones staggered, coughing, his false teeth clacking furiously. Meeks said Jones could get a chance at Sutherland when the Scotsman was down. Jones wheezed, and the sailor laughed again, a dry, grating laugh that expressed scorn and pity for weaklings.

At forty-five, ten years younger than Jones, Hugh Meeks was a remarkable contrast to the bent, sickly clerk. Ruddy and clean-shaven, his square chin jutting forward, Meeks rocked on his heels, placidly gazing at the frontiersmen ashore, the way a feudal lord might contemplate condemned prisoners. Unlike most men of the day, whose hair was long and worn in a queue, Meeks had his gray hair cropped close to his scalp. A sharp early winter wind flapped the man's coat collar, but he paid the chill no mind. Jones, watery-eyed and sniffling, bundled a tattered scarf more closely about his own neck, and took note of that haunting white scar that ran from the seaman's left earlobe down his neck. It seemed to be a burn, a rope burn, that stood out more starkly when Meeks was excited, red in the face.

Meeks was muttering distantly, "Been too long since I swung a pin ... Last time was off Jamaica—aye, Jamaica it was, an'

we took a smart Portugee brig full to the gunnels with slaves
... Sold good, they did, them that lived ..."

As Meeks spoke, Jones guessed a noose had indeed been
at work on his throat; Bradford Cullen had known what he was
about when he engaged Meeks to go up against Sutherland.
Jones shuddered again, hoping he would never be the object
of Cullen's revenge. It just might be that Meeks was the man
to even things up between Cullen and Sutherland once and for
all.

Meeks leered at Jones, cackled once more, and slid the
belaying pin magically out of sight inside his greatcoat. Without
another word, he strode down the gangplank and onto the
landing. Jones watched him go, brass buttons polished, buckles
shining, even his stockings clean. The seaman attempted to
give the impression of being a respectable citizen anxious to
hear news of the colonies and Congress, except that his rolling
gait made the cutlass sticking out from the back of his greatcoat
swing like a devil's tail. Nothing could mask the menacing
aura that surrounded Meeks, and as he pushed into the crowd,
men moved aside, women looked away, and he was left room
to stand close to the platform where Sutherland would rise to
speak.

Not far from Meeks, a loud argument was going on, and
Jones noticed one of those involved was the giant former soldier, Jeb Grey. A settler and partner in the Frontier Company,
Grey was an outspoken opponent of Parliament and a supporter
of Congress. He would be close to Sutherland when fighting
broke out, and would be a tough man to contend with. Jones
felt even more uneasy to see Tamano, the big Chippewa warrior, carrying his weapons. In his company was the young Sioux
brave, Little Hawk.

These Indians were friends of Sutherland and were partners
in the trading company. With them were their wives—Tamano's pretty Lela, and Little Hawk's shy, plump White Dove.
Like Jeb Grey and his wife, Lettie—a portly, cheerful woman
who had married Grey after her husband was murdered by
white renegades in the pay of Bradford Cullen—these Indians
had children at their side. The parents seemed not to anticipate
serious trouble. What would happen to the young ones when
it began, Jones did not care to guess.

But at least one of these young people familiar to Jones was
nearly full grown, and the clerk spat in anger to see him:
Tommy Morely, son of Lettie Grey, had been a boy when

Jones last served at Detroit. Now, almost twenty, Tommy was as tall as Jeb, his stepfather, though not yet as wide. Handsome and dark, Tommy seemed hardly listening to the argument going on, but was watching for Sutherland or for someone in Sutherland's party, which was approaching the platform as the crowd parted to let them through.

Like Little Hawk, Tom had been a bane to Jones, often teasing and causing trouble for the bitter little clerk. As far as Jones was concerned, Meeks and his men could do whatever they liked to the Indian and Morely. He would be happy if those two young good-for-nothings were battered senseless or done for, never mind what happened to Sutherland.

Jones was sure that partisan violence running rampant in the eastern settlements and cities could be stirred up in Detroit to benefit Cullen's activities, for people had brought their traditional likes and dislikes here with them. Most in the surging crowd had already heard that the Continental Congress had called for a total boycott of goods from Britain, and there was much anger here over the prospect of essential British trade goods being cut off from the northwest. Many traders would be ruined if that happened. Yet on the other hand there were others who raged against Parliament's new plans to seal off the frontier at the Allegheny Mountains and forbid all future settlement of Indian lands.

Added to this grievance were suspicions that Parliament would never permit free elections and civil government in the northwest, because it was the intention of Parliament to keep the entire country west of the Alleghenies under England's firm, despotic military rule—a rule that would favor only a few wealthy fur companies and manufacturers in the mother country across the sea. There were even poisonous rumors of a French Catholic plot to gain control of Parliament, to stunt the growth of expanding British colonies in eastern America, and to subvert the standards of liberty and human rights that had been hard won in the English civil war of the last century.

Doubts, rumors, lies, fears, ancient mistrust, and new resentments burned and quickened in the hearts and minds of people in Detroit. No one knew whom to believe, whom to obey, and what would happen to them if riots and mob brutality in the east broke out into a full-scale rebellion against the crown. That was why they so anxiously awaited Owen Sutherland's message, for they trusted him above all others and wanted to hear his opinion on such matters as the acts of

Congress and the agreement not to import British goods.

If Sutherland hinted he might take a side with the Congress, Meeks would have an opening, a chance to swing much of the Tory crowd to his side against the Scotsman. If this were to happen, it would be a sharp fight, for many on hand would stand by Owen Sutherland.

Jones saw another Sutherland ally: Dressed more like an Indian than a white man, with feathers and a red *voyageur* waistband, was stocky Jacques Levesque, a French partner in the company. With him were the stout merchant, Jean Martine, and Angélique, Martine's pretty, raven-haired daughter, Levesque's wife. The French of Detroit liked Sutherland, too, but it was uncertain which side they would take in any general battle between the *Anglais*, whom they despised.

Jones was no fighting man, but he had seen enough to know that Hugh Meeks needed to be as crafty as he was tough. It would take more than his crew with clubs to tame Sutherland and the Frontier Company. There had better be a hard core of Tory loyalists who opposed Congress and were willing to fight what had been done in Philadelphia. Otherwise it would be Meeks, not Sutherland, in jail or nursing a broken skull before this day was done.

Jones looked along the deck to the narrow door of his cabin. It was open, and that was good, for in case things got too hot, he could make a quick retreat and lock himself in. If heads were going to be cracked, Farley Jones intended keeping his own safely out of reach.

As Owen Sutherland made his way through the corridor that opened toward the platform, he turned over and over the words he would say to the worried people of Detroit. He hardly noticed the many new faces in the crowd, for his mind was full with the crisis breaking over the three million people in British America—a crisis that affected remote Detroit as much as it plagued miserable Boston. That city's port had been forcibly closed to commerce and its provincial assembly forbidden by Parliament to meet until the Massachusetts Colony had been punished for violent disobedience to London's rule.

It was not only the stirring acts of a defiant America that troubled Sutherland, however, for many collecting here on the brown grass above the wide Detroit River knew what had been done by Congress in Philadelphia. That news had traveled fast. Everyone had heard of the four thousand English soldiers quartered on unhappy Bostonians, of the colonists' destroying British tea rather than paying duties on it, of the boarding and burning of a royal customs vessel. As far as Sutherland was concerned, the demands of Americans that they be fairly represented in Parliament were questions for lawyers to debate and resolve; however, this civil conflict coming upon the land, the bloody riots, attacks on government officials, and the counterraids of loyalist supporters were forcing matters to a climax.

It was no longer a question of intellectual theory or abstract concepts of natural law, but a matter of whose side an American took when the fighting broke out in his own community. There were many already standing on one side or the other simply because their dislikable neighbor had chosen a stand. There were others whose hatred of all authority and whose poverty had driven them to desire a change of rule, no matter how turbulent the change became. They had nothing to lose.

Then there were those who were prosperous, who had much to lose, and wanted peace for its own sake, no matter if the rule of law kept the British bootheel on America's neck.

It was time for a decision, and Owen Sutherland had made his already. When he confronted these people, who had asked him to represent them as a neutral in the raging turmoil torturing America, he would not stand before them now as the same man they had sent to Philadelphia. He was no longer neutral.

Hands reached out to touch him, to grasp his own, and words of encouragement and greeting came from every side, from dozens of familiar faces. But Owen Sutherland knew that in the next few moments, he would have many enemies where there had been friends. He might be despised and cast out by those very folk whose respect meant much to him. Even Tamano might turn his back, and surely many Indians would consider him their enemy.

Sutherland was taller than most, lean and graceful, with a curly head of black hair. His commanding presence gave no hint of how utterly alone he felt. Then there was someone by his side. He half-turned, sensing Ella at his shoulder, and he lightly touched her hand. She alone knew the decision he had made in the long journey home from Philadelphia. Ella, Owen's beautiful fairhaired wife, would support him in this, for she, too, shared his vision of America, a united America with its own government that represented colonists fairly. They would no longer be a subjugated, disjointed number of quarreling colonies without a voice to shape their destiny.

Just as he reached the plank platform and prepared to go up the steps, Sutherland took his wife's hand in his, and the children—Benjamin and Susannah, ten and eight—clutched at his waist. At that moment his name was shouted and the crowd began to applaud. His heart skipped.

"What will they say after they hear me?" he asked Ella, the noise of the crowd almost drowning out his voice.

She drew a shaking breath. "Many will think you damnably wrong. The rest will know you are bound by love for our country. But, Owen—" She gripped his arm. "—Have you seen the men from Cullen's ship? They're in among the crowd."

He took her hand again and said, "I've seen them and know who they are." He released her hand and eased the children away with a kind word. His pale eyes meeting Ella's, he said, "Have a care. If worse comes to worst, get the youngsters away immediately."

Ella promised with a nod, and drew the children to her. Owen turned and stepped up onto the platform, the claymore hanging at his side, seeming part of him. As he stood before the shouting and cheering mob, he slowly raised his hands. In that moment he was grateful for the presence of friends so close by, even though the Chippewa, Tamano, and the Frenchman, Levesque, would be distressed to hear him speak, to learn that he had chosen to support the Continental Congress against Parliament. Still, Sutherland knew they would stand by him if there was trouble this afternoon.

From this day on, nothing would be the same for the Frontier Company or for Owen Sutherland, who would be called a rebel against the king.

ROMANCE, WAR, HONOR AND ADVENTURE AT THE DAWN OF A NEW FRONTIER!

NORTHWEST TERRITORY

Not since John Jakes' <u>Kent Family Chronicles</u> has there been a series of books like the NORTHWEST TERRITORY, which vividly chronicles the forging of America and the men and women who made this country great. These are the stories of the Sutherland family and their founding of a great trading company along the frontier and in the cities of the Old Northwest—America's heartland. Facing the perils of Indian attacks and the threat of Revolution, the Sutherlands fight for what they believe, helping to shape America's destiny.

_____ 05452-7/$2.95 WARPATH (Book 1)

Owen Sutherland—Scottish-born frontiersman, soldier, and trader—leads the men of the Northwest in putting down the most brutal Indian uprising in America's history. In the midst of this turmoil, he meets and falls in love with Ella Bently, a beautiful young Englishwoman at Fort Detroit.

NORTHWEST TERRITORY

_____ 05532-9/$3.50 CONQUEST (Book 2)
Owen and his new bride Ella journey through the Northwest wilderness to the great city of Philadelphia, which is endangered by bloody civil war. Owen meets with Benjamin Franklin, and together they confront rebellious mobs. Then follows a perilous wintertime journey over ice and snow to get home to Fort Detroit and the Sutherlands' young and growing trading company.

_____ 05846-8/$3.50 DEFIANCE (Book 3)
Owen Sutherland's Frontier Company rivals even the well-known Hudson's Bay Company. Fighting against unscrupulous businessmen and renegade outlaws, Sutherland, his family, and friends now face the greatest threat of them all: Revolution in America.

Buy these books wherever Berkley Books are sold. Or use this handy ordering coupon: